HEROES ꓥꓲLLAINS

POLICE SCOTLAND
BOOK 11

ED JAMES

To James —

Thanks for all of your help over the last few books in trapping my stupid mistakes. Click. But also thanks for the stupid chats about beer and metal, which keep me as sane as it's possible to be.

You're one of the best.

DAY 1

Monday
10th August

1

Detective Sergeant Scott Cullen kept his gaze on the silver Range Rover three cars ahead as they followed it past the Scottish Parliament, which still looked like a municipal swimming baths from provincial Scotland, just with some Catalan window dressing stapled on. Showed where the country was these days.

DC Paul 'Elvis' Gordon was behind the pool car's wheel, giving off the vibe of his namesake's final hours in Vegas, rather than his Hollywood pomp. He scratched at his massive sideburns, keeping the car a steady thirty as they passed through two roundabouts and two sweeping bends along the busy road from the city's political heart to its social armpit, Dumbiedykes. He stopped to wait for an old man to cross, drumming his thumbs off the wheel, then headed into the former council estate. The high-rise blocks still seemed like a junkie haven, even though the flats were mostly leased to MSPs and bankers, and filled with designer furniture and bespoke kitchens. Mostly.

The Range Rover pulled up outside a beige-and-grey tower block, the blacked-out windows hiding the driver.

Cullen gestured for Elvis to drive on by the target – no slowing down, no turned heads, no suspicious behaviour. As they passed, Cullen angled the wing mirror.

Dean Vardy hopped out of his pimp ride, his disco muscles and skin-tight T-shirt a cocky challenge to the afternoon's fourteen degrees, the Edinburgh wind lowering the temperature. He strutted up to the front door like he owned the place. Not far off the truth – his legal businesses owned twenty flats inside. God knows how many his illegal ones did.

Elvis cruised around the turning point at the end, doubled back to the neighbouring block and slowed to a halt at the side of the street. He killed the ignition and yawned, releasing a blast of coffee breath. 'Hope you're pleased I haven't made a joke about you being the dumb guy in Dumbiedykes?'

'Very pleased.' Cullen reached for his Airwave radio and put it to his ear. 'Suspect has entered premises at Holyrood Court, Dumbiedykes. Want us to follow him in?'

'Negative, Sundance.' DS Brian Bain's Glasgow rasp hissed out. 'We've got eyes on you from up here, so sit tight. Your front-left headlight is buggered, by the way.'

'Look, she's in that flat alone.' Cullen tightened his grip on the 'oh-shit' handle even though they weren't moving. 'We're just letting Vardy walk up there?'

'It's called a plan for a reason, Sundance. Boss's orders. Now you make sure he doesn't leave without us knowing.'

Bloody hell.

Cullen ended the call and slid the Airwave back into the sleeve pocket of his battered green bomber jacket.

Across the street, by the entrance, some neds were playing football – none of them looking any older than ten.

Nothing else happening.

Elvis was stroking his lamb chops, a look of puzzled constipation stuck on his face, like the King of Rock 'n' Roll on his resting toilet. 'So we're just to sit here?'

'Those are the orders, aye.'

'Tell you, this undercover stakeout's been dragging on longer than one of Wilko's morning briefings.' Elvis shook his head. 'Here we are, sitting on our arses, while that Vardy bastard runs around like he owns the place, raping and killing. And I'm only here because you pissed off the boss.'

'You don't need to remind me.' Cullen gave him a glare, hoping it would warn him that a constable should watch what he says to a sergeant. Elvis looked the other way. 'Fine, I'll say it if it makes you happy. You're here because I messed up Wilko's case, but I did solve a murder in the process. And, for my troubles, I got a second-ment to Operation Venus. Along with the rest of the Special Needs class.'

'Very funny.' Elvis chuckled despite himself. 'Just saying, that's all.'

'You could put in for a transfer, you know.'

'How did you...?' Elvis settled even deeper into his seat, blushing. Something groaned. Could've been the back rest, could've been his stomach. 'Sorry, Sarge. Might want to open a window.'

Cullen held his breath as he got out into the blustery wind and leaned against the car.

The sky looked like it had been in a fight. Hard winds from the North Sea pummelled grey clouds across the horizon. One seemed beaten up, a lumbering purple mass like a bloody bruise.

Edinburgh in August. Got to love it.

The car rocked as Elvis got out. He stepped around and settled his bulk on the bonnet, upwind of Cullen. 'Look on the bright side, though. You've got me for company. Dragged me into this unexpected career development opportunity and I haven't resented you for one moment. Must be my sunny deposition.'

'You mean disposition.' Cullen stuck his hands into his jeans pockets. 'And you don't mind this new gig because it means you're not gawping at CCTV all day.'

Elvis pushed himself off the bonnet and puffed up his chest. 'Hold on a—'

'Alright, Scotty?' A big guy in a shiny blue muscle-shirt slapped Cullen's shoulder with one hand, holding a two-litre plastic bottle with the other. 'Alright, my man?'

'Aye, just walking the daftie here. What's up?'

'Your daftie looks fair exhausted, Scotty.' Big Rob grinned at Elvis, killing any attempt at a witty comeback with a confused wink. 'You boys doing interval sprints?'

Elvis rolled his eyes. 'Aye, that's what we're doing out here.'

'Good effort, my man.' Big Rob waved the bottle around, splashing water on the pavement. 'Been working hard myself all morning. Today's target is ten litres.' He flexed a pair of bulging biceps. 'Need to hydrate these bad boys.'

'Ten litres?' Cullen smirked at him. 'Isn't that going to dehydrate you?'

'Science.' Big Rob tapped his nose and wandered off.

Elvis watched him go. 'That your ex-boyfriend?'

'Just some old CHIS.'

Elvis did that particular frown, his features squishing up like a used chip wrapper. Usually meant he was thinking of something funny. 'There's nothing covert, human or intelligent about him, is there?'

Cullen glanced at the heavy clouds pressing down on the tower blocks. 'Elvis, you'll need to drive me to A&E, I think I've split my sides.'

'Come on, mate. That was funny. Got to admit.' Elvis crossed his arms and did his best impression of a petulant toddler, huffing and puffing.

Cullen closed his eyes, wondering what he'd done to deserve this. Then he remembered, in exact detail. When he opened them again, the dreich weather made him sigh for the four hundredth time that day.

'Looks like a right cloudburst's on the way.' Elvis elbowed Cullen in the ribs. 'Bet you've pulled yourself off so much in the shower, you get a hard-on every time it rains.'

Cullen couldn't even muster the energy to turn the radio back up. *I need out of here. Or to get shot of this clown.* 'Me and Craig Hunter busted a steroid ring in a gym a few years back.'

'Sounds like a great excuse for you pair to hang around with a load of naked blokes.'

'That's Craig's thing, not mine.' The first raindrops battered off the pavement, so he got back in the car and scanned the radio. Had to settle for *TalkSport*. Even though the caller sounded off his head, it was better than listening to *Elvis in the Afternoon*.

Elvis got behind the wheel again, stroking his sideburns as he turned off the radio. 'Load of pish.'

In one of the towers, Dean Vardy was meeting a young woman. Unprotected, unguarded, and alone. With *his* record.

It didn't feel right.

Elvis cleared his throat and spat out of the open window. 'I was reading this article in the New Yorker by this boy called Art Oscar. Heard of him?' He took Cullen's silence as an instruction to keep talking. 'Said the war on drugs was a political ploy cooked up by

Nixon to take out people who weren't going to vote for him. You know, blacks and anti-war lefties. Think that's true?'

Cullen cocked an eyebrow. 'I didn't know that.'

'Said it was heroin and marijuana at the start. Makes you wonder what this war on drugs is all for, eh?'

Cullen paused. 'I mean, I didn't know you could read.'

Elvis rolled his eyes.

Sod this for a game of soldiers.

Cullen opened the door and pointed at Elvis. 'Stay here and wait for Vardy. I'm going upstairs.'

CULLEN KNOCKED ON THE DOOR THREE TIMES, THE SECRET SIGNAL that was about as subtle as a brick in the balls. Or one of Elvis's jokes.

The door cracked open and half a face appeared in the gap: round suedehead, receding hairline, deep frown, squinty eyes, and a limp moustache. DS Brian Bain. 'Sundance, I told you to wait downstairs, you tube.'

'You did.' Cullen looked down at him, letting Bain feel his height disadvantage. 'How about you go and babysit Elvis?'

'How about you piss off?'

Cullen stared at him, then lowered his eyes and unzipped his jacket to give his hands something to do other than punch the little bastard. 'I need to speak to the boss. Move.'

'You could ask nicely.'

'You wouldn't understand nicely.'

Bain stared at him, an uneasy smile twitching under his moist moustache. He recovered his cool, stepped back and swung the door open. 'You charming bastard.'

Cullen walked straight past him into the flat. Boarded-up windows, grotty old furniture, cold strip lighting making the place feel as inviting as a mortuary. Must be the last place in the tower block that hadn't been turned into an IKEA showroom.

In the kitchen, an Armed Response Unit loitered with intent. Four men, two women, dressed head to toe in black tactical gear, handguns strapped to their thighs, semi-automatic rifles slung tightly over their chests, index fingers resting idly on the trigger guards. The sight alone made Cullen twitchy.

DI Paul Wilkinson sat at the kitchen table, fussing over some recording equipment. Well, one of his hands was. The other was busy stuffing his mouth with chocolate raisins. A pong of stale sweat radiated off him. He caught sight of Cullen and dropped the smudgy paw to give his balls a good scratch. The guy seemed to gain at least a stone of flab every week, his manboobs straining at his latest checked farmer's shirt. 'Well done, Cullen. You found us all the way up here.' His Yorkshire accent was hiding behind an acquired Scottish one, just a few syllables off here and there. He gathered another handful of raisins and hoovered his wee sweeties up with a wet sucking noise. 'Despite being told to stay down there.' He chewed open-mouthed, a mess of brown and pink and purple.

'I'm worried about Amy Forrest, sir.' Cullen looked away from his jowly face. 'More specifically, about Vardy murdering her.'

Wilkinson stared at him for a few seconds. 'We're sticking to the plan. End of.' He popped another chocolate raisin in his gob.

Cullen glanced at the men and women standing to attention. 'Come on, you've got this lot hanging around with their thumbs up their arses, while Vardy's downstairs, right below our feet. With *her*. She's alone. With *him*. We know where he is, what he's capable of, and what he'll do if we don't stop him.'

Wilkinson snorted, then rolled his eyes at the figures in black. 'I said no.'

'Come on, let's just get in there. We can pick him up for the assault charge and collect evidence on the murder allegations while he's in custody.'

'Cullen...' Wilkinson took another mouthful and chewed slowly, really taking his time with it, like he was provoking Cullen to do something rash. And get himself kicked off another case. 'This isn't a simple murder investigation, the sort you're used to. You're in the drugs squad now and you need a bit more of this.' He tapped his temple, repeatedly, then kept his finger there.

Even the ARU cops became so restless they started running unnecessary checks of their equipment, rustling in the awkward silence.

'You need strategic thinking in this game.' Wilkinson

dropped his hand and leaned back on his chair. 'That girl is risking her life for this operation, seducing Vardy into some dirty pillow talk, while we record it. You want to do him for some assault that'll get him, what? Five years? Out in two? I want him bragging about his drug deals, I want him off the streets for life.' He gave Cullen a stern look, then reached for his raisins and popped another load into his mouth. 'That little enterprise nets him seven million quid a year, right? And you want him inside on assault charges. Leave the thinking to the big boys, yeah?'

Cullen stared at him. *Playing power games while an untrained mark lured a violent misogynist into a honey trap.* He flexed his fingers and zipped up his bomber jacket. 'Understood. Sir.' He turned away and stepped over to the wall to await orders.

I know all about your kind of 'strategic thinking'. Throw bait to a shark, then wash your hands of any responsibility if the shark kills the bait, just as long as you catch the predator.

The audio recorder on the table burst into noise. A door creaking, followed by a female voice: 'Why... why don't we slow things down a wee bit, eh?'

'Slow down? *Slow down?*' Vardy's voice, guttural and deep. 'You having a laugh? Thought this was a booty call.'

'Sure, but I want to get to know you first, Dean. I see you at the club all the time, but you're my boss. You're so distant. I mean you're cool and that, but I want to get to know you. What you're thinking.'

'Right now, I'm thinking that I want to smash your back doors in before I get back to work. How about you get to work on this rager, eh?'

'Okay, then. But I've got a wee surprise for you.' Amy Forrest's voice was close to the mic. Sounded like a door opening.

'Now we're talking!' Bed springs creaked, followed by some slobbery noises. 'Aye, that's the game. Cup the balls, nice and hard. Work the shaft. Just like that. Oooh. Bite it. Aye, you too.'

Cullen left Wilko glued to his recorder and stepped out of the flat into the dank corridor.

'Here, Sundance.' The door closed behind Bain. 'What a farce.'

'We need to stop it. Right now.' Cullen powered over to the stairwell. One floor down, Vardy was in a flat with Amy Forrest.

'We've got way more than enough on Vardy. We should be arresting him.'

'Wilko's having a laugh if he thinks that wee lassie will get Vardy to incriminate himself.' Bain was up close, moaning into his ear. 'I should still be running this. Load of—'

A gun shot, echoing up the stairwell. Cullen froze. Felt the pressure in his chest, took a sharp breath, glanced around, tried to—

Another shot.

Down there.

And another.

Shite, Amy's flat.

Cullen sprinted down the stairs, a rush of blood like static in his ears, disembodied voices shouting, then along Amy's floor, combat boots hammering along the corridor behind him, the door rushing towards him, his shoulder crashing through it, the force carrying him several paces into the flat before he stumbled to a halt. He jerked his head around to get his bearings.

There – bedroom door wide open, Dean Vardy's back framed by the doorway, motionless, head bowed, arms loose by his sides, trousers round his ankles, a gun dangling from his right hand.

Cullen felt like he was staring at a picture – a perfectly composed still life.

Then Vardy spun around. His eyes shot to Cullen, fury flashing. But, just like that, it was over. He dropped the gun, grinning. 'I found her like that.'

Cullen charged at him just as the first ARU cops piled into the flat, their shouts deafening in the confined space. He flew through the bedroom doorway, pushing Vardy sprawling onto the floor.

But Cullen's gaze was drawn to the bed.

A woman lay tangled in the blood-soaked sheets, naked but for her torn underwear. It felt wrong to look at her exposed body, even more wrong that her chest was burst open by a gunshot wound. Her head was like some overripe piece of fruit used for shooting practice.

Amy Forrest.

Cullen's mark.

Cullen's fault.

He grabbed Vardy's T-shirt and yanked him up. Fist poised,

ready to strike – but didn't. It took all his strength to stop himself from smacking that smug, smug face. 'You're going away for a long time.'

Vardy glanced around to make sure no one else was looking at him. Then he winked at Cullen, whispering, 'Sure, sweetheart, you keep telling yourself that.'

2

SILENCE.

Then strained voices and the blur of movement – two of the Armed Response Unit pushing between Cullen and Vardy, cuffing the suspect. Vardy flashed another smile as they rushed him out of the room.

What the hell is he up to?

On the bed: Amy Forrest, shot through both breasts and once in the head.

This is my fault.

For the longest time there was nothing, just him and this cooling corpse. Used to be alive, but now she was decaying, another consequence of his failure to stop Dean Vardy.

A knock at the door. A haggard figure in a white boiler suit shuffled into the room. Jimmy Deeley, Edinburgh's chief pathologist, his cheeky expression just visible through the goggles. 'Afternoon, Sergeant. Standing there a while?' He walked up to the bed, whistling, and set his case down as he started examining the gunshot wounds. He straightened up, the cracking of his spine loud, and made a gun out of his fingers, aiming at the body. 'Tap, tap, tap. Clinical.' With another crack of his spine, he took a Dictaphone out of a pocket and went back to work, muttering into the device.

Cullen left Deeley with his dead body. Out in the corridor, he barged through a crowd of masked faces, tugging on crime-scene suits like they were dressing for PE at school. He stopped outside the safe flat they'd been using – Wilkinson's base.

Inside, the inspector was hunched over on the sofa, elbows resting on his knees, brooding.

Cullen cleared his throat. 'Looks like our friendly neighbourhood drug baron is modelling himself on Baltimore's worst.'

Wilkinson's stare went from brooding to blank. 'What are you talking about?'

'Deeley reckons Dean Vardy has copied the MO of a fictional villain from *The Wire*.'

Wilkinson's face remained a perfect blank. Either he hadn't got the reference, or he was too busy contemplating the smoothest way of shifting the blame for this botched operation.

Cullen didn't care to find out, and he cared even less about playing politics, especially at a crime scene. 'Look, this is my fault. I should've prevented it. But I didn't. I want to make sure this stops right here. Let me get a ballistics expert to match the shots to Vardy's gun. Please make sure this bastard doesn't get off, again.'

Wilkinson bristled. 'Again?' He exploded to his feet. 'Who do you think you are, you arrogant little shit? You want to make sure Vardy doesn't get off again? AGAIN? Let me tell you something about—'

'Sir?' Elvis stuck his head in through the door. 'Hate to interrupt, but you'll want to hear this.'

Wilkinson let his arms drop. Still kept his glare locked on Cullen. 'What?'

'Got uniforms going door-to-door like you asked, sir, and I was just speaking to a certain Sammy McLean, the neighbour from across the hall.' Elvis thumbed behind them like neither knew where the hall was. 'Says he saw Vardy do it.'

'MR MCLEAN?'

No reaction. The guy was sitting at his rickety kitchen table, his eyes roaming the Formica like he was counting the cigarette burns.

Cullen leaned back on his plastic chair.

The flat was a dump. At least it looked and smelled like a

dump, since everything in it seemed to have come from one, including the tenant. Sammy McLean was supposedly forty-two, but the booze on his breath and the broken veins on his nose showed how hard those years had been.

Cullen cleared his throat, loudly, but the guy was too drunk to notice. That, or he was too used to police enquiries. 'Mr McLean?'

Again no reaction. Seemed miles away.

'MR MCLEAN!'

'I made this when I got back, I'm fine.' Sammy looked up from the table and reached a trembling hand for his tea cup. He looked from Cullen to Bain and back, a puzzled frown on his face. 'I've no idea who you are or what you want from me.'

'We're here about the shooting next door.' Bain slammed both hands on the table.

Sammy jumped at the loud bang. 'Sorry, lads, you seem to be very upset. Is it about the shooting next door? Maybe you should talk to the polis. I'm sure they'll be here any—'

'WE. ARE. THE. POLICE.' Bain threw his hands up.

Sammy glanced from one to the other. 'You don't look like polis to me.'

Cullen took his warrant card from the inside pocket of his bomber jacket and showed it to Sammy. 'DS CULLEN.' He pointed at Bain. 'THIS IS DS BAIN. WE'RE PLAINCLOTHES OFFICERS.'

'Oh, aye, like on the telly. Undercover, eh? Good stuff.' Sammy gawped at them, more gaps than teeth in his mouth. 'Sorry, I'm a bit deaf. Somebody got shot next door and my hearing's been shot ever since.'

Cullen patted Bain's arm before he could fly into a rage. 'COULD YOU TELL US WHAT HAPPENED, SIR?'

'Oh, aye, I was just getting back from work. I'm working nights the now. Went for a couple of scoops with some of the boys after. But I'm back on at ten, eh? Absolute killer, this. Already had my key in the lock when this bloke comes strutting down the hallway. Big lad, eh? Waltzes straight into the flat over the way there, not even a nod of hello. Queer thing is he left the door open. So I left mine open. Anyway, I came in here and I must've been making the tea in my kitchenette, so I got a good angle out of my front door and into the other flat. I could see right into the bedroom, not that I was perving or anything. Like I said, I was making my tea, but next thing I know there's a gunshot, so I turn round and there's the bloke in the bedroom door and *bang bang* he shoots the girl again.' Sammy looked from one cop to the other, wide-eyed. 'Shot her in the tits. One then the other. Jesus, it was so *loud*.'

Cullen glanced at Bain, then back at Sammy. 'You saw him shoot the woman?'

Sammy frowned at him. Seemed to give the question some serious thought. Then he shrugged and pointed at his ears.

Cullen took a deep breath. 'YOU SAW HIM SHOOT THE WOMAN?'

Sammy nodded gravely. 'With my own two eyes.'

Bain reached into his denim jacket, pulled out a stack of photographs and laid it in the middle of the table. 'DO YOU RECOGNISE THIS MAN?'

Sammy looked at the photo. 'Nope.'

Bain put down another one. 'HIM?'

'Sorry.'

'This guy?'

Sammy froze.

'You know this guy?' Bain tore it off Sammy and showed it to Cullen. Not Vardy.

What the hell is going on?

Sammy took it back.

'That's my cousin. He looks like shit.'

Bain chuckled. 'Sure he does.'

'What was that?'

Bain laid out another mug shot. 'What about his guy?'

'That's him there.' Sammy tapped a mug shot with his index finger. 'That's your man.'

Cullen and Bain leaned forward.

Dean Vardy.

Bain took the photograph like he was stealing the conviction – slipped it back into his pocket and held out his hand for the rest of the pictures. Sammy reached over the table to return them to him.

Cullen shoved his chair back, hard enough to make the rubber stoppers squeak on the linoleum. He paced over to the other side of the small room and stood by the sink, forcing Sammy to look back and forth between him and Bain. 'WHAT DO YOU KNOW ABOUT YOUR NEIGHBOUR?'

Sammy glanced over his shoulder. 'Which neighbour?'

'WHICH ONE DO YOU THINK?' Bain put the photos together and chapped them off the table. 'THE ONE AT THE CRIME SCENE!'

Sammy turned back to him. 'Oh, aye, they're a pair of hoors so they are. Filthy slags.'

Cullen frowned. 'PAIR?'

Sammy twisted around, a dirty leer on his face. 'Huge pair. Like they'd hurt their backs.'

Bain barked out a laugh. 'WHAT THE SERGEANT MEANT IS WHETHER THERE ARE TWO WOMEN LIVING IN THE FLAT?'

Sammy turned back to Bain, almost drooling. 'Aye, two big lassies.'

'AND HOW DO YOU KNOW THEY'RE *HOORS*?'

Sammy stared at his coffee table.

Bain waved a hand in front of his face. 'MR MCLEAN, UNLESS YOU USED A BROTHEL, WENT KERB CRAWLING OR WERE INVOLVED IN SOME FORM OF PIMPING, YOUR RELATIONS WITH THESE WOMEN WILL HAVE NO LEGAL CONSEQUENCES.'

Sammy folded his arms, eyes still glued to the table. 'Okay. I paid both of them for a shag. But before you ask, they didn't tell me their names. Didn't want to get personal, apparently. Wouldn't even stick a fing—'

'Okay.' Cullen glanced into the sink and spotted a tea cup. Full. Still warm. Sammy's cup was still on the table, also full.

'MR MCLEAN, DO YOU LIVE ALONE?'

Sammy peered over his shoulder. 'I do, why?'

Cullen strode over to the bedroom door, yanked down the handle and pulled the door open.

There, sitting on the bed with her knees drawn up and her arms slung around her legs, was Amy Forrest.

3

'Amy, Amy, Amy.' Cullen stared hard across the table of the brightly lit interrogation room. 'How well do you know Mr McLean?'

Amy Forrest glanced down at her chest and tugged at the hem of her tight white top to reveal even more cleavage.

Cullen ignored them – not something that Elvis was able to do. 'I asked you a question, Ms Forrest. How well do you know Sammy?'

Amy looked at her fingernails. Took her time with it. Then she started nibbling at a cuticle.

Cullen cleared his throat. 'Is your hearing okay, Miss Forrest?'

'What?' She looked up at him. 'Why wouldn't it be?'

'You're not answering my questions. A certain Sammy McLean's hearing seemed greatly impaired by the gunshots fired in the flat opposite his. Yours.'

'Sammy's just having you on.' Amy rolled her eyes. 'His hearing's fine, and so's mine.' She kept staring into space, like she was replaying something.

'In that case, may I—'

'Why am I here? I've done nothing wrong.'

'Then I'm sure you won't mind telling us what happened at the crime scene?'

'You think you can intimidate me?' Amy glared at him. 'I've

dealt with way worse punters at the club than some copper with a tiny knob.'

One of the few cases where having a lawyer in the room would speed things up. 'Why did you decide to change the strategy?'

'I don't know what you're on about.'

'Amy, you switched places with someone. A girl we've yet to identify. Due to your actions, she's dead.'

Amy recoiled. 'I'm sorry, I really am. I had to improvise.'

'You've got a lot of explaining to do.'

'Look, I finished my morning shift and, like, I promised Dean a threesome with me and my flatmate. He's always going on about how much he'd fancy it, so I reckoned it was the best way to get him to talk and—'

'That wasn't the plan.'

'Aye, and that's why I didn't tell you. I'm the one with the brains here.'

Cullen bit his lip. 'And this girl, your flatmate?'

'Xena.'

'Xena?'

'As in the Warrior Princess. From some ancient TV show. Her mum liked the name.' Amy swallowed. 'Xena Farley. She's from Elgin. Works at Wonderland with me.'

'Worked.'

Amy took a sharp breath and held it for a moment. She closed her eyes and exhaled, long and slow. When she opened them again, she looked straight at Cullen. 'I know, but...'

Cullen held her gaze. 'Do you know any of Xena's family?'

'Eh?'

'Amy, I need to know her next of kin. I need to inform her parents of their daughter's death.'

'No, I didn't know her that well...' She broke eye contact. 'She talked about them, but it's not like they were in the flat every week, you know?' Then she made eye contact again, her tears smudging her make-up. 'I'm sorry.'

Cullen leaned back and crossed his arms. 'For what?'

Amy pursed her lips and cocked her head to the side. Stared into space again, like she couldn't get far enough away from her memory.

Cullen kept staring at her like he'd seen it all before. 'In your own time, Ms Forrest.'

She did a double take on Elvis. Another man in the room.

But Elvis was too busy ogling her breasts to notice.

She crossed her arms over her chest and looked back at Cullen. 'I'm sorry for ruining your operation – sting – whatever it's called.' Her voice was a monotone at a hundred miles a minute, like she was six years old and had been caught stealing biscuits. 'I'm sorry for putting Xena at risk. I'm sorry for thinking I could play Dean. I'm sorry I did you guys a favour by inviting him over to mine. I'm sorry I let you talk me into wiring my flat. I'm sorry he copped on when I kept asking him about drugs. I'm sorry he pulled his gun and aimed it at Xena, rather than me.' She paused. 'You'd have liked that better, wouldn't you?'

Cullen didn't even blink. Played it all through his head again, trying to focus on why the hell they were sitting in a stale little box down in Fettes. A woman was dead, someone who wasn't supposed to even be there. He hadn't heard anything on the tape that indicated someone else was engaging Vardy.

'No, wait.'

'I've got a wee surprise for you.'

'Just like that. Oooh. Bite it. Aye, you too.'

Oh crap. There it was.

Amy had let Xena in. And Vardy was into it.

But it cost Xena her life.

Cullen leaned forward on the table, his forehead inches from Amy's. 'Why did Vardy shoot Xena?'

'He said she'd been selling drugs on the side, and when she started freaking out, he—' Amy shook her head, lips sealed.

'Miss Forrest, I dare say even you'd be surprised at how many inches thick your police file is. We know you had a sideline dealing drugs at the club. You sold a gram of coke to one of my colleagues.'

'Mind, that was after we had a dance.' Amy giggled. 'Are you sure DC Simon Buxton was on duty?'

'Aye, funny.' Cullen reached for a manila envelope on the table and pulled out a stack of photographs along with an A4 sheet of paper. 'For the benefit of the tape, I am showing the witness the evidence marked P01 through P12, and laboratory test results of a related case noted D01.' He fanned out the pictures. 'Miss Forrest, this is you selling the coke.' He slid the paper across the table. 'And here are the lab results on its purity. Admittedly, it's not high-grade quality, but quite enough to warrant a few years at her majesty's pleasure in Cornton Vale.' He let the evidence soak in for a bit. 'The old deal was, you help us nail Vardy, you walk away from these charges.' He pulled the pages back. 'This is no longer on the table, so you need to talk to us.' He paused to let Amy picture what might happen to her should she refuse to co-operate. 'Starting with whether Vardy shot Xena.'

Amy picked an imaginary key out of the air, locked her lips and threw away the key.

Cullen reached for the envelope again. 'Let me show you something else. For the benefit of the tape, I am showing the witness photographs P13 through to P20. Miss Forrest, perhaps you'd like to have a look to see if these change your mind.' He drew out the photos and carefully placed them in front of Amy, one by one. 'This woman was a lap dancer who worked in Vardy's strip club a couple of years ago, the same place you work. Wonderland on Lothian Road. Miss Forrest, this is what happens when Vardy finds out that one of his girls is turning tricks on the side.' He looked up at Amy, waiting for her to meet his eye. 'Do you see where I'm going with this?'

Amy didn't move a muscle, but the pulse in her neck throbbed.

'You see, if *we* know about your other sideline.' Cullen looked at the photographs of the brutally slain prostitute. 'Wonder if Vardy knew. Easy for him to find out, I suppose.'

Amy gave him a meek nod. Cullen expected her to vomit. But no. Calm as you like. 'Why... why wasn't he put away?'

'Because Dean Vardy leaves no traces, Amy. He's run a criminal empire for five years, going from street dealing in Leith to running half of Edinburgh's drugs, all laundered through his bookies, his taxi firm, a pub and a club on George Street as well as your strip club. Not to mention the number of hits he's ordered. And he's progressed to murdering people himself. We're going to take him down. The only question is, who's going down with him.' Cullen gave her a pointed stare. 'We were going to prosecute him for his drug empire, but now we can get him for murder. But we need you to help.'

Amy flinched. 'I can't.'

'Then when Vardy gets off with Xena's murder...' Cullen pushed the worst picture even closer to Amy.

Amy stared at the photograph. 'I... I don't know what to do.'

Cullen lowered his voice. 'If you don't testify against Vardy, he'll get off. Again.'

She just shut her eyes, turned in on herself.

Cullen leaned forward and tapped the photo. 'You can make sure this never happens again. To you or any of your mates at the club.'

Amy shuddered. Something in her seemed to give. She shoved the photo back across the table and opened her eyes to look up at Cullen. 'Right, I'll do it. I'll testify.'

Cullen leaned back. 'You'll confirm that you saw Vardy shoot Xena?'

Amy nodded. 'Right in front of me.' Her eyes shifted back to the photographs and shuttled between them, faster and faster. 'He... he shot her right in front of me. So I ran out of the flat and straight through the next open door and into Sammy's bedroom and that's where... that's where I heard another two shots.' She jerked her head up as though waking from a violent nightmare. 'And then you showed up.'

4

Cullen knocked on the door and waited. Took a look around the office space, still empty. The rest of the team must still be at the crime scene.

What a bloody mess.

The security door clunked open and Wilkinson stood there, glowering. 'Congratulations, champ.' He play-punched Cullen's shoulder. 'This one's on you. Only a year to kibosh a long-running undercover investigation and get an innocent woman killed in the process.'

Cullen gritted his teeth. 'Sir, I wanted to move in on Vardy before he shot the woman, but you overruled me.'

'Doesn't change a thing.' Wilkinson slouched into his office and collapsed into his chair. He leaned back and gave Cullen the once over. 'It's plain to me that you don't suit this kind of work, Sergeant. In the drugs squad we don't close cases with your strong-arm tactics. We close them with due diligence and patience. A shit ton of patience.' He paused.

Cullen knew the power play – had seen it so many times over the years. Wilkinson was waiting for Cullen to say something, to give him the satisfaction of an argument, to offer some fightback that might distract him from his own failings as the lead investigator.

So Cullen just stood there. 'Sir, we've tried nailing Vardy any number of times, and from any number of angles, but he always slips away.'

'You know the second bloody recorder packed in? Can't hear shit on it. Supposed to be in the bedroom so we can hear it all, get Vardy on the record, but no. Did you have anything to do with that?'

'What? No, of course I didn't.' Cullen put his hands in his pockets, tightening them into fists. 'I've persuaded Amy Forrest to go on the stand.'

'Under other circumstances I'd buy the team enough beer to get Brian Bain grinding his hips. A woman's dead, so it doesn't feel like the time to celebrate.'

'No, sir.' Cullen folded his hands behind his back, waiting to be dismissed.

'Alright then, back to—'

Someone put a hand on Cullen's shoulder. 'Scott, do you mind?' DI Bill Lamb stood there, hands on hips, chin jutting out. With the goatee, sharp suit and striking pose, he looked every bit like a Musketeer challenging Cullen to a swordfight. A sharp flick of the wrist made Cullen step aside. Lamb charged over to the desk and went forehead-to-forehead with Wilkinson. 'Need a word about my case.'

'What?' Wilkinson stood there, hands on hips like he was drawing his own sword. 'Since when was this your case?'

'Since Xena Farley got shot.' Lamb took a few steps back, not quite a hundred paces. 'Your remit ends the minute you let someone get murdered, you daft bastard. This is now an MIT case.'

'My arse.' Wilkinson puffed out his chest. 'Like I just told Sergeant Cullen here, I've been working this case for donkeys and I won't have anyone interrupt my—'

'Enough!' Lamb spun round to Cullen. 'Going to give us a minute?'

~

CULLEN SAT DOWN AT HIS DESK IN THE OPERATION VENUS BULL PEN. The open plan office was now buzzing with activity, phones ringing, fingers clacking against keyboards, the usual suspects scrawling on a white board like that was work. He plugged a pair of headphones into his computer and played the audio they got from the wire in Amy's flat.

The sound quality was woeful. Distorted, tinny, quiet. He turned the volume up as far as it would go, tuned out the background office noise, and focused. Someone had knackered the recorder in the bedroom, which made this next to useless. Most of the dialogue sounded like it was from the bottom of a well.

'Why... why don't we slow things down a wee bit, eh?' Amy, sounding like she was setting up Vardy, now Cullen knew of her plan.

'Slow down?' Vardy hadn't cottoned on yet. 'Slow—'

Bain yanked the headphones out of Cullen's ears. 'What are you listening to, Sundance?' He stood right behind him, holding the cans up to his own ears. 'You filthy bastard. Your ongoing quest to complete Pornhub, eh?'

'Piss off.' Cullen twisted around and snatched the headphones back. Two female colleagues turned their heads the other way. Didn't recognise either. One looked a lot like Yvonne, Craig Hunter's ex-girlfriend, but at a glance he couldn't be sure, and he didn't want to stare at her after what she'd just heard. He looked back at Bain and dropped his voice to a murmur. 'What are you doing here?'

'My job, Sundance.' Bain snorted. 'Anyway, what's all the shouting in Wilko's office about?'

'Wilko and Lamb pissing up the wall to see whose dad would win in a fight or something.' Cullen turned back to his laptop, took a headphone splitter from the top drawer of his desk and plugged in a pair of pink earbuds, which he handed to Bain. 'The wiretap on Vardy.'

'Like I'm interested.' Bain smirked at him. 'Look, I'll help you analyse the recording if you take a wager on who wins that handbag fight in there.'

'A tenner on Lamb.'

'I'll take that action. Wilko's no mug.' Bain sat next to him and took about a year to press the buds in his ear. 'Sure these are made for humans?'

'No, which is why I gave them to you.' Cullen clicked play again, but he couldn't hear anything.

Bain pulled his left earbud out. 'This is shite.'

'Just listen, will you?'

'I've half a mind to walk into Wilko's office right now and tell him—' Bain paused. 'Although, who am I to interrupt the bollocking he's giving that twat.'

'Shh!' Cullen gave him a hard stare.

Seemed to work. Bain returned his attention to the recording, frowning and listening hard. More muffled conversation, more rustling and popping. Then a third voice was audible, a female voice, faint at first, then shrill – too shrill to make out many of the words.

Bain looked at him and said something, but Cullen couldn't hear what.

On the recording, the woman was shouting now. Cullen thought he heard 'rapist' and 'kill'.

Then a gunshot.

Cullen hit pause and looked at Bain. 'The shouting must've been Xena. But why was she threatening Vardy? Did it look like he was raping her friend?'

'Search me.' Bain shrugged. 'Why did Vardy shoot her for shouting a bit of abuse at him? What did that wee lassie say?'

'Her name is Amy. And she didn't. She said Vardy shot Xena.' Cullen shook his head. 'She didn't say that her friend started yelling at him about rape in the middle of a consensual blow job.'

Bain gave his best lecherous grin. 'Course you'd know what it sounds like to consensually suck a—'

'Gentlemen.' Lamb clapped them on the shoulders. 'DI Wilkinson and I just agreed that I'm taking lead on the Xena Farley murder.'

Cullen pulled out the remaining earbud. 'What about Operation Venus?'

'What about it?' Lamb pumped their shoulders. 'We've got Vardy for murder. Going away for life. Need you pair and all of the seconded MIT officers back to Leith Walk, pronto.'

'Aye?' Bain passed the headphones back to Cullen. 'Wilko agreed to that?'

'Well.' Lamb stifled a laugh. 'Alison Cargill kicked his boss's arse.'

Cullen held up both hands and spread out all ten fingers. 'I worked there for almost a year and never met his boss.'

'Your reputation precedes you.' Bain shook his head, but reached into his faded-black jeans pocket for a crumpled tenner.

Cullen palmed it from him and looked back up at Lamb. 'By the way, Bill, we'll have to have another word with our eyewitness, Amy Forrest. We just listened to her wiretap recording. It took a turn for the weird just before the shooting. Xena started shouting about Vardy being a rapist.'

'Well, he is.'

'I know, but if he raped Amy or Xena, then—'

'She's really called Xena?'

'Her mum was a fan of the TV show.'

'Christ. I used to watch that.' Lamb stared into space. 'How time flies, eh?'

'Bill, our entire case hinges on Amy Forrest's testimony. We need to get it nailed down.' Lamb shifted his attention to Cullen. 'You two need to get it nailed down. Have another word with Miss Forrest. And this time, Scott, make sure you get the truth from her.'

CULLEN OPENED THE INTERVIEW ROOM DOOR.

Bain's jaw dropped. He shoved Cullen out of the way, grabbed the handle and shut the door again. 'Sundance, the tits on her!'

Cullen kept his hand on the door. 'When are you going to grow up?'

'Seventh of never.' Bain grabbed Cullen's wrist, but tenderly. 'We should do this off the record?'

'What?'

'If we want her on the stand, the last thing we need is an interview where we discuss her ability to lie, okay?'

'Fair point.' Cullen barged past him and dropped on the chair across the table from Amy Forrest. 'Okay, Amy, let's try this off the record, okay?'

She didn't look at either of them. 'Can I get out of here or what?'

'What, I'm afraid.' Bain took a seat next to Cullen and leaned in to whisper: 'Why did you lie to us?'

Amy swallowed. 'What?'

'You told us Vardy shot Xena for dealing drugs on the side. You didn't mention that Xena called him a rapist, did you? Now, why would she do that?'

She kept her focus on the table.

Cullen looked at her. 'You want a lawyer, Amy?'

'Should I have one?'

'You need to give us the truth. So, we bring a lawyer in, or we don't. But you're going to stop lying to us.' Cullen leaned back and waited.

Amy looked him straight in the eye and shrugged. 'So what am I lying about?'

'I listened to the recording. Xena called Vardy a rapist. Now, why didn't you tell me that earlier?'

'She... I don't know.'

'That's bollocks. You knew, didn't you?'

'Okay, so I knew. But she pulled a knife, and I freaked out. Didn't expect it. But Dean... shit. He pulled a gun and... shot her. And I just ran. Then I heard the other two shots.'

Cullen waited until Amy looked back at him. 'Why did Xena call Vardy a rapist?'

Amy squirmed in her chair.

Cullen leaned forward again. 'Amy, why did Xena call Vardy a rapist?'

'Because he raped us!'

Cullen sat back. 'When?'

Amy trembled, her breathing a series of stifled sobs.

'Amy, when did he rape you?'

Bain held a hand in front of Cullen's face. He stuck a finger to his lips, then cleared his throat. 'I'm sorry, Miss Forrest.' His voice was unusually warm. 'Sorry for the anguish you've suffered and sorry for having to ask you to face the memory of it once more. But you're taking back control. By speaking with us, you'll help us put Vardy away for a long time. Away from you and away from other women who might suffer in similar ways.' He paused, letting the words sink in, watching her calm down, slowly but surely. She looked up at him. 'Would you tell us what happened, please?'

Amy blinked away a tear and took a deep breath. Then she nodded. 'He... raped Xena three months ago. Me last week.' Her eyes went out of focus, like she was no longer looking at Bain, but rather at the memory. 'It wasn't the first time for either of us. He pinned me against the wall in the dressing room and raped me from behind. Then made me have a shower to wash away the evidence.' She shuddered. 'He knew I'd been dealing, knew the cops were involved.' She fell silent, hardly breathing at all. 'He would've done it to us again. Could've done it whenever he wanted.' She sounded like a different person, hoarse, haunted. 'So I spoke to Xena about it – about what you'd spoken to me about last week. She said we should confront him, should get a confession. That's why I agreed to the wire. It's why I...' Her breath caught in her throat. She was silent again – longer this time. Seemed to have said everything there was to say. She looked up at Bain. 'But at least I got him to admit the rapes, so it wasn't all bad, right?'

Bain couldn't look at her.

Amy shifted her attention to Cullen. 'What's happened?'

Cullen pressed his lips together. 'I'm sorry. The recording's too muffled to hear a confession. We'd placed the microphone in the living room, but you took him into the bedroom.'

Amy stared at him. 'Are you kidding me?'

'No. We can't make it out.'

'Are you telling me I sucked that bastard's cock for *nothing*? After what he did to us?'

Cullen sat up straight to show he was taking her outrage seriously. And to demonstrate they were still in control of the case. 'No, Amy. Your actions weren't in vain. Xena's life wasn't in vain. But, I need you to go on the stand and testify against him. Tell the court what he did to you and Xena. And what you were prepared to do to aid this investigation.'

Amy was still staring at Cullen, confused, furious, hurt. She had no words to express the chaos of her emotions.

Bain leaned forward and drew her attention with a kind smile. 'Perhaps we can close this case from a different angle. Perhaps if you can let the court see how deranged he is. I mean, what would make a man who had raped you think he was visiting you for a *booty call*? That much we did hear him say on the recording, but that's not how a sane person would think, is it?'

Amy bit her lip. 'No. It isn't.' A drop of blood appeared on the lip. She wiped it away, then looked at her red fingertip as though it belonged to someone else. 'I told him Xena and I are into rough stuff. Told him I came when he raped me. It was a fantasy of mine. He loved it.'

Cullen closed his eyes. A wave of nausea hit him in the stomach. Hard. But not nearly as hard as he vowed to hit Dean Vardy.

—————

5

CULLEN OPENED THE POOL CAR DOOR AND JUMPED OUT INTO THE Leith Walk station garage. He paced over to the stairwell, his running shoes squeaking on the naked concrete floor.

'Hang on, Sundance.' Bain scrambled after him and caught his arm. 'Don't do anything daft now.'

Cullen stopped and stared down at Bain's hand on his sleeve until he let go. 'You know what's daft?' He looked Bain square in the face. 'Letting Vardy anywhere near those women. Giving him the opportunity to kill—'

'That wasn't your call, Sundance. That was Wilko's disaster, so don't blame yourself for it.'

'I wish it was that easy. Amy's my mark. I should've known she wouldn't stick to the plan. Or at least noticed something was off about the way she was talking to Vardy, and just the way she—'

'Scott.' The voice came from behind him, clipped, rough, familiar. PC Craig Hunter held the door open, a car key dangling in his other hand. His shaved head almost touched the top of doorjamb.

His shoulders didn't used to be that broad, did they? They weren't quite touching the frame, but there wasn't much light getting past him.

Must be that kettlebell training he mentioned a while back.

Look at the size of him. And look at me, staring at him like a love-struck gym bunny.

Hunter cleared his throat. 'How are things?'

'Aye, fine, yeah. Didn't expect to see you here, Craig.'

'Me neither.' Hunter sniffed, scanning the garage for his car. 'Hear about that shooting?'

'Our obbo.' Cullen looked at Bain, then back at Hunter. 'We were upstairs when the gun went off.'

'Seriously? It's all over the telly news.'

'I managed to nail Dean Vardy, mind. If you want to come out for drinks later—'

'You the man, Scott. See you when I see you.' Hunter strode past them, heading to the back of the garage.

Cullen watched him go. 'Is it just me or was he acting weird?'

'Was *he* acting weird?' Bain laughed. '*You* lost the power of speech at the sight of him, Sundance, then near enough shagged him with your eyes. It's like Top Gun, without all that straight shite.'

Cullen placed both hands on Bain's shoulders and looked him dead in the eye. 'Oh, sweet Brian, I don't fancy Craig. But if my sexual orientation does ever change, you'll be the first to know.'

'Piss off!' Bain swatted his hands away. 'Seriously, what's going on between you and him?'

Cullen glanced at the garage entrance. A black Audi skidded to a halt, the tyre-screech echoing off the walls. 'Let's just say that I wasn't always such a gentleman with the ladies, and unbeknown to me, one of them was...' He looked back at the Audi. 'Well, here's your dear friend Bill.'

Bain groaned.

Lamb leapt up from the driver's seat, swung the car door closed with obvious delight and strutted towards them. 'Scott, good to see you.' He walked right up to Cullen and stuck out his hand. 'Congratulations.'

'What for?'

'Amy Forrest?'

'What have I done now?'

'You got us the long-awaited break. As we speak, DC Gordon and DC Zabinski are taking a detailed statement on Vardy.'

Cullen shook his hand. 'Thanks, Bill, but...' He inclined his head at Bain. 'Much as I hate to say it, you need to extend your praise to old silver tongue here. Couldn't have done it without his sweet talking.'

Lamb narrowed his eyes at Bain. 'What?'

'I'm not just a pretty face.' Bain nodded. 'Dealt with a few poor wee lassies in my time. Always pays to empathise, you know?'

Lamb stared at him for another second, his face a mask. Then he offered his hand.

Bain took it and returned the squeeze. Seemed to wince.

'Well, thanks, Brian.' A smile crept into the corners of Lamb's eyes. 'You've done a cracking job.'

Bain nodded at him, deadpan.

Lamb focused on Cullen. 'Anyway, all that's left to do is the paperwork, but that can take as long as it needs to.' He clapped Cullen on the shoulder. 'Good to have you back in the land of the living.'

'Thanks.' Cullen tried for a smile. 'I still have massive regrets about what I did back when—'

A horn honked, the loud boom echoing round the close confines of the garage. A white Daimler sped up to them, much too fast for comfort.

'Shite!' Bain squeezed his eyes shut and braced for impact.

The car stopped, with a tight little squeak of the tyres, no more than a foot in front of him.

The driver's door swung open. 'German precision engineering.' A posh male voice. Then nothing. He seemed content to just sit there, obscured by the glare of the overhead strip lighting that turned the windscreen into a distorted mirror. But Cullen would have recognised the smarmy git's haughty tone anywhere.

Campbell McLintock, lawyer of the rich and ruthless. Bain and Lamb were squinting at the windscreen as McLintock heaved his bulk out of the seat and stepped out of the car. He gave a throaty chuckle, the sort he'd given to any number of juries over the years. Late fifties and grossly overweight, he wore a purple suit with a lime shirt and a yellow tie. He cleared his throat and took a surprisingly dainty bow. 'I aim to please, and my aim is as true as my word.'

'What brings you—? Oh, no. Don't tell me you're—'

'Dean Vardy, yes.' McLintock pointed his car key at the

Daimler and locked it with a smug little *blip*. 'Gentlemen, if you'll excuse me, I'll need a few minutes with my client.'

∾

THE BRIGHT LIGHT HURT CULLEN'S EYES. HE SQUINTED AT McLintock's fat fingers, folded on the interview table like a bunch of bananas. Cullen blinked and tried to focus on Lamb's voice, but it was just a drone, sending Cullen to sleep. He was crashing – hadn't eaten in hours, dehydration making his head throb. So he closed his eyes and rubbed his temples.

'DS Cullen?' Lamb's voice.

Cullen opened his eyes and looked at him. 'Aye?'

'As I was saying, you were the first officer on the scene.' Lamb gave a Cullen a good look, up and down. 'As such, would you like to start the questioning?'

Cullen squared his shoulders and glanced at his notes, pretending to search for the best opening gambit. He blew out his cheeks, reached for one of the plastic water cups and drained it. Then he scrunched it up in his hand and shot a sharp look at Vardy. 'Why did you kill Xena Farley?'

McLintock puffed out his chest. 'Sergeant, how dare you—'

'Campbell, it's cool.' Vardy laughed as he rested a placatory hand on McLintock's chest. 'Haven't done anything wrong, have I?' He winked at Cullen. 'Just went to Amy's flat for a nice quickie.' He glanced at his lawyer. 'That French thingy with the eggs and onions, right?'

McLintock sniggered. 'I believe the word you have in mind is *quiche*.'

'That's the one. So, I'm having my *quickie* with young Amy, when in walks Xena, acting all sexy. Who knows, maybe she'd brought some dessert, if you know what I mean.' Vardy nudged McLintock and got another snigger. Sounded like he'd poked an old set of bagpipes.

'Let me refocus your attention on the reason you're here, Mr Vardy.' Cullen grabbed Lamb's water and sipped at it. *Starting to feel a bit more human.* 'Why did you murder Xena Farley?'

'I didn't—'

'Easy now.' McLintock patted Vardy's arm. Looked like he was trying to calm down a bloodthirsty pit bull.

'Yes, Mr Vardy, easy now. It's a simple question. Why did you—?'

'I heard you the first time.' Vardy hissed at Cullen through clenched teeth. 'I didn't kill that bitch.'

'Here's the thing, though. You did.'

Vardy was panting hard now, trying to control his anger. 'You think?'

'Always. You might want to try it.'

Vardy stared at him, a spark in his eyes. It wasn't humour, though. 'Aye, funny. But you're wrong. I didn't kill her.'

'So who did?'

'You're the cop, you tell me.'

'Okay, so before this cunning escape artist vanished into thin air, they magicked the murder weapon into your hand, right?'

'He didn't magic anything!' Vardy's voice was a hoarse roar. One glance at his frowning lawyer and he took a few quick breaths to cool his temper. Then he was calm again, his breath slow and shallow. Like switching off a blow torch. 'I was busy with Amy, right, and Xena went to get this candle. Wanted me to pour hot wax on her. Kind of into that sort of thing, you know what I mean? Then some guy broke into the flat. Never seen him before. Old boy, wino nose, rotten teeth, face like a melted welly. Amy seemed to know him, but he didn't give her a chance to introduce us. Just pulled his gun and shot Xena. No idea why, man. Looked like a bampot to me, though. Real headcase, if you know what I mean.' He twirled his finger next to his forehead, like he was concerned for the man's mental wellbeing.

Cullen put a hand to his own throbbing forehead. 'You know him?'

'Amy said he was her neighbour from over the way.' Vardy pursed his lips and put on a comical frown, then slowly nodded his head. 'Aye, now you mention it, Amy called him Sammy. She tried talking him down, like "Hey, Sammy, it's okay. Just put the gun away." Christ's sake, man. The boy didn't, did he? Just shot her. Would've done Amy and me if I hadn't disarmed him.'

'Of course. And are we to believe this gun I saw you hold is his, not yours?'

Vardy grinned. 'Now we're on the same page, pal.'

Cullen dropped his hand from his head and let it land on the table with a bang. 'Then why were you holding it?'

McLintock whispered: 'Careful.'

'Like I said, I got it off the boy.' Vardy kept grinning. 'But I tell you, I was traumatised, Sergeant. That bastard killed Xena, man. I made him drop the shooter but the prick ran out of the flat before you lot arrived. It all happened so fast. I was confused, acting on autopilot, know what I mean?'

'I can see how deeply it has affected you, Mr Vardy. Unfortunately we've been reliably informed that you – how shall I put this to spare your delicate feelings? – well, allegedly you RAPED THESE WOMEN!'

Vardy flinched.

McLintock opened his mouth. 'Sergeant, that is completely—'

Vardy was laughing. 'You were reliably informed, were you? That's priceless, that is. How reliable do you reckon that source is? You've met these girls, right? Little tramps to a woman. How could I have raped them? Hoors like that, they're always ganting for it—'

'Enough.' Lamb clapped his hands. 'Mr Vardy, we're charging you with aggravated assault, rape and drug conspiracy. We've got a team of forensic accountants going through your books as we speak. It's a hell of a lot of paperwork, but trust me when I say this. You'll be going away for a long time.'

Vardy's turn to open his mouth.

Lamb cut him off with another sharp clap of the hands. 'Now, do you wish to add anything before we conclude this interview?'

Vardy took a breath.

McLintock patted his arm again, a lot firmer this time.

Vardy glanced at him, then looked back at Lamb, gritted his teeth and shook his head.

'For the benefit of the tape, the suspect shook his head.' Lamb checked his watch. 'The interview ends at eighteen forty-four.' He switched off the audio recorder and hauled himself up to standing.

McLintock hefted his bulk up. 'I wish to hear both recordings from the flat in question.'

Cullen stared at Lamb, saw his confusion mirrored. 'Both?'

'Yes, both. I gather young Ms Forrest had two radio microphones in her flat?'

'You knew one of them broke, didn't you?'

McLintock chuckled. 'How imaginative, Inspector.'

Lamb took one last look at McLintock then went out into the corridor.

'The Custody Sergeant will be along shortly.' Cullen joined Lamb outside, wedging the door open with his foot to keep an eye on them. 'What was that about?'

'Search me.' Lamb looked off down the long corridor. 'Time to celebrate. Take the team over to the Elm for a few, aye?'

Cullen groaned. 'I'm not drinking these days.'

Lamb clapped him on the shoulder and led the way. 'Sure, Scott. Just the one.'

6

'—*OF THE FAAAAAMOUS IN-TER-NA-TIONAL PLAYYYBOYS!*' BAIN WAS swaying on the tiny stage, bellowing into the microphone at the top of his voice, mangling Morrissey almost beyond recognition.

Cullen looked around the crowded pub, blurry figures everywhere. A pair of uniforms pushed past him to the bar, jostling for attention as they shouted their orders, waving cards at the busy staff. Somewhere along the way he'd asked someone to hold his jacket, Bill Lamb probably, he couldn't remember, but it was too hot for more than a T-shirt and even that was soaked with sweat. The bright lights behind the bar stung his eyes, all those multi-coloured optics, a whisky collection as wide as the wall, countless shiny golden taps of lager and beer. Someone pushed from behind.

What the hell are all these people doing out on a Monday night?

August in Edinburgh. Festival season. Sod that, I'm going home.

Cullen turned to the door and pushed his way through the noisy hordes, head down, elbows out.

'Watch it, you prick!' An athletic brunette in a fitted white blouse and snug black trousers spun around and froze, her scowl melting to a puzzled smile. 'Scott?'

'Sharon?' Cullen gawked at her. 'I, um, I'm just heading home.'

DI Sharon McNeill held her hand behind her ear. 'I can't hear a word you're mumbling.'

Cullen stepped closer and spoke into her ear, wrapping his arm around her shoulder. 'I was saying, I was just about to head home.'

'Were you now?' She smirked. 'I've just got here. You looked like you were fighting your way to the bar.' She leaned in closer. Cullen thought she was going for a kiss and went to meet her half-way. Instead, she sniffed his breath and pulled back. 'Jesus, you smell like a brewery.'

He straightened up. 'What? I only had—'

'Save it.' She gave him a hard stare. 'You're not supp—'

'It was alcohol-free.'

'Believe that when I see it.' She turned away from him to look at the woman next to her.

DS Chantal Jain nodded at him. 'Scott.' She kept her expression neutral, just stared at him. Her delicate features gave away little about what she was thinking. Her jet-black hair was tied back – her cappuccino skin flawless as ever.

Shite, is that racist?

A cheeky smile crept into her almond-shaped eyes, then she gave him a quick hug – only to pull back even quicker, wiping both hands on her cream skirt. 'Eww, you're soaking.'

'Aye, well, it's roasting in here.' Cullen glanced at Sharon, then quickly back at Chantal. 'Anyway, I saw your boyfriend today.'

'Craig?' Chantal raised her eyebrows. 'That's weird. I was just talking to him and he never mentioned it. Did you piss him off again?'

'Hardly.' Cullen kneaded his temples to cover his discomfort. 'Must've just slipped his mind.'

Over the far side of the pub, Lamb was waving at him, beckoning him over to the huddle near the gents, a few colleagues Cullen only vaguely recognised. He turned back to the ladies. 'Have you spoken to Lamb yet?'

'We've just got here.' Sharon looked like she was about to turn around and leave.

Chantal gave her a nudge. 'We're only here because we heard you'd cracked that big case. Thought we'd join the celebration.'

Sharon let him take her hand, gently lift it to his lips and kiss it. She rolled her eyes, but let him lead her through the crowd.

'Jesus, Brian.' Lamb shook his head as Bain clambered off the stage. 'Someone call the police. You murdered that song.'

Bain took a theatrical bow. 'I gave it a good bash, eh? But I left it alive just enough to give it another go next time, if you catch my drift.' He thrust his groin out with all the grace of a horny terrier looking to mount a slipper. Then he noticed Cullen. And Sharon. And Chantal. 'Sundance! You've been propping up the bar so long, you missed my karaoke performance.' He pouted. 'I'm hurt.'

'I didn't miss a single thrust.' Cullen laughed. 'You need someone to pop your pelvis back in?'

Bain blew him a kiss, just as he caught Sharon's eye, peering around Cullen's back. He treated her to his best leery stare. 'Butch! Lovely to see you.'

'You know that I'm a grade above you now?' Sharon examined him from head to toe, making sure to be obvious about it. 'Sod it. You know what? Whatever. Just point me in the direction of Elvis. I need someone for a bit of surveillance work.'

Bain grinned. 'Sorry to disappoint you, darling, but Elvis has left the building.'

Lamb got in on the act. 'What surveillance do you need?' He thumbed at Cullen. 'Catching lover boy sneaking off for a pint or five? Eh, Scott?'

Cullen groaned. 'It was alcohol—'

'Aye, aye, Scott, you've never been a man for a drink.' Lamb slapped him on the shoulder, again. 'It's just not your thing, is it?'

Sharon shot him a pointed look. 'Cut it out, Bill.'

Lamb stepped back. More of a stagger. He steadied himself on a colleague, but seemed less interested in what she was trying to tell him than in hitting her with another gag. 'You know what they say about the typical copper – he's a policeman with a drinking problem. Scott, on the other hand, he's a drinker with a policing problem.'

More howls of laughter, more backslapping.

'Is that why you two haven't got any kids yet, is it? No time for a family when there's so much drink—'

Sharon slapped him.

Stunned silence from the lads. It seemed to hit them like a shockwave.

Lamb touched his hand to his burning cheek.

All around, the song and dance of the crowd continued, but Cullen just stared at his girlfriend, lost for words.

Sharon stepped forward, her nostrils flaring wide. 'Bill, how *dare* you try to embarrass a woman for being unable to have children.'

'Sharon, I—'

'Do you think it's *funny*? Just because you can stick your little maggot up someone and knock them up doesn't mean it's—'

Cullen reached for her hand, but Sharon shook him off. 'Go on, Bill, say something. I mean, nothing's off limits with you, is it? Just as long as your idiots here laugh. Right?'

Lamb bit his lip.

Cullen tried to get between them.

But Sharon shoved him out of the way and got right in Lamb's face, snarling. 'Don't you like it when a woman talks back? Are you worried I might have a go at one of your many, many embarrassments? Like your piss-poor arrest record? You were a shambles out in East Lothian and you've been worse here in Edinburgh. You're just relying on the old boys' network to keep your career afloat, aren't you? And let's talk about that big Vardy collar Scott got you today.'

Again, Cullen tried to get between them. Again, she shoved him out of the way.

'Let's be honest, if you're the one preparing the case for court, Vardy won't get convicted.'

Lamb took a step back, raising both hands to signal he meant no harm. And to fend off another slap, which was looking likelier by the second.

Instead, Sharon turned on her heel and made her way to the front door, cutting right through the swaying crowd.

Cullen started after her.

Lamb caught his arm. 'Scott, I'm sorry. I had no idea. I wasn't trying to have a go at her.'

'Bill.' Cullen turned to face him. 'Instead of taking the piss out of me, maybe you should've put yourself in her position. She even tried to tell you, but you were too busy acting the big man. Now I have to pick up the pieces.'

~

'SHARON!' CULLEN BURST THROUGH THE FRONT DOOR. IT FELT LIKE breaching the water surface after a deep dive. The fresh air hit him in the face. The image of his girlfriend slapping his boss flashed across his memory. Then the door closed behind him and cut the pub's drone to a dull throb. White and maroon buses rumbled up and down Leith Walk, multicoloured rickshaws weaving through gaggles of pedestrians, a family with painted faces, a burly man with two black eyes. A black cab darted in and out of the nearby parking bay to pick up a group of drunks, trying to open the doors before he stopped.

Cullen shook his head and focused on the faces around him.

Sharon was standing at the bus stop across the road, watching him with a blend of disbelief and disgust.

Cullen took a step towards her, but stumbled as the sudden movement sent a rush of blood to his head. He staggered to a stop, and leaned over, hands on knees, waiting for the black spots in front of his eyes to disappear.

Sharon was still standing at the bus stop, arms folded, tutting. 'Look at the state of you, Scott.'

'I'm not drunk. Just three bottles of Nanny State. Half a percent each. I'd need to drink ten to get a slight buzz.'

'So why are you stumbling like you've been out with Rich and Tom?'

'Because I'm knackered and I've not eaten and because a woman was shot right in front of me.'

That got her. 'Shite.'

'Bill's running a murder inquiry and it's my fault. Supposed to be easy, but...' Cullen ran a hand down his face. Made no difference. Instead, he concentrated on her disapproving stare, using it like a taught rope to pull himself up and all the way across the road to the bus stop. 'Look, Bill's a wanker. He's acting like the big man because his team just caught the bad guy and he's had a few too many pints and he's feeling all invincible and—'

'Stop rambling, Scott! It's not him I'm pissed off at.'

'But that joke about us not having kids and—'

'Scott, listen to me.' Sharon grabbed his shoulders and shook him. 'The joke was tactless, sure, but it's you who's pissed me off.'

Cullen frowned. 'Me?'

Sharon glared at him. 'Bill's right, you know, I might as well hire a surveillance expert to follow you around. I just can't trust you.'

'What?' Cullen wracked his brain, replaying the scene in the pub.

I didn't do anything wrong. Did I? Or is she talking about something bigger? Does she suspect me of cheating on her?

He cleared this throat. 'What have I done?'

'You're plastered.'

'I had two bottles—'

'It was three a minute ago.'

'Shite.' Cullen leaned back against the bus stop. 'Okay, so I had a pint of beer. Alcohol and all that. Bill forced me.'

'And you just took it?'

'He said it's what a team leader does.'

'You're sure it was just the one?' She let go off his shoulders. 'Scott, you can hardly stand up.'

'Might've been two. But I switched to the—' He burped into his hand. 'Christ. I switched to the alcohol-free one.'

'What was it you had?'

Cullen couldn't help but smirk. 'It was Elvis Juice.'

'This isn't funny!'

'I know, but Bill was going on about drinking pints of Elvis's piss.'

She pulled out her phone and started thumbing the screen. 'You stupid bastard. That stuff is six and a half per cent. You've not touched a drop in months, no wonder you're bladdered.' She put her phone away and looked around for a bus. 'Scott, you promised me you wouldn't start drinking again without a discussion.'

'Sharon, I—'

She cut him off with a look as sharp as broken glass. And as glittering. She blinked away the tears, then dropped her gaze to the ground. 'I'm not even sure we're doing the right thing anymore.'

'What do you mean?'

'Scott, you know I can't have children. That's all under the bridge. Yeah, yeah, we can adopt, but I just don't know if you're fit to be a father.'

That stung like a punch in the gut. 'What?'

'You're a child. I don't even need to ask if I'll be a decent mother, because I'm looking after you.'

Cullen put his arms around her and drew her in for a hug. 'Come on, that's—'

'Scott!' She held up her hand like she was going to invite him into Lamb's slapping club. 'Back off.'

Cullen stepped away.

Jesus Christ. What a bloody mess. What the hell do I do?

A bus rumbled towards them. A couple of drunks counted change in front of them, jostling for position.

Cullen took her hands and went down on one knee. 'Sharon McNeill, will you marry me?'

DAY 2

Monday
13th February

18 months later

7

CULLEN COULDN'T LOOK AT AMY FORREST.

So he looked at DC Simon Buxton instead. Watched him stroke his goatee, seemingly lost in thought, giving his groomed beard a break to swipe his floppy fringe from his forehead.

Cullen took a deep breath, made sure his most encouraging smile was fixed firmly in place.

Amy was sitting in an armchair, her baggy grey leggings sagging around her knees, hugging her oversized grey fleece jumper tight, the material splattered with food, snot and puke stains, trying to calm a baby boy with a tired rocking motion. Trying and failing. The child kept whining, not a proper cry, but the sort that couldn't be ignored for long before the floodgates would burst. Despite the nine months practice as a mother, Amy seemed to have no idea about what to do with her son. Still looked like a child herself – just eighteen.

Hard to reconcile the image with her previous life as a stripper.

Cullen cleared his throat. 'Thanks for agreeing to see us this early in the morning.'

'Aye, no problem.' Amy didn't even have the energy to look up at him. Just left her blank gaze resting on the coffee table between them. 'It's not like I'd be sleeping otherwise. Zak's up at the crack of dawn. Every single day...'

'Right, well, we'll not keep you anyway. Our visit is to make sure you have no further questions about the trial proceedings. I take it you're still okay to testify?'

Amy reached for the wee one's bottle on the coffee table, then leaned back on the couch and tried to plug the rubber teat in his mouth. He turned his head away and cranked up the noise. 'Aye, no problem.'

Cullen glanced at Buxton, but it was clear Buxton also doubted if she had understood the question. So Cullen looked back at Amy. 'So there's no problems?'

Amy paused. Seemed to think about it. Then closed her eyes. 'What was the question?'

'I asked if you're still fine to testify at the trial.' Cullen measured his voice, matching it to her slower cadence to establish an unconscious rapport. He paused, just like she had. 'Are you?'

Amy opened her eyes again and met his concerned gaze. 'You think I don't look fine?'

Cullen saw exhaustion. Self-loathing. Regret. And an utter lack of hope. In the deep shadows under her eyes. In the hard set of her mouth. In the sallow tone of her skin. He had to look away. Silence settled between them, and Cullen didn't know how to break it.

Buxton leaned forward on the couch, switched on his cockney charm. Not too much, not too little. 'That's the great thing about having a nipper at a young age – both nans will all still be alive, right? You must get lots of support from family and friends?'

Amy snorted. 'Are you serious?'

'Well, I mean, both my brothers have got boys and girls. Both nans love looking after their grandkids. I bet yours do, too, right?'

'You're a special kind of stupid.' Amy stared at him. 'I was a stripper when I got pregnant after that animal raped me. Exactly how excited do you think my family were when they found out, eh? And how many pals do you think stuck around when the baby came? Eh?'

Buxton swallowed. 'I... I hadn't thought of that.'

Amy's eyes said she was about to flare up, but she deflated quickly. She turned back to the baby and tried to coax him into accepting the bottle, waving the little teat under his nose. The boy just screamed louder.

Cullen cleared his throat. 'Is there anything we can do to help you?'

Her head snapped up. 'You got a time machine?'

She had a lifelong habit of rejecting polite offers of help with equally polite reassurances that she was fine, just fine. She wasn't fine. And someone needed to tell her that was okay to not be fine.

'I wish I did. We're here to help you.'

She stared at him. Gradually, the fire in her eyes went out. Then she thanked him with the tiniest of nods, grabbed the baby and held it out to him.

Cullen froze, unsure what to do. *Am I supposed to look at the boy or hold him?*

'Here, take him. I need to get a jar of mush from the kitchen, since he won't take the bottle.'

Cullen jumped up from the couch, rounded the coffee table and took the squirming boy from her hands, her slippered feet padding through to the kitchen. He looked down at the little thing in his arms. The baby's right eyebrow was circled by a faint birthmark. Couldn't weigh more than a stone. *Is that normal for a nine-month-old? Seems very light, but what do I know?* He hugged the baby to his chest and started swaying, silently at first. So he started talking to the boy, his head bent low. 'Hey, little man. It's not always this cold outside, you know? It can even get quite warm.'

Buxton was frowning at the stream of nonsense.

The little eyes looked up at him, puzzled. Then the expression hardened and all Cullen could see was the steely grey of Dean Vardy's eyes. Made him flinch, made bits of him clench tight.

It can change as they grow up, but Jesus, I hope that's all he's inherited.

Buxton was still watching.

'Your mummy's just gone to get you something to eat. She'll be back soon enough.'

The boy settled down, shut his eyes and puckered his lips. Then fell asleep.

Cullen gazed at the slow rise and fall of his small chest, the warmth of his tiny body, the looseness of his short limbs.

The silence was shattered by a single, piercing sob.

The baby jumped with fright. Cullen clamped on to Zak, fast and tight, and felt it take a shuddering breath, then unleash a high-pitched scream.

Amy was standing in the kitchen doorway, a hand clamped

over her mouth. In the other she held a jar of baby food, useless and forgotten. She watched Cullen snap out of it and soothe her son with a gentleness that was as far beyond her reach as the stranger across the room. Her trembling hand dropped to her side and she started crying, her face twisted up and red – like mother, like son.

Cullen walked over to her and gently placed the boy in her arms. He tried to put some cheer into his expression, let her know that her life wasn't always going to be like this, but he couldn't make his face lie and Amy wasn't looking at him anyway. She was looking at her child, like a prisoner looks at her warden.

'Excuse me?' Buxton over by the coffee table, an impatient question in his eyes. 'Can I just wind back a bit? You implied you don't have a support network, yeah?' He frowned, as though to prove he really had been thinking. 'Those animals will ask this in court, so this isn't me being harsh, yeah? If it was so obvious to you that you'd be raising the little guy alone, why did you have him?'

Amy's eyes widened.

Cullen mouthed, 'What the hell?'

Buxton tried his cockney geezer act again. 'I mean, I know you didn't *choose* to have him. But when you found out you were pregnant, you decided to keep him, and that *was* your choice, and I'm wondering why. Dean Vardy's lawyer is a real nasty piece of work. In court, he might suggest that you having the child indicates a certain desire to be a mother, and he might claim your relationship with... your child's father is a little more complicated than that of victim and rapist. He'll certainly ask the jury to question the validity of your testimony, so I want you to be prepared for that, yeah?'

Cullen could only stare at him.

Amy didn't say a word, just sobbed even harder, the baby responding to his mother's anguish by arching away from her and screaming so loudly his eyes bulged. She trudged back to the couch and slumped down on it, letting the child squirm and scream on her until he tired himself out. She settled him on her lap and opened the jar as if on auto-pilot, looking around the other scraped-out jars and scrunched-up wet wipes on the coffee table. She reached over and picked up the least-dirty teaspoon, rubbing it on her fleece jumper. Then she spooned some of the bright yellow fruit mush out of the jar and held it in front of the boy's closed mouth. His eyes opened, followed by his mouth, and she stuck the spoon in.

In the awkward silence, Cullen sat down on the chair across from the mother and child. Buxton looked ready to continue the questioning, so Cullen got in first. 'We're here to help, Amy. We're sorry we can't do more, but we can help you prepare for what you'll face at this trial.' He shot a glare at Buxton that hopefully read, 'Keep quiet,' then smiled at Amy again. 'Could you maybe talk us through your thoughts when you found out you were pregnant with Zak?'

Amy looked up. A shadow fell on her tired face. 'Suppose.' She looked back down at her child and continued feeding him. 'I was working at Wonderland at the time, but you know that. Anyway, after... after *that* happened, one of *his* partners took over the day-to-day management and the show went on, and so did my life. At least I thought so, until I got sick on stage one night. Took a sick day, felt like shite. Went to the chemist, got a pregnancy test and that was that.' She paused.

Cullen didn't want to jump in – wanted her to explain it. Her own words, whatever that meant.

Amy held Zak up to her face, making eye contact with him. 'I told my best mate about it and she told me to get an abortion. Course she did. She'd had one herself. No big deal. Right?' Her eyes burrowed into Cullen, her stare vicious. Then she shook her head and her focus went back to her son. 'Or so I thought. I mean, I'm not religious, and it was the only way to keep my job and my friends and my lifestyle and...' She swallowed, a brief flicker flashing over her eyelids. 'Just after I started there, one of the girls got knocked up and had the kid. Last we saw of her. I tried to stay in touch, but it's hard when you're working all night. Means you're asleep when the mothers are up, and we ran out of stuff to talk about in ten seconds flat. Not like you can laugh about the sad wankers trying to grope your tits all night while she's breast-feeding her kid, eh?' She looked up and laughed, her eyes staying dead. 'When I found out, I was most scared about being alone. I was used to being judged and, one way or another, I've always been alright for money. But I've never been alone.' She went back to feeding her baby. 'But something changed. Maybe it was the hormones. But maybe this was my chance to do something that wasn't about *me*, something selfless. Something good.' She looked up at Cullen again, but the ghost of a smile had vanished. Instead, fresh tears welled up in her eyes. 'But this isn't good. I'm not good. I'm failing every day.' She looked back down at the baby. 'And he reminds me of *him* all the time. And of what *he*... did to me. Because my child looks just like... like my rapist.' She shut her eyes as a sob wracked her body.

Cullen couldn't look at her.

Buxton was, and Cullen could've sworn they were thinking the same thing.

This was useless.

They were useless.

There was nothing they could do to help this woman, and in all likelihood, there was nothing she could do to help herself.

Her testimony alone wouldn't secure a conviction for Vardy, and they were making her put herself through the ordeal of reliving the violence he made her suffer, and in a courtroom full of strangers. And the system required more than her word against his for a murder conviction.

Cullen glanced at the kid. DNA evidence showed that Vardy was the father, but he'd said the sex had been consensual. Normally, it would be her word against his, but of course they had an audio recording of them having sex after the rape. For whatever reason, Amy wouldn't pursue it. Too busy getting on with things.

Cullen's phone rang. DI Bill Lamb. He raised a hand in apology to Amy as he got up. 'What's up?'

'Scott, someone's got to the witness.'

8

CULLEN SLAMMED HIS HAND DOWN ON THE DOOR HANDLE AND charged into the hospital room, Buxton hot on his heels. He scanned the room, four beds, all occupied.

Sammy McLean was lying in the left one at the large window, breathing through a tube. But at least he was breathing.

The attending doctor stood by his bedside, her hair in a severe bun, her back to the door. She seemed to be examining the stats on the machine, and seemed to be in no hurry about it, as she made a series of adjustments. Then she turned around to inspect the new arrivals with a grim-faced scepticism.

Cullen flashed his warrant card, Buxton following suit. 'DS Cullen, DC Buxton. How is he?'

'My name is Dr Helen Yule.' She folded her arms, cracking the starch of her white coat, and peered over her glasses with a stern frown. She took the glasses off and breathed on the lenses, polishing them on her short sleeves. Her right eyebrow was half missing, an old scar intersecting it. Then she put her specs back on, the strip lights turning the round lenses into mirrors. 'Mr McLean is in no fit state to take visitors.'

Cullen looked down at the patient next to her, but it could've been anyone. White bandages covered most of his head, the rest was purple skin obscured by a breathing mask. 'Look, we really need to speak to him, if you don't mind?'

'I do mind.' Yule took a step towards him, arms folded even tighter. 'Mr McLean here is in a critical condition. In order for him to make a full recovery he must be spared any and all forms of stress. And something tells me stress is all you brought with you today.'

Cullen recognised a trap when he saw one. So he got a grip on his temper. 'No stress at all, Doctor. We need to ask Mr McLean about the circumstances of his assault. As an eyewitness in a forth-coming trial—'

'And it'll have to wait.' Dr Yule stuck her hands on her hips. 'He has sustained considerable head injuries and—'

'Seriously—'

She cut Cullen off with a sharp shake of the head. 'Just look at him! Does this look like a man who can focus on your questions?'

Cullen took another look at the body in the bed and could only agree with her.

'Even when he's well enough, I can't promise he'll remember enough about the incident to answer them. The brain...' Yule frowned as though wondering whether Cullen even had one. 'The brain is a complicated machine and memory's a fickle thing at the best of times.' She clasped her hands together. 'Now, I must insist that you leave. Now.' She ushered them out of the room and closed the door firmly behind her. 'Your questions will have to wait.' She reached into her pocket for a small device and grunted at it. 'Keep out of that room.' She walked down the corridor, as brisk and sure-footed as a drill sergeant. No mean feat in a pair of Crocs.

Cullen waited until she turned a corner, then reached for the door handle to Sammy's room.

'Scott!' Lamb was striding towards them from the other end of the corridor like some souped-up muscle-car bearing down on them. He'd been hitting the weights hard, put on at least two stone in the last year, all of it around the chest and shoulders. 'Glad I caught you.' He stopped far too close to Cullen, making him step away from the door. 'How is McLean?'

Buxton grinned. 'Scott tried to ask him, but a doctor got her teeth into him before he got a chance.'

'He's not in a good way, Bill.' Cullen peered through the glass into the room. The hiss of each breath rattled the frame. 'Dr Yule refused access. She doesn't know if he'll be in a fit state to testify at the trial.'

'Shite.'

'Reckons he may have suffered some memory loss.'

'The guy wasn't the full shilling anyway.' Lamb leaned against the wall, kicking his left foot back against the paint as he strummed his moustache. He nodded to Buxton. 'Stay here, okay? The minute McLean wakes up, I want you in there to take his statement. Until then, nobody gets in that room without your approval.'

Buxton gave a nod. 'Noted.'

'Now, Scott, I need you to find me whoever assaulted Sammy. Head back to the station and go through the CCTV.'

'Come on, Bill—'

'No, Scott.' Lamb cut him off with a cheeky glint in his eye. 'Someone's tried to murder a witness. Vardy's name's all over it. Now, prove it for me, okay?'

～

'HERE YOU GO.' CULLEN ENTERED THE CCTV SUITE, TWO PAPER bags in his hands. 'A decaf cappuccino with extra cream and caramel sauce, and two haggis paninis with extra cheese.'

'Breakfast of champions.' Elvis glanced around from the bank of flat-screen monitors and snatched the bigger of the two bags. 'Ah, buggeration, it's all spilt.'

'To your good health.' Cullen pulled a polystyrene cup of black coffee from his own bag and toasted him. 'You obviously value it.'

Elvis laughed, bits of semi-chewed haggis flying from his mouth onto his keyboard. 'Good health's overrated. What's the point in living to a hundred, if you have to give up all the things that make living worthwhile?'

'Never change, eh?' Cullen took a pot of porridge from his bag and sniffed at the grey slime. Burnt. 'You getting anywhere?'

'Kind of.' Elvis checked his watch. 'I need to get back out to Bathgate for my shift soon, but this is another favour you owe me.'

'Add it to the pile.'

'Okay, well I've made a wee film for you.' Elvis slurped coffee, then rinsed his mouth out with it and swallowed. 'Should really have some popcorn.' He took another bite of panini as he moved the mouse and clicked.

The blank wall-mounted screen lit up, showing Sammy's beige-and-grey tower block in Dumbiedykes. Down below, a heavy-set man in a dark hoodie approached the front door, pushed through and disappeared inside the building.

Elvis clicked again and it cut to another camera. Inside view of a stairwell. The same man trudged up the steps, hood pulled down low, casting his face in shadow. Kept looking behind, below, took a few seconds to clear the first floor. Watching everything, every detail, his neck in constant movement like a midfielder looking for the next pass and the one after that. The man climbed up to Sammy's floor.

And kept on walking.

Cullen frowned. 'Is that not him?'

Still chewing, Elvis pointed at the screen. 'Never take your eye off the ball, my man.'

On the screen, the hooded figure stopped halfway up the next flight of stairs and pressed himself against the inside wall. He stayed like that for just short of half an hour, according to the clock in the corner racing through the minutes as Elvis sped it up. The guy shifted his stance a little every so often to relieve the strain of sustained alertness, each small movement looking like a muscle spasm in fast forward.

Then Elvis switched it off and the guy was perfectly still again. Five seconds later, another man appeared in the frame, jogging up the steps from below. Sammy McLean stopped on the landing, clutching two shopping bags. He put one down as he opened the door to his corridor.

The recording seemed to snap into fast forward again, but Elvis hadn't touched it. This was real-time.

The hooded figure shot down the stairs, grabbed Sammy from behind and hurled him over the landing. By the time Sammy reacted, he was already airborne, flying head first down the stairs. He tried to cover up, but his hands didn't make it all the way to his face. His shopping bag caught in the railings and he crunched hard on the lower landing, his head cracking off the banister. He went limp, his legs buried underneath him. Burst milk cartons sprayed all over him, ready-meal boxes splatting a red tableau around him.

At the upper landing, the hooded figure stood and watched for a few seconds. Then he rushed down the steps, jumped over Sammy with surprising ease for such a big guy and ran down the rest of the stairs.

Elvis cut back to the outside camera. The front door flew open, the man raced out, jumped into a car parked kerbside and sped out of shot. The video froze on the empty street.

Cullen stood there, sipping bitter coffee. Looked like a professional hit, though more attempted murder rather than sending a message. Sammy's milk and spag bol saved him from going all the way down. 'Can you trace the number plate?'

'Sure, but you won't care about that when you see what else I got.' Elvis flexed his fingers, reached for the keyboard and let them hover over it. 'Expect to be amazed.' He hit rewind and the images replayed in reverse, the car speeding back into shot and the door flying open. The hooded figure jumped out backwards and stopped on the street. Elvis adjusted the jogwheel until it slowed to a crawl then stopped. 'Tada!'

Cullen leaned forward and narrowed his eyes. A gust of wind had caught the guy's hood just before he ducked his head to get in the car. Blink and you'd miss it.

But Elvis hadn't missed it. And it was a clear shot. 'Gareth Irwin. Vardy's bar manager.'

DI Lamb pushed through the swing doors and Cullen followed him into the Debonair. The doors sucked shut behind them but someone stopped them.

'Hoy!' Wilkinson marched in. Cullen hadn't seen him for months – barely recognised the guy. He'd lost at least three stone and looked well for it, like he'd been attending the gym rather than just paying the monthly direct debit. 'You pricks think you're going in without me?'

'This is my gig, Paul.' Lamb stopped him with a hand to the chest. 'You're here to advise.'

Wilkinson stared at him for a few seconds, then nodded. 'Go on, then. You make an arse of it and I'll pull a rabbit out of a hat.'

'Believe that when I see it.' Lamb led through to the bar area, the morning's cold half-light slanting through the frosted windows. The place was mostly empty, save for two cleaning ladies who had been mopping the hardwood floor to a wet gloss. Now they just stood there, framed by the bar on the one side and the window booths, where a group of lads tucked into a fry-up. Rows of round tables lined the far wall, stacked high with chairs, as motionless as the cleaners.

Lamb flashed his warrant card. 'Good morning, ladies. DI Lamb, Police Scotland.'

Neither woman replied, instead staring at the card, frozen in the moment, an obvious question in their wide eyes. The lads in the window continued their breakfast.

Lamb slid his ID back into the breast pocket of his suit jacket and tried again. 'Either of you seen the manager?'

The cleaners glanced at each other. Neither spoke.

Lamb checked his watch, then nodded at Cullen. 'Go through to the back and check the office.' He paused. 'And be careful. Irwin's a big guy.' He turned back to the cleaners. 'Don't worry, ladies, we're not here to—'

Cullen stepped through the door marked 'Staff Only' and the overhead closer swung it shut behind him. A bright strip light illuminated a narrow hallway with several closed doors. If the signs could be trusted they led to a toilet, a cleaning cupboard and an office. Bingo. He stepped up to the last door and tugged it open.

A small room, darker than the hallway. Stale air, the quiet hum of electrical appliances, a desk stretching almost from wall to wall. And there was Gareth Irwin, leaning back in a chair, his face lit up by a laptop. Like a kid on a camping trip, reading monster stories to his friends with a torch held under his chin. But this ogre didn't need dramatic lighting to frighten kids. He filled his lungs with a big breath. 'What the f—'

'DS Scott Cullen.' Cullen took a step into the room, holding up his warrant card. 'We're arresting you on suspicion of assault—'

'No!' Irwin slammed his hands down on the desk, vaulted over it and charged.

Cullen just about dodged him with a late sidestep and Irwin shot past him, head first like a battering ram.

And straight into Wilkinson, smashing the DI in the solar plexus and yanking him clean off his feet, wrapping his arms around the backs of his knees, pulling tight and letting gravity do the rest. Textbook rugby tackle. Wilkinson went down hard, flat on his back, Irwin landing on top of him with a crushing thud. Game over.

Irwin started untangling his arms and made to scramble to his feet. Cullen lunged, pushing Irwin through the office door into the narrow hallway. The big man sprang back up and sprinted towards the door to the bar.

Cullen tried to jump over the prone Wilkinson, but Cullen tripped, landing on his hands and face. Cullen rolled over his shoulder but pushed up to standing, hitting the ground running – just when Irwin yanked the door open and made for the bar.

Cullen kept running, then the door started to close. Decision time. He put his head down and powered on, five more steps in an all-out sprint, four, three, two, one, he threw his right hand out like Superman to go through the gap at an angle, tucking his face behind his shoulder as he dived for it. The closing door grazed his hip and leg, but he was through, and with another quick roll he was on his feet.

Irwin was halfway across the room, but the sound of Cullen's squeaking shoes made him check behind.

Lamb broke from the cleaning ladies and charged at Irwin, who ducked under his wild roundhouse punch, weaved around, straightened up and kicked him between the legs. Lamb doubled over with a breathless groan, all in one smooth motion.

But Irwin stayed where he was, breathing hard. Lamb twisted around and loaded up another punch. He fired it off, and hit nothing but air, but Cullen heeded Irwin's lesson and he flew past Lamb, lower and with a longer run-up and hit the big guy below the waist, driving his shoulder into his relaxed hamstring and felled him like a tree.

Right at Wilkinson's feet. He didn't have far to go to get his revenge. Just pitched forward and collapsed on the guy's face.

Smothered by Wilkinson's big belly, Irwin's voice was barely audible: 'Vardy made me do it.'

9

WILKINSON PULLED UP OUTSIDE ST LEONARDS STATION, GLOWING IN the morning sun, the reflection of his BMW X5 shining bright in the building's glass front, a mosaic of colours in an inviting range of different-sized glass doors. Behind was the brown mountain ridge of the Salisbury Crags; the ancient rocks like some primordial sentry, cloaking the station in shadow. Seagulls rode the thermals – a snow-white condensation trail cutting across the clear-blue sky. 'Right, out you get. I'll catch up with you inside.' He paused, looking straight at Cullen. 'Oh, and thanks for taking Irwin down.'

'Just make sure to put it in your report. "Detective Sergeant Cullen showed extraordinary grace under pressure to neutralise a severe threat to a senior officer. I therefore recommend him for promotion to Detective Inspector." Something like that.'

Wilkinson slipped the car into Drive and revved the engine. 'Like I said – get out.'

Cullen jumped out, struck by a blast of fresh February air, and stepped onto the kerb.

A squad car pulled up, the Battenberg blue-and-yellow pattern catching the sun, and Lamb got out of the passenger seat and stuck his head over the roof to look at Cullen. 'Give us a hand with Irwin, would you?'

Cullen walked up to the car's rear wheel and waited for Lamb to get into position. Then he nodded and Lamb opened the door. Cullen reached in, gripped the back of Irwin's neck and angled his own body to give him space to get out. 'Mind your head, sir.'

Irwin swung his feet on the pavement, placed his cuffed forearms on his knees and levered himself out of the car. His eyes were only half open, his cheeks about as pale grey as the piles of snow skirting the pavement.

Lamb closed the door behind him. 'You got a lawyer—'

'No need. I'm already here.' A slender man in a pinstripe suit stood at the station's front door, hands in his pockets. Hamish Williams, with the calm confidence only a shitload of money could buy. 'Braw morning, is it not? My very favourite type of weather, this. Now, I should like to hold a brief private conference with my client ahead of any interview?'

Lamb gave him a curt nod.

Cullen gave Irwin an equally curt shove and walked him towards the building. On cue, two uniformed officers stepped out of the front doors and took over, guiding the lawyer and his client inside.

Lamb locked his gaze on to Cullen. 'Why was that lawyer here so fast?'

'Always got his ear to the ground, hasn't he?'

Cullen looked away. 'Coffee?'

'Dying for one.'

'My treat. Not that it's—' Lamb stopped dead.

Angela rounded the corner, her flat heels clicking off the flagstones, and stopped dead. She glanced at her husband. 'Bill.'

Lamb looked at his wife, his face hard to read. 'Angela.' Then he got out his massive Samsung smartphone and put it to his ear, walking off with a tight nod. 'I'll see you inside, Scott.'

'Good to see you, Scott.' Angela towered a good few inches over Cullen and took his outstretched hand, giving it a brisk shake. 'Still no wedding ring?'

He cringed. 'You know what it's like. We're both busy, got lots of work... And of course you and Bill would be invited.'

'Wouldn't miss it for the world.'

'What brings you here?'

Angela flashed him a coy smile. 'You'll find out.' She opened the glass door and stepped inside the station. The door closed, but the glare of the sun turned it back into a mirror.

HAMISH WILLIAMS LOOKED AT LAMB AND CULLEN LIKE A CHESS grandmaster who has considered every possible move on their part and knows for a fact that this little game can only go one way – his client would refuse to provide a single answer, he himself would parry every question, and then the interview would be terminated with zero gain. See you in court, hope you get a favourable jury.

Lamb knew it, but he was still giving it his best shot. 'Why were you here so quickly, Mr Williams?'

'A laudable attempt at asserting control over the conversational dynamic with a sudden change of direction, Inspector Lamb, but as I'm sure you'll appreciate, my availability to my client, prompt or not, is not the subject of this interview.'

Lamb grabbed a biro and sublimated his frustration into a rapid beat of the table.

Williams glanced at the pen and his smile broadened.

Time for an intervention.

Cullen cleared his throat. 'Mr Irwin, at your arrest you stated that, "Vardy made me do it."' He kept his voice in the same narrow band. 'Can you please confirm this in the presence of your lawyer?'

Irwin just sat there, head bowed, just like when Cullen asked him to get out of the car.

'Mr Irwin, you are under no obligation to answer my questions, but do please indicate that you have heard me.'

Irwin glanced at his lawyer, got a casual nod, and shrugged. 'Alright, I heard you.'

'And do you wish to answer?'

Irwin dropped his head again. Sat there like that, sticking to the silent treatment. 'I heard you.'

Cullen scratched his nose to hide his reluctant appreciation of the guy's sense of humour. 'Very well, let's move on to the nature of your relationship with Mr Dean Vardy. Can you confirm that you work for him in the capacity of bar manager at the Debonair on West Port, Edinburgh?'

Pause. 'I heard you.'

Cullen folded his hands on the table. 'Are you aware of the criminal charges brought against Mr Vardy?'

Another pause, but this one was longer.

'Did you—?'

Irwin shot another glance at his lawyer, this time with a hint of uncertainty in his eyes.

But Williams dropped his gaze to his manicured fingernails and calmly shook his head.

Irwin turned back to Cullen, stared him right in the eye and resumed his tried and trusted strategy. 'I heard you.'

Cullen could see it in his stare. *I've lost him. Bloody hell.* 'I asked if you are aware of the criminal charges brought against Mr Vardy?'

Irwin didn't even blink. 'I heard you.'

Cullen leaned back.

Someone knocked on the door. A female officer whose name Cullen couldn't remember stuck her head through the door. 'Need a word.' She held the door for him.

Lamb gave a nod, checked his watch and leaned over the voice recorder. 'DS Cullen left the room at ten twenty-six—'

Cullen stepped out into the hallway and closed the door behind him. The woman whose name he couldn't remember offered her hand and he shook it. He tried to remember her name, or her job, or a possible reason why she had asked him to step out of the room midway through an interview.

She smiled. 'Shall we go?'

'Where?'

She pointed down the hallway. 'To the interview?'

He threw his thumb over his shoulder. 'Didn't you just interrupt the interview to have a word with me?'

She laughed, a high, happy sound that seemed about as at home within these walls as her bright orange wool jumper.

'I'm serious. What interview?'

She hesitated. 'The job interview? The one DI Methven delegated to you?'

Cheeky bastard...

'With Angela Lamb.'

10

'Morning.' Angela stepped into the room and closed the door behind her and took a seat across from Cullen and the mysterious HR lady. 'Again.'

Cullen looked up from the thick file in his hands and laid it back on the table. 'Why didn't you tell me you were here for a job interview when we bumped into each other?'

'Just wanted to check you're still the formidable detective I worked with all those years ago.'

The HR woman giggled.

Cullen reached for the file to dodge their looks and gestured around the grim interview room. 'I can only apologise for conducting this interview in here. The office space upstairs is struggling to cope with the move up from Leith Walk. Three big teams in one place and all that.'

'No problem. Not my first rodeo. I'll miss the old station...' Angela paused, biting her lower lip. 'That is, if you'll have me back.'

Cullen shot the HR woman a side glance to see if she wanted to take this one, but he just got a nod. So he focused on Angela and narrowed his eyes. 'Why do you want to return?'

She stared at him, not blinking. 'Because motherhood isn't enough. Not for me. Don't get me wrong, I love my kids to bits. But... The baby brain, the childcare dramas, the mother groups, the competition and stress of when your kids hit which developmental markers and what to do when they're off the chart…'

She's clearly thought about this for a long time.

'I had my first last year.' The HR woman was beaming with joy. 'But being with them all day? I get that.'

'Don't get me wrong, it's so rewarding. But… I need a bigger purpose to my life.' Angela's eyes went out of focus. Then she took a sharp breath. 'I want my old job back because I miss it. I didn't think I would when I left it to have kids. But I value it more now, not just because of the balance it offers to my domestic life, but because…' She cringed a little. 'Sorry if this sounds naff, but having children has changed how I think about community and individual responsibility. But I want more. I need more.'

Another giggle from HR. 'Okay, so the interview will form a series of competency-based questions.'

∼

'ANYTHING YOU WANT TO ADD?' THE HR WOMAN SCRAWLED ALL over her form, spiderweb handwriting that even she couldn't read. Cullen had no hope. 'Anything at all?'

'I just want to say…' Angela cringed again. Then she gritted her teeth. 'I always thought my forte was hard facts, analysis, interviews, reviewing CCTV, but I want to make a contribution to my community.' She took a quick breath and looked Cullen straight in the eye. 'The thought that my kids get to live lives as safe as anyone could hope to make them… Every day that thought gives me a feeling of deep gratitude and reassurance, because parenting is hard. Being responsible for two little human beings that are utterly defenceless and who look up to you with complete trust, that's hard. But I can give other people that same feeling, then that's why I'm here today and why I'm asking for my old job back.' She sat back and folded her hands in her lap.

Cullen looked at her, saw that her slight discomfort had given way to her previous calm certainty. 'Well, thanks for that. We'll, uh, we'll think things through and… You know how it is.'

Angela nodded. 'When should I expect to hear?'

'Be in the next fortnight.' Another laugh. 'Thanks for your

time.' The HR woman gestured at the door. 'You know the way out, I'm sure?'

'Sure.' Angela frowned at Cullen.

'I need to have a quick word with...' He swallowed. 'With my colleague here. You got time for a coffee?'

Angela glanced at her watch. 'Mum's minding the kids, but sure, a quick coffee should be fine. See you in the canteen.' She grabbed her bag and coat, then left them to it.

As the door closed, Cullen got to his feet, clutching his file. 'Right, that was super easy. Can you fast-track it?'

The HR woman puffed up her cheeks. 'That's not how this works and you know full well. I'll discuss this with DI Methven and he can advise you on the outcome.'

Cullen nodded. 'But she'll get the job, right?'

'No comment.' HR lady clapped her hands and rubbed them together. 'Now, I must be off.' She offered Cullen her hand. 'And like I said, nice to work with you again.'

Cullen shook her hand, squinting at her. 'Sorry, I've got to admit, I can't remember when we did before.'

She stuck her hands in the pockets of her skirt and laughed. 'Well, I won't spoil the fun of you working that one out for yourself. Like Angela said, you're the detective. I knew all along that you couldn't remember my name.' She walked out of the room.

Cullen watched the door close behind her, a blush creeping up his neck. *This is going to annoy me all bloody day now.* He opened the door and stepped out into the corridor. And bumped straight into Bill Lamb. Like hitting a brick wall. *Christ, the guy is built these days.* 'Jesus, Bill, what the hell are you doing?'

Lamb dismissed the question with an irritated scowl. 'How did Angela's interview go?'

Cullen dodged his hard stare. 'What makes you think I was interviewing her?'

'Got her name on your pack, you idiot.' Lamb nodded at the file under Cullen's arm. 'Besides, I saw her come out of the room. So, how did it go?'

'You know I can't tell you anything. But do you know the sugar plum fairy's name?'

Lamb frowned. 'Donna Nichols?'

Cullen clicked his fingers. 'That's it.'

Lamb laughed. 'And you thought you shagged her, didn't you?'

Cullen's blush made a comeback. 'Wouldn't be the first time.'

'You're not her type, Shagger.' Lamb laughed. 'She's the better half of my boss.'

'Cargill?' Cullen's turn to frown. 'But she's a...'

Lamb laughed even louder. 'Aye, last I checked she was a woman. Yes, Donna is gay and no, it's not very likely that you shagged her. No need to worry.' He gave a wink then walked off, throwing his parting shot over his shoulder. 'Now, Shagger, you need a lift to Tulliallan?'

Cullen stood rooted to the ground, the third blush in ten minutes creeping up his neck.

Tulliallan? What?

Ah shite, that training course. Bloody hell.

11

Cullen floored it as he overtook the tractor, cruising past the golf club. No time to enjoy the view, and not the right season for it anyway. He couldn't remember seeing more than three colours the entire way here – brown, grey and... brownish grey. February hadn't opened up to spring yet, still stuck in winter. He slowed for the turning to Tulliallan Castle – the castle a plain grey, matching the drab barracks behind it. He pulled into the car park and screeched to a halt.

Twelve, on the dot. *One minute to my next bollocking.*

He jumped out of the car and speed-walked to the building, reluctant to arrive out of breath and sweaty. He stepped through the doors and checked the gleaming foyer, packed with lumps in cheap suits, looking for a sign to—

'You're late!' Bain was leaning against the floor-to-ceiling window, his petulant frown drawing attention to his shaved head, his full beard weirdly starting below the ears. Made him look like a painted egg. 'One minute late, Sundance. Tut tut.' He pushed off the wall and grabbed Cullen's arm to guide him to a quiet corner of the grand reception area. 'Here.' He held Cullen's gaze. 'What's Methven got against me?'

'Methven? Other than the usual?'

Bain's grip hardened. 'What's that supposed to mean?'

Cullen slapped his hand away. 'I need to sign in.' He started to walk towards the registration desk.

Bain caught up with him and got in his way. 'Come on, what's his problem?'

Cullen tried to push past.

But Bain was like a terrier, scuttling around him and getting back in his way, chin cocked and teeth bared. 'Methven got another one of those helper jobs for the Rape Squad for your better half. Guess who he seconded. That prick McMann. Not me, oh no, never me. You've been given *two* of those gigs. TWO! But—'

'Stop shouting.' Cullen glanced around, but nobody seemed to care about the commotion. Too many dark-suited figures with clipboards and conference packs. Two detective sergeants from Dundee stood in the registration queue, like they were in the middle of a lovers' tiff.

Cullen stared at Bain. 'Fine. Sharon told Methven anyone but you.'

'What?' Bain stood there, his slack mouth hanging open. Then he swallowed and found his voice again. 'That *bitch*.'

'That's my girlfriend you're talking about.'

Bain shrugged and his aggression fell off him like a bag he was tired of carrying. 'Well, Sundance, you know how I feel about her.'

'Remember that Methven sent us on that case in Glasgow.'

'Aye, those South African pricks. I tell you, Sundance...' Bain started a slow walk over to the classroom door.

BAIN LEANED OVER TO CULLEN, SQUEEZED IN AT THE BACK OF THE classroom with all the other late arrivals. 'I know it's only been half an hour, and I never thought I'd hear myself say this, but I've learnt something.'

Cullen knew there was some lame joke in the offing, but couldn't help himself. 'Aye?'

Bain leaned back, not bothering to lower his voice anymore. 'I've just learned that this clown has absolutely nothing to teach me.'

The room fell silent. Lamb was staring straight at Bain. 'I'm sorry, Brian, am I boring you?'

'Aye, you are.' Bain folded his arms and looked out of the window, his bravado yielding. 'The rest of these muppets are hanging off every daft word coming out of your mouth, so don't mind me.'

'Excuse me?' Lamb put a hand to his ear. 'I didn't catch that.'

'Nothing.'

'Well, let's chat about this *nothing* during lunch.'

'Have I been naughty?'

'Brian...' Lamb looked at his watch, a gesture he was clearly enjoying these days, the snap of the wrist making his arm flex just enough to pull the jacket tight over his muscles. Again. 'And would you look at that, it's lunch time already. The day's just flying by. Back here at two.' He pointed at Bain, then at the door, then headed out into the corridor, cutting a swathe through the class as they got up.

Bain sighed, deep and loud. 'Ah, shite.' He stood up and followed Lamb out, head shaking like this was all beneath him.

Cullen took his phone from his pocket and started typing a text to Sharon. *'Out at bloody Tulliallan on—'*

'Scott!' DI Terry Lennox grinned at him. Heroin thin, lank greasy hair. 'How's it going?'

'Aye, not bad.' Cullen got up and slid his phone back in his pocket. 'Been a while.'

'And then some.' Lennox glanced around the now half-empty room. 'You still in Edinburgh?'

'For my sins. You still Glasgow?'

'Nah, I transferred to Livingston when they restructured. Working the MIT now, like the rest of us here.' He looked around. 'Bain doesn't get any better, does he?'

'Gets worse. Every day.'

Lennox chuckled. 'And what's he doing here anyway? I thought this course was for detective sergeants only?'

'You're a DI.'

'I'm teaching.' Lennox groaned. 'Don't tell me he is as well?'

'Hardly.' Cullen paused. 'He's a DS again.'

Lennox frowned. 'Don't tell me his chickens have come home to roost?'

'Still got a few left in the hen house.'

A woman's laugh made Cullen turn around. He did a double take. 'Hold on, you're...'

'Yvonne Flockhart.' She looked like a model from the cover of a glossy magazine. She leaned in for a kiss on the cheek and whispered, 'And I remember you very well, Scott Cullen.' She straightened back up, the consummate professional again, straight-faced. 'Didn't know you two were acquainted.'

'Worked a few cases over the years.' Lennox looked back and forth between them. 'How do you know each other?'

Cullen dodged his gaze. *I just know her in the biblical sense.* 'We worked for Ally Davenport at St Leonards, back in the good old Lothian and Borders days.' He looked at her, losing count of how many times he'd blushed that day, his skin burning under his collar like sunburn.

Yvonne returned his look, deadpan. Just stared at him like she was wondering whether to be amused or insulted by his denial of just how well they'd known each other back then, at least for one night. A cheeky glint lit up her eyes. 'This guy is so much fun on nights out.' She winked at Lennox. 'Scott used to be quite the party animal.'

'Bloody roasting in here.' Cullen stuck a hand under his collar and loosened it, pretending to peer at the nearest radiator. 'Must be spending half the Police Scotland budget on heating this place. Lunch'll be a deep-fried Mars bar and a cup of tea.'

'Oh, I quite like it.' Yvonne shrugged. 'The temperature in here, I mean. But you know how hot I like it.'

Cullen did his best to focus his attention on Lennox, who was looking like he'd walked into a porn shoot. 'Turns out, Yvonne and I used to keep emailing facilities – me getting them to turn it down, her to turn it on.' Another blush flared on his neck. 'I mean up.'

'Right.'

Cullen cleared his throat. *Really need a glass of water. To pour over my head.* 'So, how do the two of *you* know each other?'

'He's my boss.'

'Been working together over a year now.' Lennox glanced at Yvonne. 'Yvonne was one of my DCs, but I supported her through the promotion to DS just last month after I kicked out a useless old bastard.' He coughed. 'I mean, after I lost a long-serving officer to retirement.'

'Congratulations, Yvonne.' Cullen looked at a spot on the wall, just over her left shoulder. 'Well deserved, I'm sure.'

'Thanks, Scott. The same to you. I heard you made DS. And apparently you also made a clean break with your cowboy ways. That true?'

'Aye, well, I'm trying. The case I'm—'

His phone rang.

He reached for his pocket, pulled the blaring thing out and glanced at it. Wilkinson.

Shite, what does he want?

'Sorry, I need to take this.' With a few quick steps he was out of the room, and out of ear shot. 'What's up?'

Wilkinson's voice was a barely restrained shout. 'Bloody spanner in the works at Vardy's trial. Amy Forrest didn't turn up.'

12

Cullen took the turn into Dumbiedykes at fifty miles per hour.

SHITE!

He hit the brake, putting his entire weight on the pedal as the anti-lock system kicked in, the tyres squealing until the car shuddered to a stop.

The football bounced past the bumper by no more than a foot, followed by two primary-school kids in red-and-grey uniforms, slamming their hands on the bonnet and squealing with laughter as they raced after the ball.

Cullen sat there, their little voices echoing in his ears, his white knuckles trembling on the wheel. He shook his head and took a deep breath, then shifted down to first and trundled over to the kerb.

∼

Cullen walked down the tower block's corridor on Amy's floor, out of breath but back in control. Until he saw Wilko's face.

The DI was waiting for him outside Amy's flat with pale lips and genuine concern in his wide eyes. 'Cullen, the flat's empty. No sign of her or the baby.'

'Have you checked with the neighbours?'

'I've been knocking on doors and talking to folks since I called you.' Wilkinson looked up and down the hallway, desperate for a new avenue to explore. He cleared his throat. 'No one's seen her or the little guy in days.'

'Shite. Me and Si Buxton were in there this morning.'

'Did you bloody scare her off?'

'We were trying to support her.' Cullen pulled his mobile from his pocket. 'Does Lamb know?'

'Lamb's teaching at Tulliallan.'

'I was just there.'

'This is my case as well. If anyone's calling him, it's me.'

'So what do you want me to do?'

'While my team's questioning her known associates, I need you to talk to the women who worked with Amy before she had the kid.'

'But they won't—'

'I know. I'm thinking they'll be too terrified to talk to us in case Vardy finds out. So, while you can open the door, I'm teaming you up with someone who's good at interviewing trauma victims and —' Wilkinson stared over Cullen's shoulder. 'Ah, here we go.'

Ambling towards them was a wee man with a broad smile. Bain. He stopped, looked at the ceiling and turned out his hands. 'Ask and ye shall receive.'

'CAN'T DRIVE MY CAR ON POLICE BUSINESS, NOT AFTER LAST TIME.' Cullen looked at his pride and joy, a bottle-green Golf GTI that was seeing its best days now, and wondered if it was wise leaving it in Dumbiedykes. 'We'll have to—'

'Catch.' Bain tossed the keys. 'I got a pool car from St Leonards. Besides, I always like being driven by you, Sundance. Like seeing one of those monkeys typing Hamlet.'

Cullen got in the maroon Volvo. Smelled like it still saw active duty as a kiddie carrier, driving smelly boys to rugby practice, a whole team's worth of jerseys marinating in sour sweat. He gritted his teeth and turned the ignition. It roared like a brand-new rally racer. He revved the engine and sped off.

≈

CULLEN HAMMERED THE HORN, MAKING A COUPLE OF DAYTIME drinkers jump back onto the kerbstone as he blared past. They both shot him a look, then went back to sucking on cigarettes, eyes glued to their phones.

'Pubic triangle, eh?' Bain chuckled as he watched the two topless pubs whizz past. 'Mind when there were three, Sundance. Should just call it the Brazilian strip now, eh?' He was looking round at Cullen, waiting for a laugh.

Cullen didn't give him one, instead winding his way up to the junction and taking the next right. Castle Terrace backed on to the block containing Vardy's lap dancing club. He spotted a gap and slotted the battered Volvo between two brand-new SUVs. He turned the engine off. All he saw was money, money, money.

Bain followed his gaze and chuckled. 'I know what you're thinking, Sundance. We fit into this part of town as well as this embarrassment of a car.' Then he unclipped his seatbelt, let it whir past his ear and opened the passenger door to step out on the pavement, as calm as the castle sitting on its volcanic plug.

Cullen got out and followed him across the road. By the time they reached the corner of Lothian Road, he was ten feet ahead.

Bain jogged after him. 'Sundance, quit running, this is important.'

Cullen kept going, but glanced over his shoulder to see what Bain was playing at now. When he saw his serious expression, he stopped to wait. 'What?'

Bain caught up and got right in his face. 'You need to slow down and get some perspective, keep the big picture in sight.' He started walking along the street, Cullen half a step behind him. 'You can't just barge into this place and expect those lassies to welcome some cop with a hard-on for truth, justice and the Cullen way. They'll be worried you're there because of some wee scam they've got going, or just because you're an arsehole.'

'Shut your face.'

'I'm serious. In their eyes, that's what we are. Prickss trying to mess them around. They've all been there before, eh? So they'll clam up and kick you out and you'll be back to square one, only without a single lead left.'

Cullen slowed down, as the three bouncers at the front door came into view, stamping their heavy boots on the pavement. 'What do you suggest, then?'

'Watch and learn.' Bain walked right up to the bouncers. 'Gentlemen. Freezing, eh?'

The two guys leaned forward to catch his quiet words. Then they eyed Bain from head to toe. Whatever they saw, they didn't like it.

The one on the right gave a sneer and straightened up, folding his massive arms over a tight black T-shirt. Didn't seem to notice the cold. He fixed a stare on some spot a foot above Bain's head.

Dismissed.

The guy on the left. Christ, his skin was inflamed and pimpled. His giant arms looked like water balloons ready to pop. Probably injecting Synthol straight in to make his biceps look like his mate's. And definitely not a man smart or calm enough for a spot of diplomacy.

The other one looked like he was made from steel wire, every muscle on his exposed arms defined and tense and vibrating with aggressive energy.

Cullen stepped in front of the likely lads and cleared his throat. 'We're just—'

'Cops.' Steel Wool waved at someone across the street. Didn't even look at Cullen. 'And you're not getting in without a warrant.'

Cullen bit his lip. 'You remember Amy Forrest?'

Steel Wool just shook his head. 'You're not coming in. End of.'

Synthol's forehead creased, like a crack in limestone. 'What about wee Amy?'

'She's gone missing. We need to find her. I'm worried about her.' Cullen nodded inside as a sheepish punter left the club, cloaked in a blast of Kylie. 'Just want a quiet word with the girls, see if anyone's seen her. That's all.'

Synthol grunted at his mate. 'Kenny, she was a good laugh.'

Kenny couldn't look his mate in the eye. For a moment he just stood there, flexing. Then he glanced around and stood aside. 'Alright, boys, in you go and... Say hi to her from me, eh?'

Cullen bit his tongue as he stepped between the bouncers and into the dim club.

The doors had hardly swung shut behind them, when Bain

slapped him on the shoulder. 'I'd no idea you were such a good actor, Sundance.'

Cullen shrugged him off and looked around for someone to ask about Amy.

Bain strode past him and met a scantily clad girl at the counter. She looked up from her phone and fluttered her fake eyelashes at him, but he was all calm authority. 'Afternoon, doll. Looking for Amy Forrest?'

The girl glanced past him at the doors, apparently wondering why the bouncers had let a cop in.

'Sorry, I should've explained.' Bain treated her to another kind smile. 'I'm not here to bother her. I'm just concerned for her and her child's safety. They're both missing and...'

The girl cocked a bored eyebrow, brushed a stray strand of sleek ginger hair over her ear. 'Right.'

'You know her, though, aye?'

'Right.'

'Listen to me.' Bain glanced back over his shoulder at the heavily guarded front door, then leaned even further over the counter. 'I'm worried she's been killed.'

The woman inched forward and stared at him, her eyes wide with anticipation. 'What? Really?'

'We're cops, right. Murder squad.' Bain paused, letting his unwavering stare imply everything else.

She swallowed and reached for a walkie-talkie from under the counter. With a nervous catch in her breath she held it to her mouth and pressed transmit. 'Pauline?'

The speaker crackled with static. Then a distorted voice came on the line. 'I'm having a smoke. Can't this wait?'

THE SMOKING AREA WAS ABOUT THE SIZE OF A TOILET, AND THE smell wasn't far off either. Pauline stood behind two big black bins, drawing on a cigarette with hollow cheeks and vacant eyes. Maybe to take her mind off the fumes. Maybe to take it off worse things. She hugged a pink puffer jacket tight, almost covering the black corset that barely concealed her. Shivering, she took another breath.

Bain stepped forward. 'Alright, darling, need a wee word—'

'Stop.' Cullen grabbed him back. He stayed at the door to avoid crowding her and triggering her fight or flight instinct. Not that there was anywhere to run to. 'Hello, Miss Quigley.'

Pauline snapped out of her daze and stared at Cullen. Her gaze dropped to the ground, followed by her cigarette butt. 'What the hell do *you* want?'

'We're here to—'

'Shut up, you prick.' Pauline looked back up at him, unblinking. 'I went to jail because of you.'

'You went to jail because you lied for Dean Vardy. On the stand. It's called perjury. Your lawyer might've warned you about it?'

She didn't have an answer for that. She just shivered.

'Surprised you're working for him again, though.'

'Turns out there aren't many jobs for ex-cons.' Pauline sniffed. 'Not when they're female, anyway.' She laughed with about as much happiness as was in the surrounding bins. 'You don't get it, do you? Vardy owes me for not telling the truth about what happened, for taking the fall, and the jail time.'

'After all he's done to you?'

Her haunted eyes refocused on him. 'Why are you here?'

'I could bullshit you about how Vardy might be getting paranoid in custody and how he's getting his henchmen to clean up any dirt we have on him by taking out anyone who might testify against him – people like you, Pauline – but I don't think that's likely to happen and I don't want to lie to you.' Cullen paused. 'I just want to speak to you as somebody who knows what he's capable of.'

'I know what that prick's capable of so I'm not—'

'What's he done to Amy Forrest?'

She closed her eyes.

'Pauline, do you know where she is?'

She looked up at the blue sky and shivered again. Then shut her eyes and kept them like that.

'Pauline, you of all people know what danger she's in.'

Her shoulders sagged. She dropped her head and looked at the floor, as though she might find a happier answer there. All she found was her cigarette butt, still lying at her feet, still glowing faintly. She stood on it, grinding it out with one sharp twist of her long heel. Then she looked back up. 'Amy hasn't worked here in ages, not since the baby. Most of the girls lost touch with her after that.'

'But not you.'

'I've made enough mistakes. Amy left this place, thought she was going somewhere better. Only… she ended up stuck in Vardy's hands. But that's life, eh? Some demons you can't outrun.'

'I know Zak's Vardy's kid.'

Pauline tugged a stray her from out of her eye. 'That's not what I meant.'

'She's dependent on Vardy for money, right?'

Pauline looked up at him again, curling up the sides of her mouth. 'You really don't know, do you?'

13

'CAN'T BELIEVE IT.' CULLEN SLAMMED ON THE BRAKES AND PULLED up on the kerb at the door of the Debonair. The pub looked deserted, just one middle-aged drinker with a ponytail and a beard standing out front, propping up the wall with one hand while clutching an almost-empty pint glass with the other. Still as a statue, even when Cullen charged past him to yank the door open. And nearly pulled his arm out of his shoulder socket.

Locked.

Cullen stood back and glanced at Bain, slowly climbing out of the car, then back at the lone drinker leaning against the wall. 'Excuse me, mate?'

The guy ignored him.

'Excuse me?' Cullen walked up to him and waved his hand in front of his eyes.

The guy flinched and dropped his empty glass. As it shattered on the ground, he flinched again.

Cullen stepped back, kicking glass off his shoes. 'When did the pub close?'

'Eh?'

'Can't have been that long ago.' Cullen pointed at the shards. 'You've only just finished your pint.'

The guy stared down at the broken glass. 'Been closed all day. Says so here.' He tapped the window next to the door.

CLOSED ALL DAY.

'So why were you standing here with an empty glass?'

'Long story. Woke up this morning with a hangover stomping around my head like an angry badger. And that little beauty was lying next to my bed. And I thought to myself, I thought, that glass is not yours. Where did you get it and why are you too blootered to even remember taking it? And then I thought, that's—'

Cullen's phone rang.

He reached for it, holding the other hand up in apology. 'Sorry, I need to take this.' He turned away, glancing at the screen. Wilkinson. 'Sir, we're on the trail of Amy Forrest. She's been working as a cleaner at the Debonair.'

Wilkinson paused. 'At Vardy's pub? Why?'

'Money?' Cullen frowned. 'Trouble is, the place is shut for the day.'

'Huh. Well. That can wait. I need you at the Royal Infirmary. We've got a problem.' Click and he was gone.

'FOR THE FIFTIETH TIME, HE DIDN'T SAY.' CULLEN GOT OUT AND LEFT the Volvo in the sprawling car park outside Accident and Emergency. He ran inside the hospital, weaving through a casting call for *The Walking Dead*. A man stood in the middle of it all, staring into the distance, the pale victim of some accident or another. Two nurses were trying to talk to him but he shook off their attempts. Cullen dashed along a corridor and stopped at the nurse's station.

No sign of Wilkinson – dead, alive or risen from the grave.

Bain elbowed his way past Cullen to the desk and flashed his warrant card. 'Listen up, pal, we're cops. Supposed to be meeting DI Wilkinson. You seen him?'

'Good afternoon, gentlemen.' The nurse looked up from his computer screen. 'You must be here for the murder. Follow me, please.'

What the hell?

Cullen glanced at Bain, then back at the nurse. 'Which murder?'

But the nurse had already rounded the counter, surprisingly

fast for a man his size. Cullen caught up with him by a large set of swing doors that whirred open at their approach.

Wilkinson and Lamb stood outside a ward, arms folded, not talking to each other.

'Thanks.' Cullen nodded at the nurse and jogged over. 'What's going on?'

Wilkinson shot him an angry look. 'Sammy McLean is dead.'

'His injuries from the fall?'

'Do you hear me?' Wilkinson glared at him. 'Our only eyewitnesses are missing or dead! This is bollocksed beyond buggeration!'

Lamb grabbed hold of Wilkinson's sleeve and stared deep into his eyes. 'Keep a lid on it, Paul. Okay?' He turned his attention to Cullen. 'Someone shot him.'

Cullen recoiled. 'What?'

'Are you deaf?' Wilkinson got in his face. 'Shot in a bloody hospital. In a bloody HOSPITAL!'

Lamb patted his arm again. 'Easy, Wilko.' He glanced around, then lowered his voice. 'You shouldn't be shouting that around here.'

Wilkinson shrugged him off. 'Don't you—'

'Here, Wilko.' A SOCO in a thin white boiler suit stepped up behind him and tugged off his mask. James Anderson, looking like he'd taken a good chunk out of his goatee during that morning's shave. He nodded at Cullen and Bain. 'The Chuckle Brothers are here, I see. God rest their souls.'

Bain frowned. 'Have they died?'

'I've no idea. Probably.' Anderson turned back to Wilkinson. 'Anyway, my lot have just completed the search of the room. We found the shooter's gun in the bin. Good news is we've got a skin fleck on the handle. If the gods are with us, we might be able to get a DNA trace from it.'

'Oh?' Wilkinson perked up. 'Anything else?'

'Deeley's in there now, doing his thing.' Anderson gestured at the door. 'The boy was shot three times at point-blank range – once in the mouth, twice in the chest.'

Wilkinson's jaw dropped. His stare wandered from Anderson to Lamb and back again. 'But... Vardy's in court.'

'So?' Cullen almost laughed. Managed to keep his face straight.

'He's not the only person to have seen *The Wire*. All we've got is someone hitting the victim with three taps.'

'Three taps?' Wilkinson got right in Cullen's face, close enough to taste his breakfast on his breath. 'You think you're some hotshot, don't you?'

'I'm just saying, sir. This obviously wasn't Vardy.' Cullen pointed at his head then at his pectorals in quick succession. 'But that doesn't mean they weren't working for him. I'll find whoever did it.'

THE CCTV SCREEN SEEMED TO SHOW THE SAME VIDEO CLIP ON repeat. Or variations on the same theme. The fisheye camera was mounted on the hallway ceiling, giving a top-angle view of the people passing in and out. Halfway along the wall, the door to Sammy's room was closed. Two doctors walked by on their rounds of the ward, then three nurses in blue rushed around with some clipboards and medication. A patient in a colourless dressing gown shuffled to the vending machine, pushing an IV-stands on castors.

And all in the middle of it was DC Simon Buxton, standing there, yawning, tapping on his phone, eating, chatting to a uniformed officer. Looking bored as hell.

A visitor shook up the monotony of the scene, walking past in multicoloured street clothes.

Then a nurse walked up to Buxton. After a lengthy chat, he let her into Sammy's room. She came out seconds later to continue her rounds. Just a quick check-up, her body language showing calm routine.

'Well.' Cullen leaned back and looked at Buxton. 'Nothing happening, over and over again.'

'Like my life.' Buxton was squinting at the screen. 'This is getting us nowhere.'

'Alright.' Cullen reached over and hit the space to pause the video. 'When did the gunshots happen?'

'That's the thing.' Buxton hovered his thumb over the space bar, but didn't press it. 'There's no audio, so it's just guesswork.'

'Keep checking it, okay?' Cullen pushed his chair back and got up. 'Every frame, every person in or out of that room.'

'That'll take forever.'

'I'll get you some help.'

'I'm such a 2868.'

'You can call yourself one.'

Buxton snapped out of his thoughts with a laugh and dropped his hand. 'This is a disaster, mate.' He glanced at Cullen. 'And it's my disaster. Before you came here, Wilko went *apeshit* at me for letting the murderer get at Sammy McLean.' He frowned. 'I had *one* job.'

'Si, you did your job. Someone got in that room and killed him behind your back. It's not your fault.'

'Of course it's my fault.'

'You didn't let anyone in. And forget about fault, just find who did it, okay? Someone got in there without you seeing. Find them.'

Buxton looked at him with glazed eyes. The words would take hours to sink in, but at least he'd started the process.

The door flew open and Wilkinson marched in. He glowered at Buxton, who didn't even look over. 'Cullen, I need you at the High Court. The judge is making a statement.'

'ORDER!' THE JUDGE SAT BACK DOWN AND NODDED AT THE CLERK OF court, a small bald man sitting at the table in front of the judge's bench. His shiny head was glistening with sweat in the sickly yellow hue of the overhead lights as he turned around, craned his neck up at the judge and muttered a few unintelligible words.

Cullen was at the back of the crowded room, but standing, so he had a clear view over the densely packed benches of the public gallery and press box, lined with journalists leaning forward to hear what was being said at the judge's bench.

Dean Vardy sat at a table next to his lawyer, both in sharp suits, both facing the judge. Vardy leaned forward to peer around McLintock at the jury box. A couple of jurors noticed his stare and turned to look at him. When he was sure of their undivided attention, he pointed at the empty witness box. Then he dropped the hand and tapped his heavy gold watch with his right index finger.

The judge pulled back the sleeve of his black gown and looked at his own watch. He nodded to himself and cleared his throat with a solemn cough. 'Ladies and gentlemen, esteemed colleagues of the Court, the prosecution has now been granted as much time as the law allows in order to produce a witness.' He glanced at the Procurator Fiscal, standing by her team. 'I have no option but to defer the prosecution's case for one month.'

A hush sailed around the room.

McLintock was first to his feet. 'My lord, I request that you dismiss this case.'

'Campbell, that is not going to happen so please do not push your luck.'

'Then I request that my client, a respectable businessman and pillar of the community, be released on bail until such time as the prosecution can present any evidence whatsoever of wrongdoing on his part.'

The judge looked at Vardy, his stern gaze lingering as the entire court seemed to hold its breath. 'Bail set at three hundred thousand pounds.'

14

Cullen drove through a flicker of street and headlights, lancing through the black February night sky, stinging his eyes like disco strobes.

When did I last eat? Or sleep?

Can't remember.

Fettes appeared ahead, the floodlights making the car park look like a massive cardboard box, same shade of brown, same brutal geometry. He slotted the Volvo into a free space near the entrance, just in time to see Lamb disappear through the front door.

Cullen killed the engine and jumped out into the cold. He rushed after Lamb, again just in time to see him disappear through a door. He flashed his ID at the reader and followed Lamb through into a small conference room.

Empty, but it felt like a graveyard.

Lamb stood just inside the door, a confused frown deepening on his forehead. 'Take it you've heard?'

Cullen perched on the edge of the table and nodded. 'I can't—'

'Bill!' DCI Alison Cargill stormed into the room, trembling with rage. 'What the *hell* is going on?'

Lamb gave Cullen a questioning look, then turned back to Cargill. 'I don't know what to say, ma'am.'

'Were you not in court?'

'I was at Tulliallan, teaching the DS cohort—'

'Silence.' Cargill stood there, breathing hard, staring at Lamb. 'Inspector, this does not happen on my watch. Am I clear?'

'I understand, ma'am. Look, DI Wilkinson was in charge of—'

'Don't you dare try and—'

'I'm not trying to wriggle out of this, ma'am. We had two witnesses. One was assaulted at his home this morning. We've got the culprit in custody but he's not speaking. I was assured by DI Wilkinson that Sammy McLean would be fit to stand up in court.'

Cullen spun around, arms in the air. 'What? He was in intensive care!'

'Well, Wilko reckoned he'd be fit to testify and because I was teaching, I didn't think—'

'Teaching is all you'll be able to do once I've finished with you.' Cargill's nostrils flared like she was about to breathe fire. Instead, she roared at him. 'Am I clear?'

'Loud and clear, ma'am. Look, I've got an email from Wilko saying Sammy was fine to stand up in court.'

'An email?'

'Aye. I honestly didn't think it was that bad. Thought he'd just tripped in the snow or something. Wilko even said the bruises would add to his testimony.'

'Someone shot him.' Cargill was still shaking. Nothing would calm her down. 'And have you found the culprit?'

'We're a long way away, ma'am.'

She shook her head hard. 'We still have one witness, though. So why the hell is this not in court?'

Lamb cleared his throat. 'Amy Forrest, ma'am. She's gone to ground.'

'The case has been deferred and we're looking like a bunch of clowns because we don't seem to be able to take people from their homes to the court.' Cargill grunted. 'Find this Amy Forrest, Inspector. I don't want to have to play the recorded statement from eighteen months ago. We don't look good in it. If we can find her, we can go into court with both balls in our own hands rather than Vardy squeezing them.'

'Ma'am.' Cullen paused, gruesome images flashing in his head

– Vardy shooting Xena Farley in the face, then in the chest, twice. Same with Sammy McLean. He swallowed. 'People who agree to testify against Vardy have a habit of ending up dead.'

'That's not what I want to hear.' She glared at him. 'This is your fault, Sergeant. And you, Bill. Both of you. You've made a dog's dinner of prosecuting Vardy *twice* now.'

'How is this *my* fau—'

'Shh!' She pointed at the door. 'Sergeant, get me that witness. Now.'

'Ma'am.' Cullen took a step back and did as he was told. He went to shut the door but it slammed, the echo thrumming in his ears. Then Cargill's voice droned through the thin walls as she tore Lamb apart with her words.

Cullen paced past the receptionist to the front door and out to the floodlit car park.

Jesus Christ.

How the hell am I going to find Amy?

And now Vardy's back on the streets, hunting for the only witness his people haven't murdered. Assuming she's still alive.

Cargill's right. This is all my fault.

I asked for this and I've made a right mess of it.

His phone rang.

Cullen snatched it out of his pocket. Buxton. 'What?'

A startled gasp. 'Umm, sorry, is this a bad time?'

'Yes. What?'

'I... well, I'm still at the hospital. Got something off the CCTV review. It's not much, but it might be useful, so I thought I'd call you straight away. There's no audio, so we can't verify the shots, but—'

Cullen clenched his teeth. 'Cut the foreplay, Si.'

'Yeah, well, I've got footage of a guy, at least I think it's a guy. He's wearing scrubs and a facemask, so he looked like a surgeon, and he waited for me to leave my post to go for a slash—'

'You left the room?'

'I was bursting, mate. It was up to my eyeballs. I asked the nurse to look after the room for me, but she let him in to check the chart or something.'

'Tell me you've found him.'

'No, but—'

'Si, come on.'

'Look, there's a high-res frame of him approaching the door on the way in. There's a bulge in his coat at the small of his back. Looks like a gun.'

'Have. You. Found. Him?'

'No, but we've got him on the way out, still wearing the surgical mask. All we've got to identify him by are the eyes.'

Cullen swore under his breath. 'Last time I looked at our criminal database, it wasn't exactly full of eye-prints.'

'Ha-bloody-ha.'

'Si, call me when you've got something better than a brief sighting of a stranger with no identifying features.'

Buxton said nothing, but his hollow breathing sounded like he was scraping the barrel. His breath caught. 'I've just got access to the CCTV from the entrances. I'll see if we can find this guy.'

Cullen bit his tongue. 'Tell me when you've got him.' He cut the call and took a deep breath, squinting up at the night sky. The floodlights burnt his eyes, but he forced himself to keep staring, to keep looking for something beyond the fluorescent mist hanging in the moist air.

He couldn't see a thing.

When the first tears blurred his vision, he lowered his head and squeezed his eyes shut until the neon halos faded.

The short walk to his car wasn't nearly long enough to clear his head.

Amy unable to look at her rapist's child in case she saw Dean Vardy.

And Vardy himself, grinning at the impotent judge, seconds before his people produced three hundred grand like it was pocket change.

And Buxton's words painting the picture of how Sammy McLean's killer had got into the room. Three quick shots and he was gone. Tap, tap, tap. Like Marlo Stanfield in *The Wire*. Quick and efficient. In and out.

But distinctive. One man's MO.

Or rather, one man's group's MO.

Someone knew who'd killed Sammy McLean. And knew where that raping, murdering bastard would be.

CULLEN WAITED IN A DOORWAY ACROSS FROM THE DEBONAIR, lurking in the shadows. Traffic squeezed through the narrowed road, walled in by flashy SUVs on both sides, each one more expensive than his annual salary. Vardy's rich friends, out to celebrate the bastard giving the courts a two-fingered salute. Again.

The drive should have given him enough fresh air to cool his temper, but the sight of all this illicit wealth on wheels fired him up even more. Every car was paid for with dirty money, either by some career criminal or by an upstanding member of the community who'd made a tidy profit from the clean side of Vardy's empire. Cullen didn't know what made him feel dirtier. Or what made him feel more frustrated. Knowing this went on, or knowing he couldn't do anything about it.

He got the pool car fob out of his pocket and flicked out the key. A minute of scratching expensive paintwork would only get so much satisfaction and a shitload of trouble.

People like Vardy got away with raping and murdering and assassinating witnesses, because people like Cullen wouldn't suspend the due process of law, even when they knew the bastard was guilty.

Each thought pulled Cullen further down a rabbit hole of vigilante fantasies. Keying their cars seemed like small beer compared with what he was going to do to Vardy.

Two men walked down the hill from Lothian Road, heading towards the Art College, their heels clipping the pavement, the sound echoing off the walls like shrapnel. They stopped outside the club and continued their relaxed conversation. The bouncers from Wonderland.

A large figure stepped from the shadow of the bus shelter and bundled towards them. He drew wary looks from the doormen, who knew what was coming.

When he was fifteen yards out, they dropped their heavy shoulders.

Ten, they settled into tense boxing stances.

Five, they—

Shite, it's Wilko.

Cullen shot off after him, dancing round the back of a black cab. 'Paul!'

All three turned to face him, the bouncers frowning.

Cullen grabbed Wilkinson's shoulders, his hands throbbing as hard as his temples.

Wilkinson glared at him, his fists clenched by his sides.

The bouncers scanned him for signs of imminent violence, then relaxed their shoulders and stood up straight. Again, they knew the score as well as he did. It was over. At least for now.

Cullen led Wilkinson across the street, having to weave between a pair of black Land Rovers as he retreated into the shadow.

The smarter of the two touched his Bluetooth earpiece and spoke into the mic. 'Hey, it's Kenny, down at the front door. Tell the boss some cop just rocked up. Looked to get handsy with us. Name wasn't mentioned, but he might be back to tell me in a minute. Got a boyfriend with him, too. That prick who was looking for Amy.'

Wilkinson's turn to grab hold of Cullen. 'What the hell do you think you're doing?'

'You were about to get into a fight with those two, weren't you? Unprovoked. They'd have sued you for harassment and police brutality and God knows what else.'

'They're Vardy's men.' Wilkinson looked back across the street. 'They're working for a rapist and murderer and—'

'I know that. Believe me. I've worked this case long enough to know. But you've got to check your temper if you want us to get a conviction. You can't just go ballistic at—'

'Gentlemen!' Across the street, Vardy stood on the pavement, a smug look on his face. Wearing the same navy suit as in court, his gold watch catching the street lights. Behind him, a posse of men with more money than taste, tailored suits, their wrists and fingers shining as well, pecking cigarettes and nipping frosted champagne flutes. 'Oh, you poor things. You're standing out here in the cold all by yourselves, too polite to ask if you can come in and celebrate with us.'

Cullen stared at him, clenching his teeth. Keeping it calm, making sure not to say anything that would have Vardy reaching for his phone to report them to Campbell McLintock.

'And what are we celebrating?' Vardy pursed his lips and

frowned at them in mock thoughtfulness. 'What did my clever barrister call it? Oh yes, the smooth workings of our incorruptible justice system.'

Wilkinson was out of the bus shelter like a rocket, powering towards Vardy faster than Cullen had ever seen him move.

The bouncers closed ranks in front of Vardy and grabbed hold of Wilkinson, leaving him hanging over one man's shoulder, pointing his finger at Vardy, roaring like a trapped wild animal.

'Just you wait! I'll burn that shithole of a pub to the ground, and I'll do it with you in it!'

Vardy just patted his pockets, took an imaginary notebook out, and made as if to write down Wilkinson's words. Then he paused, scrunching up his forehead in cartoonish concentration. 'How do you spell shithole? Is it hyphenated? Oh, wait, stay like that. I'll just draw a wee picture of your mouth.'

Amid the boisterous laughter of Vardy's entourage, Wilkinson roared and started flailing with both arms to get at their leader, but the bouncer whose shoulder he was leaning over had already had enough. With a quick dip of the knees, he got under Wilkinson's centre of gravity, bear-hugged the large man and simply lifted him off the ground. Wilkinson yelped with surprise, then kicked out at his shins. And missed. He tried again, and missed again, even worse. He looked like an enormous toddler having a tantrum.

Cullen raced across the road and yanked Wilkinson free of the doorman's grip. Wilkinson thrashed around, nearly knocking Cullen off balance with a wild roundhouse punch aimed at Vardy.

Before he could have another go, Cullen grabbed Wilkinson in a headlock and hustled him up the road.

∼

'Are you cool yet?' Cullen sat in the driver's seat, staring at Wilkinson. 'Eh?'

Wilkinson was counting his change, hands between his legs, his lips mouthing each new number.

Still can't believe this. I came so close to committing property damage, came so close to barrelling inside like Bruce Willis in a Die Hard *film, but without the clue as to how to take out a building full of armed thugs.*

And I let Wilkinson hand Vardy another victory, another humilia-tion. And good old Wilko did it at the top of his voice with words so filthy they should have come out of the other end.

'Have you been drinking?'

Wilkinson looked over but didn't say anything. He went back to his change. 'I've bloody lost count.'

Cullen grabbed his wrist, stopping him. 'When you were watching Vardy's pub, were you drinking?'

Wilkinson laughed. Minty breath covered Cullen's face. Was he covering alcohol?

I can't tell. And I couldn't care less. I've got my own problems.

'You need to tell Cargill about this.'

'I'm not speaking to that bloody witch.' Wilkinson reached into his pocket for some more change. 'Two eighty-five. Two ninety-five.'

Any other night, Cullen would have laughed, but not tonight. 'Get out.'

Wilkinson looked over. 'You're not going to drive me home?'

'No. You've got enough for the bus. Get up to Lauriston Place and you can get a 47 most of the way home.'

'You should give me a lift.'

'Get out.' Cullen reached across him and flung the door open. 'Now!'

Wilkinson gave him one last glare then complied. 'You're making a mistake here.'

'Just pissed off.' Cullen shut the door and drove off, leaving Wilkinson to rail at random strangers like a drunk idiot.

Cullen walked into the World's End Close and stood there in the dark, staring up at the bright windows of his flat.

Shite.

My car's still in Dumbiedykes.

He yawned into his fist. *No chance I can be arsed getting it tonight.* He let himself into the communal stairwell and trudged up the steps. He stuck the key in the lock. It was pulled from his hand.

The door swung open and Sharon stood in front of him, looking right through him.

'Sorry it's so late, but I—'

'Don't.' Sharon's face was ice. And venom.

He frowned. 'Don't what?'

'Don't bother, Scott. I want your stuff out. I want you out. I want out. Full stop.' Sharon looked at him, long and hard. Then tossed the engagement ring at him and slammed the door in his face.

15

'SHARON!' CULLEN KEPT KNOCKING UNTIL SHE OPENED UP. 'COME ON, let me in.'

The door cracked open, the chain rattling, an eye peering out. 'Scott, go.'

'Look, I don't understand.'

'Just leave me alone.'

'If you want me and my stuff gone, you need to let me in.'

'Find somewhere else to sleep tonight. We'll sort this out later.'

'Sharon, come on.' Cullen opened his palm, showing the engagement ring. The thin light from the flat caught it, making the diamond sparkle. 'I want you to have this.'

'I don't want it. Didn't throwing it—'

'Look, can you hear me out?'

The door closed.

Shite. Well done, champ.

What the hell's going on? What have I—

The door opened wide and Sharon stood there, hands on hips. Fluffy sat behind her, the cat's chest all puffed up, his usual disappointed look even worse tonight. She turned and followed the cat through. 'You've got five minutes.'

❦

'OKAY, FINE.' SHARON STOOD IN THE KITCHEN, AVOIDING EYE contact with him, stroking the cat on the counter until a huge clump of fur collected in her hand. 'Look, when we got engaged it was already too late for me.'

Cullen couldn't speak. She'd finally said out loud the words he'd only heard in his head, all the shit she'd left unsaid, at least verbally. The coldness, the distance. 'But it's been bad for longer than eighteen months.'

'Scott...' She took his hand, cold against the warmth of his. 'You didn't ask me to marry you because you thought you'd always love me. You only proposed because you were afraid I'd break up with you.'

Cullen felt like he had walked on stage in the wrong act. She was pages ahead in the script and had cut through his preamble, his bullshit. But he didn't know his own lines. *And bloody hell, she's right.* And deep down he knew it. 'You're wrong.'

She pulled her hand away and opened a bigger gulf between them.

'We're good for each other, Sharon. And I had good intentions when I asked you to marry me. The best.'

'The best? You sound like Donald Trump.' She at least gave him a smile, if only a bittersweet one. 'Intentions are one thing, Scott, but your heart was never in this engagement, right?'

He bit his lip. 'You know what I think? Most people aren't with their first choice of partner, just the first one who comes along, or the best one at a point in time. And I just realised I'm not your first choice anymore.'

Her gaze flickered. 'Hold on a minute, *you* are not *my* first choice anymore? How is this about me?'

'You're the one breaking up with me.'

'How long have we been engaged now, Scott? A year and a half? And what have you done since proposing? We're still living in my flat, you're still not pulling your weight in cleaning and cooking and even just tidying up. I'm still waiting for a sign that you've at least thought about making wedding arrangements.' She exhaled long and slow, all her energy seeming to drain from her. She was past caring.

And this silent proof of her withdrawal hurt more than anything she could've said.

She took another breath, short and sharp.

Cullen watched her mouth moving but couldn't listen. Wished he was somewhere else. Back in time. Forward in time. Anywhere – just not here.

'—Yvonne Flockhart, right?'

'What?'

'Scott, Chantal told me what happened. Yvonne was going out with Craig Hunter and you shagged her after some Christmas party.'

'That was in the dim and distant past, before I even met you. I've changed.'

'Really?'

'Really. It was disgraceful, I know it was, but it was ages ago and I was out of my skull. Couldn't even remember doing it.' He looked away. 'It's one of the reasons I stopped drinking.'

She got up with a huff and walked over to the sink. And just stared into it. He knew her too well to be taken in by this jealousy act. It was the kind of thing you said when you needed a decent reason to break up.

When the truth was that she just didn't care anymore. When she knew that would've been too hurtful.

'Sharon, please. You're talking about a mistake I made when I was someone else, when I still thought life was just about shagging and getting hammered so hard I didn't mind who I was shagging. It was bad, I know, really bad. But I've apologised to Craig, we're friends again, and I'm better than that now. I know I am.'

She half-nodded like she knew he was right, but then she sighed with a tiredness that had nothing to do with the time of night. 'Don't make this harder than it needs to be.'

'Look, I had to interview Angela Lamb this afternoon.' Cullen caught a flash of her giving her speech, seeming embarrassed by it. 'I want what her and Bill have.'

'You want it with me?'

'Of course. It's why I proposed, Sharon. I want to spend my life with you. I want to have kids with you.'

'But I can't have kids.'

'We can at least *try*. You've been pregnant once. We can do IVF, we can—'

'I'm not doing IVF, Scott. And I don't want to try for kids with you. I feel like we're in opposite corners of a shared prison cell. I feel trapped, Scott, and I want out. I want to be someone else.'

'You want to be with someone else, is that it?'

'For God's sake.' She pointed out of the small kitchen towards the front door. 'Scott, do the right thing for once and give me some space.'

THE FOOTBALL THUDDED OFF THE DRIVER'S DOOR AND THE LITTLE toerag stepped forward, arching his body to deliver the perfect volley on the follow-up, smacking the ball off the window, then wheeling away, arms in the air like he'd just won the World Cup for Scotland, his hissing cheers like the buildings of Dumbiedykes were the crowd at Hampden.

'You little shite!' Cullen grabbed him by the arms and lifted him clean off the ground. Little bastard couldn't be any more than eight. 'That's my car!'

'Sorry, mister!' His eyes went wide, his breathing hammering out of his lungs. 'I didn't know!'

'You didn't care, did you? Didn't give a shite.' Cullen dropped him on the pavement, but kept a tight grip on his shoulder. 'That's my car, you little bastard. Cost me ten grand. You know how long it takes to save up for that? Or how long it takes to pay the loan off? Do you?'

The kid was crying now.

Cullen gave him a shake. 'Do you?'

'Sorry, mister.' Thick snot bubbled in his nose.

The ball trundled over to them. Cullen let go of the little sod, picked up the ball and battered it high in the air, arcing over to the lower flats across the road. Seemed to take ages to land, but it thumped against a garage door. 'Now piss off.'

The little shite sprinted off in the direction of his football and hopefully his home. *Shouldn't be out at this time.*

The driver's door was splattered with marks where the balls had hit. He'd even knocked the wing mirror out. At least it was still attached. A quick adjustment and it was back.

Cullen reached down for his old gym bag and tossed it in the passenger seat. Then got in the Golf and rested his forehead on the steering wheel.

Where the hell am I going to sleep tonight?

CULLEN PULLED UP IN THE HALF-EMPTY CAR PARK. TULLIALLAN STILL looked like a cardboard box caught in the floodlights at this time of night. The bar was glowing, the sound of a load of drunk cops laughing and joking bleeding out through the open window. Must be a lot of them in there to need to open the window in mid-February. Made the place feel less like a police training college and more like a lonely hearts club, filled with the sad pricks who didn't have families to go home to, seeking refuge in the subsidised booze, drinking enough to drown out the world.

And there were the ones not even down in the bar, the ones who sat in their rooms toasting dead souls with their bottle of single malt, only stopping when the bottle was empty and their supply ran out. Nothing left to drink.

Nothing left to do. Over and out.

Like it was with Sharon.

All that bullshit about Yvonne and Craig... She'd left the building years ago. Her heart was no longer mine way before I proposed. Had been since... Since she'd lost that baby. And I hadn't helped, had I? I should've been there for her, but she couldn't even bring herself to tell me that she was infertile. Took her a year, maybe less, maybe more. But I should've been at the doctor with her, not finding out way after the event.

Two cops staggered out of the front door, trying to light cigarettes as they walked. They leaned against the side wall, hidden from the lights, just two tiny red dots glowing.

The last thing I want is to be back on the piss with those jokers, scoping out talent, drinking to the point of not caring about rejection, charming my way into some woman's knickers, for one night only.

That's not me, not any more.

All too depressing to even get out of the car, let alone into some strange bed. But Cullen climbed out of the car and took his time walking over to reception.

Just thinking about it made him tired. The projection of his best characteristics. The pretend enthusiasm for non-existent shared interests. And the inevitable dissatisfaction of the first sex. But the surprise intimacy of the second, caused by an errant stroke of her hips as they woke up or her getting back into bed after going to the toilet and spooning into—

Cullen stopped at the front desk. No receptionist, not even a bell. A door opened and wild laughs drifted through from the bar, and a greasy guy settled into the chair behind the desk, arched an eyebrow and gave Cullen the once over. 'Mm?'

'I'm on the MIT Sergeant Development Programme.' Cullen laid his warrant card on the desk, letting the corner snap down. 'Need a room for the night.'

The receptionist glanced at the card, then consulted his computer with the kind of aloof snort you'd expect in an Edinburgh luxury hotel. Not a police training college. 'You're in luck.' Thick smoker's voice. '*One* room left. Will you be here all week?'

Rest of my life, mate.

'Probably. Stick it on the Edinburgh MIT account.'

'Certainly.' The receptionist produced a keycard and tossed it onto the desk. 'First floor. Breakfast is served from six. Enjoy your stay.'

'Thanks.' Cullen took the card and let his feet lead him down the well-trodden path to the bar and annihilation, his mouth already wet with the taste of the night's first pint.

His phone vibrated in his coat pocket.

Sharon? Has she changed her mind?

He snatched the ringing mobile and peered at the screen.

It wasn't Sharon.

Number withheld.

He took the call. 'Hello?'

A short pause filled with a quick breath and slight groan. 'Sergeant, it's Campbell McLintock. I'm Mr Vardy's—'

'I know who are you. What the hell do you want?'

Another pause.

'Well? What do you want?'

A nervous cough. 'I need you to come to my house. Eighteen Clinton Road.'

'How did you get this number?'

'Please. Now. I have come into possession of some highly sensitive information pertaining to the criminal charges levelled against my client. I'll be waiting.'

'—DEFINITELY HIM.' CULLEN KNEW MORNINGSIDE, BUT COULDN'T for the life of him remember which one was Clinton Road. The SatNav guided him past a lively boutique restaurant, the couple in the window looking like they were having a similar chat to the one he'd just enjoyed. A huddle of lads stood in the doorway of the designer bar next door, laughing and joking and sucking on fizzing pints of lager. 'What do you think I should do?'

'Tough one, Sundance.'

Can't believe I'm asking him for advice.

Still, if this is a set-up, they'll believe my worst enemy over my best friend.

'You thought of calling Lamb or Methven?'

'Tried. Neither are answering.'

'So I'm your third choice? Thanks a bunch.'

'So what should I do?'

'Sod it, go on, see what the boy's got to say.'

'Right.' Cullen took the next left, and it was like he'd turned into another century. Georgian mansions lined both sides of a quiet street, each set back behind large front gardens, illuminated from below by ground lights, like they were exhibits in an architecture museum. Then the smooth asphalt gave way to a cobbled road, the houses shrouded in dark shadows, the soft glow of each lamppost hinting at the silhouette of a house, glimpsed through bare trees shaking in the February winds. The Golf's headlights swept along a narrow curve, catching on the high stone walls, until a dark gateway yawned at him.

'You have reached your destination.'

Cullen took it slowly through the gateposts and pulled up on a wide pebbled drive. Beyond, the house lay in darkness. He killed the engine and stepped out into the dark, then started crunching his way up the long drive. His eyes started adjusting to the monochrome half-light outlining the driveway's thick foliage in cold silver.

He checked his Airwave radio was in his jacket pocket and glanced up at the canopy of stars. Something sharp grazed his cheek and Cullen dropped to the ground. A massive figure loomed over him, slightly less dark than the night sky. A sharp pain stung his face. *Bastard's cut me with a knife!*

Cullen rolled back over his shoulder and was up on one knee, hands raised in a double guard to protect his face against the next swing of the blade.

But it never came.

Cullen squinted through the darkness, shuffling back to create more distance, but all he could make out was the attacker's swaying arm. Right to left, left to right. He seemed content just standing there, playing mind games with his unarmed prey. Like that bastard with the hammer. The thought made his shoulder throb.

Then Cullen realised why his attacker wasn't coming after him.

Because he was a tree – sprawling and towering with low-hanging branches and scale-like, razor-sharp leaves.

Cullen straightened up and touched his cheek, feeling the wet warmth at his fingertips, now covered in inky black smudges. He wiped his fingers on his trousers and set off again towards McLintock's house, a four-storey mansion glowing in the moonlight, nestled between two massive oak trees. Not a single window lit, and something else about the place made him wary. No motion sensor lights, but two front doors. The one on the right was wide open.

Cullen covered the rest of the distance in a crouched run and skittered up the grand set of stairs. Sure enough, the door was open but the hallway beyond it was even darker. He pressed himself against the door frame, the smooth ridges pressing through his thin suit trousers. He cocked his head to the side and strained his ears. Quiet music drifted down from upstairs – sounded like the smooth cheese of Sade. But no voices talking anywhere in the house.

And no sign of Campbell McLintock.

Cullen slid his phone from his pocket and switched on the torch, angling the spotlight to the floor to ensure he didn't trip as he tiptoed towards the music. The staircase was carpeted with a long Persian rug, swallowing the sounds of his footsteps. He stopped on the first-floor landing and listened. Still Sade, but there was also a faint noise of rushing water. Sounded like it was upstairs so he set off again and stopped on the second floor. The noise was louder, spilling out through the crack of light under the swing doors down a hallway.

What the hell?

Is McLintock having a shower?

Cullen tiptoed up to the doors and touched the handles, checking if they were locked. They swung open on well-oiled hinges, inaudible and smooth, all the way in. The bedroom beyond was grand in every sense, the indirect lighting soft and warm, the antique wooden furniture polished to a rich gleam, the cream silk sheets on the king-size bed spread wide like it was an upmarket hotel.

No sign of any speakers, but Sade sang about travelling coast to coast, LA to Chicago. The shower noise came from behind a closed door.

No sign of a disturbance, just a man getting cleaned up after a long day of rubbing shoulders with filth like Vardy.

Another noise, almost faint enough to be drowned out by the sound of rushing water. Almost. Sounded like wheezing, coming hard and fast from inside the bathroom.

Cullen froze, holding his breath. *What the hell?* He stepped across the thick shag rug and tried the door handle. Starting to worry he might bust into some asphyxiation sex game.

Wrong.

He stumbled into a blood bath, the tiles slick and red, a blood trail smearing across the tiles to the fogged-up shower unit, the door hanging open.

Campbell McLintock lay face down on the floor, stark naked. Through the steam, a figure in a black gimp suit straddled his back. A man, his entire body covered in glistening wet latex, including the head, wheezing as he pinned McLintock down.

Cullen stepped closer.

The gimp stopped dead and stared at Cullen from behind his gleaming mask, one hand holding McLintock's head up by the hair, the other raised high above him, a blood-stained blade catching the light in neon brilliance. He swung the blade down in a flashing arc, deep into McLintock's throat, opening the neck like a dropped can of Irn Bru, spraying red mist over the white tiles instead of orange.

16

CULLEN LURCHED FORWARD, BUT THE GIMP LASHED OUT WITH THE knife, missing his face by millimetres. He slipped on the blood and went down hard on his front.

The gimp was standing in the open window. Then he disappeared.

Cullen scrambled to his feet and slid across the smeared tiles. Like trying to run on oil. He braced himself against the door and knelt down next to the dying man. He tried to turn him over onto his back and stop the bleeding from his neck, but the crimson puddle underneath him kept pooling out further and the slick skin slipped out of his grasp. He let go and jerked his head around to look for— There! He hit the tap and the shower stream stopped.

Silence.

No rushing water thrumming in his ears, no suppressed wheezing, no choked gurgling. Nothing.

The gash in McLintock's throat had stopped bleeding. But it was over. The lawyer was dead.

Cullen stared at him, at the glazed eyes, at the countless stabbing wounds all over his pale, limp body, already washed clean by the shower, the forensic evidence all down the plughole.

Stuck at square one.

Unless I catch the gimp. And he's getting away.

Cullen climbed to his feet, careful not to slip and fall and scramble in the wet shower. He stuck his head out the window the gimp had used to escape, expecting to see the same pitch black as at the front of the house, but the back garden was lit up by bright spotlights.

The gimp was limping across the lawn, dragging his right leg.

Judging by the trail of destruction, the gimp had jumped down to the greenhouse's slanted glass roof and tumbled through it. A shower of shards covered a collection of exotic plants. So he must've scrambled through the back door into the garden.

I've got time to catch him.

Cullen climbed on the window ledge and pressed his back against the wall. With a deep breath, he edged along to the black iron drainpipe. He reached for it with both hands, ready to abseil down. But it was February. The pipe was cold and moist, impossible to hold on to. His fingers lost grip. All he could do to avoid taking a headlong fall was to kick off the ledge and jump, out and away from the wall, unable to see when or where he would—

Shite!

Cullen hit the ground with a jarring thud, the momentum knocking him back over his heels, breaking his balance, sending him reeling on to his arse. He tried to roll with it but went straight into a flowerbed and banged his head on a stone. Everything hurt, huge black spots swirled around in front of his eyes. He vomited, harsh acid burning his throat. He struggled back to his feet, trying not to keel over again. Deep, steady breaths. The spots started disappearing, all but one. He blinked to bring it into focus. Not a black spot. A black gimp. In the bright light, his latex getup looked more like a cheap Batman costume, but without the cape or anything to grab hold of. Either way, the guy was standing at the open doorway of the garden wall, rooted to the spot.

Amateur.

Cullen made a dash for him.

Batman spun around and sprinted through the gate. Then he screamed, his right leg collapsed under him and he went down like he'd been shot, grabbing his injured knee and rolling on his back.

Cullen ran over to the prone man, but Batman's hand slid from his knee to his ankle, sneaking his knife from its holster. Cullen was already in the air, diving for him, as the guy brought the weapon up. The blade flashed in the spotlights. Then it disappeared in Cullen's shadow. He was swooping down for the tackle, coming down hard, forearms crossed to brace his heavy fall on the guy's broad chest and knock the air out of him. Too late to change direction and dodge the knife coming at his throat, so he swiped his left forearm up and out to parry the blade, then crashed, hard.

Air escaped from his lungs.

The pain in his shoulder like an electric shock.

The blade sliced through his jacket, the fabric tearing.

Cullen rolled and tumbled, thudding his head against the stone wall. Black spots swirled through his eyes, fast, dizzying, all over the place.

One of the black spots got up and hobbled through the gate.

Cullen let his head drop back on the cold hard ground and closed his eyes until the rest of the spots disappeared.

A BRIGHT LIGHT BURNT INTO CULLEN'S LEFT EYE, LEAVING A GLOWING trace as it shifted to his right. It lingered there and he tried to close it, but rubber-gloved fingers pried it open. Then something clicked and the light died.

'He'll live. Mild concussions don't kill people.'

Cullen groaned as the paramedic's head came into focus above him, hiding behind the burnt-in red blotches. He reached for his searing shoulder and his fingers explored it, looking for the knife wound or even a bandage. Just the combination of a hard landing and an old injury. Felt like it needed to click back into place. 'Batman does.'

Silence, as the paramedic exchanged a concerned glance with her colleague kneeling down beside her. 'Maybe it's worse than I thought.' She crouched low. 'Sir, do you think I'm Batman?'

Cullen laughed, then winced at the stabbing pain in the back of his head. His vision went blurry, nausea creeping up his throat. He took two fast breaths and tried to focus on the woman's face, the chestnut skin, the black curls spilling down over her green uniform, the deep concern in her eyes and the quick, easy smile that danced around the corners of her mouth when he kept staring at her. He coughed. 'No, I don't think you're Batman.'

Now the smile danced in her eyes, too.

But a brash voice barked across the garden. 'Get in there, Sundance!'

Bain. *Bloody hell.*

'Now, I need you to take your clothes off and put them in this bag for me.' She held it out, but it looked like there were three of them. Aim for the middle.

'Why?'

'You're covered in another man's blood. You're a suspect.'

'I'm—' Cullen bit his cheek. Hurt like hell. 'Fine.' He hauled off his top, the cold air biting at his bare skin. He had to use the wall to keep upright. He tossed the jumper into the bag but it seemed to land on the ground.

'In the bag, not in the vague direction.' The paramedic crouched and picked it up.

Cullen handed her his trousers, leaving him in his boxers, in a Scottish February evening.

'Looks very cold tonight.' The paramedic raised her eyebrows as she passed him a navy tracksuit. 'It should fit.' A pair of shoes dropped in front of him.

Cullen stepped into the bottoms and tugged them up. He shivered as he zipped the jacket up.

'I'll be inside.' The paramedic turned her back on him and walked over to the door.

Cullen gazed up at the sky, the shiver out of control.

Bain's shiny bald head blocked the view. He held out his hand. 'Squared it with Lamb.'

Cullen took it and let Bain help him to his feet. 'What?'

'The phone call. You'd left your phone unlocked up there too so he's heard the call from Campbell. You're in the clear, Sundance.'

'Thanks.'

'You won't thank me when you see the texts I sent.' Bain laughed. 'Still, your phone's in evidence, so you'll get it back tomorrow. Maybe tonight if you're lucky.'

Cullen hugged his arms tight round himself. 'Have you found Batman?'

'What the hell?' Bain frowned at him. 'Have you lost your mind?'

'The guy who killed McLintock and stabbed me in the shoulder was dressed as Batman. He—'

'Batman doesn't kill. Think about it, Sundance. His parents were shot and...' Bain laughed. 'Bill!' He turned around to the greenhouse, where a few SOCOs searched the crash site. 'Bill! Cullen reckons he was attacked by Batman.'

One of the suited figures walked over and tugged his mask free: Lamb, looking at Cullen with the same concern as the paramedic. 'Give us a minute, Brian.' He dismissed Bain with a bored flick of the wrist. 'Scott, are you okay?'

Cullen stood up tall, though it was a struggle. Now the adrenalin was wearing off, he was stiff as a post mortem. 'Bit dazed, but I'll live.'

'What was Bain on about? You were attacked by *Batman*?'

'Jesus Christ.' Cullen huffed at Bain over the rear door, doing nothing to hide his broad grin. 'No, I was attacked by somebody *dressed* as Batman. Some guy in a black latex suit and mask, and don't bother asking. I can't ID him. He slit McLintock's throat in the bathroom, right in front of me, then—'

'Brian said you were here.'

Cullen huffed out a painful sigh, sending a spasm across his aching shoulder. 'I got a call from McLintock. Said he had something on Vardy.'

'Vardy? What was it?'

'I've no idea. When I got here, this Batman guy was on top of him in the shower, sliced his...' Cullen swallowed down the image of McLintock's death. His murder. 'Then he jumped out of the window.' A SOCO was leaning out of it, high up. 'I almost caught him, but...' He pointed at where he had just been lying. 'He escaped through the archway there. I couldn't even tell you how long ago it was. No idea how long I was out for.'

'Don't worry about him getting away, Scott. Be glad *you* got away, too.' Lamb paused, glancing up at the brightly lit bathroom window, then gave Cullen's uninjured shoulder a squeeze. 'And don't worry about not catching the guy, either. You called it in as soon as you could. Besides...' He motioned at the wrecked greenhouse and the trampled grass leading to the garden gate. 'The guy left enough destruction in his wake to point us in the right direction. I've already got uniforms picking up the trail.' A cheeky glint sneaked into his eyes. 'Now, let's go up to the bathroom and see if the shower hasn't washed away all the evidence. You never know, there's a one-in-a-million chance we might find something to reveal the secret identity of your dark knight.'

'You think I'm joking, don't you?'

'Get over yourself, Scott.' Lamb marched across the lawn towards the house.

~

CULLEN STEPPED INTO THE BEDROOM, HIS TYVEK SUIT CRINKLING, the mask tight around his swelling cheek. Everything seemed to be the same. The sound of rushing water had gone, but the suppressed wheezing was still there.

What?

Cullen froze.

A suited figure was leaning over the dead body in the shower, the baggy suit shaking with wheezy laughter. 'The *size* of it!'

Lamb joined Cullen in the doorframe. 'What the hell is—' Then he roared loud enough to make the SOCOs in the room jump with fright. 'BAIN! Get out of there, now!'

Bain looked across at them and rolled his eyes, but he obeyed the order, joining Lamb and Cullen in the master bedroom, his leer still creasing his eyes through the goggles. 'What a sight, lads.'

'Jesus, Brian, what the hell is wrong with you?'

'Bill, have you not—'

Lamb grabbed his arms. 'What the hell is so funny about a dead man?'

'Should see the—' Bain burst out laughing again, as close to a bellow as the mask would allow, '—see the cock on that guy. Hung like a donkey, I tell you.'

'Sergeant!' Lamb shot a glance into the bathroom, where the SOCOs were still photographing the crime scene, bright flashes throwing hard shadows into the bedroom. He turned his attention back on Bain. 'The last thing I need is for one of my officers to get a reputation for ogling dead men's cocks!'

A sharp cough came from inside the bathroom, then a figure the exact shape and size of Jimmy Deeley stepped through the doorway, a stern look glaring through the goggles. 'Now, I know you'll want to perform a thorough examination of the body, but our friend Mr Anderson there,' he pointed at another crouched figure, 'is in a race against time to preserve any forensic evidence. Most of it was washed away in the shower.'

Lamb just grunted. 'That's it?'

'Hold on.' Deeley raised a hand. 'Anderson's collected a big clump of hairs from the drain, mostly the victim's, but judging by the colour, some may have come from the murderer.'

'Some good news, then.' Lamb gave him a curt nod. 'I know you don't like—'

'He died just after I burst into this room.' Cullen checked his watch, not that it was much use. 'Must've been around eleven twenty.'

Deeley nodded. 'Sounds about right.'

Lamb let out a loud sigh. 'I was going to ask when he was first attacked.'

'Right. Sorry.'

Deeley peered back into the room and frowned. 'Well. You're in luck, Bill. There's some scabbing on the wounds, so he was at it for a while. Hours.'

'Any idea of the—'

'If I had to give an educated guess, I'd say the first cuts occurred at about nine pm last night. Give or take half an hour.'

'Jesus Christ.' Cullen closed his eyes. 'He was tortured for over two hours.'

Lamb stood there, staring into space. 'Okay, Jimmy. Need the PM done first thing tomorrow.'

'Come on, Bill, I've got—'

Cullen left them to it, walking out of the master bedroom into the mansion's cold hallway and outside the inner locus. He kicked his CSI suit off, but got the leg caught.

'Wait up, Sundance.' Bain shuffled out after him. 'Oh, I know that look. Come on, Sundance, don't tell me you didn't find that claymore of a—'

'Shut up.'

'—need at least two hands to—'

'I swear—'

Lamb barged past Bain, tearing his facemask off and taking a sharp breath. He looked at Cullen's scowl, then at Bain. 'Are you still—'

'Not me.' Bain's leer became even more lecherous. 'Cullen was just saying how erotic he finds McLintock's massive man sword.'

'Enough.' Lamb gripped Bain's shoulders. 'I need one of you to go next door to interview McLintock's business partner.'

Bain smirked. 'Me and Hamish go back a long, long way.'

'Brian, I doubt you have the necessary emotional intelligence to deal with a man in shock.'

'Eh?' Bain puffed up his chest. 'I'll have you know—'

'Shut up!' Lamb focused on Cullen. 'Scott, can you go next door and speak with Hamish Williams. An FLO's broken the news to him, but he's taken this the hard way.' He frowned and a shadow fell over his eyes. Could've been sympathy. Could've been tiredness. Could've been something darker. 'Even though he's a bastard of a criminal defence lawyer, he's still a human being who's just lost a close friend. Treat him like one.'

17

———————

CULLEN SCUFFED DOWN THE FRONT STEPS OF MCLINTOCK'S mansion, turned right, jogged twenty paces up the driveway and skipped up an identical set of stairs and rang the bell. It chimed a solemn tone.

The heavy oak door swung open with a loud creak and a stony-faced man looked out, wearing an acid yellow police uniform. 'Cullen, is it?'

'Here to see Mr Williams.'

'Follow me.' The FLO hurried down the hallway as fast as he could, which wasn't much above a saunter. The walls were lined with pictures, all preserved for posterity in gilded frames. Class photographs from Loretto School in Musselburgh. The under-graduate degree certificate from St Andrews University alongside graduation photos in sepia. Then the doctoral diplomas from Oxford and Yale Law School, followed by countless portraits of a flabby pale man slipping into middle age with thinning blonde hair and an ever-changing array of gaudy fashion disasters. Williams was a lifelong fan of cravats, and a tireless grinner when posing alongside celebrities, major and minor.

'When you're finished...' The FLO gave an impatient cough and motioned at the swing doors to the lounge. 'Williams is through there. I'm trying to figure out how to get his bloody espresso machine working. Need a PhD in Astrophysics, I swear.' He slouched off back the way.

Cullen opened the doors and peered through.

Williams sat on his Chesterfield wingchair, his slippered feet resting on a golden silk footstool in front of a grand fireplace. He put a cognac glass to his lips and sipped. Didn't even glance at him, his gaze set on the dancing flames.

Cullen cleared his throat with a wet cough.

Williams lifted his hooded eyes to lock on to Cullen's. 'Oh hello there, darling. Who might you be?' He was swaying and his eyes struggled to stay open.

'Detective Sergeant Cullen. Police Scotland.' He slipped his warrant card from his chest pocket and held it out for Williams to inspect. 'We've met several times.'

'Ah.' Williams craned his neck and peered at the small writing in the mellow glow of the fire. 'Pleasure's all mine.' He relaxed into the backrest and let his eyes feast on Cullen, tucking his flabby neck folds into his golden silk cravat.

Cullen crossed in front of the fireplace and took a seat in the companion armchair, another oxblood Chesterfield, the leather warm from the fire. 'I gather you've been informed of the events next door?'

Williams flinched. Tears welled up in his eyes. 'Tragic.'

'I'm sorry for your loss. I know that Mr McLintock was your business partner. Was he a friend as well?'

'Yes, you may say that.' Williams tried for a smile. Looked like he had seen one once. From across the room. 'We were friends, of course. You don't split a mansion like this unless you're very close friends.' He looked sidelong at Cullen. 'Then again, I don't expect somebody with the rough temperament of the street to understand what he was to me.'

'When did you last see Mr McLintock?'

'At the office first thing. But then, you see, I had a power brunch with an important client and from there I had to rush to a lunch meeting with another highly important client and...' Williams trailed off, glancing at Cullen. 'I NEED MORE COGNAC!'

The shout was swallowed by the heavy leather furnishings and the heavy brocade curtains. The crackling of the fire emphasised the awkward silence.

Williams was looking at Cullen like he was supposed to deliver the drink.

So Cullen looked around the dark room. There, resting on a large book shelf filled with leather-bound law books. A bottle of supermarket cognac. 'Sir, may I have your—'

'Not that piss, you—' Williams bit his tongue. 'The Frapin Cuvée, if you will.'

'You need to—'

'Oh, Hamish, but that was over five thousand pounds, wasn't it?' Williams broke from his silly voice. 'And if I can't drink it on the eve of Campbell's passing, when can I?' He hauled himself up and staggered over to the bookcase and pulled a hidden door open at the third attempt, before disappearing inside.

Cullen let his gaze wander around the room. The hot air from the fire was getting to him, making him more lightheaded by the minute.

Living next door to each other. That seems weird. Almost too weird.

'Then again, I don't expect somebody with the rough temperament of the street to understand what he was to me.'

What did he mean by—

Oh. Oh, man.

The door creaked open again and Williams staggered through, clutching a fresh cognac and wearing a fresh dressing gown of purple silk, paired with a lime paisley cravat. 'Sorry, dear boy.' He collapsed into the armchair and spilled half the glass down his front. Didn't seem to notice, or mind if he did. 'I'd offer you some of the cognac, but I know about your battles with the demon drink.'

Cullen held his gaze, sweating in the oppressive heat. *How the hell do you know that?* 'Right, let's cut the shit. You and Campbell were personal partners as well as professional?'

Williams stiffened. For a moment he sat there, his face set in a rictus of that phony smile. 'If you must know, and I do hope this is of relevance to your investigation, Sergeant, for I *will* check with your superiors and believe you me, they owe me. If you are merely asking in the hope of shaming me or outing my partner posthumously for some filthy lucre from the gutter press, woe betide you, boy. Woe betide you. I will prosecute you to the full extent of the law.' He forced his face to relax, and sucked down a glass of five-grand cognac. 'Now, to answer your question... Yes, Campbell and I were lovers.' He dwelt on that last word like a final farewell to his one true love.

Then again, there was a performance element to everything he said or did, so Cullen kept a check on his sympathy. 'Thank you, Mr Williams.'

'You have no idea how hard that is to confess. Even harder for Campbell. I wish we'd come out years ago.' Williams struggled to his feet and puffed out his chest, a fat turkey in purple foil and Cullen had ruffled his feathers. 'I need more cognac.'

'Hamish!' Cullen motioned for the lawyer to retake his seat. 'If you want me to find his killer, then I'll need all relevant details on the nature of your relationship with Mr McLintock.' He got out his notepad and leafed through it, page by page, until he found a blank one. He took his time with it.

Sure enough, the air went out of Williams like out of a punctured accordion. He dropped back into his armchair with a deep groan. 'You know, Campbell wanted to remain a committed bachelor. Even though that's been code since biblical times, he wanted to keep up the pretence that he hadn't found the right woman yet. I found that challenging, but those were the terms we'd agreed on back when we first started stepping out together at St Andrews. Of course, we studied at Oxford, separate colleges naturally, then both went to Yale. It was much more liberal in New Haven, but still Campbell insisted on his *privacy*. When we returned to Edinburgh to set up practice and bought this mansion...' He waved a tired hand around the room. 'Well. We split it in two, but there are doors between them, if you know where to look.'

Cullen didn't want to risk interrupting his flow, so he waited. And waited.

Williams nodded forward and jerked back. '—not asleep!' He blinked hard a few times. 'Anyway, as I was saying, Campbell seemed his normal self the last time I saw him. In fact, he called me up this evening. He'd taken the team out to celebrate Mr Vardy's verdict. I gather that Mr Vardy was bailed. And you lost your witnesses, didn't you?'

'One of them.' Cullen tasted bile in his throat. 'How did—'

'I gather the other is with the wind, mm?'

'Can you think of anyone who would want your partner out of the picture?'

'Any number of police officers, yourself included, I'm sure.' Williams took a steadying breath. 'Well, Mr Vardy wasn't best pleased with Campbell.'

'Go on?'

'I believe that Campbell and Mr Vardy had a brief discussion in chambers at court while the bail was arranged. Campbell told me that Vardy was yelling about the injustice – about it not being an acquittal. Campbell tried to persuade him that the case was as good as dead, but Mr Vardy was more upset about the injustice of spending eighteen months in custody only for the case to fall apart. He had lost all this time because his lawyer was, and I quote, "*a fannybaws who couldn't get this stinking jobby of a case thrown out last year*". Campbell was protesting that he had done all he could, but Mr Vardy was... Well, he's an ungrateful bigot and he was incensed.'

There was no sign of McLintock at Vardy's shindig at the Debonair that evening. Odd.

Wait a second...

Cullen tried to overlay Vardy's physique with the figure in black. Got a good enough fit.

'Did you get the impression that Vardy might've—'

'Sergeant.' Williams gave him a long hard look. 'You've met Mr Vardy, correct?'

Cullen gripped the arms of the chair. 'Several times.'

'Listen, while Campbell was out celebrating, I had a business dinner and didn't come home until late. And we have an... agreement. If Sade's playing in Campbell's bedroom, that means Campbell is entertaining on his own.'

'You mean?'

'Christ, do I need to spell it out for you?' Williams hugged his arms tight. 'Having sex with another man. I don't like it, but I love Campbell, so I've always left him to it.' He gave a scornful snort. 'Now, it's getting rather late and—'

'And do you know who Mr McLintock was enjoying a spot of Sade with?'

Williams drew a sharp breath, and held it. But after a tense silence he deflated. 'Touché, Detective. I see we can both hit below the belt. As for Campbell's companion for the night, I can only hazard a guess. How shall I put this? Campbell had certain sexual appetites I found it impossible to satisfy.' He averted his eyes and with a bashful wave indicated his flabby physique. 'Campbell had rather extreme muscle-boy fantasies which he fulfilled by calling on a local escort agency. Very tasteful establishment, I assure you. All above board and the rent boys are regularly screened for STDs and...' He fell silent, staring into the fire, perfectly still, nothing stirring but the flames dancing in his wet eyes.

Cullen leaned forward on his chair. 'Did Campbell have a regular rent boy?'

Williams gave him the smallest of nods. Then he closed his eyes. And kept them closed. Seemed to never want to open them again.

Cullen couldn't blame him. He let the silence sit between them for another moment. Then he nudged it aside with a quiet cough. 'Did Campbell ever mention this man's name to you?'

'This is none of your business.'

And just like that, I've lost him.

Christ, this man's lover had his throat cut right in front of me. Jesus. Focus. The gimp suit.

'Hamish, was Campbell into cosplay?'

A leer settled on Williams's face. 'Cos-what?'

'Cosplay, short for costume play. The man who killed him was dressed like Batman.'

'What the hell are you talking about?'

'I saw it.' Cullen got up and wheeled round to lean on the back of his chair. The room's cold air nibbled at his scratched cheek even though he was standing right by the fire. 'I was in the room when it happened. A man in a black costume. A big man. And he'd been torturing Campbell, maybe for hours.'

Williams stared into his glass. 'Campbell had a superhero phase a few years ago. Don't judge him, Mr Cullen. Everybody has their kink, and I won't apologise for Campbell's.' His eyes started flickering, like he was watching a highlight reel of McLintock's adventures in spandex. 'Truth be told, it brought out the best in me. We used to dress up as various heroes and there wasn't a dry cleaner in the city that would clean up my Robin costume. Campbell had such formidable control that he kept his Batman one spotless. What a man...' His hand dropped into his lap and he started an absentminded rub.

'Mr Williams.'

The hand froze and a puzzled frown appeared on his forehead. 'Yes?'

'Did anybody else know of this?'

'Not especially, no. We had a Superman join us once—'

'Do you remember his name?'

'I...' Williams pursed his lips, his eyes flickering again. 'Campbell arranged it. Sorry.'

'Come on, we're trying to find your partner's murderer.'

'I can't remember.'

'Hamish, I know you. We've sat across meeting room tables hundreds of times. You've got a mind like a steel trap. You know. I know you know.'

After a few seconds, Williams looked back at Cullen. 'Campbell called him Big Rob.'

Cullen grabbed the chair back tight.

Him? That idiot with biceps like thighs?

I haven't seen him since...

Crap. That day. When Xena Farley was shot. Big Rob, sluicing water on the pavement.

And I have no idea where to find him.

THE NIGHT HIT CULLEN IN THE FACE LIKE A WET TOWEL, FOLLOWED by the kind of rain you could hardly see but which soaked your clothes in an instant. He turned up his collar and slouched down the driveway to the dark gate.

Out on the road, a car flashed its headlights.

He legged it across the slippery cobbles and got into the dry of the back seat, slicking his sodden hair as he slammed the door.

'What kept you so long?' Bain twisted around in the passenger seat. 'Were you sucking his co—?'

'Stop!' Lamb stared through the windscreen, gripping the steering wheel.

'I was going to say cognac!' Bain held up his hands. 'Heard he's got a bottle that cost double my month's salary.'

Lamb sighed like he just wanted to go to sleep. Or slap that look off Bain's face. 'Did you get anything, Scott?'

'He offered me some of his five-grand cognac.'

'See?' Bain swivelled round to focus on Cullen. 'Bet that's not all he offered, eh? Pretty boy like you, Sundance.'

Cullen shrugged it off. 'Not far off. McLintock and Williams were lovers.'

'Seriously?' Bain's mouth hung open. 'What, Campbell was a bummer?'

'Brian, would you—'

'So they did share this house.' Bain gasped. 'And with a hammer the size of McLint*cock*'s, I dare say *he* was doing the pounding.' His eyes went out of focus.

'Would you just shut up?' Lamb put a hand over Bain's mouth. 'Scott, did you get anything else?'

'Campbell had muscle-boy fantasies, satisfied by rentboys.'

Lamb let Bain's mouth go. 'How the hell did we not know?'

'Because any indiscretion might've shagged big Campbell in the arse, him being a respected lawyer and all.' Bain shook his head. 'One thing being a bummer, quite another seeking out rent boys, eh? But those itches, eh, they scream out to be scratched long and hard. Good old Campbell had the cash, didn't he? If I were him, I'd call an escort agency and have my pick of the finest crop, get a contract, stick to one or two regulars... The opposite of Williams. Young and virile muscle boys, like sex toys fresh from the box.' He blinked. 'How am I doing so far?'

Cullen stared at him, dumbfounded.

Bain started laughing. 'I'm on the money, right?'

'Aye, you are, actually.'

Lamb turned round. 'What? He's right about—?'

Cullen nodded. 'Aye, and—'

'Course I am!' Bain clapped his hands with delight. 'And Williams was a bottom.' He gave Lamb a leering look. 'That means receiver, sir.'

'I know what—'

'And given the size of McLintock's plonker, it's fair to assume Williams isn't such a tight arse as—'

'Enough!' Lamb's shout hit Bain like a punch in the mouth. 'Sergeant, we're investigating a man's murder, and all you can think of is the size of his penis?'

Bain turned back to Cullen with a petulant frown. 'McLintock had a much better weapon—'

'Get out!' Lamb was trembling with rage, wringing the steering wheel as though picturing his hands around Bain's neck. 'Now! And grow up or I'll have you on a disciplinary before you bring up McLintock's—'

'Aye, aye.' Bain stepped out into the rainy night, chuckling. But then he leaned back in to peer at Cullen over the head rest. 'Little birdie tells me you checked into the Tulliallan Ritz, Sundance.'

'You heard him, Brian. Piss off.'

'Charming. I'll wait in your motor, Sundance.'

Lamb reached over, but Bain slammed the door shut, hard enough to rock the car. Lamb watched him go, counting to ten under his breath. 'Have you got any leads?'

'Well, my number one suspect is Vardy. He's pissed off with McLintock for spending eighteen months on remand.'

'Even though the case is falling apart?'

'Even so. Maybe especially so. Pissed off that he was inside for so long.'

'I don't buy it.' Lamb turned around and fixed Cullen with an unreadable stare. 'Who's number two?'

'Bain's rent boy theory. It was like him and Williams were singing from the same hymn sheet.' Cullen stared at the dark gate. 'I got a name for the rent boy.'

'Someone we know?'

'Big Rob.'

Lamb drew a sharp breath. 'Him...' A tense silence settled between them, until Lamb took another breath, this one short and sharp. 'You think he's this Batman figure?'

'You don't believe me, do you?'

'I don't, Scott. Sorry. It just seems...'

Through the rain, the other car's lights flashed. Bain, impatient to get going.

Cullen patted Lamb on the shoulder and cracked the door open. 'I know Big Rob from a case me and Craig Hunter worked back in the dim and distant. Guy looks like he's chiselled from marble.'

'You know where to find him?'

'Know where to start, anyway.'

'Get on it, first thing tomorrow. Forget about Tulliallan. Okay? You're on this full-time. Need you in bright and early.'

DAY 3

Tuesday
14th February

18

A PHONE RANG SOMEWHERE.

Cullen opened his bleary eyes and scanned around the bright room looking for the bastard thing. Things weren't where they usually were. And neither was he. He was in a room at Tulliallan, lying on the luminous white sheet, still wearing his crumpled suit from the night before. Alone. Hadn't even managed to turn off the light before he passed out.

And his phone was still ringing and ringing and ringing and nowhere in sight.

He felt a sharp tingle in his chest and a thick vibration, drilling into his ribs. He fumbled his phone from the inside pocket of his suit jacket and answered the call. 'Cullen.' His voice sounded like he'd been shitfaced the night before.

Just silence in his ear. 'Scott?' Buxton's voice. 'Did I wake you?'

Cullen glanced at his watch. Six oh one. 'I'll forgive you. What's up?'

'You seen Lamb?'

Cullen sat up on the bed and caught sight of himself in the wall mirror. He looked as rough as he felt. He yawned into his fist. 'The only Lamb I've seen is a load of sheep jumping over stiles in my dreams.'

'Right. Well, tell him I'm looking for him.'

'Where are you?'

'I'm up at Morningside. Some big mansion. Big group of us and no sign of Lamb.' A pause. 'Oh, here he comes now. Catch you later.' Click and he was gone.

Cullen shook his head, then sat up and yawned again. *Too bloody early. And I've got to find Big Rob. Could be anywhere. Could be nowhere.*

He kicked open his suitcase and picked up a fresh shirt, badly crumpled. No sign of an iron in the room.

He lay back on the bed and yawned again.

I wish I could go back a year and a half. Sort Vardy out once and for all. Stop him getting in that flat, in that bedroom. Take the gun off him and shoot him. Stop all this bullshit.

And while I'm at it, I could sort myself out as well. Keep my mouth shut, instead of proposing to Sharon in a panic to patch up a broken relationship.

Or I'd grow a pair and go through with it, but this time I'd go for broke. No hanging about, no holding back, no backing out. Be a different person.

Shite, I've no idea know what I want.

He caught a pong of stale sweat.

But a shower would be a good place to start.

∿

'SORRY, SIR.' THE GYM RECEPTIONIST FOCUSED ON HIS COMPUTER screen, the cross trainers grinding behind him as early-morning mentalists sweated pints. The receptionist's University of Edinburgh polo shirt was soaked through with sweat already. Roasting in there. 'Robert hasn't swiped in for a few months now.'

Cullen yawned into his fist, spraying saliva. 'But he is a member here, right?'

'That's correct. Robert has been a member since, oh, 2011.'

Right after we shut down his previous place.

'Does he still pay the monthly membership?'

'Annual, I'm afraid.'

Cullen used the desk to push up to standing. 'Can you give me an address or—'

'Sorry, sir, we don't hold that information. You need to check with the university.'

'Right.' University gym meant the membership database was held centrally. Meaning a warrant. 'Okay, thanks for your time.' Cullen stepped out into the cold morning.

So he's been here, but isn't here at the moment.

I know Big Rob – spends all day in the gym. Well, when he's not posing for some muscle magazine.

A parking attendant was taking an interest in his Golf. 'Police!'

That got a nod, making the wee nyaff scamper off like a rat down a drainpipe.

So, where now?

No idea.

⁓

CULLEN SLOWED BEHIND THE BUS, PULLING OUT TO PEER ROUND. A solid queue of traffic barred him from overtaking. An even thicker queue waited to get on the bus.

Bloody hell. He leaned back in the seat. *Be quicker walking. Not that there's anywhere to park.*

His phone rang. The dashboard display read *Budgie calling.* He hit the answer button on the wheel. 'What's up?'

'Just spoken to a neighbour who claims she saw a man fight some superhero in McLintock's garden last night. That was you, wasn't it?'

Cullen felt a stab of pain in his shoulder. 'Don't remind me. Did she follow where he went?'

'She's an old dear in her seventies. Says her eyesight ain't what it used to be, but she's adamant she saw you two fighting. She wants to talk to the "valiant policeman who fought that ghastly black man". Her words, not mine.'

'Jesus.' The bus set off and Cullen trundled up St Leonard's Street.

'I know, right?' Buxton sighed. 'Anyway, she heard a loud commotion in McLintock's garden. So she looked out and saw a black-suited figure open the greenhouse door and hobble towards the garden wall. Seconds later, you climbed from the rear window, fell from the drainpipe, cracked your arse open, gave chase and wrestled the black-suited escapee to the ground. Not losing your touch, are you?'

'Did she recognise him?'

'Nah, but she reckons he was a man, couldn't tell how old but he was physically fit and, I'm putting words in her mouth, but he was well-practised in hand-to-hand combat. Although he seemed to be clumsy with his knife. That, or you showed great skill in disarming him. Know which one my money's on.'

Cullen had to wait while the bus pulled in for another gang of commuters heading south. 'That it?'

'Nah, there was something else. Something weird, mate.' Sounded like Buxton was shuffling through his notebook. 'She recorded it on her phone. Bit shaky, but there's a video of the fight. Queer thing is, when you knocked your head against the garden wall and lost consciousness, this Batman geezer didn't take advantage. She thought he was going through your pockets, but it turned out he was moving you into the recovery position.'

'What?'

'Like I say, very peculiar behaviour. Maybe you were just too sorry a sight, lying there at his feet, passed out and—'

'Si, that guy slit McLintock's throat right in front of me.'

'Shit.' Buxton sighed again. 'Weird as hell, mate. Either way, she says this black fella ducked through the gate and disappeared into the trees.'

'She confirmed that we're looking for a big guy in a Batman costume.'

'Look, I've got to go, mate. Catch you later.'

Cullen took his chance and cut down the back street, finally clear of the bus. 'Have you told Lamb?'

'Can't find him. Catch you later, mate.' And he was gone.

Cullen pulled into the car park behind St Leonard's and got out. He yawned into his fist yet again. *Badly need a coffee.*

'Scott!' Lamb was charging towards him. 'You got him?'

'He's not at the gym.' Cullen screwed his eyes up at the grey sky. 'I'm fine, by the way. Nice to see you.'

Lamb frowned. 'That was your lead? Hoping he's there at the same time as you? Give me strength...'

'He's a gym bunny like you, Bill. Lifts so much every day that I'd prolapse just thinking about it.' Cullen nodded at Lamb's bulky form. 'You wouldn't.'

'So, you got any other leads?'

'I checked and he's not been there in months. So I'll dig deeper after my—'

'Scott, you need to focus.'

'Bill, I've driven over here from Tulliallan to get to the gym at opening, which is usually when Big Rob turns up. I've not had breakfast or a coffee. What else do you want from me?'

Lamb just stood there, flexing. 'Well, I just caught up with Bain. He's managing the street team, God save us. Says Si Buxton took a statement from a neighbour who saw you chasing a guy wearing a Batman costume.'

'You believe me now?'

'Well, a seventy-four-year-old lady with glasses thinks she saw a black-suited man run away in the night, from a distance, and she's convinced it was Batman. Give me a break.'

'Bill, are you saying you don't believe her?'

'Someone's lost their mind, Scott, and I hope it's not you. How can I explain this to the press, eh? Has anyone seen Batman? We're looking for him in connection with a brutal slaying because we're trusting some old biddy who thinks she might've seen him out of a high window in the middle of the bloody night. What do you reckon?'

'Actually—'

'Exactly. Now, I need to focus on the only suspect we've got.'

Cullen frowned. 'I'll find Big—'

'Vardy!' Lamb threw his arms up in the air. 'Scott, pull your head out of your arse. You told me Vardy was pissed off with McLintock. Do you really need me to spell out our next move here?'

∼

Vardy was sat at the Debonair's bar, taking a very long sip from a pint of lager. Looked like the whole thing went down in one. He slammed the glass off the bartop and licked his lips.

Cullen walked over and sat next to him. 'Ah, there you are.'

Vardy didn't look at him, his eyes obscured by black sunglasses, on a dull February morning. Indoors.

Lamb scraped back the stool on the other side and sat, leaning his bulky arms on the bar. 'I'd ask if that's your first taste of freedom but we all know you got absolutely battered last night.'

Vardy focused on his pint glass. 'What do you want?'

'I want to know who killed Sammy McLean.'

Vardy pushed the sunglasses down his nose and stared at Lamb for a few long moments. 'You want to repeat that?'

Cullen shrugged. 'You're only sitting here because someone shot him. In a hospital.'

Vardy took his glasses off and threw them on the bar, where they dinged against the glass like a silver bell. He looked round at Cullen, dark shadows under his bloodshot eyes. 'And there's me thinking you're here to follow up on the death threat I reported last night.'

'I hadn't heard.' Lamb snorted. 'Sounds like bullshit, though.'

'It's not bullshit.' Vardy clicked his finger at the barman to get another pint. 'Why are you here, officers?'

'We're here for your alibi, but since that also concerns last night, why don't you repeat your wee report?'

'Alibi?' Vardy looked around at the two security guys standing behind them, their hands folded in front of them, so things still looked civil. Their tight smiles told another story. 'Why would *you* of all people ask me about my alibi?' He frowned at Cullen. 'You *are* my alibi. You and that big palooka, what's his name? Williamson? Wilkinson?' He looked at Cullen like he'd walked into the wrong film. 'Don't tell me you can't remember? That fat bastard kicked off outside. Looked like a farmer with a fuse as short as his mother's cock. You had to march him off before he made an even bigger tit of himself.'

Cullen could feel Lamb's look burn a hole into his face, so he kept his eyes front and centre. 'I remember, but that was early evening. Right?'

'Between seven and eight.' One of the doormen nodded. Kenny or the one pumped full of Synthol. Cullen couldn't tell because of the large bomber jackets they wore. 'Got it on CCTV.'

'Well, there you go. My alibi.' Vardy burped as his barman handed him a fresh pint. 'Cheers. Matter of fact, I woke up on this very bar about five minutes before you walked in.' He picked up his pint, glancing back and forth between his visitors. 'So, I'd appreciate if you could let me get back to my breakfast.'

He held up the glass and took another long sip, taking it below halfway.

Lamb smiled at him, but only with his mouth. 'Sorry to be a bother, sir. We'll be on our way, then.' He stood up from his stool and swept his hand off the bar to offer Vardy a handshake, but when Vardy saw what was coming, it was already too late. Lamb backhanded the glass, his wedding ring clinking, and knocked it clean out of Vardy's hand. Straight into his lap. Beer showered over Vardy's trousers. The glass smashed on the floor, the golden liquid sloshing over his shoes, pooling in a puddle. Wide-eyed, he looked back up at Lamb. 'What the—'

'My mistake entirely, Mr Vardy. Please don't feel stupid.' Lamb patted him on the shoulder. 'Can I get you a new one?'

'Get your hand off my shoulder.' Vardy stared at him, seething. He took a sharp breath and narrowed his bloodshot eyes at Lamb. 'Listen to me. Some prick made a death threat. I need to know who to kill.'

Lamb wiped his hand on his suit jacket. 'Certainly, sir.' He glanced at Cullen, then at Vardy. 'You must get a fair few death threats. What's got you pissing your pants about this one?'

'Aye, it's not the first.' Vardy glanced down at his wet crotch and started rubbing at it. 'But some arsehole projected a video onto the wall of my nightclub.' He gave up on the wet patch and pulled his phone from his pocket. 'Here, I've got it on video.' He held up his phone and played the video for them.

A shaky image showed the side of Vardy's club on George Street, his own head projected on it, a cartoonish knife slicing his throat, over and over again.

Vardy put the phone back in his pocket. 'I sent a couple of my boys up the building opposite and they found a projector rigged up. Got them to take it to the police.'

Cullen laughed. 'Sure you didn't do that yourself?'

Vardy stared at him. 'Look, you prick, I'm shitting myself here. You need to do something about it.'

'Top of our to-do list. Promise.' Lamb clapped him on the shoulder and flashed him another one of his shark smiles. 'I need a wee bit of information from you first. Starting with where you were between nine and midnight last night.'

'Told you, you donkey. I was right here. Fell asleep at the bar.'

'You got witnesses for that?'

Vardy pointed at his two goons. 'You need statements? Take them from these boys.'

'Anyone I can rely on?'

'I'll give you the CCTV footage. That do you? As you pointed out, I've been at her majesty's pleasure for a year and a half so it's not like I can tape over it with Monday's, is it?'

'Fine. So your defence is that you were here?'

'Defence of what?'

'You really don't know?'

'You need to stop being a prick, mate. Might help you do your job. Who's died? Anyone good?'

Lamb stepped around him, careful to avoid the beer puddle on the way out. 'Campbell McLintock.'

Vardy stood there, clenching and unclenching his fists.

19

LAMB PUSHED HIS WAY INTO THE STATION CANTEEN, CULLEN following in a daze. 'What you having, Scott?'

Cullen flinched.

'What's up?' Lamb walked right up to the counter and looked at Cullen with that familiar concern in his eyes. 'You not getting enough sleep?'

'Something like that.' Cullen looked for a seat. At this time of the morning it was quiet – that perfect window between shift patterns, just that uniform superintendent fuming away at her laptop. 'Coffee. At least two shots.'

'You look like you need it.' Lamb caught the barista's attention. 'Too busy shagging around, no doubt. You do know it's Valentine's Day, right? Might want to get a wee card for Sharon to apologise for… I'm sure you're due her an apology for something, right? Get her something classy.'

'Right.' Cullen walked over to a small table in the far corner, facing away from the door. That morning's *Argus* was smeared with brown sauce and dusted with brown sugar. He flipped it over and attacked the sport section. Usual Rangers–Celtic shite. You'd be forgiven for thinking Edinburgh didn't have a football team, let alone three in the league nowadays. He put the paper down and glanced back to see what was taking so long.

Lamb was deep in conversation with the barman, a gym buddy

judging by the guy's physique. No doubt discussing food supplements and protein shakes. No sign of Cullen's espresso, though. Guy looked like he knew where to get any flavour of steroid, and how to use it.

'Alright, Scott?' Yvonne Flockhart was frowning at him, looking like she'd just left the salon, even at this time of the morning. 'You okay?'

'No.' Cullen cringed. 'Yeah, I'm fine. Just tired. You know how it is.'

Her frown turned into a pout. 'One of those days, is it?' She pointed at the empty chair next to him. 'Is that free?'

'Go ahead.' He got up and helped her out of her fluffy coat.

She hung it over the back of her chair and took a seat.

Cullen stayed on his feet, wondering whether she had meant to brush his hand when she took the coat.

'Scott? Are you going to sit with me or should I stand up again?'

'No, no, I was just thinking about...' He cupped his hands round his mouth. 'Hey, Bill, get something for Yvonne.'

Lamb didn't even break stride with his gym buddy, just gave a casual salute. 'English breakfast, loads of milk. Got it.'

Cullen sat back down and pretended not to notice the smile twitching in the corner of her mouth. 'So, how you doing, Yvonne?'

'Fine, aye. You know how it is. I was looking for Ally Davenport. He said he'd be here. Needed a wee chat for a while now, and seeing as how that bloody course is cancelled this morning, I thought—' She leaned forward. 'Whatever's on your mind, Scott, you can talk to me about it.'

'Talk about what?'

'Come on, Scott, cut the shite. The whole "I'm a Scottish man" bullshit. We don't talk about our feelings. We buy them drinks, and then we get them so shitfaced they forget where we live.' She arched an eyebrow. 'Or who we're shagging?'

Cullen wanted to crawl off into the corner. Staring at the sugar dusting the table was as close as he could manage. 'Alright. I'm going through relationship hell.'

'Tell me about it.'

Does she mean she's going through that circle of hell herself, or is it an invitation to actually talk?

Bugger it.

'Ever since you and I...' He bit his lip and glanced at the counter. Lamb was facing away from him, absorbed in his chat. No danger of being overheard – apart from the lone superintendent fizzing away at her laptop, the place was still deserted. He averted his eyes from Yvonne's. 'I've had a guilty conscience ever since I found out that I messed up your thing with Craig. I was... so drunk at the time that I couldn't even remember until... Never mind, it's no excuse for not being able to walk past a beautiful woman without trying to shag her.' He glanced up at her.

She just raised her eyebrows.

So he dropped his gaze again and carried on. 'I didn't mean that to sound like you were just one of many. It's just that this whole part of my life's... well... it's over, you know. But... that sort of behaviour, I'm doing it because there's something wrong with me, somewhere deep inside. And I've tried, believe me I've tried, but I've got serious commitment issues.' Again, he looked up at her, hoping for... he wasn't sure. Some token of sympathy? Some form of absolution? Something to suggest that he wasn't doing so badly after all?

'Don't flatter yourself, Scott.' Yvonne laughed. 'You didn't ruin my relationship with Craig. That was doomed or I wouldn't have hooked up with you.'

'Was there anything in what we did?'

'I don't know.' She narrowed her eyes, her little ski-jump nose twitching. 'But if you're thinking about past conquests, I imagine your current one isn't going too well.'

'Understatement of the year.'

'Want to talk about it?'

'I don't know. It's... Christ, it's complicated. When you're with someone for a while and you think you're going to spend the rest of your life with them and you talk about having kids and you propose and... aye, she kicks you out. Doesn't even explain herself. It's not like I was shagging around behind her back. I was just... me.'

'When was this?'

'Last night.'

'Shite.'

'Aye. Shite. I just don't know what the hell to think.'

'Join the club.' Yvonne scraped her chair back and snatched her jacket. She pursed her lips. 'It is shite, but then you get over it. You realise that it's better not spending hours of your life in that toxic environment. I've been single for three months now and I don't miss it. None of that shite. Who squeezed the toothpaste from the bottom? Who drank the last of the milk? Who didn't fill up the car with petrol? It's all shite and I was just as bad as he was.' She shook her head, though less at him than at herself, it seemed. 'Anyway. It gets to you, but then it gets easier.'

'Yvonne, I'm—'

'Shh.' She put a finger to his lips. 'Scott, stop making everything about you. It's not a good look.' She walked over to the counter and grabbed her tea off Lamb before walking out, her angry steps striking the hard wood floor like a series of exclamation marks.

What! The! Hell! Is! Wrong! With! Me!

Cullen picked up a newspaper and buried his head in Rangers melodrama. He stared at the newsprint, watched it become blurrier the harder he tried to focus on it, but that was the least of his problems.

She was right.

I'm such a selfish prick. All that shagging around... it was just a cry for attention. Looking for rejection in all the wrong places.

And Sharon was right to break up with me. We were just bored. That's no way to live your life. And you only get one. Just this – the here and now. There's nothing else.

He could still taste her hand cream on his lips.

You idiot, don't fall in love with her.

Softer footsteps walked towards him. 'Well done, Shagger.' Lamb plonked two paper cups on the table, the one marked C bubbling through the lid. 'Classy.'

Cullen looked up. He had nothing to say.

Lamb sat on the vacated chair. 'Yvonne had the—'

'Shut up.'

'Is it your time of the month again, you—'

'Seriously, Bill. I'm not in the mood.'

Lamb just looked at Cullen, his eyes wide. Then a flash of rage lit them up. 'Listen, you're not the only one feeling the stress of this investigation, so—'

'Don't make everything about me? Don't worry, I hear you.'

Lamb leaned back on his chair and folded his arms over his broad chest. 'Tell me.'

'Tell you what?'

'Why you look so pissed off. I mean, I joked about you shagging around and needing to apologise to Sharon. But you've been shagging Yvonne, haven't you?'

Cullen took a sharp breath to put a bit more oomph into his *bugger off*. Then he realised that Lamb was asking as a friend. 'No, I haven't. I mean, we had a... thing, a few years back. It was messy. A drunken fumble behind a mate's back and...'

'You idiot.'

Cullen reached for his coffee. 'You don't have to tell me.'

'Sure that's all it is? I saw the way you look at each other. The way she shushed you. Very sexy.'

'Bill, I swear. It was just a one and done thing. That's all it was.'

'So Sharon hasn't kicked you out then?'

Then Cullen's phone rang. He let his breath out again, reaching for his mobile and glancing at the screen. *DI Colin Methven*. He looked back at Lamb, shrugging an apology as he took the call. 'What's up, sir?'

'Get to St Leonard's.'

'Already here, sir.'

'I thought you were— Never mind. You're late for my first briefing on Operation Knightfall.'

'Operation what?'

'Knightfall. With a K. I've caught the McLintock case.' The line went dead.

CULLEN WAS ABOUT TWO STEPS OUT FROM THE INCIDENT ROOM when the door opened and a miserable crowd filed past him, eyes front, teeth clenched, not one word said between them. He clutched his coffee tight in case one of them tripped over their own shoelaces and spilled it.

Methven was last out, more relaxed than the rest. Better

dressed, too, in his silver-grey suit which matched his short-trimmed hair and designer stubble. Today his usual dour look was replaced by a broad grin. His wild eyebrows hadn't read the memo, though. 'Cullen, smashing to see you.' He eyed Cullen from head to toe, taking in the tired eyes, the crumpled suit, the scuffed shoes. 'You look like your wife's just left you.'

Cullen managed to keep the smile going, but his clenched teeth were giving him a headache. 'The troops looked like they were off to a funeral.'

'They might well be, and it'll be their own.' Methven sneered at him, but slowly he started nodding. 'But no.' He grunted. 'Now, in lieu of you attending a briefing—'

'I was in the canteen with DI Lamb, so—'

'Campbell's murder.' Methven leaned against the door jamb. 'I gather you have a suspect?'

'Two. First, Dean Vardy and—'

'I know all about him.'

'Bill and I spoke to him first thing.' Cullen clenched his teeth. 'He reported a death threa—'

'And have you investigated it?'

Cullen raised his hands. 'Hold your horses, we just got back.'

'Well, Bill sent me a text while you were reading the papers.' Methven flared his nostrils. 'So I checked with Control and it turns out Mr Vardy hadn't reported any death threat. Unlike he claimed. Which makes me suspect he's our prime— Well. And who is the other?'

'It's a long shot. Campbell McLintock—'

'This is the muscle-boy trade who cosplayed with them, yes?'

Cullen stared, wide-eyed. The conversation was about six steps ahead of him and his head was swimming. 'Right, Big Rob. I know him.'

'And?'

'And I'm tracking him down and—'

'Hold that thought.' Methven elbowed his way past Cullen and held out his hand. 'Good morning, James. I hope you've got some good news for me.'

'Morning.' James Anderson looked at Methven like he had just stepped in a steaming pile of dog shit. 'Just got the DNA results back from the clump of pubes we found McLintock's shower.'

Methven winced.

'You're in luck, big man. We got a hit, some Polish boy who got busted for drugs a few years back. His name's unpronounceable, though. So many consonants. Must give the lad a sore throat every time he says it out loud.' Anderson held out the file he was carrying. The top page contained a headshot and a list of personal data, including this supposedly unpronounceable name.

Cullen peered at it and groaned. 'Nice and slow: R-o-b-e-r-t.'

'I can manage that part, you tube.' Anderson snarled. 'The surname, you bam.'

Cullen took a second look. Then it was his turn to laugh. 'Robert Szczepański.'

'How the hell do you know that?'

'Because I know him. And he's not Polish, and that's not his real name. Robert Woodhead was born in Manchester, but changed his surname to Szczepański. The guys at his gym kept saying he looked like the strongman competitor.'

'What, Geoff Capes?'

'Right sport, wrong era. Szczepański was the champion in 2009, and that became his stage name. And he's the kind of nutter who changes his name by deed poll to mess with people.'

'Sounds like you married the prick.' Anderson scratched at the missing chunk of goatee. Up close, it looked like the hair had been burnt off. 'He your type?'

'Oh, he's a big hunk of rock-hard muscle, James. More your type than mine.'

'Piss off.'

'Six foot tall, seventeen stone, can bench-press double my weight.' Cullen pulled out his wallet and looked through it. 'Here you go. He's got it all listed on his calling card.' He handed it to Methven but kept looking at Anderson as he spoke. 'He was a CHIS in a case me and Craig Hunter worked a while ago. We busted him for dealing steroids, flipped him and took down a whole drug ring.'

'Get you.' Anderson was still staring at the card. 'So you know how to get hold of him?'

Cullen scratched his neck. 'That's the thing – he wasn't at the gym this—'

'He-Man Nights.' Methven snatched the card off Anderson.

'I've had dealings with this gentleman for... other crimes.' He started heehawing with laughter. Sounded like a donkey in distress. 'He-Man are a security firm, but we all know what they really do. But before that, he got himself into bother doing a bit of street trade, most of it with old men in public spots. Calton Hill, the Dugald Stewart Monument. You know, the thing in all the Edinburgh postcards. Looks like a miniature Athenian temple with loads of columns. One night we get an anonymous tipoff, so we climb the hill and there he is, his sweaty nakedness glistening in the moonlight while he's banging someone senior at Alba Bank, pinning him against one of the pillars, arms flailing like a horny monkey.'

Anderson gave a wry smile. 'This is that Zhe—? That guy?'

'Indeed.' Methven kept his eyes focused on the business card. 'When we arrested Mr Szczepański,' his pronunciation was perfect, 'he tried to tell me his name four times, and I didn't get it. Eventually, he had to write it down for me. Turns out he couldn't pronounce Szczepański either.' He squealed with laughter, much louder than the anecdote warranted, almost choking on his delight before he took a long breath. 'Long story short, he goes by Big Rob.'

Silence.

Anderson leafed through the file. 'I really need to get back to work.' Without making eye contact with either of them, he nodded a vague goodbye and paced back down the corridor.

Cullen clenched his teeth and the dull pain returned. 'So, what do you—'

'I want Big Rob in a room within the hour.' Methven glanced down at the calling card in his hand as though he had to jog his memory. 'Might be best starting at He-Man Nights, mm?'

20

'No, that's not the kind of service we offer here, and I resent the question.' The bald steroid abuser in his fifties had a gold earring and forearms the size of small children. At the moment, he had them folded over his tight T-shirt, a garment that was about two sizes too small. He was sitting behind a desk but seemed like he would have felt more comfortable squatting or lifting weights. 'We're a respectable security firm.'

A giant He-Man Nights logo filled the right-hand wall. Behind him was a spectacular view over the Firth of Forth to Fife, sandy beaches, choppy waters, wheeling seagulls, far horizons, big skies. Inchkeith Island brooded in the middle.

'Sure?' Bain pursed his lips and waved at the walls which were draped in crushed velvet.

Mood-lighting glinted like candle flames on a series of portraits mounted at head height around the room. They were headshots, all with name plates, all male, and all of the gentlemen seemed to be doing their best to look as raunchy as physically possible – their heads cocked at rakish angles, carefully groomed beards and pursed lips.

Bain unpursed his own lips and looked back at the reception-ist. 'Sure you're not running a knocking shop here?'

The receptionist huffed and glared at him some more.

But Bain walked over to the nearest display, cocking his head to the side, inspecting in great detail. His eyes flicked between Cullen and the receptionist. 'Is our pal Robert Szczepański up on your wall of shame here?'

No response.

'He is one of your boys, right?' Bain stepped up to the desk. 'Listen, we're not here to drill deep into your business, okay? We just need to speak to Robert.'

The receptionist narrowed his eyes. 'What's this about?'

'Just an old case that's resurfaced.' Cullen got in front of Bain. 'I know Big Rob from back in the day. He helped us bust a drug ring at Rock Hard Gym.'

The receptionist looked back and forth between the detectives, then checked his computer. 'Right, Big Rob is due to meet a client this evening.'

'This is kind of urgent, mate. Any chance you know where he'll be before then?'

A huff. 'If I know Rob, he'll be torturing himself at his new gym.'

~

ULTRAMAN GYM WAS THE SIZE OF A WAREHOUSE, SEVERAL FLOORS and split levels dedicated to all manner of self-abuse from squash courts to yoga studios. In deepest, darkest Niddrie.

Cullen followed Bain down a long corridor, lined with glass on both sides, grunting men hitting heavy bags on the left – the right a room full of panting women in spinning classes, the nearest standing up on her pedals as they passed. Mirrored walls everywhere. A gang of six early twenties lasses strutted towards them, all dressed in lycra, lots of naked skin on display, all of it glowing with perspiration.

'Kids, eh?' Bain nudged Cullen. 'They can pass out in the drunk tank one night and be back in here the next morning.'

'Getting old must be difficult.' Cullen laughed. 'Maybe Big Rob can sort you out with some Viagra. How many are you on now? One for a semi, two for a—'

'Piss off.' Bain strode off down the steps from yet another dance studio, loud club music thrumming through the stairwell.

Cullen sped up and caught him at the bottom of the stairs. 'Where you off to anyway?'

Bain stopped and stared at him. 'Searching for Big Rob.'

'Sure you're not just ogling a few sweaty men on their backs, moaning and straining and—'

'Very funny.' Bain's eyes wouldn't quite meet Cullen's. 'You're acting like you know where Big Rob is. Quit being a prick and just tell us, eh?'

'Try thinking like a detective for once. We know he's a male escort, so he needs to look good naked. We also know at least one of his clients liked him to role play some superhero sex game, so we can also assume he needs to be strong to act out all those rescue missions in a leotard with his pants over the top, right?'

Bain was still avoiding Cullen's eyes. 'So where is he?'

'In the basement. That's where they keep the big weights for the big boys.'

'How do you know that?'

'I can read signs.' Cullen pointed at the floor plan next to the stairs and headed down.

The basement was a whitewashed cavernous space with a low-arched ceiling. A double row of twenty-five benches filled it, each with a rack of plates, the incessant clanging and banging of metal bars on metal brackets like they were in a factory. They passed two gorillas in tank tops, one pressing an overloaded barbell, the other spotting the trembling lifter. 'Come on, come on, come on, bring it, you're nearly there, it's all you, mate, I'm hardly touching the bar, come oooooooooon... You the man!'

'I'm the man!' Then the lifter vomited all over himself. Lying down.

Cullen led the way down the narrow corridor between the rows of benches, checking each grunting face.

Big Rob was impossible to miss, standing at the water cooler, guzzling from a two-litre bottle, blissfully unaware of his surroundings, happy with himself and his place in the world. King of the iron jungle, decked out in knee-length black shorts and a neon-yellow muscle-shirt so tight it looked like a crop top. At least a C-cup, but maybe triple figures on the chest measurement. And he was massive now, almost doubled in size since Cullen last saw him eighteen months ago. And he was huge then.

Cullen tried to overlay his physique on the masked killer in the Batman costume. Rob was way too big – the sort who could carry a Mini half a mile, not jump through a window. So Cullen gave him the thumbs-up. 'Nice shirt, Rob. Do they make it in your size?'

Big Rob laughed, a deep, rumbling sound full of confidence and testosterone. 'Alright, Scotty. The shirt's that size on purpose, you cheeky rascal. Want to show off my gains, don't I?'

'Here, pal.' Bain pointed at his naked shoulder. 'Is that Didier Drogba?'

Big Rob gave the tattoo a fond caress and tutted at him. 'Now, now, that's quite obviously Tracy Chapman. My queen, don't listen to the jealous wee policeman.' He looked back at Cullen and motioned at the bench next to him. 'Been playing five a side, if you know what I mean. Five twenty-kilo plates either side of the barbell. Bar included, that makes it... a sexy one-eight.'

Bain laughed. 'Two-twenty, you big fanny.'

Cullen rested a hand on his chest. 'I could listen to you do sums all day, but I need to ask you a few quick questions.'

Rob held his bottle over his lips. 'Like, police questions?'

'Aye. Questions about Campbell McLintock.'

Big Rob dropped the water bottle, and barged past Cullen towards the exit, sending him spinning. Bain stepped out from behind him and ducked under Big Rob's centre of gravity, seized the oncoming man around the waist, thrust his pelvis forward and up, arched his back, twisted his torso to the left and let Big Rob's momentum do the rest. Glued together at the hip, they went over Bain's shoulder in a slick wrestling move that put Big Rob square on his back.

Bain landed on top of him with a sickening crunch, straddling Rob's heaving chest.

'SORRY, BUT IS THERE ANY CHANCE WE COULD SPEED THIS UP A BIT?' Not So Big Rob sat on the smallest chair in the station, his chest level with the table top. 'And could I get a sandwich or something? Bottle of water? I just had a massive chest workout and I'm on this hydration regime—'

'Still? I remember you telling me about that last year.' Cullen looked down at him. 'You're a cucumber with anxiety issues.'

Bain started wheezing with laughter.

Cullen motioned for them both to settle down. 'Now, Mr Woodhead, we're still waiting for your lawyer to turn up, so—'

'Just get on with it.' Big Rob shifted on his wee chair. 'Not got all day for this, eh?'

'I'm happy to wait, you know?' Cullen folded his hands in his lap, the very image of casual patience. 'Should be here in an hour or two. Be better to do this properly. So there's no rush if you want to—'

'Get started. I've nothing to hide.' Big Rob puckered his lips as though he had bitten into a lemon.

Cullen knew where to focus. 'If you've nothing to hide, why did you try to run away when I mentioned Campbell McLintock?'

'Because... because you said he'd been killed and it sounded like you were trying to fit me up for the murder.'

'Mr Woodhead, if you have nothing to hide, why did—'

'Because I was there, okay?' Big Rob flinched like the admission put him square in the frame. He glanced back and forth between the detectives, rubbing at the twitches in his face. 'I mean, I was at his place early in the evening. He'd hired me for some... work around the house. Check-ups on his security system, that kind of thing...'

Cullen stared him straight in the eye. 'Of course...'

'Honest to God, Scotty, I didn't kill him!'

Cullen just kept staring at him, nodding, waiting.

Big Rob looked like he was about to spill the rest of the story, but the strongman dropped his gaze to the table and let the breath back out with a sullen humph.

'Rob, cut it out. We all know what you were up to at that house.'

Bain snorted. 'Aye. Laying pipe.'

'Christ.' Rob stretched out his massive chest. 'Right, fine. I was at McLintock's house for the usual service...' He bit his tongue, then glanced down at his hands and lowered his voice to a mutter. 'I was there to help Campbell celebrate some job thing. No idea what, I never listen. Does my head in. I'm there for a job, not to sort their heads out. They can go to a shrink for that. I'm not paid enough. Anyway, last night he wanted me to dress up as Batman.'

Cullen felt his heartrate quicken. He did another take of Big Rob's physique.

It was dark – really dark – so maybe. And him putting me in the recovery position...

He knows me.

Christ.

'Even had the costume, right size and everything.' Rob stretched out his massive chest. 'Bit of a sexed-up gimpy version of the original, but it fit, eh? Like a glove. So I put it on, did the, eh, deed and went home to my girlfriend.'

Bain cleared his throat with a wet cough. 'Your *girl*friend?'

'Straight for play, gay for pay, you know? The gay stuff is my job, man. I've got three kids to support.'

'Three fu—'

'Okay.' Cullen put his hands up. 'You were saying you went home to your family?'

'Aye?' Big Rob frowned. 'Aye. I was saying I was home before nine. Date night with the missus. Anniversary, eh? Dinner, flowers, bit of romancing, you know the drill.'

Bain sniggered. 'Why so coy now? So you'd just been ploughed by Campbell's monster cock and now you—'

'What?' Rob screwed his face up. 'No, I didn't say. Not at all. I'm a giver, not a taker. And I just told you I'm not gay.'

Bain looked mystified. 'Have you seen the harpoon—'

'Aye, I've seen it. Frightening. This is... Christ, I can't believe I'm saying this out loud. Mr McLintock said his partner's penis isn't big enough to get destroyed.'

Bain burst out laughing. 'And yours isn't shrivelled up from all the steroids?'

'I'm alright down there, mate.' Big Rob looked up and maintained steady eye contact with Bain. Then he nodded, the tics and twitches now playing havoc with his face. 'His words, not mine.'

'Alright, alright.' Cullen gave Big Rob a stern look. 'I'd rather you focused on your alibi. Can you prove what time you left Mr McLintock's house?'

Big Rob stared at Cullen, dead still, his facial tics disappearing with the admission of the truth. He fixed his gaze on Cullen, leaned back and took a calm breath, somehow managing to look dignified for a strongman squatting on a kid's chair. 'I'll give you the facts and you can give it your best shot finding proof. Glad that you're the cops, and not me. I'm just the rich man's rent boy, and once I'd done my job, I got changed back into a pair of ripped-off tracksuit bottoms and left through the front door. I didn't grapple with anybody who didn't pay for the privilege. And that's the end of it.'

~

CULLEN STEPPED INTO THE OBSERVATION SUITE EXPECTING A PAT ON the back, maybe even two. One for getting Big Rob to admit he was at the crime scene on the night of the murder and perhaps another for getting him to corroborate Deeley's estimate that McLintock was unharmed until at least nine pm.

'What a sodding disaster.' Methven had shaken off his calm demeanour. 'I expected you to get a confession, Sergeant.' He stared at Cullen, a calculating meanness in his eyes, then shot the same look at Bain as he entered the room. 'Gentlemen, you just took a shot at an open goal and missed. You interviewed a man who refused legal counsel and who outright confessed to having been at the crime scene around the time the victim sustained his first injuries. Oh, and he admitted to having had sexual relations with said victim. He even implied a degree of resentment.' He took a sharp breath and spread his arms wide. 'Bottom line, our man had motive, means, and opportunity, and you got sodding nothing.'

Cullen counted to ten as Methven lowered his arms, like a tired father who wasn't really mad at his incompetent boy, just disappointed. He pointed at the screen, at Big Rob still sitting at the table, not fidgeting, not twitching, not doing anything that might reflect a guilty conscience. 'He's clearly not the murderer.'

Methven fake-laughed. 'Forgive me if your verdict doesn't inspire me with confidence, Sergeant. I'll have to continue the interview myself.' He looked back and forth between Cullen and Bain. 'You two can get off to Tulliallan for your course. Seems like you need the extra lessons.'

Cullen swallowed his pride and the verbal abuse he felt like giving. 'Sir.'

21

Cullen killed the engine, taking a few seconds to unclench his fingers from the steering wheel. He rubbed his eyes, then blinked away the red sunspots in his vision and glanced at Bain.

Asleep.

Of course. Untroubled by thought or conscience, like a bearded baby.

'FIRE!'

Bain jolted awake, flailing his arms in panic and somehow managing to hit his hands off pretty much everything within reach – dashboard, window, roof, even his own head.

Cullen burst out laughing.

Bain stared at him, wide-eyed. When he stopped hyperventilating, he sagged back in his seat with a sigh like a death rattle. 'You arsehole.'

'Oh, come on, that was beautiful. Does make me wonder how someone who just smacked themselves in the face managed to take out Big Rob. That must've been a bit of a fluke, right?'

'That wasn't a fluke, you wanker.' Bain closed his eyes. 'It's called Judo. Been doing it since I was a wean.' He got out of the car and stomped across the car park.

∾

'FIRE!'

Cullen opened his eyes and shot to his feet. 'What?'

A classroom, low light, a projector screen glowing white with the Police Scotland logo.

The course. Right.

And the only thing on fire was his face.

Bain stood next to him, laughing. 'See how you like it.'

Cullen yawned into his fist and sat back down again. Could easily fall asleep again. He took a deep breath, his head throbbing, and blinked crystals out of his eyes.

'School's out for summer, Sundance.' Bain pushed past Cullen. 'I need a drink. You fancy one?'

Cullen got to his feet and followed him over to the door. The noise from the bar spilled out into the corridor.

Been so long since I had a drink. A proper one.

But there's nothing tying me down now. Nobody to tick me off for staggering in after ten pints with Buxton.

But over two years sober, give or take. Is it worth giving up that milestone? Can I trust myself?

Cullen reached into his pocket. 'I'm buying.'

CULLEN SIPPED THE PINT AND SHUT HIS EYES. THE COLD, CRISP nectar slipped down his throat. So easy. Too easy. Then the immediate hit of alcohol, spiking his veins in a way that wine or spirits couldn't. He opened his eyes again and the college bar seemed to glow, the comforting atmosphere of an old man's pub. Maroon wallpaper, beer-themed mirrors and detective sergeants from all around Scotland drinking the taps dry.

'Christ's sake, Sundance, you look like you're going to come.'

'Feel like I have.' Cullen took another drink and rested his glass on the bartop. 'And without any Viagra.'

'What the hell are you talking about.' Yvonne was frowning at him.

Cullen spotted Bain over her shoulder, now talking to the barman about whisky. 'Oh, hi. I was just winding Bain up.'

'Like he needs any more.' Yvonne smiled at him like seeing him here wasn't the worst thing in the world.

So he took another sip of beer. 'Been in here a while?'

'Your chat is rancid, Scott.' She clapped a hand on his shoulder, but missed by a few inches. 'Aye, how can you tell? Just waiting for the party to get started.' She winked at him. 'Have a nice sleep?'

Cullen blushed. 'You noticed?'

'Someone chain sawing at the back of the room is a bit offputting. Poor Terry had to shout to make himself heard.'

'Ah, shite.' Cullen tried to smile, but it was coming off as so fake. So he hid it by drinking his pint. 'Can I get you a drink? White wine, right?'

'Well, if you're buying.'

'Alright, don't move. Back in a sec.' Cullen joined the queue, a backlog created by Bain's intimate analysis of the whisky stock. He tried to nudge past the guy ahead and get to the bar.

'Hoy!' He got an angry glare from Lamb. 'Oh, you're awake.'

'Aye, aye.' Cullen sank the last of his pint and raised the glass. 'Can I get you one?'

'Least you can do. Get us a Talisker.'

'If Bain ever makes his mind up.' Cullen caught the barman's attention and mouthed the order.

'Cheers, Scott.' Lamb held up his whisky glass, still full from the previous round, left it near his lips, savouring the smell. He put it down without a sip. 'So how's Methven getting on with the case?'

Cullen groaned. 'Come on, Bill, you're off the clock.'

'Doesn't mean I don't want to talk about that case. Not often one of the biggest deterrents to our conviction rate gets murdered.'

'Well, I don't want to get between you and Methven's swinging dick competition.'

Lamb clenched his teeth. 'Don't...' He held up his hands. 'No more chat about dicks, okay? Bain just won't just shut up about how blessed the late Mr McLintock was.'

Cullen was already shaking his head as the barman rested his beer and Yvonne's wine on the bartop. Lamb's whisky followed. The barman named his price but Cullen couldn't hear. He reached for his wallet, anyway.

But Lamb grabbed his arm, shaking his head. 'Leave it. I'll pay for those. Glad to see you're back in the land of the liver abusers.' He took out his mobile and held it to the card reader. 'Isn't technology wonderful?'

'Cheers, Bill.'

Cullen led over to Yvonne. 'You guys know each other?'

'Worked together over the years, aye.' Yvonne drank a big chunk of her fresh glass of wine. 'I'm starving.'

'ANY MORE DRINKS?' THE WAITER CLEARED HIS THROAT AGAIN. Sounded like he had something stuck in there. 'Or the dessert menu?'

'For the fifth time, pal, can we just get the bill?' Even Bain had lost interest in where this evening could still go. He shook his head as he watched the waiter limp off. 'Can't get the staff, eh?'

The curry house was near enough empty now, much like the empty Cobra pint glasses littering the small table. They were squeezed into a corner booth, Yvonne's leg pressed up against Cullen's. His hand crawled towards hers, but she pulled it away. A brief flash of her eyebrows at Bain and Lamb sitting opposite made her message clear. The way she rubbed her bare foot up his leg muddied it.

'You rude bastard.' Lamb shook his head at Bain. 'What's the magic word?'

'Bugger that.' Bain gave him a shrug. 'I'll tip the boy, don't you worry.'

The waiter returned with the bill and Bain scowled at it. 'Right. Forty quid each.' He tossed two twenties on the table. 'And here's my tip.' He daintily placed a tenner down. 'Christ, even drinking's expensive these days.'

Cullen chucked his money down. 'You can't get a bargain every time, can you?'

'What's that supposed to mean?'

'It means you were lucky to get that Thai bride of yours in the sales.'

'You what?' Bain glared at him, but when Lamb and Yvonne started laughing, he couldn't help himself from joining in. He got up and grabbed his coat from the back of his chair. 'Thanks for the concern, Sundance. Better get home and tend to my investment. Bye, bye, my lovelies.'

Lamb was on his feet too now, placing his money on top. 'Get a taxi, aye?'

'Course. Think I am?'

'An idiot?' Lamb clapped his hands. 'And that's my cue.' He hung his leather jacket over his shoulder and curtseyed to Yvonne. 'Good evening, madam. Sir. Make sure you don't leave it too late, aye?' He winked at Cullen, then followed Bain out.

Silence.

Then they both spoke at once.

'So, what do you fancy doing n—'

'So, what did I miss—?'

They shared a laugh.

'You first, Yvonne.'

'No, I'll answer yours.' She pouted. 'Nothing. You missed absolutely nothing. The entire course is as pointless as Bain's existence.' She put her money in. 'Sounds like your day was much more satisfying?'

'Hardly.' Cullen paused, the memory of last night's crime scene hitting him again. 'And to answer your question, seeing as this place is closing, we can either go our separate ways or...'

Cullen sat in the corner, watching Yvonne at the bar, the view obscured by two locals playing pool. The pub was busy, with the benches around the walls filled with half of Kincardine's retirement homes on some kind of evening release programme. The two old guys next to him were stuck in a game of dominoes that was heading towards violence.

Yvonne caught his smile and returned it with a wink.

At least we're away from the college. No sneaky photos shared around WhatsApp groups...

'Barman's bringing them over.' Yvonne slumped in the chair next to him, hooked her arm under his and pressed her leg up against his. 'So, tell me about your fun adventures in fighting crime while the rest of us spent the day trapped at Tulliallan.'

'It's hardly a fun day when you spend it with Bain and Methven. And besides, we got sent back here, didn't we?'

'Fair point. He's awful. Thank God he's been away working for most of today.'

'I disagree. Got saddled with him all afternoon.'

'What did he do?'

'Nothing too bad.' Cullen laughed. 'Actually, he's... Bollocks to it. He's not as bad as he used to be. Nowhere near as bad. You know that thing where people get promoted beyond their competency?'

'The Peter Principle.' She looked up as the barman deposited a glass of white and a pint of something murky. 'People in a hierarchy tend to rise to their "level of incompetence". Right?'

'Right. Well, he's living proof.' Cullen took a sip of beer and it felt like he'd been hit by a tanker full of grapefruit juice. 'This is *fantastic*.' Another sip. 'Aye, so Bain was a nightmare as a DI. Red-faced all the time, effing and jeffing like nobody's business. Trying to frame people. Now he's a DS again, he's just annoying. Back to being competent.'

'Bill said he was obsessed by the victim's cock?'

'Right. I mean, it was *massive*, but you get over it. He hasn't.' Another mouthful of citrusy beer. 'This is lovely, by the way. Ooh.' Another sip. 'You know, if it was anybody else, I'd reckon they'd suffered some kind of psychological trauma in childhood or whatever. The knob gags could be gallows humour, but...' He thought about it, then shook his head. 'Some days it seems to be all Bain talks about. Few months back, we did this case through in Glasgow and...' He laughed. 'I'll just leave it there.'

She patted his arm, letting her hand linger there. Still held it there when the barman returned, depositing two glasses on the table. Fizzy amber liquid, each with a shot glass inside, filled with a dark liquid. Jägerbombs. 'Thanks.' She winked at the barman, walking off with a 'Cheers'.

Cullen stared at the Jägerbomb like it was napalm. A dark shot sat inside a fizzing glass of energy drink. *Drinking beer is one thing, this shite is really crossing the line.* 'You trying to get me pissed?'

'Maybe?' Yvonne held hers over her mouth. 'You ready?'

Cullen picked his up and stared deep into the shot glass. 'Bugger it.'

'Go!' With a practised flick of the wrist she necked the Jäger-

bomb, slammed her empty glass back on the table and reached for
her wine.

Cullen chucked his down his throat, the shot glass bumping
against his teeth, the energy drink dribbling down his chin. 'Ah,
shite.' He set down the empty glasses and took another sip of beer.
'I forgot how rank that stuff is. Bleurgh.' He stuck his tongue out,
as if the stale pub air could take the taste away.

'You big jessie.' Yvonne looked him straight in the eye and
clinked her glass against his. 'Did Bain really buy a Thai bride?'

'I don't know if she's really a mail-order bride, just that he
claims she's from Thailand. I've never met her, but, then again, I
put Bain's son behind bars, so he's unlikely to tell me the truth
about anything.' For a moment, Cullen got lost in his thoughts,
then he shook his head and they were back on track. 'Now, if you
want me to be sober enough to walk you to your door, I'd better
stop drinking.'

She took the pint from his hand, smoothly laced her fingers
between his and stood up. 'Off we go, then.'

YVONNE GIGGLED AS SHE FUMBLED THE KEY CARD. IT FLOPPED ONTO
the splotchy carpet. She bent down to pick it up, taking a couple of
goes to stand up again, and swiped it through the lock. It clicked
and she froze, frowning. She took a step back and looked up at
Cullen with dead serious eyes, the giddy smile fading from her
face. 'Are you sure this is a good idea?'

'I thought we were—'

'What I mean is, are you sure you're man enough for this?' She
cocked her head at the door. 'After the last time, you bitched out
on me. Kept blanking me. Have you grown a pair since then or am
I wasting my time here?'

Cullen could think of nothing to do other than return her
stare.

'Well, are you coming in or are you too scared?'

Cullen snapped out if it. 'Of course, I'm scared. Back when I
was a cadet here, I got caught smuggling a local girl into my room.
Next morning, five laps of the playing grounds and two hundred
press-ups. Almost tore a pectoral.' He touched his chest as if it still

hurt. 'Now you've got me wondering what suffering awaits me this—'

She put her hand over his mouth. 'Shut up, Scott. You love it.' She dropped her hand to his chest and gave his manboob a playful squeeze.

Cullen leaned in for the kiss. It all ended. The smiles, the flirting, the night. And his old life. A new one starting, her tongue in his mouth, pushing against his. Her teeth biting his lips.

Then his phone buzzed and he tried to ignore it but the bastard thing kept ringing. He broke off the kiss. 'Sorry.' He pulled it out and glanced at the screen. Methven. 'Shite. It's the boss.' He leaned against the wall and put the phone to his ear. 'What's up?'

'Dean sodding Vardy is dead.'

22

'RIGHT, BEFORE YOU GET OUT...' DI TERRY LENNOX DROPPED THEM off under a street light outside Vardy's flat in Bruntsfield. 'Listen, I don't care about what's going on between you pair, and nobody's going to hear about it from me, but the state of you...' He shook his head. 'You're *detectives*.'

Cullen didn't say anything, just got out of the passenger seat, careful not to spill the bottom half of the acrid coffee he was using to camouflage the reek of booze on his breath. And to sober the hell up before Methven clocked how pissed he was.

Yvonne got out and Cullen had to catch her to stop her falling over.

Lennox was on the phone to someone, behind the windscreen of his squeaky clean Škoda Yeti.

An approaching car made Cullen squint, the headlights lighting up Yvonne's face. One of those squashed new Range Rovers, gleaming white even in the faint glow of the street lamps. Methven. He parked next to Lennox, his face like stone.

Cullen groaned. 'Just when I couldn't feel any sicker.'

Yvonne snorted into her cup, making the lid burst off and a jet of coffee shoot out, just as Methven stepped out of his car.

'Ah, good evening, Sergeant. Nice to see you back in Edinburgh and on such a joyous night.' He clapped his hands together. 'Dean sodding Vardy is dead!'

Cullen cleared his throat. 'Might have been even funnier if you hadn't already told me the punchline.'

Yvonne choked on her coffee and had to walk away in a coughing fit to catch her breath. 'Sorry, sir.'

Methven looked after her, seething. Then he looked Cullen up and down, his focus settling on his curry-splashed shirt. 'I thought you'd stopped drinking.'

'I wasn't on duty, sir.' Cullen faced Methven's glare with one of his own. 'Look, can we see the proof that Vardy actually is dead?'

~

CULLEN TOOK THE CLIPBOARD FROM BUXTON AND SIGNED HIM AND Yvonne in. 'You get all the good jobs, Si.'

Buxton took it back and thumbed behind him, clearly not in the mood. 'Body's in the bathroom off the hallway.'

Cullen hauled the mask over his head, snapping the goggles in place. He gave Yvonne a nod, then led the way into the flat, his own breath hissing in his ear, the crime-scene mask making his boozy sweat circulate. He stopped by two figures, shrouded in white boiler suits, examining the glossy red paint on the open front door. One of them looked up and shuffled out of the way, letting him move on to the next obstacle.

Another SOCO worked away at the varnished floorboards in the broad hallway. 'For crying out loud.' Anderson.

Cullen pushed past them and stepped into Vardy's flat, his heart hammering.

What if this is like when Vardy killed Xena Farley? No chance of recognising her, so he assumed it was Amy Forrest. What if this time someone's mistaken Vardy for someone he'd killed?

'Christ.' A figure stepped through a door and groaned. Jimmy Deeley, judging by the timbre of the groan. 'Good evening, detectives.' He gave them each a grave look. 'This is ugly.'

Cullen joined him by the door, but another pair of SOCOs blocked his view into what he assumed was a bedroom. 'How ugly?'

'Like Bain on the toilet.' Deeley stared at the floor, his eyebrows twitching like he'd seen such a thing. 'I'm estimating the time of death as *roughly* an hour ago, with half an hour each way. Same MO as with Campbell, though.'

'Seriously?'

'No, I'm joking at a crime scene. What do you think?' Deeley stepped aside. 'I'll let you see for yourself. I'm off to repeat myself to your boss.' He headed down the hallway, stopping to talk to one of the SOCOs kneeling on the floor.

Cullen set off, slowing as he passed a huddle of SOCOs working around a doorway. 'Coming through.' He stepped over them and their tuts into the bathroom, all glossy white marble and shiny gold fixtures. For a moment, Cullen felt like he was in a posh hotel.

Then he saw the body in the bath. Dean Vardy, naked, lacerated with cuts, lying in a congealed puddle of his own blood. Whatever else Vardy had been, he had always been overflowing with life, but now every last drop of it had left him. Looking at this corpse was one of the hardest things Cullen had ever had to do.

I've wished this kind of death upon him for over a year. Now a genie's granted my wish, it's just... another life taken... more suffering. And what good will it do? Another bastard will rise up to take his place and—

'Look at that.' The figure standing in the doorway, shrouded in white, pointed at the dead man like some avenging angel. Bain – no mistaking him. 'Cock like an acorn!' Then he squealed with delight. 'I really expected him to have a bigger wanger, you know? Driving all those shagging wagons, running a massive gang of drug pushers, acting the big man...' He shook his head like he was disappointed. 'Guess he never saw old Campbell in the gym locker room, eh? Poor wee guy.'

Cullen looked at Yvonne, shaking with the effort of suppressing her laughter. 'And here was me saying he was better.'

Methven stepped between them, a twitch in the corner of his mouth. 'Alright, Sergeants. I appreciate that you've had a hard day and clearly a much harder evening, but I need you to go the extra mile again for me.' He gave them a brave smile. 'Sergeants, can you please speak with Mr Vardy's girlfriend.' He closed his eyes and motioned at the bathtub. 'She's the one who found him. Neighbour heard her screaming and called the cops.'

~

CULLEN GAVE THE DOOR A TENTATIVE KNOCK, THEN WAITED IN THE stale corridor that smelled of third-hand cigarettes and cat piss. Down the spiral stairwell, the bedlam still engulfed Vardy's flat.

Yvonne leaned against the wall. 'He deserved it, right?'

I don't know. Maybe. Maybe not. Vardy deserves to be off the street, paying for all the suffering he's caused. Is this really that bad, given our complete inability to put anything resembling a case together? He can't destroy any more lives. Someone's done us a favour.

Cullen gave Yvonne a shrug. 'Maybe.'

Footsteps thumped towards them inside the flat and the door opened slowly. Sheena Douglas, a Family Liaison Officer Cullen had dealt with a few times, peered out. Mid-thirties with twinkling eyes. 'Hey, Scott. Yvonne? Long time, no see.' She stepped out into the stairwell. 'She's holding up remarkably well, considering. Trouble is, I can't understand a word she says.'

'What?'

'She's Polish. I think. Can Vardy speak Polish?'

Cullen frowned. 'No. Wilko had an informant who was from Krakow, said he could talk about Vardy in front of his face in Polish, never let on.'

'So Vardy's in a relationship with someone he can't communicate with?' Sheena nodded. 'Guy like that, he's not after a nice chat, is he? Just all about the body and the face.' She frowned at the door. 'This is her flat, but Vardy owns it, from what I can gather. I *think* her name is Wioletta Pawlok.'

'Mind if we have a word?'

'By all means.' Sheena led them into the flat. The place was battered and tattered, seeming a thousand miles from Vardy's polished bachelor pad. 'These detectives need a word, Wioletta. Is that okay? Can I get you a coffee?'

Wioletta was sitting on the sofa by the window. She gave Sheena an abstract nod but didn't acknowledge the detectives. 'Coffee, yes. Please.'

Cullen nodded a silent thank you at the FLO, then crossed the large room, nice and slow so as not to startle her. 'Miss Pawlok... may I call you Wioletta?'

She reacted to the sound of her name with that vague nod. No signs of guilt or insincerity. Her shock seemed real, even if nothing else did – the bleached blond hair, the pouting lips, the inflated breasts. Vardy sure had a type.

Yvonne took a seat next to Wioletta, careful to keep a respectful distance while still communicating a sympathetic presence. 'I understand this is a difficult time for you, so I'll make this brief. Okay?'

Wioletta turned her head to face Yvonne. 'Yes.'

Yvonne registered her reply with a warm smile. 'Wioletta, may I ask where you're from? I only ask in case you'd like a translator present.'

A slight frown crept on Wioletta's vacant face. 'Yes?'

Yvonne nodded. 'Your country?'

The frown disappeared and Wioletta went back to her vacant gaze. 'Poljska.' She blinked a few times. 'Poland.'

Yvonne pointed at herself, then at the door. 'I'll get you a translator. Back soon.'

No reaction.

YVONNE SKIPPED DOWN THE STAIRS. 'GOT OUR WORK CUT OUT FOR us, Scotty boy.'

'I'm struggling to keep that curry down.' Cullen followed her, the petrol station coffee burning in his gut.

'If you were going to lose it, it was when you saw Vardy.'

'Thank Christ for Bain's penis obsession.'

On Vardy's floor, Methven was making an arse of taking his crime-scene suit off. 'Sodding, sodding hell.' He finally kicked the second leg off and passed it to the attending SOCO for processing. Then he clocked them. 'Well?'

Yvonne just shrugged. 'She's Polish.'

Methven frowned. 'That's a bit harsh, Sergeant.'

'No, no, I mean she hardly speaks a word of English, so I haven't been able to question her.'

'Ah, I see.' Methven shook his head. 'I can never understand how—' He peered downstairs. 'Is that Paula Zabinski? Paula! It's Colin!'

Footsteps clambered up, then DC Paula Zabinski stopped on the stairs. Pale blonde hair, her rosy cheeks dotted with freckles. 'What's up, sir?' Spoke with all the boredom of someone who'd fended him off for years.

'Do you speak Polish as well as your surname suggests?'

'It's too late to wind you up for offending me, Colin.' A smile crept over her lips. 'Yes, I'm bilingual, if that's what you're asking.'

Methven chuckled. 'Let's see if you're as quick getting answers as you are giving them. I've a special mission for you. Let's see how fast you can get Miss Pawlok to tell us about the circumstances of her discovery here. Extra points for any details of Vardy's criminal enterprises.'

Zabinski trudged up the stairs towards Wioletta's flat.

Outside, Cullen took a look around to make sure nobody was in earshot, then glanced at Yvonne. 'So, how about when we get back to—'

'Scott?' The flat door slammed and Zabinski stomped across the path towards them. 'Is Crystal still about?'

'He was just here a—'

'Paula!' Methven bounded over, grinning from ear to ear. 'Did you manage to—'

'Of course I did.' Zabinski yawned. 'She says she was working at Sunset Beach, a tanning studio in Dalry. Left at eight to meet a friend for a drink in the Debonair. Vardy was supposed to meet them, but she didn't see him. Then she came home, found him in the bath around eleven. She screamed out and the neighbour came in. They called the cops.'

Methven checked his watch. 'How the sodding hell did you get all that out of her so fast?'

'Told her if she helped, you'd find the murderer by the end of the week. Extra points if you can do it by Friday.'

'How...' Methven stared at her. Then laughed out loud. 'I like the cut of your jib, Constable. Excellent work. Excellent. I don't need to ask you to validate the timeline, do I?'

'You know me, Colin. Remember, extra points for Friday.' She winked and walked off towards the huddle of plainclothes cops standing around doing bugger all.

Methven watched her go, a confused look on his face. When she was out of earshot, he leaned over to Yvonne and made sure his voice was a whisper. 'As a woman, would you say she was flirting with me?'

Cullen rubbed his face.

Yvonne bit her lip, her forehead creased. 'Well, I think you'll find out on Friday, sir.'

'Quite.' Methven dropped his gaze to his feet and cleared his throat. 'Now. The delightful DC Zabinski gave us a timeline for tonight, assuming it can be validated. Between that and Deeley's estimated time of death, we can narrow down the murderer's window of opportunity.'

Cullen nodded. 'Problem is, sir, we've got far too many suspects. You could go through the phone book and—'

'I know, Sergeant.' Methven's eyes were shut, the lids flickering. 'But this is a standard case. We have suspects, so we can see if they fit the timeframe.' He opened his eyes. 'And I just so happen to believe there's an obvious one we've been ignoring for a long time.' He looked at them expectantly.

Cullen saw his blank look reflected on Yvonne's face. 'Who?'

Methven shook his head. 'Sodding hell. Amy Forrest, of course. She went against Vardy, even promised to go on the stand. He probably threatened her and her friends, but the trail went cold. We never found her. Maybe she became frustrated enough to take matters into her own hands.'

'Makes sense, I suppose.' Cullen nodded. 'Especially after the other witness who agreed to testify against him was killed. That might've tipped her over the edge. Trouble is, we've no idea where she's hiding. Or if she's still alive.'

'Sergeant, a year and a half ago, Ms Forrest tried to kill Vardy. Her and her friend Xena Farley, who ended up dead by his hand.'

Cullen exhaled slowly. 'Makes you glad somebody finally got to him.'

Methven gave him an uncertain look. 'Does it?'

'No.'

Methven took another sharp breath and cleared his throat.

'Right, we need one more stab at finding her...' He let that hang in the air between them. 'Can you—'

Cullen's phone rang.

'Sorry, sir.' He pulled it out and checked the display. Buxton. 'What's up, Si?'

A crackle on the line: 'Got another vigilante sighting.'

23

CULLEN'S SCUFFING FOOTSTEPS ON THE STONE STAIRCASE SOUNDED as tired as he felt. He reached for the door handle and stepped out into the night air, half of his brain still processing what was going on between him and Yvonne and what the hell he was—

'Watch out!' Buxton grabbed his shoulders. 'Steady, mate.'

'Si.' Cullen did a double take. 'What are you doing here?'

'Eh? Waiting for you? I just spoke to you.'

'What?' Cullen stared at him. 'No I mean—?'

'Are you drunk?' Buxton jerked his head forward and sniffed Cullen's breath. 'What the hell, mate? You can't interview a witness like this.'

'I'm fine.'

Buxton lowered his voice to a hiss. 'Not like this, mate, seriously.'

'Mate, come on.' Cullen let out a deep breath and watched it mist in the air. Then almost toppled over. *Maybe he's right.* 'Fine. Just tell me what this witness saw.'

'Right...' Buxton pointed at the building over the road. 'Dear old girl, lives over there. I was waiting here to go back in with you, but... Mate, you should hear her. She said she's some *grande dame* of the publishing world, runs her own agency with *fabulous* writers to wine and dine *everywhere*. That's why she's up this late. Jetlagged from a transatlantic flight, hashing out some *hush hush* deal she *really* couldn't tell me about, *darling*. Course she did and—'

'Si, did she see Batman?'

'She's as pissed as you are, mate, going off on a tangent every other sentence and they just go on and on and on and—'

'Si, for *Christ's sake!*' Cullen stared at him, narrowing his eyes. 'Did she see a superhero?'

Buxton glanced back over the road. 'She saw someone dressed in a black leather costume sneak out of the block, a well-built man by the looks of it, but he was wearing a mask, so she couldn't see his face.'

'Get a full statement. I'm off to brief Methven.'

CULLEN RUSHED UP THE STAIRS.

'Scott!' Lennox was skipping up the stairs after him, hardly making a sound he was so light on his feet.

Cullen reached for the handrail and steadied himself before his wee wobble. He gave Lennox his most professional frown. 'What's up?'

Lennox raised his hands in mock apology. 'Simon Buxton has a—'

'I just spoke to him.'

'Right. Have you told Methven?'

'If you'll bloody let me!' Cullen turned, his sole scrunching on the stone step, and started up the stairs again.

'Chaos, mate.' Lennox was on his heels, mouth-breathing all the way up. 'Absolute chaos.'

Methven was standing in the doorway, frowning at Lennox. 'Terry?' He held out a hand and, rather than some mason's hand-shake, they did an elaborate slapping ritual, like two blinged-up footballers celebrating a goal. 'Been a long time.'

'Got another witness saying she saw a superhero flee the scene.' Lennox gave a polite smile. 'That's two, isn't it?'

Methven's scowl turned into a sneer. 'Is it?'

'Last night.' Cullen patted his scraped cheek. 'At McLintock's.'

'Heaven help us.' Methven shot a glare at Lennox. 'Can you escort DS Cullen and DS Flockhart back to Tulliallan?'

Cullen got in first. 'Don't you believe me?'

'Sergeant, I need to ruminate further.' Methven pushed past them and started walking down the stairs, delivering his parting shot over his shoulder. 'Get some sleep. I'll see you at St Leonards at seven on the dot. Sober, if you can manage that.'

THE KNIFE SLICED THROUGH THE AIR IN FRONT OF CULLEN, SLICING through his jacket, cutting his chest open. Pain screamed in his ears.

Batman was licking his lips. 'You okay, Scott?'

'Get away from me!'

Batman slashed out again, jabbing the knife in Cullen's throat. 'You okay, Scott?' He leaned forward and started lapping at the blood spilling from the wound, like a thirsty dog.

'Get—'

'—off me!' Cullen jerked awake.

Lennox and Yvonne were both staring at him from the front seats. The Tulliallan car park glowed behind them, far too bright. The dashboard said it was the back of two. *Up in five hours. Shite.*

'Christ.' Cullen glanced at them in turn, then rubbed his eyes and got out of the car. Had to brace himself against the door to stop himself falling. He held on to it until the world stopped spinning.

A phone rang. Cullen patted his pockets, found his phone in his trousers. Not ringing, at least not any more.

Lennox put his mobile to his ear and signalled that it was a private call. 'Sir, we're just—'

Yvonne got out and put her hand on his. 'Still want to go back to my room?'

DAY 4

Wednesday
15th February

24

THE SENSUOUS MOANING WAS DOING CULLEN'S HEAD IN. THE purring with pleasure he could take, but when she lowered her head and started making slurping noises as well...

'Excuse me?' Cullen glared across the table. 'Can you—'

'Mmf?' The woman froze, a sausage poking out of her mouth, grease dribbling down her glistening chin. Her plate looked like a crime scene: chopped-up meat splattered with ketchup, a congealing pile of baked beans like spilled brains. 'What?' She took the sausage stump out of her mouth and thrust it at him, like some piece of evidence. Like a bloody severed finger. 'Does this offend you? Are you *vegan*?' Said like the worst swear word.

Cullen had to look away to keep his own breakfast down. He pushed his porridge bowl away. 'No, I'm just—'

Hungover, like an idiot.

He swallowed. 'You were being a bit loud, that's all.'

'Oh, I'm sorry, princess. Was I too noisy sucking my meat?' She stuck the sausage back in her mouth and started fellating it.

Cullen got up and left the table, coffee in one hand, cupping his porridge bowl in the other. Then his phone rang. He set the bowl down on another table and checked the display. Angela Lamb. *What does she want?* He sat. 'Cullen.'

'Hey, how you doing?'

'I'm okay. What's up?'

'Just wondering if you've heard anything about the job?'

'Jesus, you're keen. Bill throwing money away or something?'

'Motivated, not desperate. So?'

'It's Methven's role, but I'll talk to HR and find out what's holding it up.'

'I thought it went well. Did I fail?'

'Angela, you know I can't comment on that. Look, I've got to go.' Cullen cut the call and slipped the phone into his pocket. He tried another spoonful of porridge. The sausage slurper walked past the table, puckering her lips. He shut his eyes, let her have the victory.

'Good to see you up so early, Sergeant.' Lennox took the opposite seat, clutching a purple smoothie.

Cullen stared into his porridge and stirred it a few times.

Lennox gave him the once over. 'After all the daft drinking you and Vonnie did last night, thought you'd be chugging the water?'

'Vonnie?'

'Yeah, she doesn't like that one. Why I call her it.' Lennox lifted his smoothie, pursed his lips around the straw and took a deep, long *SLURP*. 'Recommend one of these bad boys. Nuke any hangover.'

'Looks like it's bruised. Like my head.' Cullen leaned back, stifling a yawn. 'First hangover in ages and—'

'Your head feels about as tender as an altar boy's arse after choir practice. Don't worry, your secret's safe with me.' Lennox took another long suck then chuckled. 'But speaking of perverts, I thought I'd see Bain here?'

'Not seen him today. He went home last night, didn't he?'

Lennox leaned in close, winking. 'Back to his mail-order Thai bride, right?'

'Never met her. Have you?'

'Nope.' Lennox rested his smoothie on the table. 'Nobody has, but Bain says he's in love, so fair play to the boy.' He sucked his smoothie right to the bottom, but kept on sucking, getting louder and louder, making the other diners look over. Then he stopped to wink at Cullen. 'I wouldn't be surprised if *she* turned out to be a *he*, mind. Dirty old bastard. Can't believe he's still dining out on that email.'

Cullen froze. 'What email?'

'You don't know?' Lennox smacked his lips. 'Got caught up with Damo McCrea a couple of years back. Used to work with him and Bain in Glasgow South, aye? Damo said that back when Bain dropped a clanger on this case with some rock star, who—'

'I worked that. Remember it like it was yesterday.'

'Well, get you.' Lennox tore open a paper bag to reveal a bagel smeared in peanut butter. Everything was – the inside of the bag, the outside of the bagel and now Lennox's fingers. 'Anyway, Bain pissed off DCS Soutar in some meeting, right? I know Carolyn and she'd had way more than enough of him, so she sent an email to Keith Graham and—' he clicked his fingers quickly, 'who's your guy?' More clicking then he pointed at Cullen. 'Oh yeah, Alison Cargill, right? Not a guy, but, anyway, so Carolyn sent them this email about Bain being inept and how she wanted him fired. Unfortunately for her, she got distracted by a phone call or whatever, and sent said email to our friend Brian Bain.'

'Seriously?'

'Oh hell yeah.' Lennox munched his bagel, rubbing peanut butter all over his lips and chin. 'Way Damo tells it, Bain threatened to go to HR, but they came to an arrangement. So Soutar's been protecting him ever since, no matter how depraved his carry-on has been.'

'I smell bullshit.'

'How?'

'Bain got demoted. He was a DI, now he's a DS.'

'Same pay, though. All part of the deal. He's out of the line of fire, just what he wanted.'

'Lucky bastard.' Cullen shook his head. Bright pain throbbed behind his eyes. He squinted at Lennox, who was busy reading a text message.

Lennox mistook it for an invitation to chat. 'So, have you seen Yvonne?'

'Not since last night.'

Lennox picked up his smoothie and rested the straw against his lips. 'Is there something going on between you two?'

'I really don't see how that's any of your business.'

Lennox stiffened. 'Fair enough.' He got up and stomped off.

Cullen shook his head, gently, to avoid another wave of nausea, and reached for his phone. Three words had never taken him so long to type and delete and retype and reconsider and, finally, send.

How are you?

He stared at them, started wondering what Sharon would read into them. The longer he looked, the more disappointed he became by how offhand they'd appear to her. To anyone. Like he'd just tapped the predictive text above the keyboard, letting a machine ask the questions. Like he hadn't shared her life for years.

The three dots started bouncing underneath his question as she typed a reply. And typed. And typed.

Then the dots disappeared. And no message came through.

One did, from Methven.

Briefing early. St Leonards. Now.

Cullen pulled into the car park at the foot of the Salisbury Crags and took the last space. He got out and raced over the car park to the back entrance. His phone buzzed. Another text message. He reached into his pocket to read it, but he was distracted by a lithe skinhead walking his way.

Rich McAlpine blanked him as they passed each other.

Cullen stopped and turned round. 'Hey, Rich?'

But he walked off.

What the hell is all this about?

What is it with people I used to share flats with cutting me off?

Cullen walked over to the card reader by the door. Before he could swipe his card, the door clunked open.

DCS Carolyn Soutar stepped out into the pissing rain and gave him a curt nod. 'Sergeant.' She powered past him, followed by Cargill and some other senior officers, heading to the waiting press gang.

There goes the reason I have to put up with Bain's nonsense.

Rich was near the front, holding his phone out to record his questions. He locked eyes with Cullen then looked back at Soutar and her gang.

The DCS cleared her throat and started talking into the microphones thrust into her face. 'Thank you for joining me. I'll be brief.'

Cullen walked inside the building and checked his text message.

'I didn't kill him. Amy'

He stopped and stared at the screen.

Why the hell has she sent me that? Is it even her?

He hit dial.

No answer.

'There you sodding are.' Methven grabbed him by the arm and walked him down the corridor. Then he leaned in close and hissed hot coffee breath in Cullen's ear: 'Livingston MIT are running both cases now.'

Cullen frowned. 'Seriously?'

'No, Sergeant, I'm just winding you up.' Methven shut his eyes, the lids flickering. 'I've just been in a sodding power breakfast with DCS Soutar and... she gave two reasons, and both are impossible to sodding argue with. First, the number of times we butted up against McLintock or investigated Vardy. We're too close, they aren't. I pointed out that he owned a gym in Livingston, but she was having none of it.' He opened his eyes again and snarl. 'Her second reason is that she suspects that Vardy has some Edinburgh cops on his payroll. And detectives at that.'

'Shite. Do you know who?'

'Nothing more than murmurings at this juncture. Alison Cargill and I pleaded our case, insisting that we stay involved to flush out the rats.' Methven gripped Cullen's sleeve again. 'But it's a matter for Professional Standards and Ethics, not us.'

Cullen shrugged Methven's hand off. 'You trying to say something?'

'No need to be so touchy.' Methven snorted. 'Your performance last night showing up half cut at a crime scene was unprofessional, to say the least, but you're not on my list of suspects.'

'Am I on theirs, though?'

Methven looked away. 'They won't tell me.'

'Great.' Cullen held up his phone. 'Look, I got a text from Amy Forrest. Says she didn't kill Vardy.'

Methven stared hard at it. 'Do you believe her?'

'I don't even know if it *is* her. Could be anyone with a burner, typing her name.' Cullen pocketed his phone. 'But I'll get the number traced. See if we can get a location.'

'Excellent.' Methven huffed out a sigh. 'There's another thing. I'm afraid that Livingston are interviewing everyone on our investigation. Starting with you.'

25

CULLEN KNOCKED ON THE DOOR AND WAITED. HIS PHONE BUZZED IN his pocket – another text, this time from Tommy Smith in Forensics.

'Ill look in2 yr nr l8r. Backlog long as yr arm.'

And here's me thinking he is an expert on phones.

Cullen tapped out a reply.

'If you could expedite? Urgent. And send the results to Buxton. Cheers.'

He put his phone away and knocked again.

The door opened and Yvonne stood there, frowning. 'Morning, Scott. You okay?'

'You're interviewing me?'

Yvonne stepped into the corridor and pulled the door to behind her. 'Standard procedure, Scott. It'd be the same if the situation was reversed. If you've done nothing wrong, then you don't need to worry.'

'I should be working this case.'

She dropped her gaze to her feet and put a hand back on the door.

Cullen whispered, 'Is this about last night?'

She stiffened, a blush creeping up her neck.

'Is this about me not coming back to your room?' He lowered his voice even further. 'Listen, I wanted to. You wouldn't believe how tempted I was, but I'm in the middle of something and I'm sorry for leading you on and—'

She pecked him on the cheek. 'I understand.' Her voice was as quiet as his. 'Let me know when you reach the end of that something.' She stiffened as she opened the door. 'You coming?'

Cullen clenched his teeth and followed her in to the room.

'Sergeant.' Lennox looked up from a file on the table and gave him a cold smile. 'Have a seat.'

∾

CULLEN SCRATCHED HIS FINGERNAILS OFF THE PALMS OF HIS HANDS. The left was still burning from the porridge incident. 'We done?'

'Well.' Lennox puffed up his cheeks and glanced at Yvonne. 'There's only one conspicuous detail here, wouldn't you agree?'

What the hell has he got on me?

There's nothing. Certainly nothing I can think of.

Doesn't mean someone's planted something. Someone in Vardy's organisation, one of those bent cops on the payroll.

Yvonne raised her eyebrows like she hadn't been listening, but before Lennox noticed, she started nodding. 'I agree.'

Lennox turned back to Cullen. 'Tell us more about this leather gimp suit.'

'At the time of night, and in the confusion of the moment, I could not ascertain exactly what the murderer was wearing, but I believe that it was a Batman costume. Maybe a fetishised version, but a Batman costume.'

'With the mouth open?'

'Excuse me?'

Lennox held up his monster Samsung phone, showing a photo of Batman from one of the films. 'He's got a mask, aye? But the mouth is uncovered, right? Did you see anything that might identify him?'

All Cullen could see was the black shape in the dark night. 'I don't know. If it was, I didn't see. All I saw was dark.'

'The Dark Knight, eh?' Lennox put his phone away with a smirk. 'You sure it was a Batman costume?'

'No, but I'm sure it was a costume.' Cullen cleared his throat. 'Look, DI Lamb and DI Methven have expressed doubts about the superhero attire, but there are two eyewitnesses corroborating my story.'

'Was there a cape?'

'I just told you that it was a Batman costume without a cape.'

'No cape...' Lennox squinted at him, like he was wondering whether Cullen was winding him up. He leaned back and nodded slowly. 'And you believe this choice of costume was meaningful?'

'I've no idea, do I?' Then Cullen frowned. 'Wait. Campbell McLintock, his partner told us he had a superhero fetish.'

'Ah, Hamish Williams.' Lennox made a note on his phone with the stylus. 'Do you think the murderer could've known about this?'

'Hamish said Campbell was private about this fetish. About their whole relationship. We spoke to a bodybuilder who regularly worked for them as a gay escort. Robert Woodhead.'

'Ah, the infamous Big Rob.'

'Right. Well. He told us he engaged in some sexual role play with Mr McLintock – had to wear a Batman costume.'

'The same one?'

'I don't know. Sorry. Look. I believe DI Methven was validating his alibi for the time of death, but—'

'Already done that. Got Mr Woodhead on surveillance camera and we've got a witness statement from a neighbour. Big Rob was nowhere near the crime scene at the relevant time.' Lennox nodded to himself. 'Begs the question of who *else* knew about McLintock's superhero fetish. You tell anyone?'

'It's all in the case file. And you know what this place is like.' Cullen waved his hand around the room. 'The canteen staff will have heard by now.'

'Quite.' Lennox flicked over a page on the file in front of him. 'But we have a statement suggesting that Batman killed Vardy too. Meaning we're looking for somebody with a motive to kill him and McLintock.' He sat back, arms folded. 'We've been advised to treat the murders as unrelated and to treat the costume similarity as coincidence.'

Cullen pleaded with Yvonne. 'Come on, it's the same guy at both crime scenes. Vardy's and McLintock's deaths are connected.'

'Why, though?' Lennox waited for an answer.

Cullen couldn't give him one, not one that he believed.

'Thought so.' Lennox shook his head. 'Look, we're treating

both as vigilante actions and investigating any connections. As I'm sure you know, frustrated cops make the best suspects.'

Cullen's jaw dropped. 'Me?'

'Where were you on Monday evening, Sergeant?'

'I was at Tulliallan.' Cullen felt a sting behind the eyes. 'Look, I checked in and, before I could get to my room, Campbell called me, telling me he had information about the Vardy case.'

'So you went there on your own?'

'I thought it might just be mischief. You know Campbell.'

'Never met the man. But you seem to have known him quite well?'

Cullen's mouth was dry. His tongue stuck to the roof. He sat forward, swallowing hard. 'Look, I fought with this Batman guy, right? Guy almost stabbed me.'

Lennox looked him up and down. 'You're quite big. You match the description of this—'

'Wait a minute!' Cullen pushed himself up to standing, leaning on the desk. 'Are you not listening to me? I fought with this guy! An eyewitness saw it!'

'Right.' Lennox clicked his tongue a few times, then made a note on his phone. 'Where were you last night between—'

'Really?'

'Really.'

Cullen looked at Yvonne, but she was staring at her notebook. 'I was at Tulliallan.'

'All night?'

'Until you picked us up and drove us to the crime scene.'

'Us?'

Cullen stared at him. Then his eyes flicked to Yvonne, but her gaze was firmly fixed to her notebook. 'A few of us went for a curry in Kincardine. Don't know the name of the place, sorry.'

'The Raj, I believe.' Lennox clicked his tongue again. 'Know it well. It shuts at nine during the week. And it definitely shut at nine last night. I checked with the staff. And DI Lamb and DS Bain left shortly before closing. Which leaves plenty of time for you to get to Bruntsfield.'

Cullen didn't say anything. Couldn't.

'You're not going to give me an alibi?'

Under normal circumstances, Cullen would've refused to

answer, if only to spare Yvonne the embarrassment. In this case, though, silence would make him a suspect, a real suspect. He shrugged an apology at Yvonne. 'After the curry, I was drinking at a pub in Kincardine.'

Lennox gave him a dubious frown. 'All night long?'

'For a while.'

Yvonne seemed to shrink down into her notebook.

'And would the barman confirm that alibi?'

'Of course.'

Lennox leaned forward and gave him another one of his squinty looks, unsure whether Cullen was having a laugh at his expense. He leaned back again, though the squint didn't quite leave his eyes. 'And what would he tell me if I asked him at what time you left the pub?'

'He *should* say that we left the pub at around eleven.'

'We?'

'Can't have been much earlier than that, because we went straight back to Tulliallan. Then I got the call from DI Methven ordering me to attend the crime scene not long after.' He took his phone from his pocket. 'Let me check. Shouldn't take—'

'Sergeant.' Lennox leaned over the table and snatched the mobile from his hand. 'Were you drinking on your own?'

'I was with DS Flockhart.'

A frown flickered across Lennox's forehead. 'I see.'

Cullen grabbed his phone back. 'Am I a suspect here?'

'Excuse me? I need to take that into evidence.'

'You don't need my phone unless I'm a suspect. Besides, you can call up Tommy Smith and get a list of DI Methven's calls and whether they were answered. You don't need my phone.'

Lennox stared at him for a few hard seconds then looked away. 'What time was the call?'

Cullen flicked his finger up the screen until he found what he was looking for. 'Here we go. Ten fifty-four.'

Lennox reached into the inside pocket of his suit for his own mobile. After messing with it for a few seconds, he looked back up at Cullen. 'My call log says you called me at eleven oh one. So, the question—'

'Seven minutes? How could I have possibly got to Edinburgh,

murdered Vardy, and got back to Tulliallan in time for you to pick me up?'

Lennox stared at him, not letting go.

Cullen threw his hands up. 'I get it, standard protocol, solid alibis... sod that. I was kiss—'

'Thank you very much for your time, Sergeant.' Yvonne clapped her hands and leaned over the voice recorder on the table. 'Interview terminated at eight twenty-two.'

Cullen stormed out of the interview room and almost knocked Methven off his feet.

Not that he seemed surprised. 'Walk with me.' He turned on his heel and strode off the other way.

Cullen fell in line behind him, catching up by the stairwell. 'What's up?'

'Not here.' Methven glanced up and down the hallway, then opened the door to an empty office and ducked inside.

Cullen followed him and leaned back against the door. 'You going to talk now?'

'What do you sodding think? Your interview?'

'WELL, THAT'S WHAT I EXPECTED.' METHVEN STARED AT THE DOOR like he was facing off against Lennox. 'Sounds like you're in the clear, but can you trust DS Flockhart?'

Cullen said nothing. Just tried to figure out whether he was being set up. He searched Methven for signs of deception. A change in his blink rate or perhaps a twitch in his hands or feet. Got nothing. 'Lennox thinks I might be the Batman impersonator.'

'You?'

'I'm in better shape than I've been in years.' The wooden door was warming where Cullen's hands touched it. 'But it's not me.'

'Well, clearly.' Methven gave him a thoughtful nod. 'I've been instructed to keep working the cases, see if we can find any leads that Livingston aren't investigating.'

'By Cargill?'

'No comment.' Methven winked. 'Livingston are interviewing everyone who's worked both cases, to identify suspects with personal vendettas against both Vardy and McLintock. They're heading down a sodding rabbit hole.'

'Doesn't mean they're wrong.'

'But it doesn't mean they're right, either. They're chasing after a load of corrupt cops who may or may not exist. Believe you me, I know Lennox's superiors in Livingston. They're always looking for glory, or at least ways to peg us back.' He fell silent but kept staring at Cullen.

Private conversation, no witnesses, vague implications, perfect deniability.

Bugger this.

Cullen squared his shoulders and folded his hands across his chest, then he set his face in a non-committal smile. 'What are you saying?'

Methven broke his intent stare, if only for long enough to roll his eyes like he was already regretting his choice of ally. 'Do I really need to spell it out for you?'

'Wouldn't hurt.'

'Keep investigating both cases but stay under the radar.'

'This is most unlike you.'

'Well...' Methven paused to give him an ambiguous look. 'I know when to use certain weapons.'

'Are you calling me a—'

'Sergeant, you're off the leash.' Methven patted his arm. 'Go and forage.'

26

_____

CULLEN SIPPED COFFEE AS HE CLIMBED THE STAIRS UP TO THEIR office space, his head still throbbing. Tasted burnt.

The door opened and a pile of stacked files walked through. 'Alright, mate?' Buxton, twisting to the side. 'You doing anything important?'

'Trying not to, why?'

Buxton jerked his head in the direction of their office, his feathery fringe flopping over his forehead. 'Got a shit ton of paperwork to go through. That Flockhart bird, Christ. She's a piece of work.'

Cullen grabbed the top few files. 'What are you doing?'

'Got me and half the bloody DCs in Scotland looking through the whole case against Vardy.'

'Operation Venus?'

'Right.' Buxton gave the pile in his hands another shake. 'This is just the bleeding start of it. If you wouldn't mind—'

~

THROUGH THE STEAMED-UP WINDOW, THEY COULD SEE THE PRESS corps were back in the car park.

Buxton poked Cullen's ear with a pen. 'Wakey, wakey!'

Cullen pushed the pen away. 'Go to hell.'

'You falling asleep?'

'I'm just thinking.'

'Oh yeah, about how you were up shagging all night?'

'I wish.' Cullen shuffled the papers on his desk and frowned at Buxton. 'Not getting anywhere with this, mate.'

'No? Well, I am getting somewhere.' Buxton handed Cullen a case report. 'Filed by a certain Detective Inspector William Lamb. A murder at a sweet shop.'

'A sweet shop?'

'Pick and mix. Classic con, mate. Cash business, so you can funnel all that moolah through the books.' Buxton fanned the pages out. 'Anyway, some geezer got stabbed in the shop a few years back and Lamb caught it. Not unusual in itself, but the stabber died before it could get to court.'

'You're sure this is Vardy?'

'Check the address.' Buxton tapped the file. 'It's the tanning salon Vardy's Polish bird works in. Vardy bought the building in 2010. Wilko's lot didn't know he owned it.'

Cullen gave a low whistle as he scanned the index page. 'Nice work.' He tried Lamb's number but it went to voicemail. 'Right, I'll speak to Bill about it.' He got to his feet and stretched out. 'Keep this between us, aye?'

CULLEN PARKED OUTSIDE TULLIALLAN, CHEWING THE LAST OF HIS tuna sandwich. He reached for the paper coffee cup in the middle console and walked over to the building, swilling a sip of tepid americano around his mouth to dislodge a bit of sweetcorn between his front teeth. He opened the front door and headed through reception.

'Excuse me! Sergeant Cullen?' The spotty young attendant shot out and caught Cullen's arm, glaring at him with a sulky frown. 'I have to ask you to vacate your room ASAP.'

'You what?'

'I'm asking you to check out as soon as—'

'I know what ASAP means. Why do I have to check out?'

The receptionist replied with a melodramatic eyeroll. 'Becauu-uuuse we're expecting a large contingent of the Dundee and

Aberdeen MIT on secondment to support the Livingston team, and they're all staying here to save on Edinburgh hotel bills.'

And that hour each way of wasted travel doesn't get a cell on the spreadsheet, does it?

Cullen gave him a stern look. 'I need that room.'

'No, you don't.' Lamb stepped between them. 'He'll be out of here.'

'Excellent.' The receptionist dashed over to his desk and set to work on his computer.

'Bill, I need that room.'

'No, Scott. You *need* to explain why you missed today's course.'

'I was over at St Leonards, meeting with—'

'Your interview finished before nine, right?'

'It did, but I got railroaded into helping Buxton pull together old cases.'

'And Lennox would back that up?'

'Methven would.'

'Scott, if you're on active duty, I have to chuck you off the course. You and Flockhart. Okay?'

'I've been trying to call but you didn't answer.'

Lamb bit back his anger. 'What about?'

'Need to ask you about Sweet Dreams.'

'Eh?'

'Shop in Gorgie. This is what I've been helping Si Buxton root through. One Declan Cooper was murdered there.'

'I sort of remember it. Why are you looking at it?'

'Turns out Vardy owned the shop. Probably for money laundering. It's now a tanning salon.'

'Scott, that case was so long ago, I wouldn't remember enough about it to answer basic questions.' Lamb's mouth hung open. 'Are Livvy going after me?'

'What? No. Not yet.' Cullen frowned at him. 'Look, did Vardy's name ever come up?'

'I do remember that McLintock was involved, now you mention it.' Lamb's eyes went out of focus like he was trying to remember the investigation but was drawing a blank. He blinked and shook his head. 'I don't think Vardy was mentioned, though.' He was still shaking his head, then stopped. 'Hold on. That case fell apart while I was on honeymoon.' He swallowed. 'The suspect died in custody, right?'

'Right. Johnny Cockburn.'

'I remember now. Now, *he* was connected to Vardy. Aye, Operation Venus became involved. Wilko took over while I was off.'

'Wait, Wilko?'

'Do you need me to repeat every second word or something?' Lamb narrowed his eyes, like it was all coming back into focus. 'You should have a word with him. Stupid bastard was in charge of that botched sting on Vardy last year, the one where that stripper got shot.'

'Aye, and Campbell McLintock got Vardy off that time, too.' Cullen puffed up his cheeks and let a long breath escape his lips. 'Wait a sec. You can't seriously suggest that Wilko's in that Batman costume?'

'Hardly.' Lamb laughed. 'Actually, a year ago and Wilko would need two costumes and that's just for his legs. Now, though... He's looking good, isn't he? Slimline tonic, or so he says. Reckon he's been fasting.'

'Either way, I need to speak to him.'

'If you want my advice, Scott, you should pass the intel on to Lennox.' Lamb's smile turned to a frown. 'Speaking of which. Lennox called me earlier. Try to keep this on the down low, but they're looking at your better half.'

'What?'

'Christ, Scott. *Sharon*. Turns out Sharon's Sexual Offences Unit in Bathgate had Vardy under investigation too.'

'You're joking.'

'Do I look like I'm joking?' Lamb stared at him, eyes narrowed, his jaw set. 'Few years back, Methven charged Vardy. A woman called Pauline Quigley alleged that he'd assaulted and raped her.'

'I remember. I worked that case.' Cullen let out a slow sigh. 'Never seen Methven that angry. McLintock got wind of her lying to another investigation and got the case thrown out.'

'Well, it didn't end there. Your better half and her Sexual Offences Unit picked it up. Way I hear it, they tried to round up a whole legion of other witnesses to build a cast-iron case against Vardy.'

'That was years ago, though.'

'You must know from your Operation Venus days how long a strategic unit takes to build a case.'

What else has Sharon hidden from me?

Lamb gave him an encouraging smile. 'The good news, my friend, is the lead DC is an old pal of yours.'

CULLEN PARKED ACROSS THE ROAD FROM BATHGATE POLICE STATION – a white box glowing in the February sun. His old station, over two years in uniform, barely making a dent in West Lothian's crime statistics. Fighting an uphill battle out here. For some reason it looked like somebody had painted a zebra crossing all the way up the front wall.

Across the road, Bain was pacing up the broad pavement, whistling to himself. Then he veered off track, skipped up the front steps and slipped in through the door.

Cullen stared at the closing door. *What the hell is he doing here?* He reached for the door handle and got out into the howling gale. So much for the sunshine.

CULLEN WALKED THROUGH THE DOORWAY INTO THE OFFICE SPACE and stopped to look around. The place stank of stewing coffee, like it'd been left on all day.

Chantal Jain looked up from her laptop, straight at him, then away.

Cullen spotted another, easier target, and headed straight past her without a word. 'Alright, Elvis, how's tricks?'

'Oh. It's you. What now?'

'That's no way to greet an old friend.'

'Can't see this old friend, Scott, it's just you.'

Cullen laughed. 'You lost weight?'

'Oh.' Elvis sat up, his chest puffed up. 'Been doing this intermittent fasting. Have you heard of it? Brilliant stuff. Wilko put me onto it.' He patted his flat stomach. 'Helped me cut my Christmas flab *and* it's boosted my energy levels. If I'd known—'

Cullen spotted Hunter working at a desk at the far side of the room. 'I'll catch you later, Elvis.' He made his way across. 'Alright, Craig?'

Hunter looked up at him, then straight down at his paperwork. 'What?'

Cullen leaned down to speak to him out of earshot of the busy office. For an awkward moment they stared at each other, their noses only inches apart, until Cullen cleared his throat. 'Is— is your boss in?'

'Nah, she's in town meeting the PF. I can ask Chantal when she'll be back, if you want.'

Cullen caught a glare from Chantal. 'Actually, it's you I need to speak to.'

'Is this one of those ones where I get a boot up the arse for helping?'

'Shouldn't be.'

'Scott.' Hunter grabbed a handful of Cullen's jacket and pulled him close. 'Listen to me. I've got a new DS starting on Monday. Clean slate. I don't want any shite from you ruining that. Okay?'

Cullen nodded. 'Great.'

'Great?' Hunter leaned back in his chair and folded his bulky arms over his equally bulky chest. 'Why's that great?'

Cullen lowered his voice. 'Christ's sake, Craig. I've no time for this shit.' He glanced around, and again caught Chantal's glare. She was on her feet, pretending to listen to Elvis, but Cullen knew what she was really up to. He turned back to Hunter. 'Listen, I'm investigating the Vardy and McLintock killings and—'

Hunter's eyes bulged. 'Scott...' He squinted at him. 'Did you kill them?'

'Of course not. I might be a dick, Craig, but I'm not a killer.'

The corners of Hunter's mouth twitched. 'Glad to know it.' He unfolded his arms and leaned forward to continue in a hushed voice. 'Struggling to see what kind of answers I can give you.'

'Pauline Quigley.'

'The case you and Methven dropped a bollock on?'

'That's the one.' Cullen clenched his teeth. 'Why didn't your investigation lead to a conviction?'

'What are you getting at, Scott?'

'Well, I'm told you found a number of witnesses and—'

'A number?' Hunter snorted. 'Well, I suppose *one* is a number.

Aye, we found other witnesses, but only one who would give a statement.'

'Then why didn't Vardy go down?'

'Officially, because she changed her mind. Right before the trial. Weird, eh?'

Just like Amy Forrest. 'And unofficially?'

'Unofficially means if I tell you, you keep it to yourself. This time, you don't go behind my back. Are we clear?'

Cullen locked eyes with Hunter, then gave him a curt nod.

Hunter glanced around and lowered his voice to a whisper: 'Unofficially, Vardy found out that she was about to testify against him and changed her mind for her.'

Cullen whispered back. 'Who's the witness?'

27

CHRISTINE 'CANDY' BROADHURST OPENED THE DOOR, WEARING A uniform of sadness. Holes in her slippers, baggy grey cotton joggers, her washed-out woolly cardigan open loose over a shapeless off-white T-shirt. All of it long overdue a wash. The odd grey strand had crept into her hair – dark roots growing out the once-glossy blonde. Her eyes stared with a dead emptiness, like she didn't give a shit anymore.

A million miles away from Candy the stripper – one of Vardy's girls.

Candy stared at the two cops looking at her and seemed to know what they saw. She grabbed the open flaps of her cardigan and wrapped them tight around her loose hips. Maybe she was just cold. 'What do *you* want?' Her ire was focused on Cullen.

He tried for a warm smile. 'Hi, Candy, good to—'

'If you've come here to talk me into giving evidence against Dean, then you can leave right now.' Her hand went back to the door, ready to slam it in their faces. But something made her stop.

Hunter glanced at Cullen, then back at Candy. 'I'm afraid—'

A baby's cry screamed out.

Candy's anger deflated like a tired old balloon, her shoulders sagging. She turned and shuffled back into her flat. 'Close the door, eh? The bairn'll get a chill.'

Cullen let Hunter go first and followed him through to the

living room. He stopped in the doorway while Hunter went over to the window, looking out on the arse end of Blackburn, itself the arse end of West Lothian.

Candy sat on a stained corduroy couch and hoisted up her T-shirt to loosen the front of her bra. She let a tiny baby attach itself to her nipple.

Cullen looked away. The place looked like a charity shop – one where all the good old stuff had been sold and nobody had dropped off anything new. Piles of unwashed laundry, an empty play pen, a sad assortment of half-broken domestic goods, mismatched furniture.

Candy looked up at him, and again she seemed to know exactly what he saw. 'I'm in the middle of sorting the place out.' Her voice was an exhausted drone. 'I just never get around to doing much. The wee one screams as soon as I put him down. He's four months now and all he does is feed, but he's still not growing as he should and the health worker said I'm to breastfeed him whenever he'll take it, so...'

He tried to make his next question sound as inoffensive as possible. 'Is his dad not around?'

Her look hardened. 'He's Dean's kid.'

Another one.

Shite.

'Only gives me the bare minimum child support cos his businesses are squirrelled away abroad. Some shite like that. He's never shown his face around here since the day this wee terror was born. Now he's not even answering his phone anymore.' She looked down at her baby, gazing at him with nothing but love in her eyes. 'Your father's an arsehole. I hope you grow up nothing like him.' Her voice was so soft, her words were hard to hear.

Cullen thought he hadn't heard right.

'What?' Candy glared at him. 'Are you shocked a mother would say something like that to her child? Shocked I hate that bastard?'

'Just makes our job easier.'

'What's that supposed to mean?'

'Well, we'd normally ask to have a Family Liaison Officer here to help you deal with the news, but—'

'What?' Her eyes narrowed. 'What the hell's happened?'

'Vardy was murdered.'

The words didn't seem to have the slightest effect on her. Maybe she hadn't heard right. Then her eyes went out of focus. 'Good riddance.' She let out a gasp. 'What do you want me to say? That I'm sorry he's finally pissed off the wrong person? I'm only sorry his payments are going to stop now...' Her eyes went out of focus again. 'Not that it's keeping me in the lifestyle I'd like to become accustomed to.'

Don't lose her. Keep her away from reflecting on her sugar daddy's demise and her impending financial doom.

He cut into her thoughts with a sharp cough. 'I'm sorry I have to ask you this, but you didn't have anything to do with it, did you?'

Her shrug suggested she'd considered it every sleepless night since her child was born, but she shook her head. 'To be honest, I'd love to have had the privilege, but—'

Hunter's phone rang, the opening riff of Pearl Jam's *Alive* blaring out of his suit pocket. 'Sorry.' He rummaged around for the mobile.

The baby latched off his mother's breast to scream the house down.

Hunter left the room to take the call outside, killing the jangly music with a curt, 'What?'

Candy stroked her baby's bright red face and cooed at him until he calmed down enough to take her breast again.

Cullen glanced away to grant her some privacy, but she didn't seem to notice, or care. 'Candy, you were saying. About Dean?'

'I had nothing to do with it. You know that, right? That prick'd never have got close enough to let me. After he raped me—'

A sour taste filled Cullen's mouth. 'He *raped* you?'

Candy blinked away the dazed look in her eyes and focused the full force of her resentment on Cullen. 'Is that so hard to believe?' She stared at him, the exhausted baby still suckling away at her exhausted breast. 'Are you surprised that he'd want to have sex with a woman like me?'

'No, no... I had no idea. I'm so sorry.'

'Wee Stuart...' Candy gestured at the little thing, eyes half shut, chin trembling in a semi-conscious feeding instinct. She snorted, shaking her head. 'My wee Stu's the only good thing in my shitty wee life.'

Cullen said nothing, just stared at the mother and child.

'I know what you're thinking.' Candy stroked her kid's cheek. 'Why didn't she get an abortion after that bastard raped her? Why is she raising a child in this shithole?'

'No, no. Not at all. I just feel so sorry—'

'Don't insult me, you prick. I've enough to deal with as it is. Listen to me, I'll tell you the truth. I thought about an abortion. Had the appointment made, but in the end, I couldn't go through with it.'

Cullen tried to reach out to her. 'You're not the only one in this situation, you know?'

'You mean Amy Forrest, right?' The tears broke from her eyes, but she didn't brush them away. Just let them run down her cheeks like silent screams of accusation. 'He did the same thing to her. We worked together at Wonderland before she... left. Even seeing what happened to her, I just...' She looked down at her tiny child, tears welling up in her eyes as she stroked his forehead. 'I wanted to protect this little bastard. Dean couldn't ruin him as well. I wasn't going to let that happen.' A tear dropped down on the wee boy. With a quiet sniff, Candy blinked her blurry eyes clear, then ever so gently wiped the tear off the child's still face. She looked back up at Cullen with a hardness in her grey eyes, like a rock face after a thunderstorm. 'I love my son, and I promised myself that he'll have a better life than I've had. I didn't act out any of those revenge fantasies so this wee sod has a mother and that bastard kept paying for his son. If Dean ever got put away, his people would take all of his money and we'd be left with nothing. And now he's dead...' Her eyes went out of focus again as she got lost in her thoughts.

Cullen wanted to do more for her, but no helping words came to him. There weren't any.

Candy looked up at him, a child herself. Then her empty gaze dropped back to her sleeping child.

There was a soft knock on the door. It opened and Hunter stuck his head into the living room. 'Sorry, mate, the boss wants us back at the station.'

∿

'—SHOULDN'T BE HERE, SCOTT.' SHARON STARED AT CULLEN. SHE didn't even look at Hunter. 'And I thought better of you, Craig.'

Hunter cleared his throat. 'Sorry, boss, but I gave Scott Miss Broadhurst's address and took him there to follow up on a—'

She gave Hunter a thin smile. 'I'll deal with you later.'

Hunter stood there.

She jerked her head at the door. 'That means leave.' She waved Hunter away with a flick of her wrist and watched him go.

Cullen waited for the door to click shut. 'Listen, Sharon—'

'No, you listen to me. You're a DS and I'm a DI. You're in *my* office and you're messing up *my* case without my knowledge, let alone my approval.' She paused, her scornful gaze drilling into him in a way he'd never seen, even during their worst arguments. 'Have you nothing better to be getting on with these days?'

'I'm following the best lead available. Since Dean Vardy got murdered, we're—'

'What?'

'You hadn't heard?'

She was quick to recover, sitting up and tucking her hair behind her ear. 'Does Methven know you're over here?'

Cullen clenched his teeth, biting back the hurt. He breathed in and out and counted down from five. 'He knows. So does Bill Lamb.'

She held his stare for a few seconds, fury burning in her eyes. 'I hear that Livingston are catching up with you and your antics.'

'Is that why you're kicking me out? So I don't smear your lovely career?'

'What the hell, Scott?'

'Shouldn't I be asking you that? You took over my case without telling me, groomed my witness when you knew full well that we'd been forced to drop the case – all while we were living together.'

'Scott, at some point in your life, you need to stop acting like a child and just—' She looked like she was about to say more but released her fury with a sigh. 'I can't deal with you any more.' She waved at the door like he was Hunter. Just some junior cop in her office. 'Get out. I'll take this up with Methven or Lamb or whoever you're pretending to work for.'

Cullen looked at her. He thought he had so much left to say, but he just felt empty. With a nod, he turned to leave. 'I'll get my stuff later tonight.'

She looked away. 'I'd rather you cleared your crap out when I wasn't there.'

Cullen waited for her to make eye contact again. 'Well, why don't you bugger off somewhere?'

28

CULLEN CLOSED THE OFFICE DOOR LIKE HE WAS PUTTING THE LID down on a coffin. He wandered through the Sexual Offences Unit, aware of their eyes on him, but he ignored them and powered down the corridor towards the front desk, bumping through a pair of uniformed officers streaming towards him.

Hunter stood in the low murmur of the public waiting area. 'Hey, Scott. Are you—?'

Cullen walked right on by with a bland nod, then stepped through the front door without looking back. He stomped across the road, the ice-cold wind cooling his face and neck, and unlocked his car.

'Scott!' Hunter dodged through the traffic, then round the bonnet of his car. 'Wait up, mate.'

Cullen stood there, grabbing the handle, ready to open the door and get the hell out of there. His heart was hammering. But he stopped and let out a deep breath. 'What do you want, Craig?'

'Never seen DI McNeill that pissed off. What did she want from you?'

'My soul.'

Hunter grinned. 'You want to talk about it?'

'Not really.' Cullen tugged the door wide open and got in. He slumped behind the wheel and stuck his head against it.

What the hell do I do now?

The passenger door opened and Hunter got in. 'Scott, you need to—'

Cullen sat up straight and started the engine. 'You probably want to get out.'

'Where are you going?'

'To our flat. *Her* flat.' Cullen stuck the car in gear, but held the clutch. 'I'm getting my stuff.'

'Wait. She kicked you out?' Hunter smirked. 'Who'd you shag this time?'

'Craig...' Cullen turned off the engine. 'Listen, I can only apologise so many times for—'

'I know.' Hunter's smile gave way to a tired frown. 'You don't need to apologise again, okay? I'm in a good place. Start the car and let's go before Sharon catches us sneaking off together again.'

∾

'So, yeah.' Cullen kicked down to fourth and pulled into the slight gap on the fast lane and overtook the coach, settling into the rhythm of rush-hour traffic. 'I didn't see it coming. Feel like such a twat.'

Hunter narrowed his eyes. 'Where are you going to live?'

Cullen glanced around the car. 'I was checked in at Tulliallan for this course, but Lamb's chucked me off it and they've kicked me out of there. Guess I'll live out of the car for a while.'

'The Lincoln Lawyer, eh?' Hunter looked around at the midden on the back seat. 'Bad news, mate, this isn't a hotel.'

'No shit.'

Hunter cleared his throat with a loud cough. 'I'll probably regret this, but if you promise not to shag my cat, you can sleep on my sofa.'

Cullen laughed. 'Seriously? After—'

'No more apologies. Just for a few nights, mind.'

∾

Cullen trudged up the stairs to Sharon's flat, frazzled from all that stop-and-go traffic. He took a moment to stare at his key, then shook his head at his daft sentimentality. 'Come on.' He opened the door and led through the hallway into the kitchen. It looked clean for an emotional crime scene, the place where she'd ripped out his heart and stomped all over it. He fetched a roll of jumbo bin bags from the cupboard under the sink and tore off a few for Hunter. 'Just shove it in a bag and we can get out of here.'

Hunter followed him into the bedroom. 'Just like old times, when I moved my bin bags into your old place in Porty.'

'Maybe we're destined to end up together, Craig. Police Scotland's odd couple.'

'Next stop, sleeping under a bridge.'

Cullen laughed. He opened his chest of drawers and start piling his clothes into a bag.

Hunter laid his empty bags on the bed and picked up Cullen's first full one. 'Tell you what – you pack and I'll take the bags down to the car.'

CULLEN PASSED THE FINAL BAG TO HUNTER, HIS PRECIOUS STEREO ALL packed away like a pro had done it. 'Be down in a minute.'

'Take your time, mate.' Hunter frowned at the cat swarming round Cullen's feet. 'That's Chantal's cat's brother, right?'

'Something like that.' Cullen knelt in front of Sharon's cat. 'Give me a minute.'

'Sure.' Hunter's footsteps rattled in from the stairwell, the door clicking shut.

Cullen sat on the floor, stroking the purring wee thing. 'Hey, boy, I know you hate me but I'm going to miss you.'

'Ma-wow!' Fluffy did his little dance, arching his back halfway through his march around in a tight circle. 'Ma-wow!'

'I know, boy.' Cullen stroked the cat, slowly and tenderly, the fluff balling up on the laminate.

It's not just leaving him, it's a whole chapter of my life. The number of times the little guy had been patiently waiting for me when I got back in, Sharon working late in Bathgate. All the times—

Cullen got to his feet. 'See you around, Fluffy.' He tore the first key off his ring and the first tear hit his cheek. He didn't wipe it as he tore the second key off. One last look at Fluffy, sitting there, staring up at him, and he forced himself to shut the door. Then pushed the two keys through the letterbox. He wiped the tears away with the palms of his hands. Felt about three stone lighter. Then he started skipping down the stairs, catching one last 'Ma-wow!' muffled by the door.

Out on the street, Hunter stood by a double-parked car, forcing the last box onto the rammed back seat, the boot long since filled up. 'It's never just about leaving a person behind, is it?'

'No.' Cullen felt a lump in his throat, the kind you can't swallow, so he didn't bother trying. 'No, it's not. Let's get going.' He got in the car and pulled out his phone. 'I'll just text Sharon.' He stared at the phone, no idea what to say to the woman he'd once wanted to spend the rest of his life with. He sat there, discarding all the platitudes people reserve for these moments, hand-me-downs from generations of thoughtless break-ups, cast-offs from soap operas.

In the end, he typed what he felt.

'Thanks for trying with me. I loved what we had. See you around. Scott X'

CULLEN DUMPED THE TWO BIN BAGS BEHIND THE SOFA. HIS NEW BED.

Bubble lay smack bang in the middle of it, and she stayed right where she was even when Cullen settled down next to her. A cat with enough confidence for two.

Cullen tickled her tummy. 'I could use some of that. Fancy sharing it?'

Bubble meowed and turned away.

Hunter stood in the kitchen doorway, a beer bottle in his hand. 'You alright there?'

Cullen settled back on the sofa. 'This'll do fine, thanks.'

'Not what I meant, but I'm glad to know it.' Hunter poured the beer into an ornate schooner glass. 'Don't mind me.'

'You wouldn't happen to have any more, would you?'

Hunter walked over and handed Cullen the glass. 'Have this one, mate.'

Cullen nodded his thanks while he took the first sip. 'Good stuff.' Another sip. *Becoming a habit.* 'Least I can do is take you out for something to eat.'

'I don't go down on a first date.'

Cullen swallowed the mouthful of beer, careful not to spray it all over his new digs. 'I'm serious.'

'So am I.' Hunter picked up a brightly coloured leaflet from the coffee table and handed it to Cullen. 'This is decent.'

'My treat.' Cullen scanned the menu, but after a couple of seconds he placed it on the sofa next to him. 'Listen, I know you don't want me to go on about it, but... Thanks for helping me out. After all the shit I put you through with Yvonne—'

'You're right, I don't want you to go on about it. Time to put that old story to bed now. I'm over it, and I'm in a much better place with Chantal.' Hunter folded his arms, squinting down at Cullen. 'Anyway, why do you keep going on about Yvonne?'

'No real reason.' Cullen covered his embarrassment with a fake yawn, but it quickly turned into a real one. 'Jesus, I'm tired.'

'Long day, I suppose.' Hunter dropped his arms again and looked around the room. 'You know what, I'll leave you to it. I sleep at Chantal's most nights, so you can have my bed. Fresh sheets in the cupboard. Some of my brother's eggs in the kitchen if you want some breakfast.' He pointed at the menu lying on the sofa. 'And I heartily recommend the banana, mushroom and chocolate pizza.'

DAY 5

Thursday
16th February

29

CULLEN BRUSHED HARD, TRYING TO GET THE TASTE OF BANANA FROM his mouth. He spat into Hunter's sink and glanced down. A shred of mushroom sat right in the middle of his toothpaste.

What the hell?

He split his lips and said cheese, but his teeth still looked brown.

That's what I get for following Hunter's culinary recommendation. Hard enough eating the thing in the first place.

He stared at his reflection a moment longer. Could've sworn it was a stranger. The haggard face, the grey hair despite being damp from his shower, the empty eyes...

He headed into the living room with a towel around his waist and started searching the bin bags for fresh clothes.

Bubble shot out of the first one and ran over to hide under the sofa.

Little bugger.

He rooted around in the leftovers of his life, finding clean underwear, socks, and a crumpled shirt next to a washed-out Pearl Jam tee that Sharon had given him as an ironic souvenir. He swallowed hard as he tugged his pants on.

Jesus Christ. What a mess. Living out of binbags.

And I've got a day of attending Lamb's course and pretending everything's normal and my life isn't falling apart.

Could be worse. Could be in Candy's situation.

Like there's anything I can do to help her.

And he was dressed, all except his left shoe. Sticking out from under the sofa. He reached down and a grey paw batted his hand. 'Hoy.' No claws, at least. Another hit and he grabbed the shoe. He slipped it on and laced it up, then made for the front door.

Definitely needed at least four shots this morning.

He turned to lock the flat door.

A fist jabbed him in the kidneys and his cheek hit the door. Then someone hauled a bag over his head, rough canvas chafing his skin. Rougher hands yanked him down the stairwell, his feet tripping over each step, then out to the street and the rush of cold air on his neck. A strong arm wrapped around his shoulders, pulling him up and onward. Car tyres screeched inches away from his face, exhaust fumes washing over him. A door clicked open, muffled voices exchanged short commands, but his own ragged breath was deafening.

The hands let go of him and he stumbled, his shoulder hitting something solid.

'—king kill you, you—' A shout blocked out the rest.

Cullen reached up and tore off the bag, whipping his head around to catch his bearings. The harsh daylight stung his eyes, making him squint through the spots in his vision. Tears blurred his sight.

And there was Hunter, head down like a battering ram, sprinting at him.

WHAT THE HELL?

Cullen tried to run, fists clenched, loading up a big left. *Shite, shite, shite...*

But Hunter diverted his path, colliding with a massive guy in a black mask.

Batman.

Here?

Shite. He's after me?

Cullen dropped to the ground and rolled left, away from the car, away from the men slamming into each other like a two-man scrum. He felt the thud before he heard it. His skull cracking off the kerb.

Everything went black.

~

'Hey!' Slap. 'Wake up!' Another slap. 'Scott, can you hear me?'

Cullen opened his eyes. A towering figure bent over him, a shaved head leaning down low over his face. He flinched back, trying to squirm out from under the hulking stranger, striking out with flailing arms, bridging his back like a—

'Scott!'

Cullen froze. He was inside again, his hands resting on rough corduroy. 'Craig?'

Hunter was crouching in front of him. 'Who the hell did you think I was?'

'That... That guy with the black mask. He sucker-punched me. Dragged me outside to shove me in a car and...' Cullen narrowed his eyes as the memory came back into focus. 'You fought him off. Did you see who it was?'

'No idea.' Hunter straightened up on the couch, averting his eyes. 'He jumped in the car and got away when I checked on you because you... knocked yourself out.'

'Doesn't sound like me at all.' Cullen cocked his head, and the throbbing pain in his temples got even worse. He rubbed his sore head. 'That pizza was rank, by the way.'

Hunter plonked himself on the sofa. 'You've got no taste.'

'Were they definitely dressed like Batman?'

'I'd say it's more like Daredevil, to be honest.'

'Dare-who?'

'You don't watch much Netflix, then?' Hunter reached over for a phone, tapped at the screen and held it up. 'Like this?'

A man stood in front of a New York skyline, wearing a dark-red combat suit, just showing his mouth. Kind of like Batman, but red. And without the cape. 'That's what you saw?'

'Without this.' Hunter covered his mouth. 'And you can thank me, you know?'

~

'Sodding, sodding hell.' Methven glanced from one to the other. 'You're serious?'

'As serious as—'

Methven's phone rang. He picked it up and answered it with wild eyes. 'Sorry, Carolyn, I promise I'll call you back.' He listened for a couple of seconds, then nodded. 'Understood, and thank you very much. Five minutes.' He put the phone down and leaned back on his leather desk chair, frowning at Cullen then Hunter. 'Are you one hundred percent?'

Cullen nodded. 'I didn't see him, to be honest. He was as big as the guy I fought in McLintock's garden.'

Methven just kept staring at him, his rapid thoughts evident in his flickering eyelids.

'I got back and saw him shoving Cullen into a van.' Hunter cleared his throat. 'Just in time. Managed to fight him off. The guy was *built*. And he knew at least three martial arts I don't.'

Methven locked his gaze on Cullen. 'Why did this assailant attack *you*?'

'No idea.' Cullen sat back in the chair. His head throbbed again. *A self-inflicted knock-out. What an idiot.* 'The only reason I can think of is that I've been digging into the... angle we discussed.'

Methven narrowed his eyes. 'Oh?'

Cullen motioned at Hunter. 'Craig's worked a Sexual Offences Unit case against Vardy. The only witness changed her mind and refused to testify.'

'Which happened with our sodding case and Amy Forrest.'

'Among many others. What's worse, sir, is there's women... Christ, there's a ton of women... Look, we found another case where Vardy has fathered another child... by rape. Christine Broadhurst.'

Methven groaned. 'Candy.'

'Right.' Cullen paused to catch his breath. 'The sick bastard relied on the fact they'd keep the babies, made them dependent on his low payments. And if they came forward, he'd cut off the child support payments.'

'Makes my sodding blood boil.' Methven looked at him with a stark coldness, then drew a sharp breath. 'It's easy to see how a frustrated policeman might have decided to take this case into his own hands, isn't it?'

Cullen pointed at his own chest. 'You mean me?'

'I don't know. I could mean somebody else.' Methven glanced at Hunter.

Cullen wanted to throttle the prick. 'It's neither of us.'

'Then who is it?'

Cullen clicked his fingers. 'Wilkinson.'

'What? You can't think—'

'No, I don't.' Cullen groaned. 'But Lamb said he was running a joint operation with Wilkinson's team. Same story. Witness dropped off the face of the earth.'

'So why am I only hearing about this now?'

'I've had a lot on my mind, sir.' Cullen got to his feet, fighting hard to ignore the dull throb at the back of his skull. 'We need to speak to him.'

Paula Zabinski looked up with a dark glower. 'What do you want?'

'Charming.' Cullen leaned over the desk and nodded over at the dark office behind her and its oppressive door-entry system that screamed GET OUT. 'Wilko in?'

She coughed when she saw Methven behind Cullen. 'Sir.'

Methven beamed at her. 'Oh, hello there, Paula. You look well.'

'And you look very dashing today, sir.'

Methven's face turned a deep purple. He cleared his throat with a tight cough. 'Is DI Wilkinson in today?'

'Nope. He said he's working from home.'

Methven's face went blank, his voice a hoarse whisper. 'He's *what?*'

'The sodding cheek of the man.' Methven rattled over the cobbles into the heart of Dean Village, past rows and rows of stone terraces and two-storey cottages, thick green ivy growing into the eaves, even in February. 'He's a sodding policeman. He can't just work from *home*.' He glared out of the windscreen, railing at the passing picture-postcard scene.

Cullen pointed out of the window. 'Anywhere round here.'

'Right, okay.' Methven slammed on the brakes, forcing Cullen's chest hard into the belt. 'What the hell?' Methven flew out of the door and raced along the street, fists clenched at his side.

Christ on a bike.

Cullen got out and jogged after him. Then stopped dead.

Just down the street, two guys in black masks were beating the shit out of a man lying on the ground.

Cullen hit the cobbles, running after Methven.

Tyres screeched to a halt ahead of the melee. A red Porsche SUV, the driver's eyes wide.

A man raced past the car, heading for the fighting men.

Wearing a Batman costume.

30

THE STRANGER IN THE BATMAN COSTUME CHOPPED DOWN THE OTHER two goons with sharp kicks to the backs of their knees, felling them like trees. He struck their heads with his elbows on the way down. They sprawled on the pavement, out cold, as the vigilante rounded on Wilkinson lying defenceless on the ground. He drew a long knife, the blade catching the cold winter light.

Cullen raced over, knowing he couldn't get there in time. The knife sliced high above the vigilante's head and came back down.

BANG!

Methven smashed into the masked man, low and hard, taking him clean off his feet. The knife clattered on the pavement, and Methven drove his shoulder into the guy's hip. The vigilante dug his heels in and dropped his weight, right on top of Methven, landing with a thud.

The vigilante was up like a shot, twisting around in one smooth motion and racing off down the pavement.

Cullen sped after him. After a few hard steps he was close enough to think about reaching him with a dive, but the vigilante was fast for his size, feinting this way and that. Batman put on a burst of speed and shot away from Cullen, clearing round a bend and disappearing.

Cullen took the same turn and stopped. An empty close. The

guy stood with his back to him, facing a garage door. Not a close, but a private driveway. A dead end, either way.

Cullen caught his breath. Couldn't speak. A strained moan came from behind. Cullen spun around. Methven was staggering towards him on unsteady legs, his pain as easy to see as it was to hear.

Cullen turned back and caught a fist in his stomach. The breath left him in a retching hiss as he dropped to his knees.

The man in black sidestepped Cullen and took a swift step towards Methven. Kicked him right in the balls. Hard. Methven sunk to his knees with a squeal.

The vigilante took one last look at Cullen then disappeared around the corner.

Wilkinson was sitting on the pavement outside his cottage, shaking his big head. 'Did you get him?'

'Does it sodding look—' Methven winced, forcing himself to lean against the wall. 'We sodding lost him!'

'The pair of you! You had him outnumbered!'

Cullen closed his eyes and swallowed bile. Then he opened his eyes. 'Methven distracted me.'

'I did no such—'

'You did. I heard you wheezing like Darth Vader and—'

'You let him get away. You pair of pricks.' Wilkinson shot to his feet and stood over the goons lying on the pavement. 'Who the hell is this?'

Cullen just wanted to lie down next to them and go to sleep. 'You believe me now?'

Methven bent over with pain, hands on his knees. 'I do.'

What the hell do we do now?

Wilkinson started kicking the goon. 'Who are you? Eh?'

Cullen stepped over and wrapped his right forearm around Wilkinson's neck. 'Stop it!' He waited until Wilkinson went limp. 'Let's get these bastards to the nearest interview room.'

WILKINSON FLINCHED, HIS EYES FLICKERING, HIS FINGERS FLEXING ON the table top. Looked like he was worried what he might do to the lowlife who had kicked him when he was down.

So Cullen took the lead. 'Well then, Mr Gallagher, are you saying you're not the mastermind of this operation?'

Gallagher nodded, his moist jowls flapping. The flabby skin folds around his face and neck wobbled, like an obese pug at a feeding frenzy. His mate next door with Methven and Buxton looked much more of a fighter. He was the leader. Or the driver.

Cullen leaned his elbows on the table and spoke into the microphone. 'For the benefit of the recording, Mr Gallagher nodded. Why did you attack DI Wilkinson?'

Gallagher looked him square in the eye. 'Vardy.' The answer was out before he could clamp his mouth shut. Wide-eyed, breathing hard, sounding close to hyperventilating. Then he gave up, slumping back in his chair. 'We were upset, you know? Upset that you and...' He jerked his head towards Wilkinson. 'You got Vardy killed, so we wanted to get revenge. Nothing personal, like.'

A knock on the door. DI Lennox stuck his head through, his gaze locked on Wilkinson. 'Sir, a word outside?'

Wilkinson hauled himself out of his chair.

'Interview suspended at nine forty-six.' Cullen got up and followed Wilkinson through to the observation suite.

Lennox gave him a nod. 'I'm very sorry, Paul, but my DCI says you need to be interviewed.'

'I'm in the middle of one here, you pillock.'

'You're a suspect for the vigilante killings.'

Silence.

'But...' Cullen raised his arms in the air. 'The vigilante pulled a knife on Wilko. Would've killed him if,' he looked at Methven, 'if DI Methven hadn't stopped him. Right?'

Methven pursed his lips. 'That's one way of looking at it.'

'What? But you were there. You saved Wilko's life.'

'I didn't need any saving, you—'

'Enough!' Lennox cut through with a sharp cough. 'This is why we need to establish exactly what happened. You can't just haul people in for interview as you see fit. This is our case, so...' He looked at Wilkinson and swept his hand in the direction of the door, like a gallant host at a dinner party. 'Shall we?'

Wilkinson clamped his mouth shut, straightened his suit jacket with a snap and marched out of the room.

'I'll be in touch.' Lennox left them to it.

Cullen watched the door shut. 'Why did you lie to Lennox?'

'Are you saying that DI Wilkinson can't possibly be the vigilante?'

'What? You were there, you saw—'

'I saw Wilkinson get attacked by the two idiots in those rooms. For all we know, the fellow in the Batman costume could've been a stooge dressed to look the part of the Vardy murderer and thus take suspicion off Wilkinson.'

'What? Why would—' Cullen broke off. 'You saw this vigilante, right? He was *brutal*. Exactly like the guy I fought.'

Methven stiffened, his usually cold smile turning sub-zero in a heartbeat. He clenched his teeth. 'Sergeant, this isn't our case.'

'Someone bloody attacked me! They tried to murder Wilko!'

'And DI Lennox and his team will get to the bottom of the matter.' Methven pulled himself up to standing with a tight wince. He put his hand in his pocket. 'Now, I'm sending you back to where you should be.'

'What? Yesterday you were all, oh let's catch this guy. Now you're—'

'Purple sodding buggery, Cullen! Get back to sodding Tulliallan. Now!'

31

Cullen opened the door and shuffled to the back of the seminar room, head down.

Lamb locked eyes on him, giving a slight shake of his head. Abject disapproval.

Bloody Methven's already got to him.

Lamb turned to smile at a female DS from Dundee. 'Now, Vicky, as you were saying?'

'—suspect in for interview.' Lamb stopped. 'Am I boring you?'

Cullen kept staring out of the window, over Kincardine to the Forth. 'I'm listening.'

'Really?' Lamb exhaled slowly, then looked around the room. 'It's your job as sergeants to make sure you've got a solid basis for the interview. And it's your responsibility to implement your inspector's interview strategy. Now, those of you who want to progress to that level, you need to start drafting the strategy, ready for your inspector to revise and sign off.'

Cullen's phone buzzed. Just once, meaning a text. He slid it out of his pocket and glanced at it under the table, checking that the great eye of DI Lamb was focusing on someone else. It was.

The text was from Sharon.

'I'm glad you're okay with it being over. Maybe we can still be friends. In time. X'

In time?

Cullen felt empty. He stared at the screen until it went blurry, wishing their relationship had meant something – that those years hadn't just slipped by.

'Okay, tomorrow we'll pick up on the latest techniques for post-Cadder lawyer management.' Lamb clapped his hands, his smile cooling as his gaze settled on Cullen. 'See you all tomorrow morning.'

Cullen clocked a couple of Perth DSs filing out of the room, mouths twisted like they'd taken in about as much as Cullen had. Square root of bugger all. He followed them out, trying to figure out if there was any point in replying to Sharon's message.

But Lamb was loitering outside the classroom door, arms folded. 'You okay?'

The bruise at the back of Cullen's skull was now a big lump. And a bloody sore one at that. 'I'll live.'

'Fancy a cheeky pint?'

'Eh? You just gave me a doing in front of the class and now you're asking if I want a beer?'

'Scott, if you've taken as many courses as I have, you'd realise that you need a friendly face to rip the pish out of. Half of that lot were asleep, the rest were too stupid to get the gist of what I was saying.' Lamb patted his arm. 'And there's a good boozer in the village that isn't full of cops.'

'I've got the car.'

'One won't hurt.'

∼

THE BARMAN GAVE A SOUR SMILE WHEN HE SAW CULLEN APPROACH. 'Gentlemen?'

Cullen tapped on the guest pump marked Paulaner Hefe-Weißbier Dunkel. 'What's that like?'

'You need a hand pronouncing it?'

'Just want a heads up if it tastes like cat's piss.'

The barman bristled, a deep frown creasing his forehead. 'It's a very sophisticated little number. Comes to us all the way from the foothills of the Bavarian Alps and, oh my, does this beer come with a thick and creamy head. Aromas of toasted bread, caramel and—'

'A pint of that, then.'

The barman's frown disappeared in a flash as he started pouring, head down. The beer trickled into the glass like he was milking a metallic cow. He smacked his lips on the final spurt and frowned at Lamb. 'Sir?'

'Bottle of Punk, cheers.'

The barman headed to the fridges with an ambiguous smile playing around the corners of his meaty lips.

Lamb sat next to Cullen and leaned in close. 'What. The. Hell?'

'You saw his shudder too, then?' Cullen stretched his lips out, the only thing he could do to stop pissing himself laughing.

The barman came back from the fridge and handed Lamb his bottle.

Lamb swapped it for a tenner. 'Keep the change.'

The barman topped up Cullen's pint with another shudder. As promised, it did have a creamy head. *Don't want to think about that.* The barman passed it over the bar and moved over to serve a group at the other end.

Lamb took a suck of his beer with a curious frown. 'Beginning to regret leaving Tulliallan.'

'Never mind.' Cullen clinked glasses with Lamb, then perched on a stool at the bar. 'To a speedy discovery of Batman's identity.' He took a hearty sip and wiped his mouth with the back of his hand. 'That's not bad, actually.'

'So.' Lamb took a sip from his bottle. 'How are the Livingston lot getting on?'

'They seem to be fitting up Wilko.'

'What?' Lamb shook his head. 'Wilko? The guy's a *shambles.* Living a double life as a vigilante takes a lot of organisation, never mind the physical fitness he clearly hasn't got.'

'Like you?'

'I wish this was muscle.' Lamb patted his flat stomach. 'The amount I drink, I'd fall arse over tit doing any of that kung fu shite.' Another swig of beer. 'I fancy someone like Hunter. Maybe even Methven.'

'Shut up.'

'Serious. All those triathlons. He does krav maga. Not that it stops him getting booted in the goolies all the time.'

Cullen nodded. 'Craig does that too. Krav thingy.'

'See? Loads of suspects. But not Wilkinson.' With a thoughtful look in his eyes, Lamb drained his bottle. 'Right, I need to love you and leave you.'

'What? We've only just got here?'

'Got to get home to see the kids before they go to bed.' Lamb buttoned up his jacket. 'Toodeloo, amigo.'

Cullen watched him leave. *God knows where he finds the energy for his banter, and his parenting, and his marriage, and his daily gym visits.*

He stared into his pint, barely dented.

Left holding the baby.

Maybe I need to make a few changes in my life, now that Sharon's made the big one for me.

He got out his phone and stared at her message. So hard not to read everything into those words.

The door opened again.

Lamb, returning with some Columbo shite.

But it wasn't Lamb.

Yvonne walked across the pub, oblivious to the leering looks of the elderly perverts watching her every step. She sat on the empty bar stool next to Cullen, like it had her name on it. Like they hadn't parted on awkward terms. Like she hadn't been investigating him for being a bloody vigilante. Like it was the natural thing to do to lean in close, place a tender hand on the back of his hot neck and whisper into his ear, 'Bill said I'd find you here.'

'That bloody—'

Her hand tightened on his collar. 'Is it true you were attacked?' She leaned back far enough to acknowledge his nod. She caressed his scratches and gazed deep into his eyes. 'I looked for you in the bar last night.'

Cullen cleared his throat with a self-conscious cough. 'Truth is, Sharon and I broke up. I'm staying on a mate's couch for the foreseeable.' He glanced away, every inch the romantic failure. 'Sorry, but I—'

'Shh.' She touched his cheekbone. Then kissed him.

And kept kissing him.

CULLEN WAS STILL PANTING, HIS PENIS ACHING AS HE REMOVED THE condom. Some semen leaked on his hand as he tied it up and wrapped it in a hankie.

Yvonne drew the duvet over her naked body, as cold and hard and remote as the moon shining through the glass.

What the hell?

He gazed at her in that white light and he felt a chill, and it had nothing to do with the draft coming from the window. 'You okay?'

She craned her neck to look at him. 'I'm just scared.'

Cullen sat up. 'What did I do?'

She averted her eyes. Then rolled away from him. 'Nothing. Just... The last time... You didn't even remember what we did.'

'Hey.' He shuffled over to her and spooned into her back, his flaccid cock touching her buttock, wrapping his arms around her, his hand on her smooth belly. 'I won't forget this time. Believe me.' He took a deep breath, pinning his stare at the duvet bunched up on her hips. 'I was a total dick back then. You must've had a screw loose to go to bed with me.'

'Or three bottles of wine in my stomach.'

'Just three?' He laughed. 'I'm serious. I mean, we hardly knew each other and it pissed off Craig. And I've just come out of a relationship that never stood a chance because, if I'm honest, I don't think Sharon and I ever loved each other, and now I'm rambling, I know, but I just want to reassure you that I'm not the same idiot I was back then, and who would want to share their life with an idiot who—'

'Listen.' Yvonne shuffled round and stared at him. 'Let's take this one day at a time, okay?'

'Right.' Cullen collapsed onto the bed, his damp hair sticking to the pillow. 'It's not easy.'

'For you or me?'

'I was meaning me.'

'You're the last man I had sex with.'

'Shut up.' Cullen frowned at her, but she looked deadly serious. 'Really?'

'I mean, I've been with like ten women in that time.'

Cullen felt his gut flutter. 'Do you think that's funny?'

'Don't you?'

'Are you joking?'

'Yes, Scott. Well, about the women. Not about the men. Why?'

'A few years back, I found out that—' Cullen shook his head. 'It doesn't matter. But I'm surprised it's been that long for you.'

'You think I'm a slag?'

'Hardly. It's just... You know.'

'What, you think I look sexy so I could just shag anyone?'

'I mean, you're smart and funny and anyone would be lucky to have you.'

'Right.' She bit her lip. 'Don't get me wrong. I've had dates and drunken fumbles and stuff. But there's something that's stopped me taking it any further.' She just looked at him for a few long moments, warm and friendly but no more than that. 'I wanted someone who I could see myself being with.'

'You can see yourself being with me?'

She grinned. 'One day at a time, but yes. I see myself being with you, you big weird failure.'

He laughed, loud, but it was cut off by her biting his bottom lip. She straddled his hips, grinding herself into his abdomen, biting and kissing and reaching over for another condom.

DAY 6

Friday
17th February

32

'WHY SO TONGUE-TIED?' YVONNE GRINNED AT HIM OVER HER COFFEE mug. The Tulliallan canteen buzzed around them with early-morning chatter, a curtain of noise keeping the world out.

Cullen peered back at her over his own cup. The two Dundee detectives firing into their breakfast at the next table seemed oblivious, but this was the worst possible place for a secret workplace romance. 'You know exactly why I'm tongue-tied.'

The mug blocked her mouth.

He sneaked a few glances over both shoulders before leaning across the table and lowering his voice even further. 'Fancy a drink after the course?'

'Wish I was doing the course, Scott.' She kept the smile in her eyes but started shaking her head. 'I'm full-time on that Vardy–McLintock case. You're lucky I got away when I did last night, otherwise...'

'Any news?'

'You know I can't talk about it...'

'You don't think I'm a suspect, do you?'

Yvonne leaned back and crossed her arms, her lips tight. 'Are you only interested in me because—'

'God no.' Cullen raised his palms, unsure where to look as her stare became even harder. 'I meant your team must know enough to clear me of suspicion and—'

'Scott, I can't talk about it. We've handed that side off to Professional Standards and Ethics. But the way you're going, I might have to report you. If I told you which suspects we've taken from the list, it wouldn't take a genius to figure out who we've got in our sights and... I don't want to create a conflict of interest for you so—'

Conflict of interest? 'What do you mean—'

'Right, back to work.' She got up from the table. 'I'll maybe see you tonight. Maybe.'

'Okay.'

Cullen's phone lit up on the table. A text, and if it was notifying him it meant it was Methven.

'THE TEACHING STAFF FOR TODAY'S FINAL SEMINAR SERIES HAS CALLED IN SICK, SO THE COURSE HAS BEEN CALLED OFF. ST LEONARDS NOW.'

CULLEN FOLLOWED YVONNE INTO THE ST LEONARDS INCIDENT Room. 'So, let me know when you finish, aye?'

The slyest wink, then she set off towards the desks at the back, where Lennox and the Livingston MIT lurked.

'Not so fast, Sergeant Flockhart.' Methven blocked her path. With a click of his tongue, he held out a sheet of paper. 'There. I knew we'd get a match.'

Cullen glanced at Yvonne, then at the paper Methven was holding in front of his nose. 'What are you talking about, sir?'

Methven stared at Cullen, wide-eyed, waving the paper around. 'This!'

Cullen took it and scanned the header. 'DNA results?'

'Well done, Sergeant. You can read.'

Cullen kept studying the report. 'You have a match on a tissue sample to a Jason Gallagher.' He looked up. 'Why does that ring a bell?'

'He's one of the goons who attacked DI Wilkinson.'

'Right. The one I interviewed.'

'Quite.' Methven snatched the page back and passed it to Yvonne. She didn't take it. He snorted. 'Mr Gallagher was arrested for a string of housebreakings in Colinton and Murrayfield ten years ago. And he was stupid enough to leave a skin flake on the gun he used to kill Sammy McLean.' He paused, frowning at Cullen. 'Our witness in the murder of Xena Farley. The reason Dean sodding Vardy was bailed.'

Cullen got that sickening tightness at the pit of his stomach. 'Has anybody found Amy Forrest yet?'

'Amy Forrest...?' Yvonne shot Cullen a curious glance. 'Excuse me, but who is Amy Forrest?'

Methven skipped over to his desk and started sifting through his files, a dour look on his face. 'She's where it all started... going to testify against Vardy... honey trap... of course it went south and her friend Xena got killed... oh, and he raped her and she had the kid.'

Yvonne gawked at Cullen. 'There's another witness who went to ground?'

'Are you hard of hearing, Sergeant?' Methven lifted his laptop to peer underneath.

Yvonne pinned the laptop down with both hands. 'Why has nobody mentioned her to us?'

'How should I know?' Methven looked up from his paperwork. 'That wasn't my sodding case.'

Yvonne bit her tongue. 'Right.'

Methven turned back to his stacks of papers and resumed his search as though she had already left.

Dismissed.

Cullen took the hint and gestured for her to follow him. He sat at one of the free desks at the far side of the room and logged in to the desktop computer.

She leaned against the desk, eyes fixed on the varnished wood. 'Is he always like that?'

'This is him on a good day.' Cullen searched through the case file on the computer and found what he was looking for. 'Yvonne, tell me you've seen this?'

She was still focused on the desk. 'Such a prick.'

'Look at this.' Cullen pointed at the document open on the screen. 'Amy's disappearance *is* logged in the case file.'

'Wait, so you're defending Methven now?'

'No.' Cullen slumped back in the seat. 'Look, we had a few leads on her, I swear.' And it hit him.

The text, saying she hadn't killed Vardy.

I sent it to the phone squad for analysis and haven't heard anything back.

'It's not here.' Cullen clicked and searched but drew a blank. 'Someone should've added the telephony report. Let me see who... Oh, shite.'

She leaned down to get a better look. 'What?'

'Gimme a sec.' Cullen got out his phone and dialled a favourited number. Listening to the ring tone. 'Come on, come on.'

'Scott, who are you—'

'Alright, mate, what's up?' Buxton, yawning. Sounded like he was outside, somewhere windy, which didn't narrow it down any. 'Thought I saw your car in the—'

'You free to talk?'

'Shoot.'

'Alright, I'm going through the case file on Amy Forrest's disappearance. Did Tommy Smith get back to you on the phone search?'

'Tell me about it.' The heavy clump of him climbing a staircase. 'Why does he want a boy from Hammersmith to join his Scotch Poetry Club?'

'Si, why is the report not in the file?'

'What?' Buxton stopped walking, his voice rattling round a tight space. 'I filed it and opened an action.'

Cullen switched windows and scanned the list of open actions. 'Si, it's not here. Did you close it?'

'This is what happens when you get a lowly DC to do your bidding, know what I mean?'

Cullen opened up the closed list. There. Completed, no further action. He tapped on the audit record. DC Simon Buxton. 'Si, it says you closed it.'

'That's bullshit.'

'Are you sure?'

'Of course I'm sure. Are you saying I bungled this?'

'I'm asking if it's maybe slipped your mind, that's all.'

'Well you can bugger off.'

'It says no further action.'

'Well, that's bollocks. Look, I told Lamb and Methven about this. Wilko was there too. This is utter bullshit!'

Need to get him to bloody focus. 'Si, what was the lead?'

'Tommy found a few calls from that phone. Matched it to a cell site in Dalry. You'll never—'

'Dalry?' Cullen's grip tightened on the phone, as Yvonne's glare tightened on him. 'Jesus, Si, you should've—'

Buxton's footsteps stopped. 'Get over yourself.'

'Look, Si. Whatever. We'll tidy this up later. Who was Amy calling?'

~

'YOU THINK SOMEONE ALTERED THE RECORD?' YVONNE GOT OUT onto Lothian Road. 'Really?'

'That's way above our pay grade.' Cullen joined her on the pavement and walked through the throng of morning commuters, almost bumping into a thickset man and his pre-school son as they marched along the road. 'You'd have to be at DI level to have the clearance to alter the record, but it would still show on the audit trail.'

'Unless your mate just mishandled a lead.'

Cullen stopped walking. 'Sorry, but I trust Si Buxton.'

'So you're choosing between an implausible excuse for incompetence or a conspiracy theory?'

Cullen frowned. 'Hanlon's Razor, right?'

'Hanlon's what?'

'Never attribute to malice that which can be adequately explained by stupidity. Or incompetence.'

'That's my point.'

'Well, Si's not incompetent.'

'Scott, if you're protecting him that'll look bad on you.'

'I know, but... You guys are investigating this as a police officer committing vigilante retribution, right?'

Yvonne started walking again. 'Right.'

'Well, this fits. A good cop opened an action on HOLMES – a credible lead against finding a witness against Vardy. And someone covered it up.'

'Or Buxton made an arse of it.'

'I'll accept that once we've got to the bottom of it.' Cullen stopped outside the strip joint – even more depressing in the morning gloom. The neon pole dancer in the front window was switched off – robbed of her glowing promise. He stepped around the over-stuffed bins on the kerb and knocked on the door. 'This place makes me sick.'

Yvonne was peering inside. 'I quite like a good titty bar.'

'What?'

'Of course I don't.' She laughed. 'What's up with you?'

'I just have a problem with lesbians.'

'What the hell?'

'It's nothing like that.' Cullen bit his lip. 'Look, my ex. Jesus, I never thought I'd say that... Sharon, she had a fling with a woman, before we got together. Made me question a few things about her.'

'Sounds like you were right to.' She caressed his arm, her brow knotted with concern. Then she was all business again, her forehead smooth. 'It's the punters I feel sorry for. Lonely posties and oil-rig workers. All confused by these lovely ladies coming up to them, rather than the other way round.'

Movement inside. The closed sign shifted to the side and a pair of beady eyes peered out. That bouncer, Kenny, or the other one, grunting as he clocked Cullen. The door flew open and the lumbering Neanderthal stepped out onto the street – his arms looking even more inflated, almost ready to burst. 'What?'

'It's Kenny, right?' Cullen smiled like he was greeting an old friend. 'Just wondering if Katie Douglas is in?'

Kenny spotted Yvonne joining them and gave her a frown. 'What's this about?'

'Just need a word with her.'

'This about the boss?'

'Trying to find his killer, aye.'

Kenny smacked a fist into the opposing palm. 'Any chance I can get a minute in the room with the guy?'

'You know there's not.'

Kenny gave a sad sigh. 'Still like to offer my services.' Then his look darkened. 'Just make sure you catch him, right?'

'That's the plan. So is Katie in?'

Kenny cracked his knuckles. 'Did she kill him?'

'No, but she might help us find who did.'

The calculus worked its way through Kenny's brain. He could deny any knowledge, then find Katie and ask her a few hard questions. But if anything happened to her, then he was prime suspect. And he had the look of a man who had experience of that. 'I've got her address somewhere. Wee flat on Dalry Road.'

THE STAIRWELL HAD BEEN CLEANED ALREADY THAT MORNING, DRYING water puddling on the marble steps. Cullen climbed up and gave the flat door a sharp double knock.

It opened to a crack and a woman stood there, just in her bra and knickers. Tall, heavily tanned, with dark tattoos covering most of her skin. Her eyes widened and she looked ready to run.

Cullen grabbed the door handle and burst into the room. A bog-standard one-bed flat – kitchen on one wall, sofa and telly by the window, two doors off.

The young woman flattened her back against one of the doors, her eyes wide, staring at Cullen and Yvonne. 'Get out!' Then she folded her arms over her chest. 'Get the hell out of here!'

Yvonne took three quick steps towards the girl and flashed her warrant card. 'DS Flockhart. This is DS Cullen.' She scanned the room with a cold gaze, then focused her attention on the stripper, staring her right in the eye. 'Who are you hiding behind that door, Katie?'

'What?'

'You heard me.'

'Nobody.'

'Don't bullshit me. You are Katie Douglas, right?'

Katie muttered something under her breath, her eyes darting around the room in search of some excuse to get the police out as fast as possible. Whatever she was hiding, she had no intention of giving it up without a fight.

A high-pitched baby cry came through the door behind her.

Yvonne walked up to Katie, a single jerk of the head enough to make her step aside. She opened the door and stood still, rooted to the spot.

Cullen jogged across to her to peer over her shoulder.

A naked boy stood up in a playpen, holding the wooden bars with his tiny fists, his face red from screaming, his eyes swollen with tears. His playpen covered in shit. The smell coming off him in the sweltering room was awful, the sight worse. Somehow, he had got his nappy off and writhed about in his own excrement before getting a hold of the bars and pulling himself up. A birthmark surrounded his right eyebrow.

It was Zak.

Amy's son.

33

CULLEN STARED AT THE WEE GUY, TOO SHOCKED BY THE SIGHT OF the mess he was in to do anything about it.

Yvonne snapped out of it faster. She walked over to a Las Vegas make-up mirror framed with light bulbs, grabbed a dressing gown off the chair and swaddled Zak in it.

The boy's tiny chest heaved in a breathless screaming fit, but he was too tired to keep up the high-energy protest for long, his screams giving way to feeble cries and convulsions. Soon, he'd calmed down enough for her to cradle him in her arms and carry him out of the room. 'The truth. Now.'

Katie tottered over to the make-up chair and slumped down, wrapping her arms around herself. 'Amy left him with me last night. Said she just had to make a quick house call. Back in an hour. The wee one was asleep and I was already off work, so I agreed to mind him. But she didn't come back and I'm running late for my shift.'

'You didn't think to call it in?'

Katie dropped her gaze to her bare feet. 'I waited overnight, even fed the little sod and turned up the heating to make sure he wouldn't get cold, only that broke the thermostat and the heater went so hot it got too much and I had to take his clothes off to make sure he wouldn't overheat and...'

'Where is she?'

'Search me.' Katie took a deep breath. 'She turned up the other night, saying her boyfriend battered her and she needed a place to stay, so her and Zak were on my couch.'

Cullen glanced at the wee one. *Welcome to the club, mate.*

Katie caught his look but misread it. 'Don't think I neglected Zak.'

'I'm not—'

'He was fine, honest to God, but I didn't know he'd get this upset so fast. And I was going to call the police, even though Amy told me not to...' She broke off, still staring at her feet.

'Katie, it's okay. I'm sure she's grateful to you for minding Zak. But you can help us by telling us where she went and who she went to see.' He smiled at her, battling the urge to shake the answer out of her.

She started nodding. 'Let me think...' She scrunched up her young face, thinking hard. Then clicked her fingers. 'She had a trick. An escort gig?'

'Who with?'

'Can't mind. But it was weird. She had to dress as Wonder Woman.'

Another superhero.

'I mean, I phoned the hotel, but they say there's no answer in the room.'

Yvonne stopped at the traffic lights in front of the Glasshouse, the church façade buried in a modern glass box housing a leisure complex. Cinema, bars, a nightclub, even a gym. 'This is weird.'

'What is?' The lights turned green and Cullen started across the road. 'Working together again?'

'Right. Methven and Lennox don't know we're doing this. And we're doing it your way. All cowboy.'

'I seem to remember a lot of reverse cowgirl.'

She stopped by the hotel's front door, her glower like a slap in the face. 'We can't talk about any of that on the clock, okay?'

'I know. Sorry. Look, I've been there before. It's not easy. Sorry.'

'Don't forget it.' She slipped inside the hotel.

Cullen followed her in and joined her at the reception desk.

'Yes.' She put her warrant card back in her pocket. 'The name was Kevin.'

The pretty boy in the slick suit squinted at his computer, tinkling the keyboard like a virtuoso pianist. He looked down his nose at Yvonne. 'Ah yes, we have one Kevin Jones staying with us. Shall I call up to—?'

'Just give us the room number.'

THE LIFT DOORS SLID OPEN AND CULLEN LED DOWN THE CORRIDOR, waiting before he knocked on the door.

Chances are, Amy didn't come back for her son because the job went bad.

He waited a few seconds before knocking. The door inched open.

Cullen glanced at Yvonne – could see they were both thinking the same thing.

Door ajar, crime in progress.

He followed her into the room, scanning the spacious lounge area for signs of violence. No overturned tables, no smashed glass on the hardwood floors, nobody rampaging through the suite wielding an axe. Gossamer curtains flickered over wide floor-to-ceiling windows, the slight breeze losing the fight with the oppressive heat in the room. Made Cullen sweat. A pile of cushions lay on the floor, behind a massive couch with its back to the door. He went over and pushed aside the soft furnishings.

No dead body, just more cushions and a used condom. He checked the couch for anything else suspicious. Nothing. The matt maroon leather sofa would've camouflaged any traces of blood anyway.

The room was empty. Spotless.

'Come here.' Yvonne was by the door.

Cullen joined her.

Hanging from a coat peg, next to a black mac, was half a Wonder Woman costume— spangly blue-and-white shorts. A pair of golden knee-high boots lay on the floor.

She walked over to the open bedroom door but not through it. She stared into the room. 'Shite.'

Cullen stepped over, and his breath caught in his throat.

Blood-soaked sheets pulled to the floor, all tangled up around an otherwise naked man, his throat sliced open.

Hamish Williams.

34

'Everybody knows that these wanky boutique hotels are turned over by professional cleaners every four minutes.' Anderson was on his knees, brushing and dusting by Cullen's feet. Two of his SOCOs bustled around, lit up by flashes from the photographer. 'And after the precautions taken at the last two crime scenes, we can be sure the murderer left a clean room behind anyway.'

Jimmy Deeley mumbled into his Dictaphone, facing away from Cullen, his notes out of earshot.

Hamish Williams lay at the foot of the bed, his limbs twisted in the sheets, his eyes glazed over, staring up at the ceiling like a dead fish lying on a stall at a seaside market. And the smell wasn't too far off, either. Deep lacerations criss-crossed his naked body, the blood seeping into the stark white sheets, staining them a rusty brown now it had dried. Some of that brown came from another source, judging by the stink.

All the hallmarks of the same killer as Vardy and McLintock. And the same ferocious rage.

'CULLEN!' A suited figure stood in the bedroom doorway, pointing a trembling finger at the far side of the room and Yvonne who was talking to a SOCO over by the window. Methven got in Cullen's face, his crime-scene mask frosted with stale breath. 'Why did you bring *her* with you?'

'Sergeant Flockhart brought me—'

'Get out, now.' Methven took a step into the room. 'Both of you!'

Yvonne just looked at him, her face as unreadable as Methven's mask. Then something seemed to click in there. She glanced at Cullen, back at Methven, and nodded. 'Sir.' She walked out of the room, leaving the door open behind her.

Cullen switched his focus back to Methven. 'What's got into you?'

'She shouldn't be here. And I told you to GET OUT!'

Cullen clenched his fists, ready to smack him one. *Sod it, that's just what the prick wants.* So he let go of his anger and walked away.

'Eh, guys?' Anderson was lying on the floor, pointing under the bed. 'There's a woman down here.'

Methven's jaw dropped. 'Dead?'

'No, no.' Anderson shifted onto his side, both hands up. 'Come on out. It's okay.'

A dishevelled ponytail of peroxide blonde hair appeared from under the bed, then naked white shoulders inched out, followed by a naked white bum and a golden bodice, barely covering her chest. Amy Forrest looked up.

Cullen grabbed one of the few clean sheets and draped it over her trembling shoulders. He helped her to her feet, seeing the same impatience flicker in Methven's eyes, and led Amy out of the room into the suite's second bedroom, where he guided her over to an oversized chaise longue. He grabbed a robe from the cupboard and handed it to her.

A smile flashed on her lips and she pulled it on, letting the bed sheet tumble to the floor before tying the belt.

Methven closed the door behind them and retreated to a leather armchair by the window.

Cullen stood close but far enough away that she wouldn't feel crowded. 'You okay, Amy?'

She gave him nothing, not even eye contact. Just tightened her grip on the dressing gown's belt.

'Amy.' Cullen waited until she looked at him, her pupils dilated with stress. *I hate myself for the stunt I'm about to pull, but the clock's ticking.* 'I promise to keep you safe. But I need to catch the guy who did this. They would've done the same to you if you hadn't hidden under that bed, am I right?'

She gave a tentative nod.

Cullen returned it. 'That was smart thinking. But now I need you to help me make sure he can't do that to anyone else.'

She gave him another one of her tiny nods.

'You're doing great, Amy.' Cullen joined her on the chaise longue. 'Let's start at the beginning. This might not seem important, but let's chat about it anyway. See if you can help me get the whole picture, eh?'

She scooted over and rested her head on his shoulder. 'Okay.'

Progress, at last.

'Thought you were finished with all this.'

'Aye, the stripping, but with Dean dead, Christ... I need to get money from somewhere. Zak isn't paying for himself, you know? And I can't go back to Wonderland. The other places in Edinburgh won't touch me. So I've got to go on escort gigs. Shagging fat old wankers like—' She gasped. 'Look, I need to get out and work.'

'This came from an agency?'

'Yes, just a regular booking.' Her voice was hollow. 'Got a text from the agency. Told to come here and ask at reception. There was a note waiting for me – had a keycard and a suite number upstairs.' She looked up at Cullen, twisting her neck to lock eyes with him. 'So I got the lift up. The door was open but there was nobody in. Seen that before. The guy trying to impress me with this big fancy suite. So I sat on the sofa in the lounge and drank a cup of tea in my Wonder Woman costume. Felt daft, but it passed the time, you know?' She waited for him to nod. 'And then...' She looked away, then shut her eyes.

Cullen gave her a few seconds but she was gone. 'What happened, Amy?'

'This guy... This guy came in. I thought it was the john, but he frowned at me, started acting all weird. Asked if this was a joke.'

Was that the vigilante?

'What did he look like?'

'What do you mean?' Amy shot a glare at him. 'It was the guy who died.' She shut her eyes, her lips twisted. 'But I thought that was his thing, you know, getting off on play-acting some story about walking into the wrong room and being seduced by a sex-starved woman, so I started taking off the costume, acting all sexy...' She fell silent, her lips slackening as her eyes started to go vacant.

Cullen knew the psychological trauma well. He had a moment to pull her back from staring into the abyss before she was beyond his reach. He grabbed her shoulders.

She gasped, her entire body stiffening as her eyes flew to his.

'Amy, imagine you're not here, not physically. You're watching from a safe place. You're high above everything, looking down at what happened in that room like it happened in a film. Tell me what you see.'

She blinked.

'Come on, Amy. I need you to do this for me.'

Her gaze shifted to some point over Cullen's right shoulder, her eyes flickering like she was sitting in a cinema, munching on popcorn. 'I... I see the door open and... This man comes in, and he's dressed as Batman. He's huge, and he's... He attacks the guy in the suit, cuts him down with a single punch.' She flinched. 'And then he went for me.' She stopped, her mouth hanging open.

Cullen squeezed her shoulders.

She shook off the shock. 'But I kicked him in the balls and ran into the hallway. Stopped by the front door, but I didn't run out. I slammed it as hard as I could and hid. There's a wee cupboard, and I hid behind the ironing board. When the guy came went out on the corridor to check I was gone, I sneaked back through to the master bedroom and hid under the bed.' She bit her lip, not seductively but like a small child. 'Learned that when my dad was drunk.' Her shoulders sagged. 'Jesus Christ.'

Cullen gave her another squeeze, gentler. 'Remember, Amy, you're high above everything. Nothing can get to you. Just tell me what you see.'

She nodded, her mind already back on the memory. 'I picked the wrong room to hide in. When the guy came back into the suite, he grabbed the man and pushed him into the master bedroom. The man kept whining at him, saying he couldn't walk, but then his voice went all gurgly.' She gasped, slapping her hand to her mouth. 'The guy cut his throat and the man dropped in front of the bed and... and...' She choked up. The first tears ran tracks through her smudged make-up and her shoulders started shaking.

Cullen didn't know what else to do but give them a gentle pat and sit back to give her space.

Methven walked over and whispered at Cullen, 'That's the FLO.'

~

CULLEN CLOSED THE SUITE DOOR AND SIGNED THEM OUT OF THE crime scene. He took a big breath. 'I probably shouldn't say this to you, but whoever killed Williams is most likely the same guy who killed Vardy and McLintock.' He made eye contact with Methven, seeing the steel reflected. 'I was thinking he might be saving us a job, but now... Killing those three is one thing, but he would've murdered her, too, leaving her kid without a parent and—'

'What's worse is that her story doesn't add up.' Methven started tearing at his crime-scene suit.

Cullen scowled at Methven. 'What?'

'I don't believe her *interpretation* of events.'

'What?'

'Stop saying that, please.' Methven tugged off his suit and kicked it into the discard pile. 'Do you really think Hamish Williams cast her for some sexy roleplay? He was a bereaved homosexual man, merely staying here because of what happened at his home, partly because we won't let him back, but partly so he doesn't have to face the memory yet. He was *genuinely* puzzled to find her waiting in his suite. He was hardly the sort to call a prostitute, let alone a *woman*.'

Cullen cringed. 'Sorry, sir. I was focusing on—'

'Her breasts? Sergeant, you should try to think with more than your penis every now and then.'

'That's hardly—'

'Try to keep your personal feelings out of your professional duties, okay?' Methven silenced Cullen with a wry grin. 'You did well in there. Amy isn't coming out of this in a good way, but you stopped it getting worse. Nipped it in the bud, as it were.'

'So what do you suggest we do now?'

'I'd *like* a bit of initiative from you.'

Cullen stared hard at him, balling his fists again, ready to—
Stop it.

He swallowed down his anger. 'Okay, someone left a card for her at the front desk, instructing her to go to this suite. Called her agency, went to the bother of arranging this.'

'You think she was a target too?'

'It's possible. I mean, she's connected to Vardy. Someone could be upset that she refused to testify against him.'

CULLEN STOPPED BY THE UNMARKED DOOR AND KNOCKED.

Through the window, the arched girders of North Bridge and the Old Town were shrouded in wet fog – the grey sea in the distance, beyond the cranes and towers of Leith. Lily's Flowers, an escort agency, high up above Edinburgh.

Some footsteps came from behind. Someone cleared their throat, then the door opened wide. A middle-aged woman stood there, heavy make-up and designer glasses, her dark hair swept back in an Alice band. Simple black dress and knee-high boots. She looked Cullen up and down, her expression unreadable. 'Good afternoon, how may I help you today?' The corner of her mouth curled up. 'Or perhaps tonight?'

'Need your help right now.' He got out his warrant card. 'Detective Sergeant Scott Cullen. Need to speak to you about one of your employees, Amy Forrest.'

'I see.' She led over to a smart desk, pulling out a leather armchair for him. She took a seat and held out a hand. 'I'm Lily. Pleasure to meet you.'

'A pleasure.' Cullen shook it. Her hand was soft. 'I believe that Ms Forrest had an appointment at the Glasshouse last night. One of your people made it for her.'

'Oh, Sergeant.' Lily gave him a coquettish look. Obvious how she avoided most police attention on her business. 'I have no people. It's just me.'

'Okay, then. Amy said she—'

'She is okay, yes?'

'Wouldn't go so far as to say okay, but she's alive, yes.' Cullen leaned forward on the chair. 'She said she got a text from someone at your agency, telling her to meet a client there.'

'Did she now?'

'Aye, is there a problem?'

'Only in so far as our employees are under strict instructions not to discuss our business.' She made her reply sound like a brush-off.

He gave her a wink, his way of letting her know he understood her coded answer. 'I need to know who made the request.'

'I am unable to. Policy.'

'Right.' Cullen got to his feet and stood in the window, making her squint. 'I can get a warrant and bring a squad of careless uniformed officers in here. We'll go through every inch of your business.'

'Detective, you're embarrassing yourself.' She joined him standing and motioned at the door. 'Now, I'm asking you to leave.'

'Do you know what Amy went through last night? A man was murdered right in front of her, his throat sliced—'

'Enough.' Lily collapsed into her seat, making it spin slowly. 'It's in nobody's interest to make a scene here.' She paused, then unlocked her laptop and let her dainty fingers dance across the keyboard. 'The request came from a mobile number. Unfortunately for you, that number is registered to a pre-approved account.'

'Meaning?'

'The client did not have to give his or her name. It's a mostly automated process.'

'So you let just anybody—'

'I'm afraid so. This business operates on a trust basis, okay? That account was introduced by one of our premium-tier members. It may even be them, you never know. But they pay a lot of money for being able to request who they want without question.'

'Can I get the—'

'Not without a warrant.' Lily flicked her tongue across her lips. 'But seeing as how you have the decency to show up here and treat me like a human being, I'll let you have the number. Good luck.'

～

CULLEN WALKED INTO THE STATION AND BARGED PAST A PAIR OF uniforms flirting by the card reader. He scanned through but got red. 'Bastard thing.' He swiped again. Red again. 'Come on, you piece of—'

'Let me.' Yvonne took his card and ran it slowly down the reader. Green. 'Et voila.' She gave him a wink then pushed through the door. 'You okay?'

'I was. But...'

'What's up?'

'Oh, you know me, I—'

His phone rang. He wanted to ignore it, talk to her about Amy and her ordeal.

And Jesus Christ, I've not even thought *about Hamish Williams.*

He checked the display. Tommy Smith was calling. He answered. 'Hey.'

'Alright, Scott, I've got bad news.'

'Oh, let me guess, you've processed the number I sent you and it's a burner.'

'Eh?' A sharp intake of breath down the line. 'No, Scott, the number belongs to DI Wilkinson.'

35

'HERE'S HOW THIS IS GOING TO GO DOWN.' METHVEN GAZED AT Lennox and Yvonne, unblinking, waiting until they broke off eye contact. 'DS Cullen and I will commence interviewing DI Wilkin—'

'No, Colin.' Lennox puffed up his chest. 'This isn't your case.'

'Terry, have you spoken to DCS Soutar?'

'Why would I need to?'

Cullen sat back and made his own eye contact, with Yvonne. She looked as bored as he did. 'You do know we've got a spree killer or an assassin on the loose, right?'

They both looked at him, as angry as each other. Methven spluttered. 'Excuse me?'

'You're playing Game of Thrones here and someone is murdering people. Hamish Williams is—'

'*Sergeant*.' Methven lurched across the room, grabbed Cullen's arm and pulled him out into the corridor, slamming the door behind them. 'Are you trying to make us look incompetent?'

'Of course not.'

'So why are you doing it?'

Cullen pinched his nose – the only thing he could do to stop from smacking him in the face. He took a long, hard breath, let it out through his nostrils, then locked eyes with Methven. 'Listen to me. Wilkinson isn't our guy. You saw him attacked by our vigilante, right?'

'Sergeant, that's immaterial. His account was used to—'

'And nobody's ever faked an account? Nobody's ever stolen a mobile phone?'

'He is prime suspect!'

'You sound like Bain.'

Methven stopped dead. He cocked his head to the side, like a dog unsure what its owner wants.

'I'm serious.' Cullen looked away. 'Few years back, he focused on the obvious suspect, locked in on them, while the real suspect did what they wanted. Murdered, escaped. You don't want to be that guy.'

'I am not that guy.' Methven turned back to his office. 'I'll work with DI Lennox and DS Flockhart to prosecute DI Wilkinson.' He turned around one last time, ice in his stare. 'But, I need to delegate a task to you, Sergeant. I have approval to offer the DC position to Angela Caldwell. Please inform her.'

'What... now?'

'Yes. Get a hold of her and tell her.'

'I should be—'

'Get out of my sight!'

CULLEN STORMED OUT OF THE OFFICE INTO THE GREY CAR PARK. Seagulls wheeled above his head. This far inland meant a sea storm was brewing. Or something worse. He got in his car and slumped in the seat.

Bloody Methven. What the hell is he playing at?

Wilko clearly isn't Batman. Clearly isn't even the bloody Joker. But they were fixating on him. Turning a lead into evidence. Someone they could prosecute. Show they were cleaning the force, but really, just killing time.

When Batman strikes again, what will they do?

Would be nice to have said all of that to his face.

Bloody hell.

He got himself straight. Or as straight as someone who'd been through what he had that morning could get. He took out his mobile and dialled Angela and Bill's home number.

Delivering some good news for a change.

The phone rang and rang. Then a hassled female voice answered. 'Two-two-six, eight-three-one-five?'

Cullen frowned as he gazed out at the grey sky. It seemed as empty as his head. 'Erm, who's this?'

'This is Sheila Caldwell. To whom am I speaking?'

'Sorry, this is Scott Cullen. I used to work with Angela. Is she in?'

'Oh yes. She's spoken fondly of you.' From the sounds of it, an entire circus was in as well, rampaging through the family home. Then the sound dampened, followed by a muffled: 'Quiet!' Not that it made any difference beyond a slight pause in the bedlam. 'I'm minding Angela's two boys and they're not usually like this. I suppose it's only normal that they're having a bit of trouble adjusting.'

'To what?'

'Don't you know?' She paused. 'Angela always talks of you as a friend. I hope I haven't spoken out of turn.'

'About what?'

'It's not my place to say.'

Cullen pushed himself back in the seat, tried his hardest not to sigh. Just about managed. 'Any idea where I can find her?'

CULLEN PULLED UP OUTSIDE THE MASON'S CROSS, NOW PROUDLY sporting a Wetherspoons logo in gold lettering. He got out of the car, Garleton sprawling around him. Sandstone cottages and climbing roses and wood-panelled shopfronts painted in primary colours. He stepped into the pub and looked around. Bon Jovi played low, but not low enough. Bare wooden tables, the nearest one surrounded by four old boys tucking into fish and chips – half-drunk pints of Guinness in front of them.

Angela was sitting in a dark booth, looking like she was fighting a losing battle with three bottles of white wine.

Cullen took a seat across from her and cleared his throat.

She looked up, her eyes struggling to focus on him. 'Scott? What are you doing here?' Her speech was slurred.

He glanced at her half-empty glass. 'You alright?'

She reached for the glass. 'No, I'm not.' She drank a couple of fingers' worth and settled back, arms folded. 'What's going on?'

'You tell me.'

'You spoke to Mum, right?'

Cullen nodded slowly. 'She didn't say what happened, but you don't seem in a good way. Want to talk?'

Angela shrugged, then topped up her glass, emptying the third bottle. 'I kicked Bill out last week.'

'I had no idea. Bill never mentioned— Angela, I'm sorry.'

'He...' She blinked hard, like there was something stuck in her eyes. 'And now I'm left with two feral boys and no job.'

Cullen sucked in a sharp breath. 'Welcome to the club. Sharon's just broken up with me.'

Angela stared in her empty glass. 'Aye, well, I can understand that. You're a wanker.' She looked up with a grin.

'Touché. And Bill isn't?'

'Well...'

Cullen inclined his head. 'What happened?'

'Bill's...' Angela pressed her lips together. 'My mother's been helping out with the kids, but I'm at the end of my tether. Bill's only staying down the road, but we hardly see him and when he did visit last night, I couldn't even be in the same house as him, so I came to the pub and got pissed. Left him with those little bastards. See how he likes it.'

'Doing the same today?'

'Sod him.' She took another drink. 'Last night, that prick was late, too. Woke the kids, and Mum had a nightmare getting them back to sleep when he left. They're all over the place.'

Cullen patted her on the shoulder. 'Is there anything I can do to help?'

She glanced at him, then back at her glass. 'You can get pissed with me.'

'I'd normally say that you know I don't drink, but... well.'

'So why are you here, Scott?'

'Oh, right, sorry. I tried calling, but yeah, you weren't in, so I came to tell you face-to-face. Methven's decided on the DC position. You start in two weeks.'

'What?'

'Make sure you sober up, aye?'

Cullen headed down Garleton's long high street, past the scaffolding around the old police station, halfway through being turned into retirement flats. He crossed the road and stopped outside Lamb's bachelor flat. Looked empty. He hit the buzzer and waited. His burp gave him a fresh taste of haggis, neeps and tatties.

His phone chimed. Angela.

Thanks. Changing my diet plan back to solids from liquids. I'll regret it, but looking forward to working with you again. X'

The door clunked open and Lamb stood there in navy shorts and a washed-out T-shirt, staring at Cullen with bloodshot eyes. He grunted and staggered inside. 'Want a beer?'

Cullen closed the door behind him and followed Lamb into the kitchen. 'Bill, it's half three.'

'So what?'

'You're half cut, Bill. So's your wife.'

Lamb stopped dead, eyes narrowing. 'If you've come here to preach to...?' He swayed as he reached into the fridge. '*You* of all people? Eh?'

'Easy now. *You're* the one who left his wife—'

'Piss off, you smug, entitled wanker.'

'You're the wanker here, Bill. What are you playing at?'

'What am *I* playing at?' Lamb stormed across the kitchen and went forehead-to-forehead with Cullen, whisky fumes wafting off him. 'What am I playing at?'

'Aye, Bill. You're acting like an idiot – leaving your wife and kids. Why aren't you teaching the course today?'

Lamb didn't have a response. Just stood there, flexing a pectoral. Hard to tell if he meant to.

'You visited your kids last night and realised what you've done, right? Become one of those dads who can't handle it. It's too much pressure. Not what you wanted, eh? So you spent today drinking yourself—'

Lamb grabbed Cullen by the throat, his grip like a claw. 'You're just out of a relationship yourself and you're fooling around with Yvonne.' He tightened his grip, choking Cullen. 'You think you're the man? Shagging some daft DS from Livingston, eh? Think you're cool, eh?'

Cullen punched him in the chest. 'What the hell is wrong with you?'

'Nothing.' Lamb sucked in breath and backed off, resting his hands on his hips. 'Absolutely nothing.'

Cullen stared at him, livid. Wanted to slap Lamb's vacant mug.

Instead, he turned around and walked out.

36

WITH NOWHERE ELSE TO GO, CULLEN'S RAGE WENT INTO THE steering wheel. By the time he got back to the station, he had gripped it so hard and long, his hands were almost numb. He uncurled his fingers and tried to open the driver's door. And failed twice. He shook some life back into his right hand and gripped the handle, feeling like a feeble old man as the door finally clicked open.

'Stay there.' Methven slid round the front of the car and got in the passenger seat, slamming the door. The same feral look as in Lamb's eyes. Another DI losing it, panicking like a cornered animal. He slumped low in the chair like he didn't want to be seen. 'They're trying to pin this on me! Vardy's murder!' He looked at Cullen like he had lost his mind. 'They're trying to fit me up for it!'

'You need to step back, sir, I'm not—'

'We were interviewing Wilkinson, but he smelled a rat. So he mentioned the video death threat Vardy received, the one that was projected on the front of his club?'

'Sure, I—'

'Charlie sodding Kidd submitted his analysis to Wilkinson, not me.' Methven's gaze flickered around the car park in search of a way out of this tight corner. 'Turns out Vardy didn't stage the stunt himself after all. The thing came from a Russian drug dealer, some guy Wilkinson's squad had under investigation.'

'That sounds... good?'

'No it's sodding not. I parked the investigation into the threat. Then Vardy turned up dead and I forgot about that sodding recording. And now Lennox has wind of it. Now. Of all times he has to get on my case... NOW! When he already has me under suspicion. Sodding hell, Cullen, I need your help!'

'I need you to calm down.'

'I am sodding—'

'No, sir. Calm.'

Methven glared at him like a bull about to charge, huffing and puffing and ready to blow his house down. Then he shut his eyes, the lids flickering.

'Okay, let's go through what we've got.' Cullen shifted round in his seat. 'Vardy, McLintock, and now Williams, were all killed with the same MO. Both lawyers have defended Vardy in multiple cases, right?'

'I don't know where you're—'

'It's safe to assume that the same person murdered all three. Right?'

'Where are you going with this?'

'I'm trying to say that those murders weren't because of some drug deal. Sounds way too complicated. Have they got anything tying this Russian to McLintock or Williams?'

'No, but—' Methven gasped. 'Everything points to that Russian mobster putting the frighteners up Vardy. Guy's out of prison for the first time in *months*. If they wanted him dead, they'd have been able to get at him inside. They sent a message, end of.'

'The Livingston lot keep saying that it might be a cop, someone on our side, someone who decided to punish Vardy and those who helped him escape punishment.'

'And I discounted the video from the investigation. Makes me look negligent.' Methven stared at him, his eyes still flickering. 'So what do we do?'

'First, we need to find out if you were right to dismiss the video death threat.'

~

CULLEN TRUDGED UP THE STAIRS, HIS FOOTSTEPS ECHOING ROUND the tight space. SOCOs were still working in Vardy's flat, the crime-scene tape still up. He climbed on up, knocked on the door and waited.

Methven joined him, straightening his suit jacket, his tie, his jacket again. 'Do I look presentable?'

Cullen frowned. 'Presentable enough for what?'

'Never mind.' Methven's blush went from faint pink to red alert as he knocked on the door and straightened his tie, again.

The door opened and Bain stared out at them. 'Alright, Col. You look like your missus has caught you having a wank.'

'Sod off.' Methven shouldered his way past him and stomped into the flat.

Bain watched him go. 'Is he off his meds or something?'

'Search me.'

'Last time I rummaged in your pants, Sundance, you got a wee hard-on.'

'Never change, eh?' Cullen left Bain outside.

Methven was in the kitchen, nodding along to whatever DC Paula Zabinski was telling him.

Vardy's girlfriend, sat by the window, staring into space as though none of this concerned her.

Cullen offered a sympathetic smile, but she ignored him.

Zabinski nodded at Cullen, then over at the girlfriend. 'Aye, so according to Miss Pawlok here, Vardy got quite a few death threats in his time. Texts, emails, phone calls. Never a video display, mind.'

'Excellent work.' Methven stepped between Zabinski and Cullen. 'Does she think that the threat level could be escalating?'

Zabinski barked something in Polish. Vardy's girlfriend returned it without looking up. Whatever she said, it made Zabinski sigh. 'She said it's the Russian. We've investigated him and he's made multiple threats against Vardy.'

Methven nodded, far too fast to look genuine.

'This is simple, Col.' Bain pulled up a kitchen chair and sat on it the wrong way round. 'Way I see it, that video means hee haw. The lassie there says Vardy got threats all the time, even from this Russian boy. Comes with the territory of selling drugs, right? Get like those you bide with. Know what I'm saying?' He got blank looks back. 'I mean, the people he associates with, they're bound to threaten each other. All the time. Every week. Keep each other on their toes. Probe for any weaknesses. Vardy will have been as bad as this Russian, whoever he is.'

'Right.' Zabinski frowned, like she was trying to make sense of Bain's insight, but either came up blank or just didn't agree with it. 'Like I was saying, he got a lot of threats. On the other hand, McLintock and Williams were known to associate with Vardy.'

Methven took a deep breath, then coughed into his hand. 'As far as we know.'

'Aye, as far as *you* know.' Bain barked a laugh, then shook his head. 'Paula, did you or Wilko ever get wind of anything?'

'Nope.' Zabinski leaned back against the counter and folded her arms. 'I spent a few weeks with Elvis, sorry, with DC Gordon staking them out for Wilko. Even interviewed some ex-employees. We were looking for their involvement in Vardy's operation, but we never breached that particular firewall.' She eyed Methven. 'I gather that you're treating this vigilante as a rogue cop, right?'

'Sadly not me, but our friends in Livingston.'

'Well, like I said, McLintock and Williams were well known as Vardy's associates. Stands to reason that if a rogue cop is really behind this, he'd have an axe to grind with them. Especially as he's killed them both.'

Methven beamed at her. 'Constable, remind me to discuss your path to DS.'

'I'd be delighted, sir.'

Cullen coughed, deliberately loud enough to get them to swing round to focus on him. 'Sir, DC Zabinski works for DI Wilkinson.'

'Well, we'll just have to fix that little mistake, won't we?' Methven's smile got wider.

Cullen stepped between them. *Christ, Methven's married and he's flirting with a subordinate. Better watch himself.* 'Sir, I think we need to speak to this Russian, get him to admit he made—'

'I've got a much better idea.' Bain got to his feet and clapped his hands together. 'Let's have a wee look at their shagging pads, see if we can get some hard evidence.'

～

CULLEN STOPPED THE CAR AT THE TOP OF McLINTOCK AND Williams's private driveway and got out.

Bain was still laughing as he joined him on the walk over. 'Tell you, I'd give that Polish lassie a little language lesson, starting with French kissing. Know what I mean, Sundance?'

'Jesus Christ.' Cullen stopped on the drive. He let the trio of SOCOs walk past. Got a nod from them. Then he glowered at Bain. 'Her name is Wioletta Pawlok. She's just lost her partner. Have a bit of decency.'

'Come on, Sundance, I'm just joking.'

'You're always just joking.' Cullen jogged up the front steps to Williams's part of the mansion and tried the massive wooden door. Open. 'Bloody hell, those SOCOs have left us in charge.'

'That's how I wanted to play it, Sergeant.' Methven pushed through the door. 'I want us in control here.'

'Talking about control...' Bain was still chuckling. 'Tell you, McLintock's love truncheon still haunts my dreams.'

Cullen entered last, if only to avoid Bain. Methven was already halfway up the grand staircase.

'Here.' Bain followed him up. 'Didn't Williams mention something about a secret backdoor into McLintock's place? So he could reach around for McLintock's wanger in the middle of the night?'

Methven didn't even bother telling him off, just stood there. 'You're welcome to entertain your fantasies, Sergeant. Just keep out of my sodding way.' He set off up the stairs, heading to the sign of the carnage in McLintock's bathroom.

'Happy days.' Bain set off.

Cullen grabbed his arm and held him back. 'What are you up to?'

'Me? Sundance, I'm just checking for secret tunnels in old houses. You heard the boss.' Bain shrugged him off and skipped down the stairs. 'Indulge me.'

'Feels like I've spent half my career doing just that.'

'You're a funny bastard, Sundance.' Bain tapped at the wallpaper near the bottom. 'Hear that?' He thumped it with his knuckles. 'Hollow as your head, Sundance.' He pushed the section of wall and a door clicked open. 'Here we go.' He put his fingers to his lips and stepped through.

Aye, I've seen everything now.

Cullen trotted up the stairs after Methven, taking the steps three at a time.

The DI was in front of a plain wooden door on the third-floor landing. In this expensively furnished mansion where every single wooden panel and skirting board seemed to be made of hand-carved mahogany or covered in gold, the door was conspicuous for being so plain. He tried the handle. Locked. 'Might be a cleaning cupboard, but the lock's a bit of an overkill if that's all it is.'

Cullen bit his lip, wondering where they might find a key or what might be found behind this plain door, if not cleaning supplies. 'Hold on.' He headed back down the stairs and had no trouble finding Bain's secret passageway. He stepped through into a brightly lit hallway, a mirrored replica of next door, even the gold wallpaper and fake candles matching. Williams's half of the house. He glanced around to find his bearings. Muffled voices floated down the carpeted staircase from one of the upper floors. Cullen rushed upstairs, up to the third floor.

Knew it.

The two parts of the mansion were symmetrical, meaning that Williams also had a door on the third-floor landing, only his wasn't plain. And it wasn't locked.

Cullen pressed the handle down, the door swung inwards on oiled hinges and—

He froze.

Bain was squatting above a gilded bathroom sink, trousers and white pants around his ankles, his face contorted, as a turd squeezed out onto the porcelain. Smelled like someone had opened up the sewer. Bain looked up from between his legs and straight at Cullen with a dirty leer. 'Christ, Sundance, you've made me snap it off halfway.'

Cullen could only stand there, open-mouthed.

Bain reached over for a toothbrush standing in a cup on the sink, and stuck it between his thighs and rubbed it around. Then he hopped off, trousers and pants still round his ankles and used the toothbrush to push the giant jobbie down the plughole, grunting away. 'Come on, you bugger.'

Cullen looked away. *Jesus H Christ. Just when I—*

Hang on.

There were three other doors to the giant bathroom, one

mirroring the one he'd come through, rattling. He tried the nearest of the other two and it opened to a luxurious bedroom.

Okay...

Cullen backed out of the room and rushed back to McLintock's side of the semi-detached mansion, taking him all of three floors – down the stairs, and back up – to process the image of Bain defiling the golden sink and refocus on the investigation.

Methven was still hunched over the lock, working away at it with a set of picks.

'Save it.' Cullen tried to catch his breath. But instead just caught another image of Bain curling one off onto the porcelain. 'Got in from the other side. It's a bathroom. Should be able to get in from the bedroom on the other side.' He paced through into a bedroom, as huge and expensively furnished as on Williams's side, and tried the en-suite door. Unlocked.

But it wasn't a bathroom mirroring the one in Williams's half. Just a dark cupboard. A smallish desk was lit up by the faint light from the bedroom, his long shadow cast over the floor. An elderly desktop computer whirred and clicked, next to a stack of paperwork. Cullen patted the wall, found a switch, and flicked it. The overhead energy-saver bulb took its time humming to life. Cullen crossed to the plain wood door, slid a metal deadbolt aside and let Methven in from the landing. 'In you come. There's a computer in here that might just be as old as y—'

Bain bounced up the stairs behind Methven, that leer still on his face. 'Here, Sundance, I got it all out of my system.'

Methven frowned at him. 'You what?'

'Ach, you know, Col. Had a good rummage around over there. I've been under the cosh lately. Felt like something's snapped off inside me. Been feeling kind of clogged up, but I've finally got the whole lot out of my system. I feel a stone lighter, I swear... Got to hand it to you, Col, you've really helped me clean up my shite.'

Methven glared at him, still frowning, but just gave up. He followed Cullen inside the hidden office and started working his way through the paperwork. 'What the hell?' He held up a piece of paper. 'This is from a case file! How the sodding hell did he get that?'

Cullen took the file off him and scanned it. 'The rape of Pauline Quigley. Wasn't that—'

'The Lamb and Wilkinson investigation that fell apart.' Methven snatched it back. 'The girl who went to prison for Vardy.' He started going through the rest of the paperwork. Then stopped. 'Oh my God.' His face went white.

'You okay there, Col? Looks like you've shat—'

'Shut up!' Methven handed Cullen a sheaf of notes.

Cullen flicked through the pages. Another rape case against Vardy where the accuser was underage, so she was kept anonymous. Another one that fell apart before getting to court. 'Who's leaking this to them?'

'That's not the bit that's—' Methven handed him another page. A PI report, dated a week ago. 'McLintock discovered the girl's identity.' He stared at Cullen, long and hard. 'Amy sodding Forrest.'

37

'WHEN DO I GET OUT OF HERE?' AMY WAS HUDDLED IN THE interview room, pulling a cheap tracksuit top tight round her shoulders. She shivered. 'When can I see Zak?'

Cullen glanced at the two-way mirror, hoping Methven was still behind it. 'I'll put in a good—'

'Save it.' Amy stared out at him, her tired gaze sliding off his face and moving to his left, where Bain was rasping his grey beard. She closed her eyes for a few seconds, then opened them again, nothing but resignation in them. 'I've heard it all so many times.'

'I imagine so.' Bain nodded slowly, then sniffed. 'People must offer to help you all the time, eh? But when it comes down it? When push comes to shove? Where are they?'

'Aye...' Amy was frowning. 'Wankers.'

From squatting over a sink to this in half an hour.

'Listen to me. You've had a horrendous time. Horrendous. I'll make sure you and the wee man are both okay. And that's a promise.' Bain leaned forward. 'But you need to help us a wee bit, then we'll get you back to wee Zak, pronto. Alright?'

'Okay.' She sucked in a halting breath. 'So what do you want to know?'

'Vardy raped you, right?'

'You know that. I've told you twice.'

'You neglected to mention that you were underage.'

'Shite.'

'It's sickening, believe me. Wish I hadn't found out.' Bain held up a finger. 'No, I wish you hadn't been raped. But the thing is, Amy, you've lied about your age, haven't you? My colleagues would never have considered you for an undercover sting if they'd know you were sixteen.'

Amy stared hard at the table.

'We would never have put you and Xena in that position if we'd known.' Bain leaned forward another inch. 'I'm not saying that her death is your fault...'

Amy continued staring at the table. She rubbed her eye and looked up at Bain, then at Cullen.

Bain sat back and folded his arms. 'Tell us what happened, Amy. Then you can see Zak.'

Amy stared up at the ceiling. 'When I started dancing at Wonderland, I lied about my age. I had fake ID from school. Thing is,' she clutched her breasts, 'these are natural, unlike most of the girls there, so Dean offered me a job, didn't seem to care that my ID said I was twenty-one, even though I was fifteen.' She nibbled at her bottom lip. 'Anyway, Dean had a thing where he'd have sex with every new girl, like some initiation ritual. Usually when he was coked out of his skull, which was most nights. When it was my turn, he let one of the bouncers watch. Afterwards, that sick bastard offered the bouncer *sloppy seconds*. Thank Christ that Liam had more class, eh?'

'Go on.'

'Anyway. A fortnight later Dean had me meet this guy he knew. Got in his car, down in Leith, where the docks used to be. Ended up in this hotel, being forced to suck off some drug dealer who worked for Dean. I did the business, then Vardy pinned me down and raped me. That's when we got caught, eh? This big bastard DI Wilkinson...'

Cullen tasted sour acid bubbling up from his gut. He got up and started pacing around. He shot a stern look at Bain. *Don't interrupt her.*

But Bain was holding his breath.

'Anyway, Wilko arrested me.'

'Was he in the room with you?'

'No, he was waiting outside. I went up to his car, to see if he wanted some business, and he slapped cuffs on me.' Amy swallowed hard. 'But then he found out I'd just turned sixteen and he was going hard at me. I told him about Dean and how he'd raped me when I started. He put two and two together and realised that the sex with Dean was when I was underage. The bouncer didn't know, so when Wilkinson told him, he agreed to testify as an eyewitness. Wilkinson got a trial date fixed and I was still working away at Wonderland, making sure that Dean didn't suspect a thing. Then the bouncer died and the case fell apart. The way Wilko told me, it would've been my word against Dean's. I was worried Dean would find out. I mean, I'd given an anonymous statement, but he must've had a contact in the cops, eh? And he'd probably have killed my mum and sister. So, I told Wilkinson I wanted out of it, and I kept quiet. And for a while nothing happened. Until last week. Dean found out I was underage back when he broke me in, as he called it.'

'This is before you were due in court?'

She nodded again. 'Prick came to my flat and confronted me.' She rubbed a tear from her eye. 'Didn't even look at his son for a second. Course, Dean didn't feel bad about abusing a minor. He just threatened me, said his lawyer found out my real name and my real age. Told me I if went to the cops, he'd gut me like a pig. Right in front of Zak.'

CULLEN KNOCKED ON WILKINSON'S OFFICE DOOR, THE FETTES CAR park gleaming through the window behind Zabinski's desk. An Audi did a slow arc as it pulled by the window.

No answer.

Bloody hell.

Cullen reached over to the door-entry system and tried the first code he could think of. 2868. Nothing.

Then the door clunked open and Wilkinson peered out like a badger in the headlights. 'What the hell do you want?'

'A mountain bike and a PlayStation 4, please Santa.' Cullen grabbed Wilkinson's lapels. 'What do you think? We need a word.'

Wilkinson shook his hands away. 'You can piss off.'

Cullen pushed him into the office. 'We know what you've done, Paul.'

'Oh yeah?' Wilkinson tried to stop him, but in the end just settled back on his desk, watching Methven shutting the door. He folded his arms. 'Oh yeah? What have I done?'

'You know.'

'Listen. I've had it up to here with people thinking I'm the bloody vigilante! Bloody Lennox and Flockhart were in here saying I booked some escort gig for some stupid tart! I lost my bloody phone, didn't I?'

'That's very careless of you.'

'What have I done now?'

Methven stood over him, inches from his face. 'We've just spoken to Amy Forrest.'

Wilkinson's mouth hung open. 'What are you talking about?'

Methven kept staring until Wilkinson looked away.

'She was the tart who I supposedly booked, right? This isn't news to me.'

'Inspector, I need you to focus, okay?' Methven reached over and dusted Wilkinson's suit shoulders. He didn't flinch. 'We just found out that Amy was underage when Vardy forced her to have sex with him for the first time. And we also found out that you knew.'

'What?'

'You were going to use her as a witness to get Vardy put on trial, but you lost another witness so she bailed on you. Seems like a repeating pattern, Paul. And you're right in the middle of it.'

'How the hell did you find that out?'

'Because Campbell sodding McLintock did.'

Wilkinson sat there, saying and doing nothing. 'Shit.'

Methven planted his hands on Wilkinson's shoulders, kept him sitting on his desk. 'So, here's what we're thinking. Young Amy cost you a career-defining case. Meaning you had a motive to take revenge against Vardy and McLintock. You're a cop, meaning you had the means and opportunity to—'

'HOW DARE YOU COME IN HERE AND ACCUSE ME OF...' Then silence. 'Hang on.' Wilkinson sat forward. 'How did that prick McLintock find out Amy's identity?'

'Someone's got loose lips, Paul. Someone on your operation.

Started out as a drug sting, but you saw glory, didn't you? Bring him down for raping a minor. But no. It all fell apart. Just like when Vardy shot Xena Farley. Just like a hundred other times. You're the sodding mole, Paul. You.'

'Of course I'm not.' Wilkinson got up and walked over to the window. 'Listen to me. As per protocol, Amy's identity was kept in a file, locked away in here.' He kicked a filing cabinet. 'Me and my superintendent were the only ones who interviewed Amy. We ran a tight ship.'

'Could he have—'

'Dave's on the cancer ward...'

'I knew Superintendent Mitchell well.' Methven rounded on Wilkinson. 'But it doesn't excuse you, Paul. You show me that file or we're marching you out of here in cuffs.'

'What?' Wilkinson blinked. 'I'm not the bloody vigilante!'

'You're the only one who fits the frame for all three murders *and* who had a grudge against Amy Forrest.'

'It wasn't me, you stupid bastard! I just... Gimme a second.' Wilkinson started rifling through a file cabinet to the side of his desk. 'No, no, no.' He straightened up. 'Where is it?'

'What?'

'The file's bloody missing! I've always kept it in here.' Wilkinson pointed an accusing finger at the cabinet, then went back to rifling through it, muttering as he searched. 'There was far more in it than Amy bloody Forrest, too. Christ on a bike. McLintock was helping Vardy launder money. Like Saul Goodman in *Breaking Bad*, but with even worse suits.'

'This isn't the sodding time for jokes.' Methven grabbed him and twisted him round. 'Paul, is there anyone else who—'

'Get your hands off me!'

'Paul, I'm just asking—'

'No. Nobody else even knows the bloody code for this room.'

'Easy, easy.' Cullen got between them, nudging Methven away from the filing cabinet, then focusing on Wilkinson. 'What about your new Super? Could they—'

'I don't trust him yet—' Wilkinson froze, his eyes as wide as when they first walked in. 'That's it. I thought I can't trust him and knew he'd find a way in here to go through my stuff, so I hid the file in the safe.' He let go of the cabinet drawer and darted over to the safe in the corner. He bent low and keyed in a four-digit code. 'Here we go.' He tore the door open and reached into the safe.

Methven put his hands on his hips. 'Well?'

'Somebody...' Wilkinson stared at Cullen. 'Somebody's set me up! The file was right there!' He pointed at the safe as though it confirmed his story. Then he pushed Methven aside and strode over to the door, his chest swelling. He flung it open and stormed out to the open plan office: 'DC ZABINSKI, GET IN HERE! NOW!'

She marched into the room and stood in front of his desk, hands clasped behind her back like she was on parade. 'Sir?'

'Whatever you're working on, put it on hold.' Wilkinson looked straight at Zabinski with an unblinking stare. 'You and DS Cullen will compile a comprehensive list of who went in and out of this room in the past week, and I want you to do it within the next hour.'

'Sir, that's going to—'

'An hour. Got that?'

ZABINSKI'S DESK WAS COVERED IN PILES AND PILES OF PAPERWORK, Wilko's paranoia about anything technology-related writ large. 'Here we are again.'

Voices thundered out of Wilkinson's office, the din of two grown men shouting at each other bleeding through the wood.

Zabinski looked over at the door. 'What's got up his arse?'

'Long story.' Cullen took the chair next to her and folded his arms tight across his chest. The desk was far from empty, a mound of papers resting under a World's Best Cop mug half-filled with tepid coffee. *So much for a clear-desk policy.* 'This is going to be a right pain in the arse, but we need to do it.'

'I get all the shite.' She logged into her machine. 'Okay, so we've got to go through the CCTV of this place,' she ran her finger round in the air, 'and we've got to go through the access logs to Wilkinson's private office.'

'I'll do the CCTV.' Cullen logged in to the machine next to her, pushing the mess of papers and stationery to make room.

'I'll speak to security and get those access logs.' Paula got up and leaned against the back of her chair with a lopsided smile. 'I saw Sharon today.'

Cullen avoided her gaze, keeping his focus on the screen, unblinking, until it went blurry.

'Aye, she seemed about as absentminded as you are now. Walked right past me on the corridor but never noticed me, even when I called after her. Or maybe she blanked me. The cheek of her, eh? To think she was on my hen weekend.' Outrage twisted the corner of her eyes, but it soon faltered.

'She's a bit preoccupied.' Cullen glanced at her. 'We split up and I imagine it's been hard for her, too.'

'Oh.' Zabinski cringed. 'I had no idea.' She pressed her lips together.

Cullen stared back at the laptop screen, his eyes glazing over again. He listened to her footsteps recede, then the office door clicked shut.

∼

GHOSTLY FIGURES WHIZZED AROUND THE SCREEN AT QUADRUPLE speed, chatting to Zabinski and the old Operation Venus team, laughing and joking. Onscreen, Wilkinson's door opened. Cullen slowed it down. It was Wilkinson and Cullen, the other day.

He wrote it down in his notebook, not that there were many suspects on the page. Certainly nobody outside the immediate team. And no tell-tale bulges as they took a police file out of the room.

Got to put myself in the frame.

Cullen set the video playing again, the apparitions speeding around the office.

'Scott?' Zabinski cleared her throat. 'Look at this.'

'You got something?'

'Maybe.' She turned the computer around and pointed at a log entry at the bottom of the screen. 'Got an entry at 18:47 on Monday.' She leaned in, still listening to the din coming from the door. 'Here's the thing, Wilko was signed out at the time.'

And I know where. Trying to kick the shite out of Vardy outside the Debonair.

Cullen keyed up the CCTV, trying to play through the consequences. 'Does nobody else know the passcode?'

'Changes it every day. He's paranoid.'

'So how the hell did the thief get in?'

'Assuming there is a thief.'

'Right.' Cullen yawned. 'Okay, gimme a sec.' He wound the CCTV to the time. Just an empty office and a shut door. 'Sure this is—'

Then a figure walked across the screen in slow time. Cullen checked it was playing at full speed. It was. The figure entered a code in the reader and looked around. Big and bulky. The door opened and they slipped inside.

Cullen leaned forward. 'Christ, can you make them out?'

'Not quite.'

Seconds later, the figure reappeared, stuffing a paper file into their coat, looking up at the camera.

38

'I CAN'T BELIEVE IT.' METHVEN COLLAPSED BACK INTO WILKINSON'S chair, his eyes locked on the computer screen and the indisputable footage. 'Bill Lamb?'

Wilkinson and Zabinski were both staring at the carpet, looking as shell-shocked as Methven.

Cullen perched on the edge of the desk and tapped the screen. 'This looks like Lamb stole the file from Wilko's safe. Then he leaked Amy's identity to McLintock's PI. Which means that Vardy knew she was speaking to the cops, so he could send some of his goons after her. Put frighteners on to make sure she didn't testify.'

Methven jerked forward in the chair and rubbed his hands together. 'Why, though?'

'Money?' Wilkinson got up and started pacing around the empty office space. 'Always comes down to money. Some PI on a retainer from a top-end law firm like McLintock and Williams, they'll have money to throw at desperate cops like Bill bloody Lamb.'

'Is Bill desperate, though?' Methven shut his eyes, let the lids flicker for a few seconds. Then he glared at the screen, like it was lying and it had stolen the file. 'There's got to be a rational explanation for this.'

Cullen cleared his throat and waited until they looked up. 'Maybe I can help with that.' He rubbed at his neck. 'When I broke the news to Angela about her job, I... Well, she told me that Bill left her a couple of weeks ago.'

'Purple sodding buggery.' Methven smashed his fist onto the desk. 'Why the sodding hell did you not brief me?'

Cullen could only shrug. 'The guy's been under a lot of stress, right? Paying for two kids. Angela's a stay-at-home mum, so he's got all that breadwinner angst. And he's not been able to rent out his flat.'

'Shitting hell.' Wilkinson was nodding. 'How did we not see it, Colin? He's not been long as a DI. All the pressure of the Vardy case. I thought he was coping, but clearly his mind is crumbling.'

'So Lamb leaked.' Methven got up with a flounce and started pacing the office. 'I never thought I'd have to confront one of our own, but...'

Wilkinson looked up at him, his eyes pleading. 'You need to take this to Lennox, Colin. Get me off the hook.'

'No.'

'Come on. Mate.' Wilkinson glared at Methven. 'That bloody arsehole Lamb has been framing me. Must've been him who took my phone, set up the escort thing for Amy. Put her through the trauma of seeing Hamish bloody Williams dying. She's lucky he didn't murder her as well. It all makes sense. She pulled out of two prosecutions, let that bastard Vardy walk free. Makes perfect sense.'

'DC Zabinski?' Methven walked over to the door and opened it with a clunk. 'Can you call DI Lennox and tell him to take DI Wilkinson into custody.'

'Colin, mate, you can't—'

'I can and I am.' Methven walked over to the doorway and gave Zabinski a warm smile. 'Please lock this door behind us.'

'Sir.' Zabinski waited for them to leave then pushed the door shut.

Methven nodded at Cullen. 'Sergeant, let's—'

'Colin, you bloody wanker!' Wilkinson was in the doorway, like an angry bear in a cage. 'You can't—'

Methven pushed the door shut and locked it. 'I bloody can.'

～

Cullen rang Lamb's doorbell with one finger, knocking on the door with the other fist.

Methven joined him, his phone clamped to his ear. 'Still not answering.' He turned to Bain and motioned for him to head down the back lane. 'Check the back door.'

'Sure thing, Col.' Bain marched off with some sort of purpose for once.

Cullen pressed the bell harder, like that would make any difference. Ground his teeth hard.

'I still can't figure out why Lamb would want that file.' Methven was slowly shaking his head. 'Him of all people, leaking to Vardy?'

Cullen saw a strip of light flash under the door, and then it opened in his face, as fast as a fist. He jumped back, caught off guard by the speed.

Bain stood there. 'Didn't mean to give you a fright, boys. Thought I smelled gas, so I smashed his back doors in.'

Cullen shouldered him out of the way, pulse drumming in his ears, and headed into the flat, three stairs at a time. Living room, clear. But four doors leading off. He started opening doors. Kitchen, clear. Bathroom, clear. No sign of Lamb anywhere, and no sign of his phone.

'Where the sodding hell is he?' Methven caught up with him. 'Do you think the vigilante's got to him? Maybe abducted him? If he's been leaking, then he's at risk.'

Cullen tried the last door on the right. Locked.

Shite, what if he's in there, dying?

'Stand back.' He pushed against the wall and launched himself shoulder first. The door cracked around the lock and toppled in. Cullen braced himself against the doorframe and stopped himself before he fell flat on his face.

Lamb wasn't dying. Wasn't even there. The walls, though. The walls were covered in newspaper clippings, police reports, pages and pages of handwritten notes. Bits of string connecting them, connecting the dots. Like a whiteboard in an Incident Room. Files everywhere – on the floor, on the bed, even on the chair by the window.

Wait a second.

Cullen lurched over and grabbed the file. The tell-tale Operation Venus typography and classification. Wilkinson's file. Lamb *had* taken it.

'Em, Sergeant?' Methven was pointing at the chair back, glowing in the yellow street lights.

Hanging off the back was a scrunched-up Batman costume.

Jesus Christ. Lamb is the vigilante.

39

CULLEN STOOD ROOTED TO THE SPOT, UNABLE TO TAKE HIS EYES OFF the evidence. He felt like somebody had paused a film at the crucial, heart-stopping moment, forcing him to stare at the scene in front of him until every damning detail had etched itself into his mind.

The police reports. Wilkinson's file on Amy Forrest's underage rape, stolen from Fettes. And the Batman costume.

All pointing to the fact that his friend was a murderer.

Footsteps thundered down the corridor and Bain burst through the open door, wide-eyed. 'Christ, Sundance, you look like someone's shat in your sink.' He snapped his head around to look from Cullen to Methven to the chair to the walls, then back to the chair. 'Holy shitballs.'

Cullen stood there, trying to make sense of it. Shock, confusion. Anything. It all just pointed to one conclusion.

All the years of disappointments, letting Vardy slip through his grasp, with McLintock and Williams taking turns to get him off like they took turns on Big Rob.

All those witnesses pulling out or dying in suspicious circumstances, never pointing back to Vardy or anyone in his organisation.

It all took a toll on Lamb, crushing his hope and his spirit, making him decide to take the law into his own hands.

Jesus Christ.

'So Lamb is the vigilante.'

'That's fairly obvious, Sundance.'

Methven shook off his daze and looked at Cullen. 'Why did he take the file, though?' He clenched his jaw. 'And why did he leak to McLintock, only to then murder him?'

'Whatever, Col.' Bain snapped on a pair of gloves and started photographing the room on his phone. 'Fact is, this murdering bastard is one of ours. We've shat the bed and we need to start cleaning up the mess.'

'Are you suggesting that we—'

'Hold your horses.' Bain crouched to get a better angle on the cape. 'I'm not suggesting anything. Just saying that Lamb's out there, right now, very possibly slitting the throat of his next victim. And we've no idea who else is on his list. Could be anyone who's ever crossed him. Could be us. Could be other people on the job or—'

'Angela!' Cullen darted out of the room.

CULLEN SCREECHED TO A HALT OUTSIDE ANGELA'S HOUSE AND jumped out of the car, leaving his door wide open. He raced up the driveway and hammered on the red wooden door with his fists.

Methven and Bain fanned out, running around either side of the house.

The front door gave way and the force of his knocking carried Cullen into the house.

Angela jumped back, scrambling out of his way. Cullen had to grab her shoulders to stop himself from headbutting her. He froze inches from her face, their noses almost touching, her eyes wide with fright as she stared straight into his.

Cullen pulled his head back. 'You're okay!'

'What do you mean, I'm okay? Of course I am! What the hell are you doing banging on my door at this time of night? I've finally got the kids to sleep and you're—'

'I'm sorry.' Cullen glanced around like they might be sleeping in the hallway, then focused back on Angela, dropping his voice to an urgent whisper: 'Sorry about this, but we thought you were in danger.'

'What?'

'Bill, he—'

'I've no idea where he is.'

'We think he's—'

She clenched her teeth. 'Have you been speaking to Stuart Murray?'

Cullen stopped dead. A name he hadn't heard in a while. 'What? Why would I?'

'Because he was going to speak to Bill about the 'roid rage.'

'The what?'

'Steroid-induced rage.'

'I know what it is.'

'Good for you, Scott. It's why I kicked him out.'

'Has he been beating you?'

'What? No.' She folded her arms. 'He was getting really angry. Never got physical but... He's been hitting the gym every day, before work or on his lunchbreak or late at night, said he needed it to let off steam. Said it was the job, the new responsibility of being a DI, and the pressure of having to support the family by himself while I was out of work to mind the kids.'

'I was slagging him just yesterday because his jacket looked like a sausage.'

'But the protein shakes led to food supplements and they led to steroids. I called him out on his rage issues and he promised he'd quit that shit months ago, but he lashed out at the boys and I went through his gym stuff and he had pills and vials and...' She went silent, the memory choking her voice. She wasn't crying yet, but her eyes were going out of focus as she saw it happening all over again.

'Angela, I'm sorry, but I have to ask you—'

'Yesterday.' She gave them a tight smile. 'I told you in the pub. He showed up last night. Wanted to see the kids, but it was late and he was all over the place. I was worried he'd had some bad news cause he wasn't like himself. Really sentimental...' She frowned, then dismissed the thought with a shrug. 'Probably just drunk.'

'After you chucked him out, has he tried—'

'No. He's been a ghost. I've only had texts from him.'

'From his work number?'

Angela looked at him as though he had asked the question in German. She stared right through him. 'No, a new one.'

Shite, a burner.

'Scott, what's going on?'

'Can you give me the number?'

'Only if you tell me what's going on?'

'Craig Hunter and I worked this case, a few years back. People in a gym, dealing steroids. One of them got ultraviolent. I'm worried about him, that's all.' Cullen got out his phone, mainly just to give him something to look at that wasn't her pleading eyes. 'I'll get that number traced.'

'Scott, cut the shite. What's he done?'

Cullen took a deep breath. Tried to think of any other options. But she was his friend, had worked with him for years. She deserved the truth, no matter how badly it stung. 'There's a vigilante in Edinburgh and—'

'That guy who killed Vardy and McLintock? You think that's Bill?'

'Come on, Angela. You're a cop. You know we have to follow wherever the evidence leads.'

She flinched. 'Sorry, you're right.'

'I need that number.'

She pointed through the open kitchen door. 'My mobile's charging...' She headed through.

Cullen started following, but his own phone started ringing. He pulled it out of his inside pocket and glanced at the screen.

Hunter.

Shite, what does he want?

Cullen motioned at the front door. 'Sorry, I have to take this.'

She just shrugged.

He felt awful, leaving her alone like this, dazed and confused, but his phone kept ringing, so he stepped outside, closed the door behind him and took the call. 'What's up, Craig?'

'Scott, this isn't what I signed up for when I let you stay on my couch.'

'What are you talking about?'

'Sharon's here. Said she wants to speak to you. I told her you weren't in, but she called me a liar. She's outside, waiting in her car. Didn't sign up for this, mate.'

Cullen looked up into the dark night sky, trying to steady his nerves. It didn't work. 'Craig, I can't deal with this shite right now!'

'Don't you *ever* shout at me.' Hunter's voice was as sharp as the winter air.

'Sorry, Craig. That was uncalled for. It's nothing to do with you. I'm just... Get rid of her, please.'

Harsh breathing. 'Right.' Then a door snapped open and traffic noises rasped out of the speaker. 'Fine, I'll tell her, but I'm not playing relationship therapist for you two if— What the hell?'

'What's up?'

'She's gone.'

'She's driven off?'

'No, she's gone. Her car's still here, but the driver's door is hanging open and—' Hunter grunted and started shouting, 'Get the hell—' Then he was cut off. Sounded like the phone fell to the ground, clattering on the asphalt with a burst of static.

40

WHAT THE HELL IS GOING ON?

Cullen gunned the engine, making the car fishtail as he clattered through Leith Links, the speedo reading eighty miles an hour, as the thirty speed sign flashed past. 'Call Sharon's mobile.'

The ringtone rattled out of the speakers. Straight to voicemail. Again.

What the hell?

If Lamb took aim at Craig Hunter...

Fifteen stone of raw power and army violence...

Lamb's not got 'roid rage, he's got a death wish.

Cullen leaned on the horn, blaring past a trundling VW Tiguan still at close to seventy miles an hour.

What if Lamb got the jump on Hunter because he was distracted by my phone call?

And what if he's behind Sharon's disappearance?

But why?

Cullen floored it, hitting the tight curve outside Queen Charlotte Street police station close to ninety, the engine roaring.

Shite – that Pauline Quigley case. Another case that slipped through my grasp, only for Sharon and Hunter to run with it. And they'd not pressed a single charge on Vardy.

Meaning they were as bad as the others, at least in Lamb's eyes.

He had to slow for the queuing traffic at the lights, but took the road down to Bernard Street and slipped through there. Another kickdown and he caught the amber lights and was on the home stretch, heading over the bridge. He slowed again, as the evening traffic weaved its way along the final—

Sod it.

Cullen stomped on the brake and skidded to a halt, the smell of burning rubber hot in his nostrils. He jumped out and sprinted along the road, then swung round the corner to Hunter's street.

Sharon's orange Focus sat there, the door still hanging open.

Hope I'm wrong. Hope that Sharon went to the shops and didn't swing the door shut hard enough and the wind blew it open and—

Who am I trying to kid?

Cullen came to a stop, bracing himself on the door with both hands. He craned his neck and scanned the car's interior, all cold and alien in the pale cabin light. Her phone sat on the passenger seat.

She'd never leave that, not in Leith.

Cullen spun around. Hunter's door was hanging open. He put his phone to his ear.

Methven only let it ring once before he took the call. 'Talk.'

'She's left her car door wide open and her phone on the seat. In Leith. Lamb's got her. Must have.'

'So?'

Cullen powered up the stairs to Hunter's flat. 'What do you mean, so?'

'I mean it's hardly evidence of an abduction, far less of the abductor's identity.'

'Are you taking the piss?'

'Where's Hunter?'

'Just checking now.' Cullen stopped by the front door. Somebody had left it ajar. 'Craig?' He walked through the flat, opening the bathroom door and peering inside.

'Meow?' Bubble peered up from inside the bath, her tail all fluffed up.

'Good girl.' Cullen walked back through and checked the bedroom. Still messed up from his sleep. 'Sir, you still there?'

'Yes.'

'The front door was left open and... Hunter's gone, too. Bill must've taken them bo—'

'Bill *may* have taken them both. You're not helping matters by jumping to sodding conclusions.'

Cullen jogged back out of the flat, counting to ten as he descended the steps. He checked Sharon's phone. Tried her passcode but she'd changed it. *Bloody hell.*

He set off back towards his car. 'Sir?'

'Mm?'

'What do you want me to do?'

'We're just going through Lamb's files. He's put together his own chronological log, detailing who did what in each of the Vardy cases and... The way he's written up our recent efforts makes it seem like he believes we've tried harder to bring *him* to justice than we ever did to prosecute Vardy of the rapes and murders, let alone the crimes of his money laundering friends in high places.' Methven paused. 'You still there?'

'Aye, just trying to make sense of it.' Cullen got in his car and twisted the key. 'We've only just found out that his lawyers were helping him launder money.'

'*Some* of us just found out about it today. DI Wilkinson's known about it for a while, but he chose to sit on the information. Reading Lamb's file, I get the sense he feels betrayed by his own side. His latest notes tar everyone who has ever worked the Vardy cases with the same brush. You, me, Wilkinson, Bain, Sharon. I suspect he's coming after all of us.'

Cullen fell silent, the engine droning away.

'Be careful out there, Sergeant. I need you to return to St Leonards.' He hung up before Cullen got a chance to reply.

Cullen slid his phone back into his pocket.

What the hell do I do now?

Go back to St Leonards?

Go looking for Lamb?

Or wait for him—

That burner... The one he'd been texting Angela with.

He got his phone back out and found a number. It started ringing through the dashboard, the tone drilling his teeth. He turned the volume down a couple of notches.

'Yes?'

'Tommy, it's Scott Cullen, you got any—'

'Aye, aye.' Tommy Smith yawned. 'As I thought, that number is a pay-as-you-go job.'

'Can you get a location for me?'

FOOT TO THE FLOOR, ONE HAND WHIPPING THE WHEEL AROUND, THE other hammering the horn. Two cars and three road bikes careening out of his way like flipper balls, as Cullen shot back out of Leith, weaving around the drivers who were too slow to react. He fought to keep the car on the road at sixty miles an hour where the council had lowered the limit to twenty, just as he skidded on to Leith Walk, losing traction in the rear. He flipped the wheel back the way. A double-decker trundled towards him, but he got control and hit the floor, shooting away up Leith Walk.

'Stay on this road for one-point-five miles. Then, you have reached your destination.'

Cullen kicked the car back up to sixty – pubs and restaurants flying past him either side of the four lanes, the Friday night crowd getting denser and livelier the closer he got to the city centre. A fight was breaking out by the Tesco Express, a group of locals chatting to a hen party spilling out of a bar, a stag do in matching pink shirts getting between them.

'After one hundred yards, take a right, then you will have reached your destination.'

Cullen looked ahead. *Gayfield Square?*

He slowed down, glancing around for signs of Lamb or his car. Nothing. He checked the location Tommy Smith had given him, checking out of the window to confirm he wasn't fantasising, then pulled up by the police station.

'You have reached your destination.'

Cullen got out and jogged down the cobbled street, the leather soles of his shoes slapping off the stones. The area was almost deserted, no sign of Lamb.

So where the hell is he?

'Must be something in the Bavarian air, aye.' A guy was sitting in the doorway of Powerhouse Fitness, huddled up against the shuttered front door, wrapped in a filthy sleeping bag, a smartphone stuck to his ear. Gleaming, box-fresh, the sort of high-end Samsung that Lamb had been toting around. 'All of it one go, aye.'

Shite. That's his phone!

Cullen walked up to him. 'Police.' He reached into his jacket pocket and pulled out his warrant card, making the guy drop his frown. 'Is that your phone?'

He put it to his chest. 'Why wouldn't it be?'

'Where did you get it?'

'I'll call you back, Lenny.' The homeless man hit the screen and put the phone away. 'What's your problem?'

'Look, did someone give you it?'

'Why? You think I can't just go into—'

'Cut the crap. That model costs almost a grand.' Cullen got a nod. 'Was it a man wearing a tight leather jacket? Looks like he works out a lot. In his early forties and—'

'Aye, it was him.' The guy looked at Cullen as though he was mentally challenged. He waved the phone at Cullen. Then he tucked the mobile into the folds of his sleeping back. 'It's mine now.'

'Don't worry, I won't confiscate it. Sounds like you got it as a gift. Nothing illegal about that.' Cullen let his words sink in, then cocked his head like he had been struck by a sudden idea. 'How about this – you give me the full story on how you came by that phone and I'll give you a tenner to top up your credit. How's that sound?'

'You some sort of pervert or something?'

'No, that guy's an old mate of mine. It's part of a wild goose chase for my stag night. He gives phones to strangers and we have to track them down and... Never mind. I just need to know the exact details of what he said and did when he gave you that mobile.'

The homeless man squinted at him hard.

Cullen pulled a ten pound note out of his wallet, like it was too bizarre to be anything but the truth. 'You got a name?'

'Archie.' The guy shrugged and took the money. 'Alright. Your pal pulled up in a black Beemer, right over there outside the polis station.' He pointed down the road. 'Just stopped for a sec and buzzed down his window. Looked like he stuck out his hand to drop something in the street, but then he saw me watching him and reversed back to where you're standing now. Must've been in a real rush to get to the next drop-off, because the boy went at it full pelt, tyres squealing and all. I thought he was going to run me over, but then he stopped and got out. That's when I saw he was built like a tank. And his leather jacket, sweet Jesus, it looked painful it was so tight. I used to look like that myself, you know...' He glanced down at his arms, stick thin despite the patched-up layers of thermals. 'Anyway, your mate chucked the phone at me and told me to make a few calls to my friends. Didn't matter who I called, just as long as I started using the phone. And then he flashed me a grin. Can't say why exactly, but I got the chills. And don't tell me it's winter. That wasn't it. I know I sound soft in the head, but... That game you guys are playing isn't bringing out the best in your friend, if you don't mind me saying so.'

'You have no idea. But thanks.' Cullen pulled another tenner out of his wallet and handed it over. 'Here, get yourself into a hostel. Going to be a cold night.' He rushed back towards his car.

Lamb must have anticipated we'd track him, so he gets this guy to make us think he's where his phone is.

Good thinking.

And good sense of humour to drop the thing off next door to a police station, but there's whole lot of extra CCTV coverage around here.

Cullen tore open the driver's door and jumped behind the wheel. 'Hey Siri, call Elvis.' He hit the start button and the car grunted to life, the dial tone switching from his phone to the dashboard speaker. *Come on, come on, come on.*

'Scott, what's up? Need a ride home from the pub?'

'Paul, I need you to access the CCTV network around Gayfield Square, about twenty-five minutes ago. You're looking for a black BMW.'

'Alright, alright, alright, I'm on it like a comet. Don't hassle me.'

Cullen clenched his teeth as he started the engine and followed the one-way system round.

Elvis huffed into his ear. 'Got it! Right, I'll track his journey and call out the route as you go.'

41

'AFTER FOUR HUNDRED YARDS, YOU HAVE REACHED YOUR destination.'

'Elvis, that's not funny!' Cullen shot through Tollcross, his fists clenching the steering wheel. The five-way junction disappeared in his rear-view.

'Sorry, Scott, didn't know you'd left your sense of humour at the office.' Elvis yawned. 'Just so you know, you're heading up towards where Ian Rankin and JK Rowling live.'

'You're sure this is where Lamb went?'

'As in DI Lamb?'

Shite.

Cullen groaned.

So much for keeping a lid on it.

A red Volvo trundled out of the petrol station, black smoke belching out of the back.

'Elvis, keep this to yourself, okay?' Cullen slowed and flicked the air circulation on. 'Lamb is the vigilante who killed Vardy and his lawyers. He's taken Sharon and Hunter.'

'Craig Hunter? Aye, bullshit.'

'This isn't a joke. Look, is he really—'

'Gillespie Place should be on your right any time soon now. Number seven. Flat three. First floor, I think.'

'You're sure?'

'Believe it or not, that's one of Dean Vardy's properties. Had to go around there once. Nice building. Vardy's flat's up on the first floor, overlooking Bruntsfield Links over the road. You know, the pitch-and-putt course. And, oh man, the Treehouse does great pancakes with—'

'Shut up!'

Lamb's black BMW was parked at the kerb, right outside a black door with a faint number seven on the glass panel above.

Cullen slammed on the brakes and skidded to a halt in the deserted bus lane, inches from the BMW's rear bumper. 'Right, I'm going in. Stay on the line, record this call and keep quiet.'

'I called for backup on another line, by the way. You can thank me later.'

Cullen jumped out of the car and stuck his phone in the front pocket of his jacket. 'Can you hear me?'

'Loud and clear.'

'Keep quiet.'

'Roger.'

'I mean it.'

Cullen tried the door to number seven and pushed it open, stepping onto a short hallway before a communal staircase winding upwards. He stopped, listening for any noise beyond the quiet creak of the unoiled hinges. Muffled shouts came from upstairs. He ran up the first flight of stairs, taking the scuffed steps three at a time. He clattered into a mountain bike chained to the banister and spun, catching himself on the railing.

Stupid bastard.

He sprinted over and stuck his ear to the heavy wooden door. Sounded like people were screaming into gags behind it.

He took a few steps back and barrelled into the wood, shoulder first. The bang echoed through the stairwell like a gun shot.

The door was still shut.

Cullen's shoulder hurt as if he had been shot. His buggered shoulder, the one some psycho had taken a hammer to. He ignored it and took a few steps back, ready to go at it again.

The door swung open and Lamb looked out at him. 'Scott? What the hell are you doing here? I thought I heard a gun go o—'

Cullen dropped his head and drove his shoulder into Lamb's gut, his feet thundering on the wooden floorboards. Lamb stumbled back into the flat, gasping for breath, and clattered into a chest of drawers. Cullen was still driving through him like a rugby flanker when he felt Lamb take the impact with a shuddering thump. Lamb slid to the ground, so Cullen scrambled over him and ran towards the muffled shouts from the back of the flat.

Two doors, both open.

Shite, which one?

He kept going straight and slapped his hands against the wood, smashing the door against the wall. Nothing in the room but a stripped double bed, an empty wardrobe and a closed window. He wheeled around to run back out, but the door hit him on the rebound, right on the point of his shoulder.

Shite!

The pain flashed white in his head. He kicked the door out of his way and went back out into the hallway. Two steps and he was at the other door, grabbing the handle this time, controlling the swing as he pushed it open.

A kitchen. Big table in the middle. Two people sitting at it, Sharon and Hunter, staring at him wide-eyed, both bound to their chairs with brown parcel tape, gagged with more tape, lengths of it stuck over their mouths to muffle their excited screams.

Cullen glanced at the kitchen counter, saw a block of knives. He grabbed the biggest one, a serrated blade, and sliced through the tape wrapped round Sharon's torso, careful not to cut her. She stiffened, her eyes watching his every move, paralysed by panic. Her arms came free and she arched away from the knife, her fingers going for the tape on her mouth, fumbling at the edges. Her wide-eyed gaze shot past Cullen's bashed shoulder.

Cullen turned at the source of her terror and caught a fist straight in the face.

42

Cullen jerked awake. A deep rumbling vibrated through him. His head hurt like a wrecking ball had smashed into it.

Not a wrecking ball. A fist.

Lamb's fist.

Where the hell is he?

And where the hell am I?

Pitch black on all sides. Cullen glanced around, opening his eyes as far as his headache would let him. Just little stars spinning around. *Must've been a hell of a punch.*

He tried to move, but couldn't. Something bound his hands behind his back. Something sticky. Parcel tape?

He was lying flat on something. The vibration was shifting up and down. Was it the back seat of a car?

He craned his neck round and saw Lamb, his tense face glowing a sickly blue sheen, lit up by the dashboard. The night outside was a wall of darkness only pierced by the occasional orange streetlight, but the sodium glow was too weak to let Cullen see where they were.

Somewhere with a lot of shrubs and trees. Somewhere remote. Somewhere nobody would find him.

He sat up and blinked a few times, trying to make his vision adjust but his head throbbed harder.

How long was I out for?

Lamb's eyes flicked to the rear-view mirror. 'Welcome back. Sorry about the punch.'

'You—' Cullen lay back on the seat. He'd expected sarcasm in Lamb's voice, but he sounded truly sorry. 'Where are we, Bill?'

'Arthur's Seat.'

Cullen caught a glimpse of city lights as they rounded a bend.

'Where are we going?'

'You'll see.' Lamb turned his attention back to the road, his mouth set in a tight line. Conversation over. Just the low rumble of the engine and the tyres whispering on tarmac.

Cullen blinked again and this time it sharpened his vision, enough to notice rows of faint silver silhouettes swishing past the windows. Bushes outlined by a smattering of distant stars, lining either side of a narrow black band of roadway that curved up a slope in a long right bend.

Must be on Queen's Drive.

Duddingston's the other side of the hill. If I can just get out of this, get over there and call someone. Methven, Buxton, hell, even Bain.

Elvis!

Cullen flexed his chest, felt his phone digging into his sternum, and whispered, 'You still there?'

No response.

Shite.

Cullen shifted round, getting a better look at Lamb. 'You know as well as I do that you can't walk away from this one. Even if you kill me.'

'I'm not stupid.' Said without emotion.

'If you knew you'd get caught in the end, why did you do it?'

'Because it's the right thing to do.' Lamb glanced in the mirror, but there was no irritation in his eyes, just purpose. He looked back out at the road. 'But there's no rush with what I'm about to do.' He pulled over into a parking bay looking down on the dark waters of Duddingston Loch. The lights of southern Edinburgh dotted the horizon like tiny votive candles. Lamb killed the engine, then sat there staring out, his face disappearing as the dash lights died. 'Vardy was a rapist and a murderer. The lowest of the low.' His voice had the dispassionate certainty of the final judgement.

Cullen lay there, hating himself for getting it right. 'You think you're above the law.'

'And Vardy didn't?' Lamb's teeth caught the faint moonlight. He was looking at Cullen through the rear-view. 'That bastard literally got away with murder, several times, all thanks to those *lawyers*. Pair of them, lining their pockets with his filthy cash, earnt by pumping heroin onto our streets. Vardy ruined lives. *Ended* them.' He paused for a moment, then gave his eyes a quick wipe and turned round to face Cullen, kneeling on the driver's seat. 'Few years back, my kid sister got snared in one of Vardy's schemes. Prick got her hooked on smack then had her working as a whore down in Leith. This was before Wonderland, of course. Way before. Debbie was a good kid. Didn't deserve what that vermin did to her.'

Cullen couldn't see Lamb's eyes in the dark, but he could feel them drilling into him with red-hot agony. 'I'm sorry, Bill. I had no idea.'

'Neither did I, until it was too late. We'd lost touch. I was busy – she was supposed to be training as a hairdresser through here. Our parents died not long before she moved. Twelve years between us. Too big a gap, you know? Debbie died of sepsis. Doctor reckoned it was caused by dirty heroin. Guess who sold her that?'

Cullen tried shifting his weight, maybe toppling off the back seat into the footwell. But no dice. He was rooted to the spot.

'Those lawyers. Pair of pricks. They kept getting him off on technicalities or when one witness after another conveniently disappeared or turned up dead just ahead of a trial. All while everybody knew why. And nobody did anything about it.' Lamb barked out a laugh. 'Nobody took that bastard off the board. They could have. I mean, Wilko had any number of minor crimes he could've nailed him for. Same with Crystal *sodding* Methven. They just didn't. But those two, with their massive mansion. Their secret love. Like they were respectable, especially repping that vermin. Kept on reducing our justice system to a farce. Makes me sick to the back teeth.'

'I share your frustration, Bill. I've tried to—'

Lamb just grunted. He leaned between the front seats, his boozy breath hissing right into Cullen's face. 'The world is a much better place without men like Vardy, McLintock and Williams. And it's a better place without people who failed to stop them.'

It hit Cullen like a fist in the back of the head.

It wasn't just Vardy and his shysters on Lamb's list.

Cops like Cullen, too. Wilkinson, Methven, even Lamb himself.

We all played a part in letting them do it. We'd all known full well that a notorious rapist and murderer was getting off by sneaking through legal loopholes or by murdering or intimidating witnesses, and yet we'd taken no personal action to plug those holes. Just hid behind professional excuses.

We let witnesses die, let prosecutions die.

We let Vardy back on the streets.

'What about Amy?'

'Amy...' Lamb chuckled. 'She had three chances to take him down. *Three.* First, when Vardy nonced her. Wilko knew, kept that from the world. Second, when Vardy raped her. Pulled out of that one, didn't she? Third, when Vardy SHOT SOMEONE IN FRONT OF HER.'

The words rattled round the car.

'Bill, she's not even eighteen.'

'Debbie was eighteen when she died. Old enough to drink, shag and vote.'

'You would've killed her, wouldn't you?'

'Amy Forrest knew what she was doing.' Lamb pushed himself forward, the outline resting between the seats. 'You may not want to hear this, Scott, but cops like your ex-fiancé Sharon and her Sex Offences Unit, they're just as bad. Maybe worse. They're enablers. They had all the evidence they needed to take one case after another to court, but they just sat on it, building a prosecution. Strategic policing, they call it. Absolute bullshit. Even lowly constables like your mate Hunter had enough information that he could've prosecuted that raping bastard, but no. Sharon should've put Vardy behind bars, but they just watched and waited and did SOD ALL. She wanted to blow the case up to secure a longer jail sentence, manoeuvring herself into position to advance her career with a big day in court. I know her, Scott. I went up against her for this job. I won, but I know the pair of you. Always moaning about your careers, like that's the important thing here. It makes no difference. If she'd acted when she could've – hadn't sat on her hands – Vardy wouldn't have raped *six* women. Six. That's just the ones we know about. God knows how many others died of ODs.'

Something's not right here.

It's like he's in court, delivering his prosecution speech.

But I'm not in the dock with the others. Sharon, Methven, Wilkinson, Hunter, Amy. I'm the jury,

He's pleading with me, rather than telling me why he's handing me the death penalty.

But whatever he's about to do, it's time to end this. Get a confession, get Elvis to play the recording in court, even if I won't be there to see Lamb get his justice.

'Bill, why are you telling me all of this? You trying to convince yourself you're doing the right thing before you kill me?'

'Kill you?' Lamb sounded genuinely confused. 'Why would I do that?'

'Didn't you just say it yourself? That old phrase – the only thing necessary for the triumph of evil is for good men to do nothing.'

Lamb sighed, a weary, defeated sound. 'That's not what I meant. I meant deliberate sabotage and suppression of evidence. And worst of all, *careerism*. Ironically enough, I don't expect cops to be vigilantes.'

Cullen couldn't help but laugh. 'Really?'

In the darkness, Lamb seemed to nod, but maybe less in agreement than in confirmation that there was no turning back now. 'I know I'm a hypocrite –putting myself above the law – but it was the only way to get to those bastards. The only way to bring this corrupt business empire down before it cost the lives of more innocent people. And the only way to expose Wilkinson.'

'What's Wilkinson got to do with this?'

'You don't know?' Lamb shifted back, his knees squeaking on the leather. 'He's the reason every case against Vardy fell apart. Every single one. Whatever others did or didn't do to secure convictions, Wilkinson leaked information to Vardy and McLintock. Protected him for years. Told him who the witnesses were and where to find them. All for money. I knew we had a mole. Thought it was you or that chump Methven. Maybe Sharon. Nah, I knew it wasn't her. So I followed you all, kept tabs on your spending. But Wilko... Now, Wilko was the only one who gave himself away. On Monday night, I followed him to Vardy's bar. Thought he was being smart, didn't he? Pretending to fight him. Got you, didn't it? Sunday night, right, he came up here. This spot. I sat in the shadows, watching that prick meeting someone. I got a note of the licence plate and ran a check. The boy's a PI. He works for McLintock.'

Felt like Cullen had been punched in the gut this time. He struggled to breathe. 'He was leaking Amy's ID.'

'See what I mean?' Lamb leaned forward, his teeth glinting in the pale moonlight. 'They gave me no choice. A bent cop selling us all out, just for a bit of shiny. Selling the identity of an underage rape victim for cash. Even the PF didn't know who our witness was. Christ knows what Wilko was playing at. Maybe some leverage over Vardy. But his incompetence let that animal back out on the street to kill and rape and poison.'

Cullen's head was spinning. 'It's not too late. You can give evidence against Wilko.'

'Scott, I've got nothing that could absolutely confirm it. No solid evidence trail. You know how hard it is to prosecute a serving officer? And Professional Standards and Ethics are useless. Bunch of clowns couldn't catch a—'

'*Now*. You can come forward now, Bill. Go on the record, take Wilko down.'

'Seriously?' Lamb snorted. 'It's way too late for that. I've murdered three people. I did the right thing by killing those scumbags, but a cop's life in prison is just about the only thing worse than death. I know I deserve it, but... but it wouldn't be right to drag my family through that. The shame—'

'For Christ's sake, Bill. You tried to kill Amy, a single mother with a young son. Nobody to look after him if you'd been successful.'

'Then he'd go into care. Roll the dice, even if it's a one, it'll be a damn sight better than that stupid wee tart.' Lamb pulled his head back through the seats. 'Amy should've testified, but she didn't. She let that bastard walk away because going on the stand might've made things a bit inconvenient for her.'

'A *bit* inconvenient? She was barely sixteen. And he threatened to—'

'I know, I know, but...' Lamb sounded like he was talking to a petulant teenager with zero understanding of the moral complexity of adult life. 'Come on, Scott, compare the short-lived inconvenience of witness protection, which she and her boy would've been guaranteed, with Vardy getting off and raping all those other girls, one after the other.'

Cullen swallowed hard, his throat thick with mucus. He didn't have any words.

Lamb took something from the passenger seat and passed it through the seats, little more than a shadow in the night. 'Take this.'

Cullen reached for the shape without thinking, but the parcel tape cut into his wrists. He hissed. 'Cut that bloody tape off me.'

'Oh, aye. Right.' Lamb's leather jacket rustled and something caught the pale light, a long triangle. 'Come on then, twist around so I can get to your hands.' The cabin light switched on and a Stanley blade flashed.

Cullen squeezed his eyes shut against the glare.

'Oh, and Scott? Don't do anything stupid after I cut that tape. We're not done yet.'

Cullen nodded, his eyes open again.

Lamb sliced the tape with one flick of the wrist, then killed the light.

Cullen blinked a few times to make his eyes adjust back to the dark.

The shadowy shape loomed in front of his face. This time, Cullen's hands obeyed his order and he grabbed a paper file.

'You asked me why I was telling you this whole story. This is why. This evidence will put Wilkinson behind bars. And so you'll understand what I have to do now. There's no other way and you know it, so don't bother arguing.' Lamb fell silent.

'Jesus, Bill, please do—'

'Get out.'

'What?'

'You heard.'

What the hell is he doing?

Oh no. No, no, no.

'I heard you, Bill, but sod this. Bill. You can't expect me to assist you in your own murder.'

Silence.

'Scott...' There was a new tone in his voice now. Disappointment. 'That night, outside Campbell McLintock's house. I'd got him to call you, set you up as a patsy. But then you saw it and... You chased me and I almost killed you. You're a good man, Scott. Too good to go like that.'

'Bill, it's not too late.'

'Listen, get out and take that file. Finish what I started. Put that scumbag Wilkinson behind bars and end this whole thing. Then at least my work will have served a purpose, even if you think I'm now taking the easy way out by killing myself.'

'Bill, no—'

'After what I've done, murdering three men... I'm just as bad as them. Sod that. If they had to die, so do I.' Lamb's voice was a hollow rasp. 'Besides, I've messed up pretty much everything else in my life. So, please. Get out.'

Cullen stared at the dark shape that used to be his friend. For a moment, they were both perfectly still.

Then Lamb jerked his head at the door and the Stanley knife caught in the light.

This time Cullen didn't object. Just got out and let the door snap shut behind him. He gazed down, straining his ears in the deathly silence until they started ringing.

But the noise wasn't in his head, it was an ambulance, powering up the hill towards them.

Elvis!

Cullen reached into his pocket for his phone.

Something sharp bit into his neck. 'Stay still.' The front door clicked shut and, from the sound of his voice, Lamb was looking straight at Cullen. 'Come on, Scott.' He pressed the Stanley blade to Cullen's neck and marched him away from the idling car. 'That'll do.'

Cullen flinched, staring at the black sky while the distant stars went blurry.

'One last favour.' Lamb barked out a laugh. 'You know, the saddest thing is that, after forty-two years on this terrible planet, you're the only friend I can trust to do the right thing.' He sheathed the blade, the leather giving a strange sucking sound. 'It may not mean much to you, coming from me, but you're a good man, Scott. I've always believed that.'

'Bill, what the—'

Lamb pushed Cullen hard, kicking his legs back so he flew backwards. Cullen's arse cracked off a rock, sending a jolt up his spine. In the gloom, he caught a blurry wave from the dark shape in front of him, then could only watch as Lamb dived backwards off the cliff edge.

43

'No!' Cullen jerked upright, frantically searching the dark scrub ahead of him for signs of Bill Lamb. But it was just darkness beyond the cliff, the hard wind buffeting him.

Below, something landed with a dull thud. Bill Lamb.

The tears stung his eyes – the wind lashing them against his cheeks and ears.

Jesus Christ.

Jesus Christ, Bill. Why? Why did you have to do that?

The ambulance roared towards him, followed by two squad cars, their lights and sirens blaring in the darkness.

Cullen patted his pocket and felt the hard shape of his phone. He got it out and put it to his ear. 'You still there?' His voice sounded thick with tears.

'Course I am.' Sounded like Elvis was yawning. 'Is he okay?'

Cullen's gaze was drawn back to the darkness beyond the vague outline of the cliff, to the shafts of light coming from Edinburgh.

'Scott? Did you hear me?'

'Aye, I heard you. He's dead.'

Elvis gasped down the line. 'Well, the good news is I heard every word. Got it all, just like you asked.'

Cullen stood there, letting the night reclaim its silence. The siren climbed the hill, making his head feel like an echo chamber.

Lamb's final words blurred with the wail of the ambulance: *You're the only friend I can trust to do the right thing.*

Cullen clutched the phone tight in his hand. 'Delete it.'

Elvis gasped again. 'What?'

'I said, delete it.'

Silence.

Cullen wasn't sure if they were on the same page. So he *made* sure. 'Promise me you'll delete the recording.'

'Alright, fine. It's done. I've sent an ambulance out to your location. I was tracking your phone. Weird how Lamb didn't take it.'

'Maybe he knew.' Cullen held his phone out to kill the call, then put it back. 'Have you found Sharon and—'

'Aye, we got them both.' A high-pitched laugh. 'Craig pished himself. Actually pished himself. Big yellow puddle under his chair. Can you imagine?'

'I can. And it's not funny.'

'Come on, man. It is. Big Craig'd be the—'

'Look, whatever. Is DI Wilkinson still in custody?'

'What?'

'Just check for me.' Cullen ended the call and slid the phone back into his pocket.

Cullen squinted as the ambulance pulled over at the side of the road, the blue lights strobing. The siren cut out mid-wail and several doors banged shut. Two female paramedics jumped out, their green uniforms and high-viz vests catching the headlights. They rushed towards him – boots slapping off the tarmac – and another car pulled up. Two men in dark suits jumped out.

Cullen waited for the ambulance crew to come within earshot. 'I'm fine!' He pointed at the cliff. 'He went down there.'

They switched direction, but kept running, their torches flashing as they tracked the path Lamb had taken over the edge. The paramedics started climbing down the steep slope.

Cullen set off towards Lamb's Audi. *Need to get out of here. Get miles away. Anywhere but here.*

'Sergeant.' Methven stood there, blocking Cullen's path, looking him up and down, the lights strobing off him. 'Are you okay?'

'Just... shocked. We had a chat. Then...' Cullen pointed at the cliff. 'Then he must have hit some ice or...'

Methven looked right at him, backlit by the car and the ambulance. 'I assume Lamb only wanted to *chat* to exonerate himself of the vigilante killings?'

'Yes, sir.'

'Of course. And would I be right in assuming you believe him?' *You're the only friend I can trust to do the right thing.*

'Aye. It was... Jesus Christ, it was an accident.' Cullen's coccyx throbbed, like when he'd last been mountain biking. 'He pushed me back. I slipped, but he saved me. Jesus Christ.'

Methven crouched down in front of him. 'What's this?'

Cullen glanced down. Lamb's file. He had forgotten all about it. 'Wilkinson.' He pulled out his phone. 'We need to get to Wilkinson.'

'What's DI Wilkinson got to do with it?'

'Have a look.'

Methven turned towards the light to take a better look at the file.

Cullen put his mobile to his ear and listened to the ringtone. 'Yvonne, it's Scott. Is DI Wilkinson still in custody?'

'What the hell, Scott? It's the middle of the night.' She sounded sleepy.

'Yes or no?'

'No. Listen, I'm trying to *sleep*, thank you very much.'

'Where is he?'

'What? Well we had no evidence against Wilkinson so Lennox said he'd just go through the motions with the interview, then send him home. That was hours ago.'

'Shite.' Cullen hung up, his eyes locked on the backlit outline of Methven's head. All he could see of the face was a dark, empty space. 'They let Wilko go. Lennox. They—'

His phone went off in his hand. He stared at the bright screen. Elvis. He held his hand up as he put his mobile to his ear. 'What's up?'

'Just calling to let you know that the uniforms I sent round to Wilkinson's house when Lamb accused him in that conversation that somehow got deleted have—'

'You lost it?'

'Aye, sarge.' Elvis sighed. 'Sorry.'

'Wait, why did you send them round?'

'Wilko got let go. Thing is, the uniforms just called in. Wilko's not at home. No sign of him.'

'Shite!'

'I know. Listen, I'll make a few more calls, see if I can locate him.'

'Thanks.' Cullen ended the call and slid the phone back into his pocket.

Methven looked up from the file. 'What's happened?'

'Wilkinson's gone.' Cullen set off away from him. 'I need to find him.'

Methven stepped in his way and put a firm hand on his chest. 'No, Cullen, you need explain everything now. One moment you're chasing Lamb, and next I know he's gone off a cliff. For all I know you orchestrated this wee *accident* here.'

Cullen clenched his jaw. For a second, he thought about barging past his boss and going it alone. But he stopped.

Methven pushed a little harder. 'Explain yourself right now or we do this back at the station.'

'You're driving.'

METHVEN POWERED ACROSS THE ROUNDABOUT BY POLLOCK HALLS, the student accommodation lit up in the night. 'What the hell were you doing up there with him?'

'We were talking. Lamb had that file. Then he...' Cullen leaned forward, the seatbelt digging into his neck. 'He...'

Methven narrowed his eyes. 'You expect me to believe that sodding nonsense?'

'You've known me for a few years now, sir. That's not the first time I've been left alone in a remote place after pissing someone off.'

Methven pulled right at the lights and joined the traffic back towards the station. 'You've got until St Leonards to talk me out of putting you in cuffs, Sergeant.'

'Lamb knew we were onto him.' Cullen was sweating in the cold car. 'But he swore he wasn't the vigilante. He gave me that file, but I still didn't believe him. So he got pissed off with me, told me to get out. Said he needed to speak to Angela.'

'And where's your car?'

'Tollcross. We met there and he drove.' Cullen was pleading with him now. 'I didn't believe him, but then... Jesus Christ, Bill's dead now. He slipped on the ice and he...' It all sounded so hollow.

Methven pulled into the St Leonards car park and took out his cuffs. 'Time's up.'

'Look, hear me out, okay? This is what Lamb told me before he drove off. Wilkinson is the leak. Sold every bit of evidence we collected against him to that scumbag McLintock. Made sure that all the Vardy cases were thrown out of court.'

'Well, that's all in the file.'

'I haven't even read it, sir. That's just what he told me.'

'He's got photographs, call records, cash paid into DI Wilkinson's bank account. It's all there.'

'So you believe me?'

'I believe Bill. Not you.'

'Look, we need to find Wilkinson. He's the one we're after. Him. Lamb's...' Cullen swallowed hard. The grief hit him again, several smacks in the face, an uppercut to the chin. 'Bill's gone. Don't let his death be in vain.'

'His little *accident*.' Methven shook his head. 'Sodding hell.' He reached onto the back seat for something. 'The thing I can't figure out is why he left this behind.' He dumped a bag on Cullen's lap.

Something black caught the light. A stale, sweaty smell. The Batman costume.

Cullen shut his eyes. 'You took this from his flat?'

'I thought it was... wise.' Methven took back the bag and dumped it behind Cullen's chair. 'So where is Wilkinson?'

'That's the thing. I don't know. He's gone to ground.' Cullen opened the passenger door but stopped. 'Look, Wilkinson was in Vardy's pocket, right?'

'Go on.'

'Two of Vardy's goons attacked Wilko, remember? Saved by the vigilante. They're still in custody. Jason Gallagher shot Sammy McLean, our witness in Xena Farley's murder. Result: Vardy walked free, again. Gallagher works for Vardy. So does Wilko.'

Methven sighed, sounding about as frustrated as Cullen felt. 'You want to speak to him, don't you?'

'You got a better idea?'

'Get away!' Gallagher covered his face with his hands. The cell was dark and cold. Just the three of them. 'I've not done anything!'

'Calm down.' Cullen crouched in front of the bunk. 'We just need a word, Jason.'

Gallagher pushed himself further away, bunching up the blankets. 'I'm supposed to have been in court by now. You lot can't keep doing this!'

'Doing what, Jason?'

'Battering me in the middle of the night! I've done nothing!'

'Look, I'm here to let you go. Come on.'

'What?' Gallagher made eye contact. 'You're letting me out?'

'Aye, come on.' Cullen held out a hand. 'We're dropping the charges.'

Gallagher pushed himself to the edge of the bunk and dangled his legs down. 'Serious?'

'Aye. Need me to call anyone?'

'Nah, I'll walk.' Gallagher got up and stretched. 'Can you pass my trackies, man?'

'Sure.' Cullen reached over to the chair and picked up the dangling tracksuit. But he didn't hand it over. 'Actually, I might have to drive you myself.'

Gallagher frowned, reaching out for his clothes.

'I'm worried about you, Jason. See, the word on the street is that you're getting out because you ratted on your dear departed boss, Mr Dean Vardy.'

Gallagher sat down again, the bunk creaking. 'What?'

'Not just on Dean, though. I mean, he's dead, what would we gain by getting your co-operation? No, Jason, his empire is being divided up as we speak. And by the kind of men who are very interested in what you've been talking about. Well-connected men. Men who've been balls deep in Vardy's various schemes. Men who wonder what you know and what you're talking about. And they're very interested in speaking to you about what you knew and what you talked about in here.' Cullen clapped him on the shoulder and left a pause.

Gallagher's eyes went wide, his mouth-breathing getting louder and louder.

'So you'll be glad that I will give you a lift to wherever you want. Make sure nobody gets to you.'

Gallagher pushed back to the wall, bringing his knees up to his chest. 'What do you want?'

'Paul Wilkinson.'

Gallagher's face filled with panic, his lip quivering. 'What?'

'You and your mate attacked him, didn't you?'

'Battered him, too.'

'That attack was a fake, wasn't it?'

'Sod it...' Gallagher huffed. 'Wilkinson organised it. Got worried you lot were on to him or some other shite. Or what the hell do I know? He just wanted us to stage an attack on him, throw the scent off. That's all that was, I swear. I never tried to kill a cop. Oh shite! Shite, shite, shiiiii—'

'Calm down, Jason. I already know that. And I believe you. I honestly do. I just need you to tell me where Wilkinson would go.'

METHVEN TOOK THE FIRST EXIT WITH SCREECHING TYRES THAT WERE still filling Cullen's nostrils with the acrid stink of burning rubber when they slalomed into Dumbiedykes. 'Which building?'

Cullen leaned forward, gripping the 'oh-shit' handle tight. 'Holyrood Court. Next left.'

Methven slammed on the brake and shot out of the car, leaving the engine running.

Cullen unclipped his seatbelt and scrambled after him, piling through the tower block's entrance, then across the foyer and into the stairwell, flying up the steps at a full-on sprint. Cullen lost sight of Methven on the fourth floor, just as his phone rang.

Yvonne.

He slowed to answer it, thankful for the chance to catch his breath. 'You okay?'

'I'm okay, but I can't get hold of Terry.' She paused, sounded like she was driving somewhere. 'He was going to drop Wilkinson off.'

Shite.

Cullen played it through. Each time he came up with the same conclusion. Wilkinson had Lennox in the flat.

'Stay on the line!' Cullen set off again and reached the fifth-floor landing, his pulse hammering in his ears as he barrelled through the door and thundered down the corridor.

Methven stood there, waiting. Not even out of breath.

Cullen put his ear to the door, sucking in deep breaths.

Silence.

He whispered: 'I think Lennox is in there. What's the play here?'

Methven gave it a moment's thought, then did the usual policeman's knock.

Cullen heard muffled voices. He stood up and got away from the door.

It opened, just a crack, but far enough to see a face. Lennox, his eyes wide with fear.

Cullen tried to lock eyes with Lennox. 'Terry, is DI Wilkinson in there?'

Lennox swallowed. Said nothing.

'Just blink once for yes.'

Lennox blinked, once.

'Did he tell you to send me away and not talk to me?'

Another blink.

'Is he armed?'

Blink.

Cullen nodded. 'Alright, go back inside and tell him I've just come to talk. I'm alone, I have news he'll want to hear, and I'm unarmed.'

Lennox stared at him.

'Go.'

The door closed. Then opened to the full width. Lennox stood there. 'Come in, but do it slowly and keep your hands up so he can see you really are unarmed.'

Cullen raised his hands, taking his time to step through the doorway.

Lennox matched his pace, keeping his distance as he retreated.

Wilkinson was standing at the far side of the hallway, pointing a gun at Lennox. 'Why shouldn't I just shoot you both?'

Cullen cleared his throat. 'Put the gun down. I'm here to talk.'

'Then talk.'

Small step by small step, Cullen was moving to the other side of the room, slowly putting as much distance as possible between himself and Lennox, forcing Wilkinson to split his attention. 'We've got evidence.'

'You've got nothing.'

'Lamb has a file. All your payments, phone calls and meetings with McLintock's PI. And I'm on an open line to... to St Leonards right now.' Cullen lowered his head and glanced at his chest. 'My phone's in my pocket. You can check, if you want?'

Wilkinson snorted. 'And come close enough for you to get handsy with me? How stupid do you think I am?' His gun hand was starting to shake.

'I'm not here to fight with you. It's not too late to stop this. As it stands, you'll only face charges for obstructing an investigation. Those charges will go up to multiple homicide if you shoot us.' Cullen inclined his head at Lennox.

Wilkinson's eyes flashed over.

Getting through to him at last.

'Sir, nothing good will come of killing two fellow officers.'

Wilkinson lowered the gun, his hand shaking. His gaze drifted towards the window next to him and he flinched. It was dark outside, but the bright flat turned the glass into a mirror. He stared at his reflection. Bloodshot eyes, large sweat stains under the arms of his checked shirt, a shiny black gun in his tired hand.

He was screwed, and he knew it.

Wilkinson turned back to Cullen, the gun twitching at his side. 'I don't believe for a second that you've got anything on me. I don't believe that you're on the phone to anyone. But it doesn't matter. My only way out is to kill you and your backup, right?' He swept the gun up in a big, wide arc and pointed it at Cullen. 'Though I do fancy my—'

Before Cullen could move a muscle, Lennox threw himself across the flat, diving headfirst into Wilkinson. A shot went off. Glass smashed and someone screamed.

44

CULLEN SAT IN THE STATION CANTEEN, ALONE WITH HIS THOUGHTS. The past days kept coming back to him in fragments...

A knife attacker slashing the throat of a naked man.

A gun going off, the bullet missing him by inches. Millimetres even.

A man tumbling from the fifth floor, not high enough to turn him into pavement pizza, but high enough to shatter his bones and kill him.

He shut down each thought, forcing them into the dark corner of his mind where he kept all of his old cases, and told himself they were in the past.

And the past can't hurt you anymore, right?

Like hell it can't.

'Thank you.'

Cullen looked up.

Sharon stood there, a blanket draped over her shoulders. She scraped back the chair and sat opposite him. 'You saved my life.'

Cullen couldn't even look at her.

'Scott, you put your life at risk to save mine and Craig's. I'll never forget that.'

Cullen gritted his teeth. 'It's nothing.'

'It's not nothing. Quit with the bullshit, okay?' She reached over for his hands. 'Bill came after us because he thought we'd let the public down. Left Vardy on the street. He tied us up, gagged us. Then he started asking us what we knew about Wilkinson. He seemed calm, reasonable even. Craig helped me try and talk him out of it. Try to persuade him to turn himself in. But Bill lost it. Raged at us, saying *we* had betrayed our duty as cops, as though *we* had just killed three people, not him.'

Cullen felt her warmth through his fingers.

'He was so determined, Scott, so convinced he was doing the right thing. We were getting somewhere with him, or so I thought, but then you hit the door. For a second it looked like anything might happen. You came in, let me go, but... but he ambushed you and, well, he knocked you out, didn't he? And then he made off with you, saying you wouldn't let him down. You'd understand. And I guess you know the rest. The uniform cops just missed him. Ten seconds, Scott. Ten. Seconds.'

Cullen made eye contact. 'What?'

'They helped me and Craig get free and... We didn't know where he'd taken you. If they'd been ten seconds quicker, Bill would still be alive.'

'He took me up Arthur's Seat. Up there on the hill.' Cullen waved his hand like he was pointing in the right direction. Pitch black outside and he couldn't see the hill from here. 'If those cops had saved me... They'd...'

'Are you okay?'

'Two people I've worked with for years died tonight.' Cullen scraped back the chair, but didn't get up. Just sat there, brooding. 'Two idiots. Two complete idiots.'

'One who took the law into his own hands, Scott. One who broke the law, helped the people we try to bring down.'

Cullen avoided looking at her.

She reached over but he pulled his hands further away. 'Scott...'

'Sharon, I don't know what the hell to think.'

'Look, I wanted to thank you. You put your life on the line for me. I'll be the first to recommend you for a promotion or a commendation or whatever.'

'I understand, Sharon. This doesn't change anything between us. It's still over.'

She nodded. 'I know. I still like you, Scott. I just stopped loving you.'

'I know the feeling.' Cullen blinked back tears. 'I'm sorry for all the bad shite I've done. I'm sorry for—'

'Get over yourself, Scott.' She was smiling at him, but tears glistened in her eyes. 'You're not that bad. I'm not either. We're just different people from the ones who got together years ago, after we caught a serial killer. Maybe that was the mistake, maybe it wasn't. But we had some good times. Some great holidays. And I want to still be friends.'

Cullen brushed the tears away. 'I do too.'

'Okay.' Sharon pushed herself up to standing. 'Christ, the Valium's kicking in.'

'Are you going to be okay getting back to the flat?'

'Chantal's giving me a lift. She's just in with Craig now.'

'I'll see you around.' Cullen watched her walk away.

Part of him wanted to rush after her, take her in his arms, kiss her like he used to, try to save their broken relationship.

But the rest of him couldn't muster the energy.

It was over.

He just wished he'd been less of a passenger as it finished. Made things happen himself, been a man about it, not a boy. Taken control of things.

His phone flashed on the table. A text message from Yvonne, the contents hiding from the prying world. His breath caught in his throat, a butterfly flapped its wings in his stomach, and he slid his finger over the text icon.

'Scott, I'm so sorry to do this by text, but I can't get into anything with you. Need time to figure out what's going on in my head. Yvonne X'

CULLEN STARED AT THE SCREEN UNTIL HIS EYES HURT.

Then someone grabbed his shoulder and took the seat next to him. Hunter, smiling. Suit jacket, shirt, grey tracksuit bottoms. 'Your turn to save me, eh?'

Cullen could only nod.

'You okay, mate?'

Cullen cleared his throat, took a few goes to get rid of the tears he'd swallowed. Then he smiled, glad to see his friend. 'I just want your couch and sweet oblivion.'

DAY 7

Saturday
18th February

45

It was still dark when Cullen woke up. Took a few seconds to get his bearings. He was on Hunter's couch, the duvet kicked off onto the floor, still as tired as the minute he fell asleep.

Then his phone buzzed again.

He reached over to pick it up. Three missed calls, all from Methven, all in the last five minutes.

What the hell's happened?

He jerked up to sitting, his fingers fumbling the commands. Trying to call him back.

But the phone flashed again with another incoming call. He answered it. 'Sir?'

'Get up, Sergeant! We have work to do.'

'Sir, it's Saturday.'

'No rest for the wicked. And I know *precisely* how wicked you are.'

Cullen lay back on the makeshift bed and grunted.

'Sergeant, I'm standing outside Craig Hunter's flat and I sodding know you're in there.'

'She'll still be in bed, won't she?'

'Hardly.' Methven frowned at him. 'The woman has two young

children. And I know for a fact that she's been up since six because she phoned me. Go on now, chap on the door, but I'm leading in there.'

'You worried I might say the wrong thing?'

'No, but you smell like you slept in your clothes.'

'Speaking of clothes...'

'Leather burns at roughly four hundred and fifty degrees Celsius. Luckily, I have access to a forge. A friend in Aberdeenshire who makes Pictish wedding rings.' He yawned. 'A long drive at that time of night, but well...'

'Thank you, sir.' Cullen avoided eye contact as he stepped up to the door and knocked.

The door opened and Angela stood there, looking as tired as he felt. 'What's up?'

Methven gave a gentle smile. 'We need to—'

Her eyes narrowed to tiny slits. 'What's happened to him?'

Behind her, two boys hared down the hallway, squealing as they swarmed around their mother's long legs. She crouched down and whispered something. The older boy slapped the younger. 'Tig!' And they were off, racing through the house again.

Angela got to her feet and leaned back against the side wall, like she was bracing herself for the bad news. 'Tell me. Everything.'

'I'm afraid—'

Cullen stopped Methven, waiting for Angela to look at him.

I can't let anyone else break the news. Bill was my friend, so this is my responsibility.

'I'm sorry, Angela. Bill was involved in an accident late last night.'

She stifled a sob, but that was all the emotion she was letting herself show.

'I was there. I know what happened. And I know what didn't happen. And I'll be here for you to talk about it all, if that's what you want, but until then you need to remember one thing. Bill was a good man.'

She nodded for him to continue.

'You're going to hear a lot of things said about him in the days and weeks to come. That he killed a lot of people, including himself, but you don't have to believe any of that. There's no evidence.'

Methven stiffened, but gave a nod. 'Absolutely. The murder inquiries remain open and DI Lamb's death was a tragic accident. I personally attended the site to convince myself of that. I understand this won't be of much consolation in this difficult time, but I will work with the Police Federation to expedite your widow's pension and life insurance payment.'

She flinched.

Methven glanced back at his car, the smile waning. 'Given what's happened, the *worst* will be that even if it's deemed suicide, Bill will be posthumously diagnosed with PTSD and... Well, we're here for you.'

Angela maintained her smile for another moment. Then she nodded. 'I appreciate it, sir.'

'Well. I know this is a difficult time, but I can arrange for—'

'I'll be fine on my own. Mum's coming over and...' She covered a sob with another smile. 'Thanks.'

'Okay.' Methven jangled his keys in his pocket. 'Let me know if there's anything I can do to help.'

'Okay.'

Methven started back down the path.

Angela was looking over at Cullen, and her eyes told him she had seen right through the lies. For a few seconds, he thought she would call him out.

Instead, she mouthed, 'Thank you.'

～

CULLEN STOPPED ON THE DAMP SAND AND STARED OUT AT THE choppy waters, towards the island in the middle distance – the beaches and hills of Fife sprawling in the distance. The icy breeze started clearing his head as the sun rose above North Berwick to the east. He watched the faint yellow rays tinge the slate-grey February sky. Watched as they lit up the sky with a blue so fresh and light it made Cullen's eyes water. As he wiped them dry, he felt the warmth of the colour spectacle spread to his face and couldn't help but smile.

Life goes on.

He stood there on the beach, wind in his hair, salt on his lips, cries of seagulls in his ears.

And thoughts of rogue cops on his mind. Of whether anything could be done against them. Of whether anything would get done without them. Of when the means justify the ends. Of Lamb and Wilkinson.

Of heroes and villains.

And not knowing which was which.

Then his phone buzzed. Once.

A text.

'Sorry about that OTT text last night. I panicked. Fancy going for a coffee? Yvonne X'

NEXT BOOK

The next Police Scotland book is out now!

"THE BLACK ISLE"
Starring DC Craig Hunter

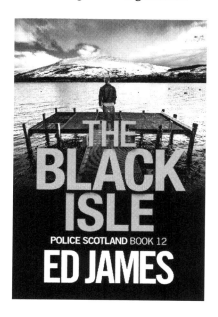

Get it now!

If you would like to be kept up to date with new releases from Ed James and access free novellas, please join the Ed James Readers' Club.

AFTERWORD

Sorry it took so long.

Book seven was released in August 2015. It's October 2018 as I type this.

Sorry. But I hope it's worth the wait. And you've had five Fenchurch novels and two Hunter books, which of course featured Cullen.

While I won't promise the ninth will be along very soon, I promise I'll try and get it out next year. I've got plans for Cullen. Big plans.

I've got a few things to do before.

Thanks again for all your support!

— Ed James

Scottish Borders, October 2018

ACKNOWLEDGMENTS

Without the following, this book wouldn't exist:

Development Editing
Len Wanner

Procedural Analysis
James Mackay

Line Editing
Len Wanner

Copy Editing
Allan Guthrie

Proofing
Eleanor Abraham

ABOUT THE AUTHOR

Ed James is the author of the bestselling DI Simon Fenchurch novels, Seattle-based FBI thrillers starring Max Carter, and the self-published Detective Scott Cullen series and its Craig Hunter spin-off books.

During his time in IT project management, Ed spent every moment he could writing and has now traded in his weekly commute to London in order to write full-time. He lives in the Scottish Borders with far too many rescued animals.

If you would like to be kept up to date with new releases from Ed James, please join the Ed James Readers Club.

Connect with Ed online:

Amazon Author page

Website

OTHER BOOKS BY ED JAMES

DI ROB MARSHALL

Ed's first new police procedural series in six years, focusing on DI Rob Marshall, a criminal profiler turned detective. London-based, an old case brings him back home to the Scottish Borders and the dark past he fled as a teenager.

1. THE TURNING OF OUR BONES
2. WHERE THE BODIES LIE (May 2023)

Also available is FALSE START, a prequel novella starring DS Rakesh Siyal, is available for **free** to subscribers of Ed's newsletter or on Amazon. Sign up at https://geni.us/EJLCFS

POLICE SCOTLAND

Precinct novels featuring detectives covering Edinburgh and its surrounding counties, and further across Scotland: Scott Cullen, eager to climb the career ladder; Craig Hunter, an ex-squaddie struggling with PTSD; Brian Bain, the centre of his own universe and everyone else's. Previously published as SCOTT CULLEN MYSTERIES, CRAIG HUNTER POLICE THRILLERS and CULLEN & BAIN SERIES.

1. DEAD IN THE WATER
2. GHOST IN THE MACHINE
3. DEVIL IN THE DETAIL
4. FIRE IN THE BLOOD
5. STAB IN THE DARK
6. COPS & ROBBERS
7. LIARS & THIEVES
8. COWBOYS & INDIANS
9. THE MISSING
10. THE HUNTED
11. HEROES & VILLAINS
12. THE BLACK ISLE
13. THE COLD TRUTH

14. THE DEAD END

DS VICKY DODDS

Gritty crime novels set in Dundee and Tayside, featuring a DS juggling being a cop and a single mother.

1. BLOOD & GUTS
2. TOOTH & CLAW
3. FLESH & BLOOD
4. SKIN & BONE
5. GUILT TRIP

DI SIMON FENCHURCH

Set in East London, will Fenchurch ever find what happened to his daughter, missing for the last ten years?

1. THE HOPE THAT KILLS
2. WORTH KILLING FOR
3. WHAT DOESN'T KILL YOU
4. IN FOR THE KILL
5. KILL WITH KINDNESS
6. KILL THE MESSENGER
7. DEAD MAN'S SHOES
8. A HILL TO DIE ON
9. THE LAST THING TO DIE

Other Books

Other crime novels, with Lost Cause set in Scotland and Senseless set in southern England, and the other three set in Seattle, Washington.

- LOST CAUSE
- SENSELESS
- TELL ME LIES
- GONE IN SECONDS
- BEFORE SHE WAKES

THE BLACK ISLE EXCERPT
CHAPTER 1

'THIS PLACE IS AMAZING.' KEITH LOOKS ROUND AT ME, GRINNING LIKE a child, his hair blowing in the wind cutting across the oil rig platform. 'There's enough here for, like, ten shows.' He winks, hauls open the door, then sticks his head inside. 'Hello?' He waits a few seconds, shrugs and slips through.

I don't follow him immediately. A fresh blast of ice-cold rain hits my face, with it a salty taste and tangy smell, and it tears the paper out of my grip, sending it flying across the platform and out into the Cromarty Firth. I train the camera on the open water, getting that perfect line of golden sun hitting the waves where it breaks the clouds in the distance, aiming right towards us. In the distance, the Black Isle looms up out of the grey, lush and green. Like something from a King Arthur story. Beyond the Moray Firth, the land rises up to meet the Cairngorms, just about visible on the horizon.

Being up this high is the perfect vantage point. Not that there is anyone about. The whole platform is dead, all signs of occupancy removed, save the living quarters Keith is peering inside. I keep the camera focused on the clouds, just as the sun slips behind.

'Hot shit.' Keith slips through the door to the living quarters and his voice is muffled by the wood. 'There's at least...' And he's gone, more noise than signal, just a tone.

I hit the stop button on the camera but leave my head-mounted GoPro running. Never know what you might catch—always good for a swift cut, or that bit of point-of-view veracity as we give our viewers a cheap thrill. I open the door and peer inside.

And I feel the metal on my neck. A faint smell of machine oil. Shit. It's a gun. What the hell?

'Stay still.' Slight accent—foreign, eastern European or Russian. The weak metallic scent of his aftershave washes over my face.

'Okay, okay!' I slowly raise my hands. 'Take it easy, pal.' I start to swivel round. 'We'll leave and—'

'Shut. Up.' He presses the gun close, digging into my skin now. 'I said, don't. Move.' He punctuates the word with a jab, making my skull rattle and my eyes lose focus.

Think fast here.

'Who are you?'

'You think you're in a position to ask that?' I see the muzzle of the gun wave at the door Keith went through, now shut again. 'Are you alone?'

I hope Keith heard enough of this to find a way back to safety. 'Of course. Who else in their right mind would come here?'

Something cracks my spine and knocks the breath out of my lungs. I stumble forward, gasping for air, and my knees thump off the steel floor.

'This is the last time I'll ask you, and I expect the truth.' The gun rasps the skin on my neck, that exact spot where the spine connects to the brain. The brain stem or something. Seen so many YouTube documentaries on it, the perfect place to kill someone. This guy's a pro. I'm messed up. 'Are. You. Alone?'

'I am, I swear!'

'I heard you speak to someone.'

'I was on the phone.' I wave north-ish towards Invergordon and its phone masts. 'Got some reception up here.' I'm reaching, hoping to hell that he buys it. 'I was speaking to the guy who brought me on the boat. He left, but he was just checking in. I had the phone on speaker. Said he'll be back in two hours. But I lost reception.'

'Then we have two hours to get you away, my friend. But I don't believe you.' He grabs my arm and snatches at my phone. 'Who is—'

I dig my elbow into his gut and he groans. I wrestle free of his grip and hurl my mobile at the open sea. But it drops a few metres shy of the edge.

Shit.

Then the phone starts sliding in the wind towards the water.

'No!' He lurches after it, but it's gone, slipping off into the deep. He turns to face me, training the gun on me. His face is riddled with scars, a diagonal knife wound cutting from the top of his right ear through his lips to his neck. Hardcore. 'Stupid.' He pushes me, then frogmarches me over to the closed door.

And all I can do is go along with it, his arm locked around my shoulder, the gun back in its place against my neck.

'Open it.'

I reach out with my left foot—he doesn't give me much choice —and nudge the door, pushing hard against the wind. A long corridor, with countless doors peeling off in both directions. He pushes me forward again and we pass a large bedroom, two bunk beds. Metallic, stripped, bolted to the wall. Adult-sized, though. The window is open a crack. No sign of Keith. My captor pushes me again and we keep walking.

Halfway down the corridor he grabs my arms to stop me. 'Stay there.' He walks into a room that's identical except for the window being half open and rattling in the gusty breeze. He checks everything with military precision, just like my bloody brother searching my flat for dope. And I get another good look at my captor. A big lump. bald and muscular, and kitted out in professional hiking gear. Outdoor wear. He stares right at me, a proper soldier's glare. Definitely ex-military.

I flash him the smile that gets me in places like this. 'Look, pal, I'm sure we can work—'

'Listen to me.' He steps forward, pinning me against the wall. 'You are not supposed to be here. As much as I would like to kill you, I have a much better plan. We are going to have so much fun.'

~

my new releases and get free exclusive content, please join for free here.

Printed in Great Britain
by Amazon

48768043R00187